OTTO
A. BERLINER

W9-CMN-486

THE COBBLER OF NORMANDY

2007

The Cobbler of Normandy

This novel was created in a historical context. The story and characters are fictitious. Any similarity between reality and fiction is purely coincidental.

Copyright © 2007 Otto A. Berliner
All rights reserved.
ISBN: 1-4196-6840-4
ISBN-13: 978-1419668401

Visit www.booksurge.com to order additional copies.

The Cobbler of Normandy

Quidquid agis, prudenter agas et respice finem!

Whatever you do, do it prudently and look to the end

Latin Proverb

ACKNOWLEDGEMENTS

When I visited the graves of the fallen American and British heroes in the Normandy cemeteries, I read the backgrounds engraved on their headstones. I was emotionally moved to tears thinking about their lives that they did not get to live. I am grateful for their sacrifices. I was able to live my life in freedom and democracy rather than under Nazi and Communist rule. These heroes, living and dead gave me the spirit to write this book as my way of saying Thank You!

I am deeply indebted to my tour guide and friend, John Flaherty, Specialist in D-day and Battle of Normandy Escorted Tours, Hand Maid Tours, his wife Elaine who not only showed me the battlegrounds of Normandy and explained all the historical events that transpired at those sites but researched little known facts for me. In addition, they cared for my room and board and transportation.

Next and foremost, I must thank my dear wife Joyce for her tireless spiritual and editorial guidance. She has been my beacon of direction helping to channel my creative thoughts to write this book. There are not enough words to express my feelings of gratitude for her involvement and understanding what writing this book has meant to me.

I am especially thankful for the literary and intellectual guidance and generous editorial assistance given by Dr. Susan Betz-Jitomir, Esq. and Dr. Howard Jitomir, Professor of English and a novelist and Gina Horowitz.

For the graphic illustration and design, I offer many thanks to Professor Judy Ross and her student Meagan O'Brien of Alfred University.

Last but not the least, I am forever grateful for the careful overview of the manuscript and editorial assistance from Kristine Klein, speech- language pathologist, and Marielle Marne, copy editor, for their exceptional talent of assessment and unwavering concentration to provide the final touches to complete this novel.

This Novel Is Dedicated To All The Living And Deceased Men And Women Of The OSS, MI6, French Resistance and Allied Military Who Fought For Freedom And Democracy And Gave Their Lives In The Pursuit of That Cause.

CHAPTER ONE

The northern wind whipped up the sea into rolling white caps. The sky lit up over the Channel with meandering lightning and frightening thunder. Although it was far out to sea, it gave warning of an impending storm.

At midnight, the telephone rang twice in the Geiheime Staatpolizei (Gestapo) Secret Police Headquarters in Caen.

"Hello," answered an officer in a faint voice.

"You have six hours to release Madam Bouquet, otherwise you will pay a heavy toll," said the voice on the other line and hung up.

The officers of the Gestapo met within twenty minutes of the phone call, and the investigation began. They didn't like threats and their nerves were already on edge.

"How do you want to proceed?" asked Sheller.

His eyes were bloody, his face partially burned. He was the most sadistic interrogator in the Gestapo. His presence alone made suspects tremble. He was a psychopathic monster who had no respect for human life.

"Identify the caller," said agent Hauptman.

"So, speak up. You received the call."

"The caller was male, perhaps in his thirties, American English. The call came from Paris."

"What do you want to do with her?" asked Sheller.

"Continue the interrogation, increasing the pain and kill her six hours later."

"We can't do that," said Freihoffer, the agent in charge that night.

"Why not?"

"Because of her background and influence," responded Freihoffer.

Madam Bouquet's company in Switzerland and Spain provides electronic equipment for the German Army. She is an American, living with her boyfriend in Normandy. She has been accused of aiding and abetting Allied commandos. Up to this point she has not been physically tortured but scared out of her wits by Sheller.

"I do not believe in yielding to threats, but the Fatherland comes first. We need her support and merchandise. Release her with a strong warning. Tell her that we are watching her villa." advised Sheller.

Meanwhile, in the fishing village, Port-En-Bessin, the howling wind and rain reached the coast. Far away from the sea, the window shutters of a rented cottage began to hit the siding and sounded like a barrage of artillery. Renee and Andre were about to consummate their marriage when a tremendous explosion shattered the windows, tore doors off the hinges, shook the bed, and broke the mirror on the wall. An additional blast of ammunition set off a ground tremor that felt like an earthquake.

There was pandemonium at the ammunition depot where the explosion occurred. The streets of picturesque Port-En-Bessin, with all its geographical beauty, were transformed as the German army, with columns of tanks and trucks carrying soldiers, moved in to investigate the explosion.

An ammunition supply had been sabotaged by the Maquis. They had put dynamite in a hole next to the building for maximum destruction. Scores of German guards were killed or injured in the explosion. The cause of explosion spread with lightning speed through the town, creating an immense fear among the residents. The people knew what the Germans were going to do next.

The Gestapo arrived from Caen and Cherbourg to investigate the incident, find the culprits, and initiate revenge for supporting the Maquis. The members of the Maquis, in possession of Spanish passports, planned to leave for Spain. Their itinerary called for using the least traveled routes, by car, horse, and foot. The Gestapo ordered the army to check the railroad station in Bayeux, the bus station, hotels and restaurants. They did not have enough men to check all the passages leading out of the country. The Gestapo hoped somebody would squeal for sympathy or money, or at best, for amnesty from harm.

Since no one came forward, the Gestapo used their maximum fear and intimidation to find the perpetrators. Two hundred and fifty citizens were randomly selected from neighboring towns and taken into the courtyard of the largest church. Everyone was waiting for twenty-four hours to find out his fate. They were not allowed to eat and drink, and had to use buckets as toilet facilities. The Gestapo demanded to know the identities and hiding places of the saboteurs, but nobody talked, they just cried and prayed. In their desperation, the Gestapo ordered the soldiers to select randomly twenty-five men to be executed in front of the others and twenty-five women to be transported to a vernichtung lager- "extermination camp"- for their support of the Maquis.

"This is outrageous and totally uncivilized, to put people to death or send them to the concentration camp of no return," remarked Marceau, the cobbler, courier and recruiter of the Resistance.

"I couldn't agree with you more. These Gestapo hoodlums think they can intimidate the French citizens. They are raving mad. Someday they'll pay for these atrocities," replied Bridget, the "adopted" daughter of Marceau, and also a member of the Resistance.

"I am worried about the Maquis. I am concerned how on earth they are going to escape," voiced Bridget.

"I'm sure they planned their escape routes in advance," surmised Marceau.

"I am scared of the Gestapo's dragnet."

"The trawl can be broken."

"I am afraid you're optimism may not work. The Gestapo is very clever."

"I understand your feelings and concerns, Bridget, but you don't know enough of the Maquis and their training. I am apprehensive too, but I have faith in their plans. They are very bold."

"Do you have any idea of their destination?"

"I believe they are headed out of France, possibly to Spain."

"Will we have a contact about their whereabouts? I would be thankful to know that they arrived at a safe place."

"I will let you know very soon. My dear, you must learn to relax. This war will bring us many surprises. You must conserve your emotional energy."

"I don't know how you can be so cool about it. We are facing a horrible danger if they are still hiding in this area. The Gestapo will comb every nook and cranny."

"They probably left immediately after the explosion. It is not unusual for them to cross dress, or take a German uniform and pretend to be officers and have companions in the car."

"Your assumptions are terrific. I hope you're right."

"You are underestimating the Maquis."

"No, I'm just trying to be realistic. Some plans don't work."

"If plan A does not work, plan B will take place. And in the worst scenario, plan C will be adopted. They are trained to escape, to become invisible, and hide until they can be rescued. They have faith in the Lord and in their mission."

"I'll keep my fingers crossed."

"You do that, my dear."

Port-En-Bessin, is situated between Grand Camp and Arromanches, and was an important fishing port and farmland in Basse Normandie. The town with all its charm and geographic beauty attracted many visitors from all walks of life. Parisians and other tourists loved to spend their sojourns and honeymoons in this seaport.

The port had been surrounded by a circular seawall with an opening in the middle. The water enters a canal where the ships are anchored and fishermen unload their wares. The main road entered from the south toward the north-east canal. The houses were mostly one or two story buildings on the main road and side streets. Gable slate roofs, facades made of stone and plaster, wood shutters and dormer windows suited perfectly into the Norman surroundings. The shops, cafes and restaurants were along the main road and side streets.

The German occupation and development of the Atlantic Wall, however, put a damper on the charm of the village. The bunkers on the hill and pill boxes on the west and east headlands overlooking the harbor took away the serenity and sense of freedom. In this atmosphere the victorious Germans used and abused the inhabitants, but respected those who catered to their needs. Among those were the hospitality workers, bakers, grocers, fishermen, carpenters, plumbers, wall paper hangers and painters, auto mechanics, and last, but not the least, the local cobbler.

Marceau Badeau was the favorite cobbler, who not only repaired shoes, but made the finest handmade boots. The German generals and officers, who were able to pay for his services, loved him. He was not only a good craftsman but a respectable character and a raconteur.

Marceau was sixty-three, five feet nine inches tall, lean and well-preserved for his age. He was partially bald, with white hair, prominent eyebrows, a small nose, and thick lips. His beard was perfectly trimmed. Marceau spoke English well and a few words in German. His French vocabulary was better than the average speaking Frenchmen. His grades were mixed in high school. He excelled in some subjects and did average in others. Marceau was born into a working class family in Paris. His mother was an Irish born seamstress and his father had worked in a cheese factory. During his late adolescence and early adulthood he enjoyed reading a variety of novels and adventure articles in French and English. Reading had become his pastime and later his passion.

He was a reliable and honest person. Marceau was a cerebral man with a keen insight and excellent foresight. Whatever he did, he did it smartly, and looked at the end. He had a cheerful personality, and a warm and giving character. Besides being an ideal husband, he was a great companion. With all these excellent qualities, his major fault was his short temper, but only when he was subjected to other people's stupidity.

Marceau had lived alone for the past twenty-four years. He became a widower when his wife died from cancer. He has had a few ladies in his life, but has been with one for the past ten years. He fathered two girls and one boy from three different mothers. Most of them grew up in Paris. He was discreet in deed and kept his private life to himself. He often visited his children in Paris as they were growing up, but they never came to his home in Port-En-Bessin.

He is a man of distinguished stature who commands respect and trust. He smokes his own carved pipe, his pride and joy, and keeps it tucked deep in his shirt pocket.

He likes to play cards with a few selected friends. He is, however, mostly an introvert and secretive. His authoritarian character is well suited for the job he is doing for the Resistance.

He learned about the importance of walking and making the best shoes and boots as an apprentice in Paris. He was called by his friend to substitute for him for three months because he had to have knee surgery. Marceau did so well that he was asked to stay for another three months. Eventually, he became the primary cobbler of the shop and was offered a managerial position. It was a very tempting offer, since the store was one of the most prestigious shoe stores in Paris. But he declined the offer and decided to work for himself.

After the executions and deportations, the tension mounted not only among the indigenous, but the Resistance at large. Revenge became the slogan and there was a reward for the head of the Gestapo who had ordered the massacre. This was a tall and ambitious undertaking. To calm the nerves of the people in town, the word assassination was forbidden to be spoken in the social circles.

Marceau had the opportunity to talk with the Gestapo agent who returned to the shop for the custom preparations needed for the making of his boots.

"Did you find the perpetrators who blew up the ammunition train?"

"Not yet, but we have good leads. We hope to grab those saboteurs pretty soon."

"Where do you get your leads?"

"People talk. We have methods to make people talk."

"I hope you'll realize that sometimes sweet enticement works better than harsh treatments, intimidation and revenge on the innocent. Those who committed the act did not necessarily share their intentions with the general public. You don't tell the German people what is happening in the concentration camps."

"You are more than a cobbler. I hear a philosopher, politician, and a wise man talking."

"Thank you for your compliment, but I am just a plain cobbler who has worldly interest for the betterment of mankind."

"We should recruit you to the Gestapo."

"I would not be good for you. I cannot squeal on people or see them tortured."

"We could have you as an interpreter and effective interrogator. You could certainly save lives. The Gestapo will handsomely compensate you for your services."

"This is very kind of you, but I would make a bad candidate."

"Look, we have very few agents who have humanitarian intentions when it comes to finding the enemy of the Reich. You certainly could sweeten the pie, and give an example of how to investigate in a fair way without physical harm."

"We all deserve a day in court. I don't know how you could find justification in killing innocent citizens."

Marceau removed the plaster and showed him the perfect form of his foot.

"This looks very good."

"Look, going back to our discussion, we try not to resort to the kinds of measures you claim, but when people do not cooperate, we must teach them a lesson."

"I did not go to Gestapo school, but I had life school. I learned a long time ago that everything has a price. There is no free lunch. You are perceived by the French people as occupiers and not victors. The war is not over yet. Things can turn around despite what you believe. It is better to impose justice on those who are the culprits rather than on innocent people."

"It is a good thing that you talking to me. My fellow agents would have arrested you for your blunt criticism of the Gestapo. You must be careful, Marceau."

"Look, we all want to live honorably and justly. All I am asking you is to have mercy on those innocent souls you sent to the camps."

"It was not up to me to decide. We have higher-ups on the officer's ladder."

"I beg you; please try to return those poor women. God will bless you!"

"I'll see what I can do. We'll be in touch. Auf wiedersehen- 'See you again'!"

Marceau calls the heads of the local Resistance together for an immediate conference to try to save the twenty-five women.

To make the situation more chaotic, the Gestapo was hunting for three Allied commandos who landed in the natural harbor of Port-En-Bessin. They were testing the soil to see if it would withstand the weight of the heavy equipment that needed to land during the invasion. The German patrol spotted them and reported the sighting to the military headquarters (HQ). Unfortunately, the commandos were late returning to the mini submarine and missed it. They were forced to hide in one of the fishing vessels whose captain was also a MI6 agent. The captain placed them down in the stern storage room. He had created out of crates and bins movable boxes at the bottom of the pile for each commando, Scott, Robineau and Olivier. Since the ship had three compartments, with the engine in the middle, they had a chance to move from stern to bow when danger called for it.

They stayed there for one day and later, with the help of other Resistance operatives, were given civilian clothes and placed in caskets in a hearse. The hearse took them to their new hiding place which was a brothel at the outskirts of the village. They were dressed in a painter's overalls with their faces smeared with paint. As the commandos were painting the rooms, the girls were teasing them with all kinds of sexual innuendos about their reserved behaviors. One girl, Yvonne, was quite bold and embraced the commando Scott.

"What do you want from me? I must complete my job before I can have fun," said Scott.

"I think you work too hard. You should relax. I can help you with that. After I am finished with you, you'll sleep like a log," said Yvonne.

"Just what are your noble intentions?" asked Scott.

"That is a trade secret," replied Yvonne.

Despite their clever disappearances, the Germans' search continued all over town. The soldiers went from house to house searching every room looking for the three commandos. The Gestapo posted a reward for sightings. Finding the three commandos became an obsession for the Gestapo. Suddenly the outside door of the brothel swung open, and two Gestapo agents barged into the living room facing the half naked girls.

"Where are those damn commandos?" demanded one of the agents.

Yvonne had the courage to respond, "We don't know what you are talking about. We did not have a customer in the last two hours. But you are welcome to have fun."

"We are here to arrest the commandos who escaped from the shores. They are spies and must be apprehended," said the other Gestapo agent.

"Well, they may show up but in the meantime why don't you let us provide you with some pleasure," said Yvonne.

"Look, we are here on official business. This is very serious. We are looking for three English speaking men who we suspect are the commandos," said the agent in charge.

"If you don't mind, we'd like to look at your rooms," asked the other agent.

"That violates our policy of confidentiality for our customers, but in this instance, certainly go ahead," said the owner of the brothel.

"But one of your girls said, 'You did not have any visitors lately,'" said the first agent.

"That is true. But we could have customers while you are combing the rooms and that certainly is not good for our business," said the owner.

"The enemy is trying to find out how we are going to defend ourselves. It is our right to investigate any unusual occurrences or individuals that we deem as a threat to our mission. Please close the brothel for fifteen minutes while we inspect your rooms or we will close you by force," said the first Gestapo agent.

"Go ahead and check the rooms," said the owner.

The Gestapo went to every room and found two rooms being painted. They were curious why the owner did not mention these men were working for him.

"When did you start working here," asked the first agent.

"Today," answered commando Scott.

"I needed the money so I could study at the University of Sorbonne."

"What about your partner?" asked the other agent.

"He is a professional wall paper hanger, but he accepts painting jobs if there is nothing else," said Scott.

"You there, can't you talk. Where are you from?" asked the first Gestapo agent.

"I was educated in Algiers and have lived most of my life in Paris." said Robineau, the other commando.

"Your French is very good. Do you have papers?" asked the first Gestapo agent.

"Yes, I do."

"Are there any more painters here today?" asked the first agent.

"In the other room," said the owner.

"How many?" was his next question.

"Just one more painter." answered the owner.

"If you see the commandos, you must let us know," said the first Gestapo agent.

"Oh yes, we will," said the owner.

The two Gestapo men exited the brothel. When they returned to their headquarters some brave Frenchwoman called the Gestapo and told them that the commandos escaped to Paris by car. The Germans did not believe the story and checked with the Paris Gestapo. The call was traced and found that it came from Port-En-Bessin. The call drove the Gestapo chief officer absolutely mad.

"Those pigs think they can fool me! But, I'll surprise them! I'll find them!"

"I know you will and you will teach them a good lesson," said his lieutenant officer.

"Didn't I teach them a lesson by executing those twenty-five French men and by sending twenty five of the town's women to the concentration camp?"

"Jawohl—that is right. The saboteurs did not come back again," acknowledged his junior officer.

"I will personally interrogate people in their apartments, homes, and businesses. No Gestapo agent will rest until I find those commandos."

"You know that we are with you to destroy the enemy of the Reich."

"Good, then let's go to work and find those guys."

The chief was embittered by the lack of investigation. He knocked on every door. His French was mediocre but it was enough to scare people to hell.

Leaving his Gestapo HQ in Caen and traveling with only a chauffeur and a guard, the Resistance saw an opportunity to remove him from further operations. Two Resistance agents with experience assumed a barmaid and waitress position in one of the local restaurants waiting for the Gestapo agent to appear. On the third day of waiting, he came into the bar and asked for a large glass of beer. The barmaid poured enough poison into the glass to kill him. The Gestapo agent drank the beer and asked for the menu. The owner politely informed the Gestapo agent that they had ran out of meat, fish, and poultry, but they had cheese if he would like a light meal. The Gestapo agent decided to go to another restaurant which was a blessing for the resistance agents and the owner. They did not want him to get sick in their place. The investigation would be devastating for everybody.

The Gestapo agent went to another restaurant and ordered the house special, but he did not enjoy his meal. He paid his bill and rushed home. Riding home became a chore for him. He felt nauseous. When he arrived home he immediately went to bed, hoping he would get better, but he did not. He was awake most of the night. The next morning he began to vomit and had bloody diarrhea. He thought it had to be the food in the restaurant which was making him sick. By the second and third day his condition worsened. He had had stomach upsets in the past. He developed a breathing problem and a fever. Other agents suggested that he be examined by a physician, but he said, "I'll be fine. I have an upset stomach. I am strong and my system will fight off whatever bug I have."

"But you have a serious breathing problem. Your facial color has turned blue," said a concerned Gestapo officer.

"We must fight on every front. That includes our bodies."

"But, please allow me to say, this is nonsense. You must get oxygen and medicine right away."

"What you are saying is nonsense. There is no medicine for the kind of bug I have. My blue color will turn pink as soon as I get over this disease."

"Sorry. I cannot order you to go to the hospital. You are our chief."

"You are damned right! I will stay here and it's my last word."

He died five days later. The cause of his death was written up as severe influenza and pneumonia.

With the help of a Resistance driver, the three commandos left their brothel's hiding place and headed to Marceau's shop for his help in returning them to England. It was not a simple request and plans had to be formulated to carry out the task.

Marceau realized that helping the commandos meant a great risk for his courier operation.

The Gestapo did not give up the search, just modified the hunt. In Caen, the Gestapo paid French conspirators with cocaine, heroine, money, and sex to comb the villages, shops, café houses, restaurants, hotels that catered to the prostitutes, and fishermen to find the commandos. They were patient, consistent and meticulous in their search. Finding the commandos was an absolute necessity to determine what the Allies were up to in Normandy.

The three commandos, on their way to see Marceau, stopped in a bar with their Resistance driver. As they were drinking their beer, they had small talk with three girls at the bar. They were French prostitutes. Since the commandos spoke French quite well, the girls did not suspect any commando connection.

"Where do you come from?" asked one of the girls.

"I was born in Algiers," said Robineau.

"Your French is not up-to-date," said the other girl.

"That is true. From there our family moved to Barbados in the Caribbean where we grew up. It's a different dialect," said the other commando.

"Are you looking for fun?" probed the third girl.

"What kind of fun?" probed commando Scott.

"We'll leave it at your imagination," said the second girl.

"Your offer is enticing, but no, thank you," said commando Olivier.

"You are going to miss a lot of fun and pleasure," said the third girl.

"Maybe another time," said Scott.

"And when is that other time?" asked the first girl.

"It all depends when we have the opportunity to see you," said Olivier.

"We would like to spend the whole night with you. You seem to be very nice guys," said the second girl.

"Well, thank you," said Scott.

"At least, we enjoyed chatting with you," said the third girl.

"We certainly appreciated your company," said Olivier.

As the four were getting into the car, they noticed two black cars and a truck of soldiers arriving. The Gestapo had received word about the commandos being in the area and asked the officer in charge of the nearest battery to provide a truckload of soldiers to capture the commandos.

Once they got outside of town, the driver stepped on the gas and drove away at a hundred-twenty kilometers per hour. He made a sharp turn to the left, then to the right, and turned in a southern direction toward Paris.

"What the heck happened? All three girls were with us all the time," asked the first commando.

"It was the bartender. He noticed that the three of you were not French. He called the Gestapo," said the driver.

"How do you know that?" asked commando Scott.

"I heard the conversation at the bar. I was close to the phone. I paid attention to certain key words. He asked about the reward twice."

"So why didn't you alert us right a way?" asked commando Robineau angrily.

"I did not know to whom he was talking. Remember, I said, I heard only certain words. But now it makes sense. He was the informant."

"What now, where are we going?" asked the second commando.

"We are making a detour to confuse them. Then back to the brothel to redecorate the walls because the madam does not like the color red. Besides the military police will be looking for us at the intersections," said the driver.

"When the coast clears in a few days, we'll go to Marceau's. But for now, we must hide in the brothel and wait until the dust clears. I'll talk with Marceau," said the driver.

The third day after their return to the brothel, the Resistance was successful in transporting one commando at a time to Marceau's place.

"We are pleased to meet you, Marceau," said commando Scott.

"The pleasure is mine. This is Bridget, my daughter, assistant, and Resistance agent of the first class."

Bridget impressed the commandos. She had a curvy figure, was five foot-seven inches tall with blue eyes and long ash blond hair. Her voice was soft and sensuous. She had a piquant smile that stupefied the commandos. Her dress was a simple two piece outfit, a white blouse with a dark blue skirt.

"Good day gentlemen, welcome to France. I take it this is not one of your pleasure trips, otherwise I would be glad to show you the beauty of this town," said Bridget.

"Maybe another time," said Marceau.

"Is there anything we can do to get back to England?" asked one of the commandos.

"I wish you could help, but you have no knowledge of the situation here. The Germans are not stupid, but they have an Achtung- "strictly follow the orders" mentality. They are good problem solvers. So we have to outsmart them to get you out of France. With the help of the Resistance and Allied Intelligence, you'll return to your HQ."

"In the meantime, you'll be housed in one of the nearby apartments that have false walls. It is a very secretive place and the Gestapo has no knowledge of it. You'll have three cots to sleep on. It is just a temporary solution while you wait for your transit."

"You'll be transported either by train or plane through Switzerland and Spain, or by plane. Either way it is a risky journey. I will be in touch with my operatives who will inform me about the Gestapo's search procedures. They shift their emphasis daily. Our stool pigeons feed them with all kinds of fantasies," said Marceau.

"We trust your judgment," said the British commando

"Good. You'll be eating dinner with us tonight, but starting tomorrow Bridget will provide food for you."

"Swell, we'll survive. We have been trained to adjust to any condition," said the US commando.

Marceau was carefully evaluating the Gestapo's daily changes in their attempt to find the three commandos. MI6 suggested flying in a modified Westland Lysander III plane to England. Marceau had to make extensive preparations for a night departure. This meant armed Resistance operatives had to watch for any Gestapo and military interruptions for landing and take-off. Also a few sharp shooters were needed for the protection of the commandos. In addition, a radio man was needed to receive coded instruction from the plane. Additional operatives had to signal the landing parameters of a secret airfield. Usually three to four operatives held a flashlight to outline the field.

Marceau was able to mobilize the technical personnel in two days. MI6 agreed to send a plane the second day at 0200 hour. Everything was ready, except the local transportation. Marceau decided to get a milk transport truck and put the commandos in one of the compartments and fill the rest with milk. They were to travel at night. By 2200 hours the truck was ready to take them to the field.

Without any problem they were dropped off at the make-shift airfield, waited until the plane landed, climbed fast into the fuselage and by early morning they were back at their commando HQ.

It was an old farmhouse. The wooden siding was broken in several places. The place was dark and looked desolate except for the barking dog in the barn. The inside of the house was sparsely furnished with worn chairs, table, and a sofa. The kitchen had a round wooden table with four chairs, an old stove, and a tiny lamp hanging from the ceiling. The curtains were drawn and no light was visible from outside the kitchen. The agents, driver, and his chief were greeted by an attractive French girl. She was in her twenties.

"Bon soir—Good evening, I'm Fran. We were expecting you." She led them to the living room area, and then showed them the bedrooms.

The men headed toward the bathroom first then entered the kitchen. Since it was in the early morning hours, she offered a light breakfast meal. Bread, butter, jam, bacon, milk, and coffee were already prepared. Everybody sat around the table except the young lady, who was standing nearby to serve the gentlemen.

"How many eggs, and how do you want them?" asked the young lady.

"Hundred, fried, over easy," replied Parker.

"Just give me two soft boiled," corrected Parker.

"The same," said the driver.

"Three scrambled with milk," voiced Shaw.

"Let's eat first, then sleep and I'll wake you up at 0900, and then we'll talk," said the chief intelligence operative.

"Can you remove your masks? I would like to see your faces." the girl asked the agents.

"No," was the answer. "Sorry, no exception. We must protect our identities. It is a must! But after the invasion, you are welcome to see our handsome faces" continued Shaw.

"What a pity," added Parker teasingly.

"It is a pity," said Fran. "But its OK," she continued, "Go to bed, have pleasant dreams. I have already prepared the beds for you."

Slowly everybody left the table and went toward their respective rooms on the second floor. Then all taking turns, they took a bath and went to bed. Captain Brian Parker was a handsome six foot two, brown haired, blue eyed, thirty-six year old engineer. His face had a tanned complexion and he had an athletic built.

He grew up in Pine Bluff, Arkansas. His mother, from German descent, remarried when he was three years old. His father was born and educated in Quebec. Parker has two step sisters and a step brother. Since the age of fourteen, he spent most summers working for a landscaper. At eighteen he was accepted at the Massachusetts Institute of Technology. There he received his B.S. degree in civil engineering, and a Master's and Ph.D. degrees in mechanical engineering. He was a keenly perceptive, ambitious person with outstanding problem solving abilities. Parker loved people. He managed to balance his introverted tendencies with his extroverted personality. His easy going personality attracted many people. Parker was a kind person, but a continuous aggravation with German military officers and Gestapo agents made him contentious. When this happened, it was wise to stay away from him.

Having served as a Captain for the US Army, Parker applied to Office of Strategic Services. He spoke fluent German and French. In addition to a diverse engineering background and passing the security clearance, he made an excellent candidate for this specific agent position.

Captain Matthew Shaw was a tall, six foot three, slim, blue eyed scientist. His blond hair was parted in the middle and always combed to perfection. He was a very pleasant looking person with a nice personality.

His mother was born in Zurich, Switzerland, and educated as a music teacher. Shaw's father was of French descent and taught violin in Aberdeen University in Scotland. Shaw grew up and was educated in Aberdeen, Scotland. He received his undergraduate degree and a Masters in chemistry with high honors and his Ph.D. in material science. He came from a family of four children where every Sunday, after church, his parents gave a concert. Shaw married his high-school sweetheart and they had two children.

Shaw has always been a serious person. Many times he was self-absorbed, but he paid close attention to his colleagues, friends, and family. He was an extremely ethical person, but did not berate those co-workers whom he disagreed with at times.

He was a Captain in the British Army and after his honorable discharge he volunteered to serve as an agent for the Military Intelligence 6. He received extensive training. Shaw managed to adjust his personality to the various demands of his profession. His language skills, fluent German and French, were great assets.

Both, Parker and Shaw were trained in intelligence work and attended a special language school for idiomatic French and German, with emphasis on geographical slang and diction. Since both were highly educated and trained, they pretended to be German born officers. Allied Intelligence had high expectations for their mission.

It was Fran. "Time to get up," said the girl.

"We'll be down in five minutes," said Parker.

Fran then asked, "What do you want for breakfast?"

This time Shaw replied, "Whatever you have."

It was less than five minutes when both agents sat in the kitchen. Parker asked for coffee and Shaw wanted tea to drink. Fran prepared eggs, bacon, croissants, butter, and jam. Roger and another Resistance agent joined the group.

"I am Jean, welcome to France. I lead this outfit, cell if you prefer. I don't want to see your faces now but later when you get dressed in the German uniforms. We have a timetable to observe. We are leaving in thirty minutes for your future apartments. There you'll receive your uniforms, papers, money and pistols. Since I was informed about your mission, I will address you only according to your designated short codes, 004 for Shaw and 006 for Parker.

Shaw looked at Jean and said in an acknowledging voice, "O.K."

Jean continued, "You'll be going first to your apartment, then as soon as you finish dressing into your new outfits, you'll meet with Marceau Badeau, the cobbler and Resistance Chief for Courier and Recruiting operation in the Normandy sector."

"Ce va bien,—that's good," answered Shaw. They finished their breakfast and Parker said, "We are ready messieurs—gentlemen. Let's go."

They got into the Renault and were whisked away. Fifteen minutes later they stopped before a three story apartment house. Jean led the way to the second floor. There were two furnished apartments side by side. Both places were identical in terms of layout and furnishings. Both apartments had a small foyer, kitchen, bathroom, fairly comfortable living and bedrooms. The walls were painted off white and decorated with a few prints. There were telephones in each of the bedrooms. Both apartments were facing the street below. Jean opened the doors and asked,

"Do you have any preference? Want to flip a coin?"

Parker answered, "I'll take the right one."

The agents entered their apartments. They looked around, opened the drawers and checked the cupboards. Roger went downstairs to get the uniforms and two medium size suitcases from the trunk of the car. Jean looked at the uniforms which were packed in brown garment bags and marked 004 and 006. He placed the uniforms and luggage in their respective apartments, Shaw's number 242 and Parker's number 243. Then Jean asked the agents to have a brief conference in Parker's apartment.

"Gentlemen," he began. "I'd like to examine your bags; just to be sure that everything that I asked for is here." So Jean opened each of the bags and found everything that he ordered.

"Here are your papers," Jean said, "and here are your pistols...just in case. You will also find your toiletries and undergarments."

He pulled the zipper on the inside of Shaw's and Parker's luggage and handed each agent ten thousand franks. "You'll receive more money as time goes by but for now you'll have enough."

Then jokingly, Parker remarked, "Are you definitely sure? No fun money?"

Jean looked at Parker and answered, "I don't think you'll need any fun money. I was told that both of you are very handsome."

"Oh yeah," sighed Shaw, "really, are we?"

As Shaw and Parker opened the garment bags they found two pair of German boots with socks stuffed inside. The uniforms were OT, Organization Todt, jackets. They were made from OT yellow/golden brown wool with gold silk interior and just the right size with an interior drawstring for sizing. The lining was stamped OT and the manufacturer's stamp was easily visible. The collars had two wavy bar insignias for the rank of Oberbaufuhrer "high construction leader." The lower part of the left sleeve had the markings of Org Todt and above that the red armband with a black swastika in a white circle. Two brown shirts, OT cap, and pistol holster were also added to the package.

Jean was quite eager to depart and asked them to get ready. "Here is the car key and car registration; I cannot be seen with you. We'll meet at Badeau's place in Port-En-Bessin," said Jean.

Oh, one more thing," added Jean. "Do you know how to get to Marceau's?"

"Don't worry, we'll find the place," assured Parker.

Jean exited and ran downstairs to meet his friend Jacques and they sped away in a Peugeot. After quickly dressing, Parker looked at Shaw, then in the mirror, and hurriedly commented, "We look like two clowns in a circus."

"Never mind, we'll live up to the Kraut's expectation," responded Shaw.

They looked just fine. Every garment was tailored to their respective sizes. They put on their boots and were ready to depart.

"Are you ready?" asked Shaw.

"Let's go," replied Parker.

They only drove a short distance when the German Military Police stopped the car.

One of the MP's approached the car, gave a salute, and said, "Papieren, bitte—papers please."

As Shaw and Parker handed over their papers, Shaw tested his German dialect, "Was ist los—what's happening?"

The soldier responded, "We are on a special assignment to be sure that nobody enters the defense perimeter. We are sorry for your inconvenience."

Shaw responded, "You are doing a fine job."

The soldier smiled and said "Danke. Danke schon! Thanks. Thank you very much."

Saluted again and said, "forthfahren bitte. Please proceed."

Shaw engaged the engine and slowly headed toward Port-En-Bessin. After a few minutes, he began to laugh, and said with considerable contentment. "We did it, we fooled the bloody fellow." He was happy. "Not bad for the first time," replied Parker.

They drove for about twenty minutes when they arrived to the outskirt of the port. Then they began looking for the location. As they drove around, the place looked more like a picturesque resort than a fishing village. However with the German bunker on the top of the hill over-looking the port entrance to the Channel, the soldiers all over, the heavy vehicles, the pillboxes it certainly took away the romantic impression of the place. There were some German patrol boats moored to the pier; French fishing boats were anchored further up the river. The traffic was slow and Parker carefully followed the map he received from Allied Intelligence. They proceeded north on Rue Du Bayeux then crossed over to Quai Felix, turned left toward Rue Letournier and parked the car. The cobbler's store was just across the street. They looked around and headed for the store.

As the door opened, tiny little bells chimed announcing the entrance of the customers. A very pretty, twenty something young woman, came out from the back and greeted them with a smile.

"Bon jour messieurs. Good day gentlemen. Je m'appelle, Bridget- My name is Bridget. What can I do for you?"

"We would like to talk with Marceau," said Shaw.

"He'll be back in any moment. You may sit down while you wait."

"That's fine," Parker responded.

Within a few minutes Marceau entered the store, looked at the two Todt construction leaders, and greeted them in a kind voice. Shaw did not wait for the usual inquiries but got to the point.

"Marceau, this 006 and I am 004."

"I am truly happy to see you. We have been expecting you. Please enter my fitting room. My daughter, Bridget, will take care of the customers while we are talking." Marceau had a younthful, healthy look. His face had hardly any wrinkles though he was in his early sixties. He kept himself thin, well preserved. His receding white hair was combed to perfection.

Marceau slowly began his smoking ritual, filling his pipe from the tobacco pouch and while he lit the tobacco several times, he asked in-between:

"I believe you met Bridget."

"We did, but we didn't know she was your daughter," said Parker. "She is very pretty and is a nice person. Is she a member of the Resistance?"

"Oui,"-"yes." answered Marceau.

Shaw emphatically indicated, "Nobody, but nobody except Jean, Bridget and you may know our identities. It is a must to protect the members of the Resistance, ourselves, and our mission."

"Don't worry. We know, we have been instructed by OSS and MI6. Let's talk. But before we get down to business I must ask you to take off your boots. Let's pretend I'm taking foot measurements. One can never be sure of my visitors."

"Let's talk about your mission," continued Marceau. "I heard about you from Allied Intelligence, but I am still in a fog. I don't know what your specific mission is all about."

Shaw curtly replied, "Total information gathering and forwarding."

"We already have a plan. We are organizing, and Andre Dewavrin, the Head of the Free French Intelligence Service in London, is directing us."

Parker took over. "This is different. We are overseeing every organization, large or small. With all due respect to Mr. Dewavrin, the US and UK are planning and executing the invasion, of course, with the help of the French and other Allies."

"We will not jeopardize any operation with electronic or pigeon messages. We have to rely on your human mail service. This operation is a super secret human intelligence mission. We must avoid talking about each other's lives, because once the Abwehr and/or the Gestapo smell our intention they go for blackmail, all kinds of torture, seduction, and murder. They are merciless. So we are going to outsmart them."

He continued, "Do you play chess Marceau?"

"Of course I play chess."

"Look, to be a winner one must have a good defense, foresight, and a strategy to check mate the opponent."

"Naturellement naturally," replied Marceau.

"But a good player is also a good observer and listener. We have to work together. Forget about the egos. I am only concerned about winning this ugly war. You are going to get all the information you need but we also have needs. The Maquis needs a variety of weapons, ammunition, explosives, and money," continued Marceau.

"Can you help us?" asked Marceau.

"I'll send a request to Allied Intelligence with my first message," answered Parker.

"How did this whole operation come about?"

Shaw took over and began to elucidate in an erudite voice.

"In April 1942, a directive was sent by the British Chiefs of Staff to British Military Intelligence 6. They wanted to collect, organize and study vast amounts of intelligence material on the German coastal defenses, topography, soil conditions, assault capabilities, landing technology, and determine the necessary equipment to successfully complete a cross-channel invasion. The American Joint Chiefs of Staff, cooperating with the British, requested the Coordinator of Information (COI) to prepare sending an agent to France. COI was the forerunner of OSS/SI—Office of Strategic Services Secret Intelligence branch. For Mountbatten and Eisenhower, Normandy was a strong invasion site. From a technical, strategic, military, and surprise point of view Normandy was an excellent choice. The reasons for close and continuous supplies at the port of Cherbourg, the limited terrain of Cotentin Peninsula, roads leading to and from Caen, but most of all, it is a brilliant subterfuge. The Germans are expecting the invasion to be at the Pas de Calais site—the shortest point between France and Britain. And that's where the Germans erected most of the defenses and positioned their personnel along the Atlantic Wall. To achieve the above mission, intelligence is the first and foremost task that has to be accomplished," explained Shaw.

"Having explained why we are here, I would like now to talk about the operational details."

"I need reliable thinkers who will also perform smartly. Gender is not important, dedication is. We need to have the execution plans for the defenses from Cherbourg to Caen, photographs of existing water and beach structures, depth and surges of tides, bunkers, and bunkers in prep, pillboxes, casemates, short and long distance guns, tanks, half-tracks, trucks, divisions, and supportive manpower including forced labor."

"That is a tall order, but we'll support you, fight with you side by side, and share the sorrow and happiness of our mission," remarked Marceau.

"Thank you."

Parker took over. "The information must reach us first before it goes to OSS and MI6. We must know what the good information is and what the disinformation is. We want all the messages delivered to a secure place. We don't want any casualties, prisoners, or the Gestapo on our necks. The drops must be in a public place, preferably in business centers where there are a lot of people around and an escape can be easy and confusing for the Germans. I want to give them hell for our treasure. They will watch us but we'll watch them also. I'll bet we'll have a touchdown. And they'll go crazy looking for the ball."

"How many men or women do you want? Where do you want to start? When do you want to begin the operations?" asked Marceau.

"Yesterday was too late," replied Parker. "We want three people in a group. We'll have small cells. All together not more than seven cells to start with. We don't want any personal relationships between members of the cells. No sex and no love under any circumstances. If it happens they must leave the cells. We will instruct them at the first meeting. The gender combinations must be mixed, one woman and two men, or two women and one man. We want pretty faces, smart and athletic types who can run and escape in an emergency."

"I hear you," said Marceau.

"By the way, do you need women who are good in bed with German officers?"

"Whatever is necessary," replied Parker.

Marceau's smiling response was, "but occasionally you can also have pleasure while playing in the dirt."

"Do you want some coffee or tea with some delicious cookies? Bridget makes them."

"I'll take tea," said Shaw. "Coffee for me," replied Parker.

"Mon amie, Bridget," yelled Marceau. Bridget was helping a customer and yelled back,

"One moment please, I'm busy right now."

Marceau got up and prepared the cups, napkins, sugar, milk, and spoons. He boiled some hot water, reached for the cookies and began to ask some idle questions.

"Did Jean give you some nice accommodations?"

Shaw said, "It's like the Ritz-Carlton. But we missed the chambermaid."

"The blonde or the brunette," asked Marceau.

The water started to boil and Marceau prepared the coffee and tea. He sat down and the serious discussion continued with Marceau complaining about the Gestapo.

"I have a problem with a young and very ambitious man whose passion is to catch people and torture them. He is a psychopathic monster. How can we outsmart him?"

"He'll eventually outsmart himself," replied Shaw.

"He comes to my store, pretending to purchase a new pair of boots and does nothing else but asks questions about my customers, people I talk to, and annoys Bridget."

"Just play the game. Make up stories. He'll love you for it," said Parker.

"But I would like to talk about something else," he continued. "We have a timetable for delivery. How soon can we get together with the cells?"

"I'll talk to Jean today and we'll be calling the people together so you can start organizing by tomorrow."

"How many confidants do you have?" asked Parker.

"My strongest confidants are Jean and Bridget. Why are you asking?"

"First, it's our job to know, and second, for security reasons. They can be captured, interrogated, and implicated," said Shaw.

"We really need you. Our mission depends on you," continued Shaw.

"Marceau, you must promise us something," said Shaw.

"You will not increase your confidential circle during our mission."

"If this is so important to you, I promise," replied Marceau.

"C'est bien, that is fine."

"We must go now," said Shaw.

"Wait," said Marceau.

"Bridget would like to talk to you. Bridget, Bridget," called Marceau.

Bridget, 26, looked nice with her slight makeup and seductively medium thick lips. Her hair style was medium length cut with bangs. She was raised in a middle-class family in Paris. Her father was a jeweler and her mother an artist. She painted beautiful portraits. They lived in a four bedroom apartment in Paris. Bridget was twenty-four when her parents were arrested by the Gestapo, charged with resistance activities and failure to wear the yellow star for their Jewish background. Both were sent to German concentration camps. Bridget found refuge by staying with Marceau and acquiring the name of Bridget Badeau.

Bridget was an industrious person. She worked very hard to help Marceau in the shop, as a Resistance agent, housekeeper, and companion. She hated the Germans and could not forget what the Gestapo did to her parents. Bridget had a difficult time coping with her memories. As a result of her early experiences, she was suspicious of any German entering the shop.

Bridget was a good hearted person and very dedicated to the cause of liberation of France. Bridget is smart, cautious, and selectively trusting. She is outgoing, but easily turns into an introvert. Her high school education helped her to understand the world and she planned to pursue her Thespian interest after the war.

Bridget came in the room and Marceau went to the store. "Gentlemen," she spoke English with a French accent.

"My papa is a good man, a smart man, a very trusted person. You don't have to be afraid of anything. He is the best shoemaker in the area. He has many customers from all over Normandy. The German officers love him. We will help you. But, of course you are cautious. He is a wise person with a lot of foresight. Marceau has a lot of passion for the cause. Merci-Thanks."

There was a momentary silence in the air.

"Thank you for telling us," Shaw replied.

"Please don't speak to anyone about our meeting. You must be very discreet about our relationship. We are at war. We'll liberate you. The invasion depends partly on how well we can outfox the Germans. You are part of our mission. At this point in time only five of us, Jean, Marceau, you, and ourselves, must know what we are doing. OK?" said Shaw.

Parker and Shaw put on their boots, got up, and walked toward the door. Bridget saw them out.

"A tout a l'heure—see you later," said Bridget.

They looked at Bridget with a smile, saluted Marceau with their hand by touching the bill of their caps and said, "Bye."

The air smelled fresh and Parker suggested walking a little bit before they return to the car.

"Splendid idea, chap," said Shaw.

They walked toward the sea and saw large numbers of gulls resting everywhere.

"It's so picturesque around here," said Shaw.

"Yes, it's too bad the Germans will build all kinds of fortifications in the coming months. It'll lose its sentimental value."

As they strolled along the seawall, a German officer asked them when and where the next project would begin.

"Erlich, Ich kann nicht sprechen uber militarishe sachen. Bitte entshshuldigen sie mich. Honestly, I cannot speak about military things. Please excuse me" said Parker with a touch of Bavarian dialect.

The officer replied, "Naturlich Naturally."

Shaw suggested walking back to the car and driving toward Bayeux.

"Why do you want to go to Bayeux?"

"Maybe we can find a good French bistro."

"That's ok with me." In no time they drove away and headed toward Bayeux.

Marceau called Bridget to make some coffee and join him for a chat. He was a little concerned about Jean. As he smoked his pipe and looked out the window that faced the street and the port beyond, he wondered about the depth of his undertaking, his loyalty to his men and women of the

Resistance, his responsibility to protect Bridget, the success of the mission, and the love and pride of his work.

Bridget came in with two mugs of coffee, some milk, sugar, cookies, and napkins on a straw woven serving tray. She put it on a small working table and sat down.

"Here I am. Drink your coffee. You seem to be far away."

"We must send him to England. He knows too much about them. He is a risk if he ever gets caught."

"How soon must he go?"

"He has to go as soon as possible. You must call and arrange the flight."

Bridget looked at Marceau with love and respect. There was something about her that was very charming and sensual. She sensed how men looked at her, but she never allowed anyone to flirt with her. Bridget was always strictly business with customers or comrades of the Resistance.

"I'll make the arrangements this afternoon and call Jean to get ready. But, you must have something else on your mind Marceau."

"Yes, I have. What do you make of the agents? You are very good at this my dear. You are good at analyzing people at first sight. It's God's gift to have this talent."

"Oh, Marceau! You're too kind. I don't really know them. What shall I tell you?

I only saw them for a few minutes and I heard little of the discussion. I think they are tough guys. My initial impression tells me that they mean business."

"I agree. We have a lot of work ahead." Marceau finished his coffee and continued his work. He was finishing a new pair of boots for a German officer. "So Bridget, do you like these boots?"

"I like the boots but not the officer. He is arrogant and mean."

"So what's new? That is how they are, those bastards."

Shaw and Parker found a small bar in the outskirts of Bayeux. The place looked like a tourist stopover, simple but comfortable. The owner's wife greeted them from behind the bar. She was in her late forties, pleasantly plump but very charming. Her husband offered them a table near the window. They were both tired and hungry and asked for the menu when they sat down.

"I am the chef; may I suggest our specialty?"

"What do you have?" asked Parker.

"We have poulet avec sauce Mediterraneen, plus pommes frites—We have chicken with Mediterranean gravy, plus french fried potatoes."

"That's good for me," said Parker.

"The same for me and bread with lots of butter," added Shaw.

"I am starving, how about you, Matt?" asked Parker.

"I am too. I love fresh, crispy French bread right from the oven."

The owner came back with warm bread tucked into a white napkin and several small little squares of butter.

"May I offer you homemade wine?"

They began to eat ferociously, like two hungry beasts which hadn't seen food for a week.

"What are you thinking, Matt?"

"What are we supposed to do next? We have no time to dillydally."

As soon as he said that, two German Gestapo officers dressed in trench coats, entered the bar, greeted Shaw and Parker, and sat down at the table next to them.

"How are the bunkers coming along?" asked one of the Gestapo men.

"The construction is progressing very well. We are accomplishing our goals. We are going to have an impenetrable defense system," said Parker.

"I hope so," responded the other Gestapo officer.

"We are very proud of you guys; you are doing a good job. The English and American guys will never get ashore. We'll kill them before they approach French soil. By the way you have a very pleasant dialect. Where do you come from in Germany?"

"I come from a small village. Thank you for your kind compliment. My mother was a great reader of story books and we just sat around with other children and listened to her. She was quite articulate," responded Parker.

The owner asked the Gestapo men what they wanted to eat and drink. He brought them wine, some cheese and bread. They ate hurriedly, got up and one of them commented, "I have to find some saboteurs of the Resistance. They are destroying our fight." They left some money on the table, said good-bye, and exited the place.

"That was good, Captain Parker. You made a swell impression."

"I just hope we don't see them again," responded Parker.

"So, where were we?" asked Parker.

"Let's finish I don't want to talk here," said Shaw.

"I don't blame you," responded Parker.

Both drank coffee, asked for the bill, and left the place. In the car they were quiet for a while then Parker asked, "Do we have to stop here to shop for food?"

"Oh, no. I saw a place before we get home to buy groceries and some other things," replied Shaw.

They headed for home. They had a long day and needed rest for the next morning. The dusk was closing in on them but the road was still bright enough to drive without lights.

"We've got to talk to Marceau first," continued Shaw.

"What time?"

"How about 0900? There are two major issues at hand. One has to do with Jean. They'll make him talk under torture or Sodium Pentothal. He must not divulge all his past and present contacts. The second has to do with cell # 1. We must know the location of the first drop," said Shaw.

"According to our instructions they can meet us without seeing us in a two room apartment where there is a door in between," said Parker.

"It is a good idea, but what if it is a trap by the Gestapo? I want pictures and identifications to check their faces plus resistance security papers with special code numbers. As way of introduction, for security purposes, we may ask them to strip," said Shaw.

"If she is pretty, why not?" replied Parker.

"Come on, Brian, we have a job to do. By strip, I mean, to reveal information that a German agent cannot."

"I agree. But do we know enough about their Resistance and personal background that we can trip a mole?" asked Parker.

"That is why we have to speak with Marceau. We must be sure that everything we do is airtight."

"I'm aware of that. But since we are working together it is a good idea to synchronize our thoughts and actions. I am just as concerned as you are about details of safety- although I kid sometimes- there are situations or there will be occasions when no matter how cautious we are, we will face a certain element of risk," commented Parker.

"I see a grocery sign at the next corner. Do you want to stop there?" asked Parker.

"Good idea why don't we?"

Upon entering the store they witnessed a very disturbing scene. One German soldier was beating the elder owner of the store while his partner was raping his young teen-age daughter. The soldiers had dragged both of them to the back of the store where they were discovered by their cries and yelling for help.

"Was machst du- What are you doing?" asked Parker of the soldier who was raping the girl.

"Macht nichts -doing nothing," answered the soldier. Both soldiers were drunk but began to realize that they were facing German officers.

"What do you mean by doing nothing? What you are doing is disgusting," continued Parker.

"They are saboteurs," shouted the other soldier.

"Then we better call the German police," said Shaw.

"Don't do that," said the soldier and he let the girl go from his arm.

"Why not?" asked Shaw.

"We have violated our military code of behavior and we could be court-martialed," said the soldier.

"Do you realize how your behavior could cause more hatred by the French people against the Reich?" said Shaw.

The soldiers straightened themselves up, apologized for their behavior and tone of voice. They saluted the officers and left the store.

"Thank you, thank you," said the elderly man and offered cheese as a gift.

Shaw and Parker picked up a few things and put them on the counter.

"I am sorry for what happened," said Parker.

Then he paid for the groceries and they left the store.

"I was ready to clobber those bastards," hissed Parker.

"I know," replied Shaw.

"But we must be careful, this is not our territory. We are not military police, and we don't want to get involved in court," added Shaw.

As they drove away both were emotionally upset and did not talk about the incident. Their training paid off and they did not lose their cool. The mission was more important than small personal satisfaction.

"Never a dull moment," said Parker

"Well said," replied Shaw.

When they got to the entrance of the house, Parker grabbed the groceries and Shaw went to park the car near the house. When Shaw entered his apartment there was a note on the floor. It was tossed under the door and was hurriedly scribbled. It read, "I could fix your boot if you come around 8:30 in the morning."

"Well, I wonder if there is telepathy?" said Parker.

"Why do you say that?"

"Because, I sensed that something was waiting for us."

"I'm going to have a few french pastries now. How about you?" asked Parker.

"I'll take a couple, please. Thanks."

While Parker was putting the pastries on a plate, Shaw heated up some water.

"What would you like to have, coffee or tea?"

"May I have coffee, please? Black," replied Parker.

Although both were ready to hit the sack, they snacked on a few pastries before bed time. As they relaxed and tied to disengage, the BBC from London reminded them of the gains and losses of the war. This in turn, increased the weight of their assignments which fell heavily on their shoulders. An army of a million, the very first wave of combatants' survival depended on their information, intelligence, and enemy planning. They had moments when their thoughts connected with their feelings, with their loved ones left behind. These moments were expressed in their silence, in their very private time.

Shaw was sipping his tea, embedded in his thoughts about developing a sound strategy for the exploration of all batteries, bunkers, casemates, pill boxes, mines and underground tunnels in Normandy. His mind focused on Marceau's cells and their responsibilities in a given area. He contemplated on how to coach them if it became necessary. He was concerned about the shortness of time and the expectations of the home office.

"I hope we'll accomplish quite a bit tomorrow," said Parker.

"Don't be so sure." I don't know what Marceau has in mind, the number of amateurs he'll recommend, and what skills they have."

"I hope we'll find out tomorrow," said Parker. "But right now I'm going to hit the sack. Please knock me up, you're an early riser."

"What do you mean?"

"It's British idiomatic English. Wake me up."

"Cheerio," said Shaw as Parker left the room.

It was 0605 when Shaw knocked on the door.

"Don't knock so hard, I can hear you. I'll be out in thirty minutes," said Parker in German.

Shaw entered Parker's place at 0640. They had a hearty breakfast of oatmeal, eggs, toast, butter and jam. They made freshly brewed tea and coffee and drank leisurely until it was time to go. While they cleaned the dishes, Parker remarked, "I love to have a good breakfast; one never knows when you have time to eat during the day in this business."

"That's good thinking." They left the dishes to dry and both exited the apartment around 0750.

"I figure it wouldn't take us more than twenty plus minutes from Fierville Les Mines to Port-En-Bessin," said Shaw.

"I guess you're right. Probably less, but let's enjoy the road and scenery. This place will be bombed to oblivion in no time."

"I hope not until we finish our assignment. I hate to live out my life in a wheelchair as a result of friendly fire."

"I don't blame you, Matt. I'm with you on that, but one never knows what will happen after we give them the coordinates."

As they got closer to the fishing village, they couldn't help but notice a long chain of slave workers flanked by German guards marching toward the shore. They looked worn and tired dressed in shabby clothes and their faces drawn to the ground. One of the workers collapsed and the guard next to him kicked him in his butt while shouting, "Get up, pig! You're a stinking pig, get up!"

Parker asked Shaw to stop the car. He approached the guard and asked him sarcastically, "Are you boosting morale?"

The guard saluted Parker and replied hastily, "No, I am disciplining."

"We need strength and good morale to build the wall. Help the man get up. Give him water; let him rest for a few minutes. He'll appreciate you and do a better job," said Parker with a mellow voice. The guard thanked him for the advice, gave a big salute, and asked the men to take a ten minute rest.

Parker walked back to the car with a smug face and asked Shaw to get going.

"That was a nice gesture. I like the way you handled it."

"I don't like brutality," replied Parker.

They were in the vicinity of Port-En-Bessin when they were stopped again by a military checkpoint.

"Papers please," asked one of the military policemen. Shaw and Parker showed their Organization Todt papers. He gave back the papers but asked them to step out of the vehicle for further questioning and checking of the car.

"Where are you going?" was the first question asked by another MP.

"Do you want to know our itinerary for the day?" questioned Parker.

"Are you playing a game with us or are you going to answer my question?"

"We respect your question but you are forgetting who we are in rank and profession."

"It is absolutely disgusting how little your military police know about what we are doing for the defense of the Reich. We are supervising the Atlantic Wall construction in its entirety of Normandy so you can live longer and hopefully go home in peace," said Shaw.

"I understand and respect what you saying and doing, but we must question you because it is our job. It does not matter who you are and what rank you hold," was the MP's answer.

"This is a matter of security," he continued. "May I look at your papers again?"

Parker and Shaw reluctantly presented their papers with the comment from Parker, "This is absolutely undignified."

"Why?" asked Shaw.

"Because of the quality of the paper," said the MP.

"We received these papers from the Organization Todt Headquarters," replied Shaw.

"These days we don't have good quality identification papers," commented the MP.

"We are old timers, we helped to renovate the Autobahn," said Parker.

"Oh so, that is a different story! You can continue your trip and work. Heil- Salute- Hitler!"

Those were the MP's last words as he saluted Shaw and Parker.

Shaw drove away disgusted. He sped to make up for the lost time. They arrived at Marceau's store five minutes later. Bridget greeted them with a big smile and a hello. Marceau was working in the back on a boot but after hearing the big "hello," he got up from his chair and welcomed the two agents.

"I'm not done yet with the boots. Do you mind waiting a little? This German officer is a perfectionist and he can find microscopic errors and blame me for the imperfections. He has faulted me so many times that I would rather make it perfect than listen to his foul mouth. My sweet daughter will entertain you while I do the last stitches."

"Don't worry Marceau, just do what you have to do," said Shaw.

"It would be an honor to talk with your lovely daughter," commented Parker.

Bridget's face got red, as Parker had made her blush. Bridget invited both of them into the fitting room and asked them to remove their boots. The three of them sat down and just looked at each other in a deafening silence.

"What's the matter?" asked Bridget.

"Nothing," replied Parker.

"We admire the combination of beauty, charm, and an intellectual mind. They are gifts of God," continued Parker.

"You are prejudiced," said Bridget.

Bridget looked very well this morning. Her deep blue eyes, pretty blond hair and natural color lipstick on her thick protruding lips would have evoked anyone's attention. Her slim figure and tight blouse made her round bosoms inadvertently noticeable. She had a very easy going but tough personality with strong conviction to win over the German army and destroy Hitler's sadistically psychopathic regime.

"I don't want you to have any preconceived notions about me. Since we have to work together for one goal to defeat the Germans, you must know something about me. Maybe I don't come across the way you think but I am not a pick-up girl or an easy pushover. I am a tough cookie. I have all the reasons to be. My parents were caught hiding in safe houses because of their Jewish ethnicities and collaborations with the Resistance. They were shipped to a German concentration camp. A couple of years ago I was placed under Marceau's protection as a step-daughter. I had to learn how to live as a step-daughter of a strange man, support the Resistance, and help in the business to avoid the slightest suspicion. So here I am, take me or leave me."

Parker and Shaw were stunned by her revelation. There was a long eerie silence, followed by a warm, affectionate gesture. Both agents got up and embraced Bridget.

"One more thing," said Bridget. "I do not flirt, fall in love, or go to bed with the men I work with or work for. I hope this will straighten out some of your preconceived notions you might have about me."

Parker and Shaw listened carefully and remained silent. The silence was broken as Marceau entered the room.

"I am done with his boots and I am ready to have our discussion. My darling, would you be kind enough and bring some coffee or tea and pastries, please?"

"We have a lot to talk about," said Shaw.

"OK, let's talk," said Marceau.

"Jean is a problem. He must leave France," said Shaw

"I'm ahead of you. He already left France this morning at 0300."

"I am glad that we are tuned to the same wavelength," added Parker.

"Well, what do you think? We are amateurs?" replied Marceau.

"We are going to divide Normandy into seven zones," continued Shaw.

"Each zone will be about ten miles long. We are measuring the distance from Cherbourg to Caen. Starting from Cherbourg where should be the first meeting and drop?"

"I arrange the meeting, you discuss the drop."

"I'll give you the names, places, and time," said Marceau.

"We want people with common sense, logic, and intelligence so we can train them," responded Shaw.

"The people I am going to recommend are all smart and intelligent. By the way, why do you need three people for a cell?"

"Two of them carry out the assignment while one is watching," replied Parker.

"What will you do with the information we are going to be providing to you on a weekly basis?" asked Shaw.

"We collect, edit, and hopefully transfer them to Allied Intelligence," replied Marceau then he queried, "What is your information delivery plan without being detected?"

"The information will be left in a drop which will change every week. We will let you know where the next drop will be with the current drop. We will try to see you on an as needed basis, but the frequency of visits may depend on the seriousness of the situation," said Shaw.

"OK," said Marceau. "I will microfilm all your written messages and take them with me to my crab boat. One of my traps has a very special cache. Only Allied Intelligence (AI) and I are privileged to know how to send and receive information.

Should the Gestapo ever confiscate my trap, they will not find the message. It is part of the chicken lure. The crab will not touch it. It burns the mouth. The microfilm is coated with a special chemical and only Allied Intelligence has the solution to read the message.

"I go out every week, whether or not I give or receive messages. Sometimes, I must go out with a German watchdog. I treat him well. He gets wine, women and sometimes fish or crab depending what I can catch that day. He becomes drunk and amorous with her, sometimes falls asleep in the boat's cabin and I can do my job," said Marceau.

"So where do we meet the members of the first cell?" asked Shaw.

"I have a friend who lives close to you in Fierville and his place is available for a few days while he is enjoying himself in Paris. Here is the key to the entrance and when you are through with your meeting leave the key under the back porch entrance mat. What time do you want to meet them tomorrow?" replied Marceau.

"We would like to meet them no later than 0900. We will wait for fifteen minutes just in case they are late, then we leave. If something happens between today and tomorrow, send a note with Bridget," said Shaw.

"I'll try to arrange the meeting, but the time is always subject to change. By the way here is the address," said Marceau.

Shaw and Parker looked at each other and agreed there was nothing more to discuss. Shaw broke the silence.

"Oh, there is one more thing," said Shaw.

"The home office is to be notified. Please send the message: 'found the spot and started fishing'

Our next communication will be the drop a week from today. It will be under my car parked across the street from where we live. Bridget can easily pretend to be looking for something she just dropped, bend down to the left of the exhaust pipe to find a magnetic box attached to the frame. She can keep it until our next personal meeting."

"This will be done and thanks for coming," replied Marceau.

On the way out Parker winked at Bridget and Shaw gave her an affectionate smile. There was a longing look on her face for both of them as she was standing behind the counter and pondering how fast their lives became interwoven with intrigue, candor, and excitement.

Shaw and Parker headed for the first inspection of the nearby bunker in construction. They got in the car and slowly drove toward the northeast direction.

"Hungry for lunch?" asked Shaw. "I wouldn't mind to have a bite and coffee" replied Parker.

They found a small roadside cafe not too far from Port-En-Bessin. The place was a simple but clean eatery. Shaw and Parker ordered fish, potatoes, and beverages. The wife of the owner prepared and served the food in no time. They were hungry and hardly talked to each other when their silence was suddenly interrupted by a rude German officer who demanded beer to be served with his meal. She kindly told him that they only served wine. He insisted that she should fetch him a bottle beer from a nearby store because he did not like wine. Parker got upset with him and told him to respect the lady and to behave like a German officer should. To make the situation worse, two German military police entered the place and the German officer complained to them about Parker's reprimanding behavior. At that point, Shaw got into the conversation and in a legalistic style of language explained to the policemen that the German officer betrayed the officer's code of ethics that was expected to be displayed by the occupying force. The German officer was asked to leave the café by the policemen, but not without a warning from the officer, "Someday I will repay you for putting your nose into my affair!"

Parker and Shaw paid their bill and apologized for the officer's behavior. It was an unpleasant incident but it happened. They were warned to stay clean and not to interfere with argumentative individuals especially when the military police was involved, but they had to protect themselves against the charge.

Parker exited first and was waiting for Shaw who stayed behind in the bathroom. He was disgusted, to say the least. Shaw joined Parker a few minutes later and Parker drove toward the Atlantic Wall. He did not have to drive too far; there was a bunker under construction about 20 miles away. Parker made a sharp left turn in the direction of the bunker. They were stopped again by German security patrol but they were let go as soon as they learned that they were on official business to inspect the site. They parked the car near the construction site and walked toward the freshly poured cement. Shaw took a sample with his hand smeared it with his finger in his palm and showed it to Parker.

The foreman came, gave a salute, and politely asked, "What's wrong? We had inspection yesterday and everything was fine."

"We are just double checking. My partner is a material specialist and he can smell the wrong stuff," replied Parker.

"I think it's just fine," said Shaw, while at the same time lightly winking at Parker.

There were a couple of workers, who had a worried look as Shaw examined the cement mixture, but soon after it was found acceptable they smiled with a hardly noticeable sigh. Parker looked at the steel construction, and found the reinforcing bars adequate for the structure. He complimented the work and the workers.

Shaw whispered to Parker that there was cheating in the mixture, definitely more sand than cement.

"Did you see those two anxious faces among the cement workers?" asked Parker.

"I was too busy telling the lie," replied Shaw.

It was enough to test their masquerade for one day, but it worked. They looked at various aspects of the construction, made mental notes of the project and location and then slowly returned to the car.

Before Shaw turned on the ignition, he took out his compass and noted the coordinates.

"So what do you think? I hope the foreman will not get suspicious," asked Parker.

"Only time will tell. As long as he does not blab about our visit to his superiors or to planted informants it will be o.k. But even if he does, our presence was certainly legitimate. Plus our spin was quite believable. Let's go home. We have another job tomorrow."

As they drove away Shaw noted that a black car was following them. It looked like an old Citroen with two passengers in the front. Shaw maintained his speed but then slowed down and stopped in front of a bakery. Shaw and Parker got out of the car and went into the bakery.

The black car parked close behind their car. There were some tense moments of waiting. Shaw was first to leave the bakery with a small package in one hand while eating a piece of pastry in the other. One of the passengers got out of the black car and approached Shaw.

"You're 004 and I am Spencer from MI6."

He showed a complicated mathematical ID that verified his identity.

"We just want to inform you that the foreman you talked to earlier at the bunker construction site was 'accidentally' killed. We had to terminate him to protect your mission. Sorry chap, but that's the way it goes. Hopefully we don't have to do it again. Cheerio."

There was no explanation as to how it happened, nor a suggestion as to how to prepare them for possible questioning. It was an accident and the less Parker and Shaw knew about it the better it was.

There was an accident and they had to leave it that way.

Parker got into the car with freshly baked French bread under his arm and was waiting for the news. Shaw told the story to Parker. There was no sentiment about the death of the foreman—the whole episode was treated as a casualty of war. The mission couldn't be sacrificed. So MI6 did what they had to do. However, they never expected the MI6 to tail them and save their necks in precarious circumstances.

They drove home tired, but more mentally exhausted. It was a full day for them with unexpected ups and downs. Shaw prepared the dinner and Parker sat down and listened to the news on the radio. Suddenly he heard a couple of knocks on the door. Bridget came with a new address in her hand.

"Marceau asked me to tell you that the Fierville address changed to Cherbourg."

"Thank you for being so kind delivering this message," said Shaw.

"Here is the address and good luck. I must go back now. Bye."

"Bye," said Parker.

They finished their meal, cleaned the dishes, and went to their separate flats to shower and sleep.

They rose at sunrise and left shortly there after in the direction of Cherbourg. Just before Shaw drove into town they stopped at a roadside café for breakfast. The place was so full that they had to wait a few minutes to be seated. Since they left early for the appointment, there was still time to have a leisurely breakfast and travel to the location.

Parker and Shaw drove around a little bit to find the street and the apartment house. It was 0845 when both entered the second floor apartment. The door was left closed but unlocked. They situated themselves in the bedroom with the door left ajar, and waited for the cell to show up. Parker looked out of the window with a pair of binoculars just to make sure that they were not followed by the Gestapo. The sighting did not indicate any problems. There were three people crossing the street, one woman and two men. They were heading toward the apartment house. The men entered the house while the woman stayed behind looking like she was waiting for someone in the alcove of the entrance.

At 0905 there were three short and one long knocks on the door which sounded almost like the BBC shortwave radio news victory pause, di-di-di-dah, during the war. Two Resistance cell operatives dressed like house painters and buckets, brushes, and paints in their hands were waiting for the response. Parker took another look out the window and then yelled, "Entrée-Enter."

The two operatives opened the door, entered the apartment, stood at the threshold, and then one said in French, "Bon jour. Marceau sent us to meet you."

Shaw, wearing a mask, responded, "Bon jour," and asked them to sit down and stay in the living room.

"Please call your partner to join us from downstairs. I think it is safe enough for the first meeting."

They waited for a few minutes until she came up. She was dressed in a similar painting overall. The men looked fairly young, in their mid-thirties, one with a short mustache and she appeared in her mid-twenties, had black hair, and a charming smile.

Shaw began talking first. "It is better to conduct our meeting in two separate rooms to protect our identities. As you were informed by Marceau, we are OSS and MI6 agents responsible for gathering overall intelligence information of the German defense strategies and structures, so we can adequately prepare for the invasion called 'Overlord.' Originally we planned to have 21 operatives in seven cells, covering the length from Cherbourg to Caen in ten sections. As time goes by and our preliminary information bears fruit, we'll increase the number of operatives. Your section, which is the first, will cover from Cherbourg to St.Mere Eglise."

"But before we go any further, we like to commend you for your outfit and finesse for our first meeting. I can see that Marceau is not only the best cobbler in Normandy but a good instructor in resistance matters," continued Shaw.

At this point Parker, also his face covered by a mask, took over and said, "Let me introduce my partner, he is 004 and I am 006. First and foremost, I would like to start with security before we begin to start with other topics of information and assignments. You may ask us any questions after each topic. As a matter of fact, we expect you to do so because we must be absolutely certain that you understand what we are doing and the meaning of it. It is a joint venture and a lot is at stake.

We try, very hard, to have a zero defect operation, but it is almost impossible, and unrealistic. The Gestapo, the German counter intelligence, and the French-German sympathizers are working overtime to destroy the Allied intelligence. We do foresee casualties among our operatives. There is this human factor of conceitedness that can be devastating. We know this from experience. There is never an absolute security. Yes, it sounds paranoid, but that is how we must play the game of human intelligence during war. We don't want you to be caught, tortured, and thrown to the wolves to be mauled to pieces. We have already lost a number of good people. The Germans are merciless at extracting information. They are masters in causing pain until one confesses, and you will talk if you get caught, because the suffering is unbearable. So we have to warn you beforehand that your mission is extremely risky and dangerous. You must always operate in threes."

Parker continued, "One person watches, while the other two carry out the mission. Have a few danger signals and change it for each operation. The Germans are good in observing your methods and they will study every move you make."

"Second, you must not discuss anything with anyone about your operation. It must be done in utmost secrecy. Do not trust anyone! Do not boast about your successes until the war ends and we have won. Just hold the gloating. Silence brings a tremendous reward!"

"We will never meet. You will connect with us only by designated drops and it will change every time. You put your information in this magnetic box that you'll find on the table. Your first drop will be the undercarriage of your car to the left of your tailpipe. You are to park your car opposite Marceau's place exactly a week from today at 0900. If there isn't a parking place, park nearby, and stay in the car. I'll give you another box with instructions for the next week. You do not wait more than 10 minutes. If we don't show up, we meet the following day at the same time and place."

"Any questions at this point?" asked Parker.

"What happens if one of us is arrested?" asked the women who introduced herself as Meghan.

"Any one of you is to immediately contact Marceau who will then inform me," said Parker.

"I'm Pierre. Is there any special interest we should concentrate on?"

"004 will talk about assignments in a little bit," replied Parker.

"I am Girard. My concern is what firearm are you suggesting for protection?"

"Possibly a concealed pistol or revolver," said Parker.

"What are your occupations and how are you making a living?" asked Shaw.

"Pierre and I are painters. We paint apartments, houses, all kinds of offices, and business places. Meghan was an interior decorator but she can't make it during the war as a decorator so she became a painter too. She works with us."

"Now I can understand where the idea came from for our first meeting. It is very clever and original. When I saw you guys from the window I really wondered whether you belonged to the Resistance or if you were here to paint the place," said Shaw.

"You asked about special assignments," he continued.

"Let me tell you that everything you notice and report to us is a special assignment. There are over a million men and women preparing for the invasion and we must know what is awaiting them. This means we must have the thoughts and plans of the enemy, the locations of all gun emplacements, pill boxes, bunkers, anti-aircraft batteries, radar stations, casemates, steel hedgehog beach defenses, wooden beach tank obstacles, command and observation posts. We need to know the various fortification designs, production sites for large quantities of concrete, the kind of mixture they use, the location of the manufacturer of steel reinforcement rods, the plans for the building techniques, the routes and means of transportation, and the nature and composition of manpower who manufacture and build these colossal defense structures."

"Am I answering your questions in terms of special assignments? I believe it is a formidable task for one cell to cover Normandy, from Cherbourg to Caen, but each cell can provide pieces to the puzzle to gain adequate knowledge in order to win the 'Overlord'."

"Thank you, we'll do our best. I think you have explained our tasks and we'll try to provide the information you're requesting from us. You'll be hearing from us next week," Pierre replied.

Meghan said good-bye on behalf of the cell and they exited the apartment.

Shaw and Parker waited a few minutes then entered the living room and locked the front door of the apartment. They sat down at the dining room table and rested their minds for a few minutes.

They left the apartment, locked the door, put the key in an envelope and placed it under the back door doormat. Then they got into the car, and drove away. For the ensuing days in the weeks ahead, Shaw and Parker met each cell at a designated location in Cherbourg, St. Mere Eglise, Carentan, Insigny, Bayeux, Port-en-Bessin, and Caen. Each cell was asked to provide the same information as was requested from the first one. They were given the same instructions regarding the rationale of the intelligence gathering, meaning of the "Overlord," and procedures for the collection of data.

The German Army High Command (Oberkommando-west-OKW) was unable to execute a coordinated plan to erect an impenetrable Atlantic Wall because Hitler had different concepts about where the strengths of the Wall were necessary. The German propaganda, however, blasted and boasted the construction of the Atlantic Wall as an impregnable rampart. The truth was that the fortifications were incomplete and there were significant weak spots where the Allied forces were able to penetrate with relatively little impunity. Therefore it was incumbent of Allied Intelligence to inform the Allied High Command where the penetration would be possible to minimize the casualties to the invading forces.

In the meantime, Marceau was busy with his work in the shop repairing boots, making new ones for the German officers which required several fittings and alterations, collecting Resistance operatives for the cells, and providing intercept-proof communications to Allied submarines via crab fishing. Life was not easy for Marceau. Had not a few German High Command officers raved about his work and personal life of the old man he would not have succeeded in all of his endeavors.

He had a commanding task to accomplish and if not for the unmitigated absolute trust in him by the Germans, he would not have been able to do what he has done so far. On the other hand, it was Bridget who provided all the help she was able to give. She was not only a helper in the shop, but she did all the necessary communications to gather the various Resistance specialists. In addition, she was a faithful and entertaining companion to Marceau. She loved him as a friend and was terribly devoted to his cause. In this unwavering spirit of trust it was inconceivable to think about accepting compliments from a German officer other than doing a good job at work. But in the midst of all the work, Bridget received an invitation from a young German officer who had been in the shop before to celebrate the birthday of a General in the High Command. To a certain extent it was an honor to be a part of such a distinguished party of the enemy and it was hard to refuse the invitation for all practical reasons.

She was picked up at 1800 by the officer. Bridget looked stunningly beautiful. She wore a black laced low cut gown with ruffles on the bottom and a short pearl necklace. Upon her entrance to the German HQ large dining room she was greeted warmly by other officers who happened to know her from the shop. After the initial formalities they sat down to eat a fairly lavish dinner that included caviar, fish, ostrich, potatoes, asparagus, French pastries, beer, wine, and champagne.

"I am so terribly sorry but I only know you as Bridget, and you hardly know me other than by my name from one encounter in the shop. Please forgive me," said the officer.

"Why did you invite me to this very private party?"

"I wanted to invite you for a lunch before, but I was afraid you'd reject me."

"What makes you think that way?"

"Let me just say, for many reasons."

"Name one reason."

"Well, it has been said, one should not mix business with pleasure." She was looking at him with a tiny smile on her face then sipped a little wine and asked, "What is the other reason?"

"Perhaps you have a deep resentment against the German army who occupies your land."

She remained silent and said absolutely nothing. He waited desperately for some answer.

Since both finished the fancy hors d'oeuvre, he felt the silence could be broken by asking her to dance.

"Do you like this music?" It was a slow ballad. "Would you care to dance?"

"I would like to dance to this beautiful music."

They both got up from the table and went to the dance floor. He took her right hand and held her close to his body. She allowed him to hold her close and let him touch her face and they danced to the music. They both felt the rhythm and sensations of each other's touch. It was a very unusual experience for both of them.

"You did not answer my question," Woerner stated.

"I am a private person and I do not go out with customers."

"So you violated your principle?"

"Yes, I did. But you are an exception. You are a nice person, and I may forgive myself this time."

The music stopped and they returned to the table. The music was very pleasant and the ambiance was just perfect.

"Would you care for an after drink?" asked Woerner.

"Thank you, I am fine."

"In your company I find myself just very happy," said Michael in a soft voice. "May I pour you some champagne?"

"Yes, you may Herr Captain Woerner."

"Please call me Michael; I don't want you to call me by my formal name."

They made a toast to this agreement and politely smiled at each other. The music continued with a faster rhythm and they were about to finish their entrée, when Woerner asked her for a second dance. She was having fun and so was he. Both had the chemistry and electricity for each other. But Bridget was very cautious and disciplined not to show her feelings or carry her behavior too far. They talked, laughed, and danced in a wonderful spirit.

When they returned to their table, there was an announcement of the occasion.

An officer got up and made a short speech and toast on behalf of the soldiers and saluted the General on his 60th birthday.

The dessert, a large birthday cake, was served and the music continued to play. After a short time Bridget felt that it was time to go home because she needed to check out the jobs for the next day.

"Do you mind taking me home?"

"Is there anything wrong?"

"I have a rather busy day tomorrow."

"I must excuse us to the General, if you don't mind. Please give my very best to the General and pardon my departure."

"I am sure he will excuse us, he is drunk anyways."

Woerner left the table and went to the General's table where he got a warm welcome by the other officers. He was excused without any problem. As a matter of fact the General gave his best to Marceau and his daughter, Bridget. Woerner saluted the General and thanked him for his understanding and kindness.

They left the table and exited the headquarters and he went for the military vehicle to transport Bridget home.

"Did you enjoy the evening?"

"Yes, it was lovely."

"What do you have planned this coming weekend?"

"I really don't know. Marceau may have plans or extra work and I must help on weekends sometimes."

"May I check back with you in a couple of days?"

"You can, but things can change at the last minute."

Michael drove the vehicle slowly to spend more time with Bridget. They were close to her home and he was very sad at having to say goodbye to her.

"Don't feel bad. We'll see each other in the shop," said Bridget.

"Not in the shop. Please."

"But I can't promise. Neither can you. We are at war!"

They arrived at Marceau's place. He stopped the car. Waited a minute then gave Bridget a big hug. She got out of the car, headed toward the shop, turned around, blew a kiss, and said, "Bon Soir. Merci!"

Michael Woerner was a Hauptleute-Captain in the German Army. He was assigned to supervise the Atlantic Wall construction. Michael was a twenty-nine-year-old, 6 foot 2 inch, slender young man. He had brown hair parted on the side and combed to perfection. With his brown eyes, and a cute dimple in the middle of his right cheek Michael was a very handsome soldier.

He was the third child of a financially well to do family. His father was a Chief Executive Officer of a steel factory and his mother was an accomplished pianist. They lived in Munich, where he finished his Gymnasium years. Michael always loved construction and studied at the University for Architecture and Civil Engineering. These two programs required an extensive education and he spent most of his adult years at the University.

Because Woerner was an outstanding student, the Todt Organization requested the Army to transfer him to Normandy. He had a double assignment: military defense and a consultant of the Atlantic Wall.

Woerner was a peace loving, kind, and just soldier. He had not shown any hatred or Nazi tendencies. Since he was drafted, he had no choice but to submit to his superior's wishes. Inside, his psyche however rejected the war and all the German atrocities in the occupied territories including the civilian discrimination. But he grew up in a German-Nazi culture and it had been difficult to shed some of his behaviors that he acquired over the years in Germany.

Woerner was able to balance his introvert characteristics with an extrovert behavior in the company of others. As a soldier, he had been tough and authoritative. As a consultant, Woerner had been strict, but compromising at times.

Marceau was still up, reading. He was a little apprehensive about Bridget.

"I hope you were careful about our side business."

"Marceau, I really don't like your comment. How can you even insinuate the idea that I would be careless?"

"When you drink, my darling, your tongue could loosen up and you might disclose important information."

"But Marceau, this is life and death you're talking about."

"So how did you enjoy the evening with him?"

"It was very pleasant. He is a nice man."

"How was the dinner?"

"The dinner was excellent."

"Are you going to see him again?"

"Perhaps I will. He is a very open minded officer, quite different from the other Germans."

"You have to be careful. German military intelligence is different from the Gestapo."

"He is not with military intelligence. He is an engineer."

"How can you be sure of that?"

"Just the way he acts. I will be careful Marceau."

"Trust is very precious."

"I agree. But you have to give me time to get to know him and build a confidence."

"My dear Bridget, I am a cautious man. I have no objection that you go out with a German, but a military officer is something different. We are at war. Thousands of agents' and soldiers' lives are in our hands."

"I am very aware of that. I will try very hard not to implicate our involvement with the Resistance."

"I want to thank you for that. Good night."

"Good night, Marceau."

CHAPTER TWO

A week went by to complete the task of meeting, informing, and assigning the other six cells. Shaw and Parker worked feverishly to start the operations of the other cells. The Germans received their orders to erect the Atlantic Wall, defend the coastline by all means and drive the Allied forces into the sea. The Allies had their orders to use counter measures through intelligence and sabotage to obstruct Hitler's plan.

Shaw and Parker collected the information from cell one at the end of the week. The drop worked well, but nothing new was found in the message. It was a confirmation of already known facts. The coastline defenses, however, were selective preparations. Hitler decided to put more emphasis on certain regions than on others. The arrival of new materials, various size gun emplacements, Todt Organization specialists and workers of all kinds were the early clues that something was in the making. Cherbourg, as a port city, was in the process of being heavily defended, but the preparations wood take some time.

"Patience is a virtue," Shaw commented to Parker.

"I know, but we must be aware of what is happening. The Germans are very good in subterfuge, hiding their big gun fortifications, pillboxes, and casemates, which house small and large caliber guns. They build fake houses and camouflage their gun placements to confuse aerial reconnaissance. The mission of Allied intelligence, with the aid of the cells, is to find these fake fortifications, report their locations, and possibly destroy them possibly long before the invasion. We must train and supervise the cell operatives to get information, take pictures and identify those various locations," said Shaw.

"So we need some special, enterprising talents among the cell members who can penetrate the German secrecy," replied Parker.

"You got it! That is very good. Now, let us do something about it!"

Parker was silent for a few minutes. Then he suggested that we should have some sexually savvy women operatives to engage in seduction and sex to obtain strategic information. Shaw agreed but recommended that it would be up to Marceau recruiting those sumptuous operatives.

"Well, let's meet the first cell again this morning and we could discuss this among the many topics," said Shaw.

"I am ready to go. Please let's not forget to talk about the weekly changeable password," remarked Parker.

"Thank you for reminding me."

They left in a hurry to meet the cell and arrived at the location just in time.

The Gestapo was searching for somebody and the house designated as the meting place was cordoned off for two hours. No one was let in or out of the house. They went from door to door and arrested three people and took them for interrogation. Parker and Shaw waited in the car and saw that the cell was walking away. There was nothing Parker and Shaw could do but to leave. Marceau was later told what happened and he immediately provided a new and better location for the next meeting. He had several locations available for such gatherings, but he was the only one who made the arrangements and provided the keys. The cell was informed in the next drop of the new location for the following week.

That same day, Marceau was readying himself for an afternoon fishing trip when two German generals entered the store and asked to speak with Marceau.

"Herren General, please sit down, and I shall look for Marceau," said Bridget.

"Messieurs General," Marceau enthusiastically greeted them and asked, "Do you wish to have coffee, tea, and cookies?"

"You are very polite," said one General.

The other general commented, "We heard about your craftsmanship from the other officers. We were told that you are the best cobbler in Normandy and your custom fitted and hand made boots are the best."

"Merci, merci beaucoup,-thank you very much, what can I do for you?"

"We want you to make custom fitted boots for us," said the general who spoke first.

"Oh, I would love to, but we must make the molds first, and I am running short of material. I must go to Paris to get more materials. How about next week at the same time?"

"That is fine; we shall see you next week. Au revoir," said the other general and they got up from their chairs and headed for the door.

"Au revoir, a tout a l'heure, see you later," replied Marceau.

"Thank God," said Marceau to Bridget.

"You were smart. I did not know how you were going to get out of this situation."

"I did not know either, but it just occurred to me as the best acceptable excuse. I have to take the boat and communicate with the Allies. I was worried because the submarine does not wait longer than fifteen minutes. Did you see my German watchdog companion for the trip?"

"No, I have not. But he should be here any minute."

"Did you buy the strong cognac for him?"

"Yes, I did. As a matter of fact it is with the rest of the provisions."

There was a knock on the door, and Marceau yelled out for Bridget to let him enter. It was not the soldier but an amply bosomed pretty girl with a tight-fitting dress buttoned only from the bust line down.

"So where is he?" she asked.

"Marceau, you are wanted," yelled Bridget.

"I don't want Marceau. I came to entertain the watchdog."

Marceau came to the front of the store, looked at the girl, and asked, "Are you Chris, the entertainer?"

"Yes, I am. Philip sent me over, do you want my resume?"

"If Philip sent you over you must be good."

"I think so."

"We don't have too much time or a comfortable room."

"That is fine. I am very skillful. He'll be in seventh-heaven in no time."

"I like your self-confidence. Where did you learn this trade of hospitality?"

"I learned this quite early in life-school, monsieur."

"What is your charge for this sort of entertainment?"

"There is no charge! I do it for the liberation of France."

"You are hired!"

"Thank you, monsieur."

The German bodyguard arrived. He was in his forties, slightly bald, and looked pale. He was offered cheese and bread. Marceau introduced Chris as an old customer's daughter who came to pick up his father's shoes. Marceau excused himself along with Bridget to go to the dock and prepare the boat for the trip. The guard and Chris were left by themselves.

"What is your name, Fraulein?"

"I am Chris and what is yours?"

"Just call me Franz."

"You are a nice looking man Franz, a little shy though."

"I don't do well with nice ladies like you."

"Oh, that is nonsense. You are a brave man and a good soldier. Girls like men who are like you. You don't come on strong, but you have strong feelings and plenty of passion."

"You are very kind Chris."

"You are kind too." Chris took a couple of short glasses, filled them with cognac and said to Franz.

"I like to drink to what you just said." Chris handed over the glass to Franz.

Their glasses touched, and both smiled at each other as they gulped down the cognac. There was a short silence which was broken by Chris, saying,

"You know, Franz, life is short, especially during war. One does not know what will happen in the next minute. Life becomes moments and we must make the best of every moment."

"I agree with you."

Chris poured another drink to Franz and invited him to sit next to her on the sofa. Franz looked around and slowly moved closer to Chris.

"Don't be shy. I will not bite you."

"I am just afraid Marceau can come in any minute."

"Don't worry. They are busy with the boat at least for another hour."

"You know, Franz; I liked you the moment I laid my eyes on you."

"I like you too."

Chris put her arms around Franz and gave him a kiss on his cheek. Franz embraced her and gave a kiss on her mouth, which was reciprocated by Chris with a French kiss. And they both lost control of their lust. She slowly unbuttoned his jacket and removed his undershirt. He opened her dress, took it off along with her bra and began to kiss her breasts, neck, and mouth. While he undressed her Chris unbuttoned his breeches. Then she stopped for a moment and reached for the glass and filled it with cognac. She offered it to Franz and he drank it down with lightning speed and continued kissing her. He began to touch her all over while Chris removed her panties and they began to make love with lust and passion. She gave him just enough cognac to enable him to climax and feel awesome. Franz wanted more sex and more drinks and Chris tried to reassure him that they would have fun later when he returned from the boating trip. She took his arm and helped him to the door. Outside they shared another kiss and hug and then Franz parted for the voyage. He was drunk and tired when he boarded the ship and was unable to observe what was really happening. This was exactly what Marceau wanted.

Marceau began cranking the engine. It was an old clunker and it took a good ten minutes before it started. There was plenty of huffing and puffing and misfire before it smoothed and was ready to sail. Marceau removed the ropes from the side and the boat started to float away from the dock.

"What is the name of this boat?" asked Franz.

"This boat is called, 'The Lucky Skipper.' She has served us well for the past ten years. Please make yourself comfortable. There is cheese, fish, bread, cognac, and wine." Franz took another jigger of cognac that finally, but slowly, was knocking him out. Marceau began maneuvering the boat to leave the harbor when he noticed that Franz had not donned the cork life vest.

"Hey comrade, you must put the life vest on."

"Thank you, I almost forgot. It must be the cognac." He tried to get it on, and with the help of Marceau, he succeeded in wearing the vest. He felt very comfortable stretching out his body on the floor and as the waves rocked the boat he fell asleep.

The circular harbor began to fade away as the boat headed toward open waters.

The Channel looked vast with patches of fog in the distance which could scare the first time traveler but Franz was in deep sleep and unaffected by the scenery and the rolling whites of the waves. Marceau watched his compass and the direction he was heading toward. There was a very short distance left toward the buoy. He slowly approached the buoy, pulled the rope twice, and lowered his crab trap containing the plastic chicken meat lure. He waited about fifteen minutes and pulled up the other crab trap. Inside the fake chicken lure was an urgent message, along with it, five crabs that they would have for supper.

Franz woke up with a big yawn and felt disoriented for a few minutes. In a kind of a mellow voice he asked, "Where are we in this vast sea?"

"Somewhere near the coast. We are heading home with some crabs," replied Marceau.

It was late afternoon when the boat arrived at the harbor. Marceau got out first with the crabs in his hand, followed by Franz with the provision box.

"Thank you for your help and company," said Marceau.

"Oh, you're very welcome. I also would like to thank you for your hospitality and the invitation to your place," replied Franz. Bridget came to help with the catch and Franz immediately asked, "Is Chris still around?"

"Oh no, she had to leave because her mother got sick, but told me to tell you hello," replied Bridget.

"Do you have her address?"

"She told me you should leave your address and she'll get in touch with you."

"Thank you." The soldier scribbled his military address on a piece of paper and gave it to Bridget.

"Thank you for coming and your companionship," said Marceau.

"Thank you for your hospitality. Bye," said Franz.

Marceau opened the urgent message which stated that one of the British agents was missing and it must be found out what happened to him. Bridget drove right away to Shaw and Parker's place and asked them to come to the shop that evening. They were not home so she left the coded message under the doors of Shaw and Parker.

There was a sense of alarm in the air because the agent was very important for the MI6. He was practically "invisible" and extremely cunning. Furthermore, he had a very delicate mission of extracting German strategic information through a labyrinth of French women hired to befriend the German generals. These women move to and came from all walks of life, from sales ladies through respected housewives. All were trained in various techniques of human frailties from drugs to sex. These ladies, recruited from all over France, were excellent liaisons from every point of view and obtained vital information for the Allies.

Shaw and Parker received the information in the early evening hours and drove to Port-En-Bessin right after their dinner. They found Marceau and Bridget quite upset.

"What is happening?" asked Shaw.

"MI6 informed me that a very important agent has disappeared in Paris."

"Do you have any information from the Resistance?"

"I had one of the local operatives here about forty minutes ago. He came back from Paris today and according to the best information he is alive but hiding. He was compromised by mistake."

"Briefly what was his mission and who helped him?" asked Parker.

Marceau described to them in detail the mission and the ladies who helped him to collect vital information. According to Marceau's source one lady was sexually overzealous and the General had a heart attack. He was taken to the hospital but the Gestapo got into the situation.

"So, what happened next?" asked Shaw.

"We do not have an accurate report yet to verify exactly what took place in the Gestapo headquarters. However, one of our operatives, working there as a cleaner, overheard some of the conversations between a young Gestapo man and the lady."

"Accordingly, she was threatened to be tortured, but she refused to disclose any information. Then, he ordered the guards to strip her clothes and she was interrogated under extreme pressure. He kept asking her whom she worked for, but she remained silent. He slapped her twice and five minutes later asked her again about her connections. She said that she was working alone for money. The Gestapo man did not believe her and she was exposed to water and electric torture. She could not take the suffering and confessed about the British agent as a procurer for sex and money."

"How did the British agent find out about her arrest?" asked Parker.

"The cleaner told her best friend what happened and she contacted the agent."

"What did the Gestapo do with the lady?" questioned Shaw.

"She is at home, but her fate is sealed. I do not recommend rescuing her, too risky and the repercussions would be mass murder. No one has any knowledge of how much she was telling the Gestapo about her mission. If she managed to lie that she needed money for sex and the British agent was a procurer, she may get off as a cleaning lady or be sent to a work camp. That is if the General did not reveal any secrets and she has no documents in her possession. She was aware of the risks and consequences of sex play with generals but she was a great resistance fighter who believed in the liberation of France by the Allies."

"So what is your recommendation now?" asked Parker.

"First and foremost, we must find the agent. If he was not found by the Gestapo and is alive somewhere we must bring him here to be sent home by plane. I know your dilemma in terms of your assignment but he is a part of us and we must find him before the Germans do. In order to spare both of you so you will not be distracted from the Atlantic Wall studies, I contacted one of our best rescue agents, Gerard Tibault, to help in this matter."

"He needs all the details and he'll proceed the best way he can," said Shaw.

Shaw and Parker spent some time with Marceau then left for home.

"So, what do you make of it?" asked Parker during the trip.

"He'll give it the best shot he can and try to save him. He has to locate him first. If you'll take me to the train station, I'll spend a few days in Paris to find him. You can run the cells by yourself in the meantime. If there is any problem Marceau will help you out. I strongly believe that MI6 is expecting me to help the chap escape and go home."

"How do you intend to find him?"

"We have safe houses everywhere we go. It is part of our training to go underground as soon as we sense potential problems. I have a few addresses in Paris."

"What about transportation?"

"Being an Organization Todt officer I am going to get some building materials and put him in between the sacks of concrete in empty concrete bags. I will surely need Marceau's connections to get a truck, driver, and a few workers with automatic rifles to accompany the load. Before I leave, we must talk to Marceau and let him know of our plans."

"I like your determination but I disagree with you. Our mission is to investigate the Atlantic Wall together. We can't spare any time to look for troubled agents on either side. We can not sacrifice our mission which involves over a million people for one individual. The invasion plans depend on our reports. I appreciate your sentimental concern, but it can not fly. It'll be a violation of our order."

"So, what's your recommendation?"

"We can stand by for consultation as it warrants."

"Maybe you're right, at least we can assist."

It was late at night when they got back to their apartments and neither of them were tired enough to go to bed. There was some concern about security on their minds especially of those who volunteered to become Resistance operatives. But help was needed and human failures were expected. It hurts when something goes wrong and dear colleagues are implicated.

"We need to leave at 0630 in the morning," said Shaw.

"That is fine. We shall start the day early so we can talk to Marceau."

Shaw and Parker parted for the night. The next morning they rose early, and after a hearty breakfast they set out to travel to Marceau's shop. Shaw gave Marceau various ideas and addresses on how to transport the MI6 agent from Paris to Normandy and prepare a night flight to London. Since telephoning was an unacceptable form of communication because of the Gestapo's listening devices, everything had to be discussed in advance and in person. Marceau promised to help getting the agent back to England.

Tibault, the rescue operative, left for Paris after the briefing by Marceau. He arrived in the early evening and stayed with a friend who was still an active MI6 operative. He was a highly respected surgeon. The German military elite were very fond of his medical knowledge and interest in the German operatic compositions. They were up until dawn dissecting every detail and discussing the various plans and options to find their colleague and rescue him.

After a few hours of sleep, Tibault began to comb the possible hideouts in Paris. He was very discouraged because the agent had disappeared without a trace. While dining that evening, he remembered a retired MI6 agent who lived somewhere in Paris. There was a remote possibility that he might be able to help him locate the agent.

This retired agent decided to reside in Paris and gorge himself with women of the arts and sculpture to avenge his wife's unfaithful behavior. His wife loved the arts, especially sculpture. She modeled nude for famous artists. One day she was so enthralled by one of the sculpture's advances that she became his mistress and her nude pictures were all over Paris.

He couldn't take the humiliation and his marriage became a love and hate relationship until a fiery divorce, but he never forgot her. She broke it off with the sculptor a year later and moved back to England.

He got a job as a security chief in a Parisian bank and lived his life in the bohemian circle. Tibault began to search for his address in the phone book, and found it at Rue de Vaugirard. He walked there hastily. It was near the Boulevard de Montparnasse, where he had been eating his dinner.

He walked up to the second floor apartment, knocked on the door with the victory signal, and to his amazement, the door opened and the retired agent greeted him.

"Hello. Do I know you?" asked agent Steve.

"I'm Gerard Tibault. I was sent here by Marceau from Port-En-Bessin. I came to save Steven. Is my friend, Edward around?"

"He stepped out for a few moments. Do you care to sit down while you wait for him?"

They looked at each other for a minute, and Steve began to question him.

"Let's chat. How do I know that you're telling the truth?"

"You'll find out through Marceau."

"How do I get in touch with him?"

"I will contact him."

Tibault then called Bridget's neighbor who asked Bridget to come to the phone. Bridget got a hold of Shaw who then talked to Steve.

"Hello my friend, this Matthew Shaw."

"You old rascal, how are you?"

"I'm fine. But you're in trouble. I cannot talk to you because it's not a secure line. The chap who is trying to save you is Tibault. He is an experienced Resistance and rescue operative. Trust him."

"Yes, I am in big trouble."

"I know. He will help you, but be patient. I must go now before this call is traced. Good luck!"

"Well, as you heard, I'm Steve. I have been hiding here since last week."

They shook hands and smiled at each other. Moments later, Edward came back and was totally surprised to see Tibault.

"What on earth are you doing here?"

"I came to save the neck of your friend."

"Good deed! I hope you succeed!

"I would love to talk to you Edward but we have to act fast."

"Never mind, do what you have to do and we'll chat later. You'll come back to Paris and we'll have a good time."

"You bet, but first I must help Steve."

Tibault turned to Steve and in a serious voice began to lay out the plans of his rescue.

"We have little time, so hear me out," said Tibault.

"It will take one day to organize your departure to Normandy. First, you will depart about 1215 tomorrow morning to an undisclosed location escorted by two heavily armed Resistance operatives. Then, you'll be taken to a cement factory and put into a cement bag. I shall accompany the shipment. We will not stop on the road. You will have provisions, something to drink, and a small waterproof bag to urinate in. Only take the absolute essentials in your pockets. I must go now. We'll talk in Normandy before your flight. Au revoir."

Shaw was absolutely elated talking to Steve even for such a short time. Phase two was about to begin. Tibault had to find Marceau's Parisian connection to get a five ton truck to carry one-hundred bags of cement and supporting boards. The Resistance had to purchase the cement and two empty bags to camouflage agent Steve in. Magicians couldn't have done it better in a theatrical showcase the way Shaw conceived the whole rescue. But timing was the major essence of the operation.

Shaw connected with Marceau later that evening and told him that the operation was progressing according to plan. Tibault was to pick up a rented car at midnight in front of Steve's apartment house. The key would be left on the driver's seat and they would proceed to Paris Concrete Products Center where he would drop off Steve. He was to wait there for thirty minutes and watch for a flashlight signal of the victory sign which would come from a Camion Renault AHR Truck. The plan seemed flawless.

The clock chimed midnight and Tibault was there to pick up his car. Fifteen minutes later Steve emerged and both drove away to the cement place. Steve said good bye to Tibault who wished him good luck and drove away. When he came back thirty minutes later, the truck signaled to him to proceed; Steve was camouflaged. It took them sometime to leave Paris but they had no problem on the way to Normandy. There was just one roadblock before they entered the Normandy region and after that it was clear sailing to the drop off destination. It was a bunker construction site and a Resistance operative was waiting there.

He tapped twice on the bag indicating that all was clear to come out. Steve cut the bag, climbed out, and slowly walked away with Tibault. The sun was shining brightly and Tibault was tempted to continue the walk in the fresh morning air but it was too risky. He drove straight to Marceau's with Steve where they would stay until departure time. Another Resistance operative joined them around ten at night and the three of them ate and drank the beer that was available. They talked about some of their experiences in France, good and bad times, cracked some jokes, and had a little nap until one-thirty in the morning.

Marceau, Bridget and the three of them drove to the airstrip where they waited together until the plane landed. The Westland Lysander III was a little late because of the foggy weather. Four prearranged Resistance operatives from Caen protected the five of them with automatic weapons under their coats and one of them directed the plane for landing. It was a very brief thanks and a good bye. An MI6 agent helped Steve to climb up into the fuselage, closed the door, and the plane left the strip into the black sky. The mission was accomplished.

Bridget took the car that had been given to Tibault and drove it back to Port-En-Bessin where another operative would pick it up and return it to Paris.

Shaw and Parker slept soundly until eight-thirty when they were awakened by a huge explosion coming from the west. They dressed and left their apartments quickly and drove away before the German military police cordoned off the road. Having driven over an hour they stopped in a roadside café for breakfast. It did not take long to find out that the explosion was caused by hundreds of mines in a storage facility. Of course, the Germans blamed the Resistance and cried sabotage. Whether it was sabotage or not Shaw and Parker listened quietly to the local chatter by the soldiers. As they were ready to leave, two Organization Todt workers approached Parker and Shaw.

"Do you happen to be a civil engineer and could you temporarily help in the construction of a bunker? The engineer who was assigned to the task had a car accident as he was coming to work and is in critical condition in a nearby hospital."

"I could help you out for a short while, but we must inspect other construction sites," replied Parker.

"We would certainly appreciate your contribution."

Parker and Shaw became separated. Parker stayed at the construction site and Shaw went to meet with cell number two since they had missed the first meeting because of the Gestapo's search of the apartment house a week earlier. Since they had only one car, Shaw had to return later to pick up Parker.

Parker left for the construction site with certain trepidation. He was not really interested in the project per se but to gain more information of the location and construction methods. At the same time he was concerned about his intimate involvement that may lead to further personal engagement, which was not his mission. It is one thing to go around pretending to oversee construction in a superficial way, but getting engaged was an entirely different matter.

The construction, in Parker's estimation, had a number of engineering and material flaws. He shut up about the engineering mistakes because it would have created all kinds of conflicts.

"Can I see your foreman?" asked Parker of one of the workers.

The foreman was busy pouring cement and asked Parker if he would be kind enough to join him.

"What can I do for you, Officer Parker?"

"You should request more steel rods and crushed stone." He was polite and curt.

"I know but I have trouble getting materials period."

"You must be more forthcoming. We cannot approve your casemates unless you come close to our expectations."

As one of the foremen directed the work, one of the slave laborers collapsed while carrying the cement mixture in a wheelbarrow. Parker tried to help the man, but one of the guarding soldiers stepped in between.

"I must ask you to leave him alone, because he is a no good French Resistance prisoner and was assigned to this work detail."

"I believe you have the wrong approach, soldier. Prisoners are human beings like you and me. They have a different political outlook and because of that they don't deserve harsh treatment."

"But they are interfering with our policies; they deserve to be punished."

"You are forgetting we are occupying their land and imposing our order on them."

"Our policies are better. It is National Socialism."

Parker listened kindly to the soldier then gave him a little more lecture in the most elegant German. He told him that one must not forget the humanitarian side of prisoner management.

"But these people are not human, they are animals, and they should be treated as such," said the soldier.

"I disagree with you. You cannot expect good labor without inspiration. By showing that you care, giving him water and a piece of bread, you will achieve more than kicking and spitting at him," replied Parker.

The soldier pondered, and slowly said, "We shall see! Heil Hitler!"

There was another guard who overheard the conversation and called his superior about the statements made by Parker. Since the military and Organization Todt operated on different levels, especially when it came to forced labor, there was a clash in the air.

The Kriegsmarine—army of offense-captain approached Parker and asked him to leave the prisoners alone because that was not his job.

"Your job is engineering and not prisoner personnel!" instructed the captain.

"My job is to see that the job is done well by the personnel you assign; otherwise you can do the job yourself! I am here to substitute not to argue with soldiers who do not know how to construct."

"We all have different assignments and we have to work together to win this war," said the captain.

"I agree that we must work together, but you must listen to me to finish this project."

"I will not listen to you, you are not my superior!"

"That is fine, do not listen to me, you can direct the project yourself!"

Parker started walking away toward his car when the captain shouted, "I shall report you to the military headquarters, Gestapo, and Organization Todt for refusing to help in wartime!"

"You do that and there will be no engineers willing to help you build the bunker. You will create such a scare that you will be court-martialed!"

At this point the captain cooled down and offered a truce. The episode left a bitter taste in Parker's mouth, but he had to play the game to shut him up. It was a memorable experience. He noted the coordinates and specifics of the bunker. Parker tended to ignore any personal questions by simply concentrating on the project. He left mid afternoon with an excuse that he had to visit another bunker for its inspection.

Shaw arrived at the construction site to pick Parker up. Parker and Shaw arrived home late in the afternoon, had an early dinner, and spent the evening briefly discussing the events of the day, catching up with the news and listening to classical music from southern England from their shortwave radio.

It was the second time that they met all the members of the seven cells who were meticulously selected by Marceau over the course of the week. The operatives varied in experience, occupation, age, and gender. But they were all chosen for their intelligence and willingness to take on dangerous assignments. All operatives received their respective code numbers according their regions (1, 2, 3, etc.) and individual names (Gene: 01, Gabriel: 02, Tom: 03, etc). This way their identities and functions were protected from the Gestapo and Nazi collaborators.

Marceau was just about ready to open his store when a courier brought him a note. He read the note with great pleasure and satisfaction.

"Thank you very, very much. You have made me very happy!" said Marceau. Bridget saw Marceau's face full of joy. Marceau gave her the note and she read it out loud.

"Steve arrived to his destination. All is well! This is wonderful news," said Bridget.

They were both elated when a German general of great respect and influence stepped in the store.

"Good Morning Marceau and Bridget. What is happening that both of you show such great happiness?" asked General von Hauser.

"A child was born to the daughter of my best friend. We heard that something had happened to her reproductive organs and she had difficulties to conceive. But miracles do happen, and this was one of those things," said Marceau.

"But what can I do for you monsieur General. How can I help you?" asked Marceau.

"I have some discomfort inside the boot. Something is pressing on my left big toe."

"Please kindly take off the boot and let me look at it."

"Could you help me get it off?"

"Of course General, just give me your left foot and I will slowly remove your boot."

Marceau began very slowly to ease off his boot and in no time he had the boot in his hand. He put his right hand inside and touched the area of complaint then very carefully palpated the general's big toe. Initially he found nothing serious but as he reexamined the boot his index finger came across a tiny sharp object embedded into the leather. With a curved pair of pliers he removed the object and showed it to the General.

"What is it?"

"A tiny stone somehow got inside. It can happen," explained Marceau.

Marceau helped to put on the boot and waited for the General's response.

"It feels much better. Thank you. What do I owe you?"

"Nothing, it was my pleasure to help you."

"You are a terrific cobbler. I will order another pair very soon."

"Thank you. Please come back and don't wait if you have any problems with your boots. Your feet are very important in your profession."

"You are a very kind man, Marceau. I will recommend you to my colleagues. Adieu, Marceau."

"Au revoir, General. Have a very good day!"

As soon as the General stepped out there was a strong knock on the door and two Gestapo men made some inquiries about a young man who was seen entering the store.

"Do you know the name of the man who entered your shop before the General entered?" asked one of the Gestapo agents.

"Oh yes, I know who you're talking about. He talked about a man who recently experienced the joys of fatherhood."

"Do you know his name?" continued the Gestapo agent.

"No, I don't. Is there any problem?"

At that point in time the General returned to the store because he forgot his gloves. The two Gestapo men saluted the General and continued to ask questions in front of the General.

"Any problem with the cobbler?" asked the General.

"Just routine questions about a man who entered his store," was the response of the other Gestapo man.

"Please, gentlemen. Marceau is an honorable man. He helps us to do our duty," said the General.

"Thank you, General," said the Gestapo agent. There was an eerie silence for a second and all three exited the store.

"Bridget, you must contact the young courier and tell him that the Gestapo is looking for him. He must disappear for a while. The Gestapo is suspicious. Please do it fast and be careful that nobody is following you. You know how to be evasive," instructed Marceau.

Bridget waited fifteen minutes then walked to a bakery, went to the back of the store, and looked through a small window for the two Gestapo men. She stayed in the store for another half an hour then rushed out toward the harbor to make contact with the Resistance. The words of caution traveled fast and the young man got the caveat by mid-morning. It was somehow worrisome for Marceau to have the Gestapo questioning him. He had been careful not to arouse any suspicion, but this time it was not his fault at all. The Gestapo had many sources of information. There were collaborators in France as well as in England. Marceau tried to be one step ahead of the Gestapo and usually asked to terminate those who tried to destroy the Resistance. Marceau did not wait to find his enemy, and asked Bridget to get in touch with the investigative arm of the Resistance. Within two days they found the stool pigeon who was giving away names to German friends for money and wine. She was interrogated by two operatives, confessed the betrayal, and was taken to a height of no return.

Marceau did not contact operatives for two weeks to allay any further suspicion by the Gestapo. He decided to lay low and work solely on shoe repairs. Only Shaw and Parker were allowed to meet with him but only for short periods of time. There was a big operation in the works, however, that had to do with identifying the mine layouts around the proposed invasion sites. The Germans had become very active in laying mines over the suspected routes that they thought the Allied forces had planned to use for a beach head. It was a delicate and dangerous investigation, but it had to be done. The burden for this job rested on Shaw and Parker while Marceau, who knew the topography helped in analyzing, describing, and transmitting the minefield terrain. Shaw and Parker sent messages via drops to every cell to be on the lookout for the laying of mines and report to them in writing via drops or personal contact.

A week went by and the Generals returned to have their measurements taken for the boots. They were very curious how Marceau could make such perfect boots that fit so well. Marceau patiently explained the process of utilizing a plaster of Paris mold to shape the leather according to cast. He emphasized the high quality of leather and the intricate sewing were so important for comfort. Bridget served coffee and some homemade pastries while Marceau took measurements and the casts. They were pleased with his skills and hospitality. He was assured for future protection and continuation of his craft.

Marceau needed some reassurance because the Gestapo gave him a very uneasy feeling. He had so much at stake.

Soon after the Generals left the store, he looked at sketchy reports of underwater beach obstacles with high-explosive mines. The Allies needed lots of underwater beach information and the pressure was on Marceau, Shaw, and Parker.

"We must contact the Resistance cells at Cherbourg, St. Mere Eglise, Carentan, Isigny, Bayeaux, Port-En-Bessin, and Caen. The areas west of these places could be deadly for the Allies if we allow the thousands of mines to explode during the invasion. We must destroy those mines before the allied forces come to shore," said Marceau.

"We are working on it, aren't we?" asked Bridget.

"We must identify the locations of those damned mines first," commented Marceau.

"Shaw and Parker are doing their best," continued Bridget.

"We have to tell the American Air Force and Royal Air Force where to bomb," said Marceau.

"We will, don't you worry!" replied Bridget.

"I love your confidence and enthusiasm!" replied Marceau. "We have a problem. There are too many enemies to watch for," he continued.

"I know, Marceau, but we are smarter. We'll beat them! We'll catch the traitors."

"Don't be so sure, my dear! You must learn not to be so trustful!"

"Oh well, I think we'll know something soon about the German minefields," said Marceau.

"Somebody is knocking; let me see who is at the door at this late hour," said Bridget.

"Go, my dear, I will prepare the supper."

One of the Gestapo men came back and politely inquired about his lost key.

"I am truly sorry to disturb you in this late hour but I must have inadvertently dropped my apartment key out of my pocket. I thought this might have happened here at your place. By the way we found the young man and he told us the same news about the newborn child. In this area we are very concerned about enemy infiltration. You must understand. Incidentally, we heard good things about you from the Officers and Generals. I could use a good pair of boots."

"We are truly sorry, but we didn't find a key after you left. You are welcome to look around. For the boots and other repair, we are here to be at your service," Bridget said in a cool voice.

"Oh well, I will manage to get into the apartment. The concierge must have a duplicate key. "Au revoir!" said the Gestapo man and walked out of the store.

Bridget politely responded by saying, "Adieu."

"What was that about?" asked Bridget.

"Who knows? I am not going to get into an investigative discussion as to why he returned. He may be lying or telling the truth."

Marceau made a delicious fish dinner with vegetables. In addition, he put bread, cheese, and wine on the table. They had a quiet dinner and afterwards read and listened to music from Paris.

It was around nine o'clock in the morning when Shaw and Parker appeared at the door. Bridget let them in, saying a big good morning and offered them coffee and croissants. Marceau had a saddened look on his face and Parker spontaneously asked,

"What's the matter, Marceau? You look so unhappy."

"The Gestapo was here yesterday. It was about the courier who delivered the message about Steve. It checked out all right, but as you know they are like sharks. When they smell blood, they don't like to let go, and swim around for a long time."

"I meant to send Bridget for you to come but now that you are here I must tell you the latest request from Allied Intelligence.

"They are requesting to identify the locations of mines at the beaches, around the batteries, and beyond. The need is urgent so the Allied Aircrafts can prepare to bomb the hell out of them before the invasion."

"I knew about those bloody mines. Some cell members mentioned them, but there were only a very few at the time," said Shaw.

"We have a task and we have to work on it," continued Marceau.

"We'll talk to the cells next time," replied Parker.

"What do you want to do with the Gestapo guy?" asked Parker.

"Let him be. If we do anything, there will be a bloodbath. We are more important to stay alive, than him being dead! We just have to play the cards right! They have to do their job, and we have to do ours. And we'll do a better job," contended Marceau.

"I agree!" said Shaw.

"We better go now!" added Parker.

"Au revoir. Gentlemen, see you again, be brave but careful. We need you badly," remarked Marceau. Bridget opened the door and smiled goodbye.

"Good boys," said Marceau and set down next to the repair table and started working on the boots for the two Generals.

It started out as a quiet morning. The sky had a few clouds and the sun was bright and strong. "What a perfect morning for an early walk," remarked Lady Renoir as she entered Marceau's place to pick up a pair of shoes she had left them there last week for repair.

"Bonjour, Madam. You're looking good," greeted Marceau.

"So do you, you're looking great," was her swift reply.

"So, what brought you here?"

"I left my black pair of shoes here. Remember sweetheart? I also have some news for you."

"I only want to hear good news."

"A young Gestapo man was hit by a car as he walked out of a bar last night."

"Where and when did this happen? Who drove the car?" asked Marceau.

"It was here, at the intersection between Rue de Bayeux and Rue de Croiseur. The car was driven by a German General. It was claimed as an accident."

"How did he look?"

"He had black hair, brown eyes, and a small scar on the right side of his face."

"How do you know that?"

"I saw the guy on the road, and I have a good memory."

Marceau's face turned from sad to happy. He was cautiously elated by the incident, but feared that the Gestapo man might have talked to his colleagues about the courier; though he might not have. This was only an assumption, but nevertheless, he was primarily involved in the case.

"Do you have some other news?"

"Yes, but it is not good news."

"After what you have told me, I can take the sad news."

"The Gestapo hung a young lady who was an important member of the Resistance in Paris."

"The undertaker is a friend of mine and he was told to pick up the body in the prison courtyard."

"Do you know her name?"

"Renee Tireau. She was only twenty-two years old. Those German bastards had tortured her to confess all the collaborators who had radio transmitters in the area where she lived. Fortunately she had some painkillers with her at the time of capture and she swallowed them all. She was practically unconscious."

Marceau had a serious look on his face as he listened very attentively to the middle age lady. But he was careful with his comments.

"I am sorry for anyone to have such a terrible death. I have repaired your shoes but your leather will not hold out very long. You better buy a new pair of shoes."

The lady took the shoes with satisfaction, paid for them, and walked out with a big thank you and good bye.

Marceau immediately shared the good news with Bridget but with a saddened face added the bad news also.

"Do you think the fear is over?" asked Bridget.

"One never knows," he replied.

Marceau repaired a lot of shoes and boots during the morning hours and crafted the new boots for the Generals during the afternoon. It was early evening when Shaw and Parker returned for another short visit.

"What's the matter?" asked Bridget with surprise.

"We have to talk with Marceau in the morning," said Parker.

"Is it anything serious?" Marceau inquired.

"It can be a potential danger for cell three," said Shaw.

"We'll talk about it in the morning. I am very tired now."

"We will see you at 0830 hour. Bye, and have a good rest," said Shaw.

"Bye Bridget, see you in the morning," added Parker as they left the shop.

Shaw and Parker arrived at Marceau's place fifteen minutes earlier than the agreed upon time and watched the people from their car. They saw a young looking man dressed in a dark raincoat although it wasn't even cloudy. He had a cigarette in his right hand and was strolling up and down the street where Marceau's place was. He finished smoking, threw the butt far away, got into his car and drove toward the seaport. Shaw and Parker followed the man and saw him getting out of his car, showing his badge to a few soldiers, talking to them, and then point in an easterly direction. He seemed satisfied and got back into his car and drove toward the Bayeux direction.

It was 0840 and Shaw and Parker apologized for being a few minutes late, but it was a justified tardiness.

"We followed a Gestapo man busy nosing around this place," said Shaw.

"I am not surprised, after the last encounter with another Gestapo man," said Marceau.

"So, what was so important last evening?" asked Marceau.

Shaw began telling the episode.

"One of our operatives, 302 by code, an attractive blonde, named Jeanette, met with one of the German officers at a friend's house who was working as a secretary for a German General. After a while, they became intimate, and she visited his apartment several times later. One evening, she looked at a map on his desk that happened to be the mine laying areas along the beaches of a section of Normandy that she failed to recognize. Because she did not read German she began asking questions that aroused the suspicions of the officer. She dropped the questions, but during their sexual play, she started asking questions about the markings on the map."

Parker took over. "That was the turning point that made the officer quite upset. According to her story, she did sexually tease him to the extreme, and he told her about the mines but not the location. The officer told the story to his friend who happened to become very curious of her motives and questioned her several times. She was smart enough, however, to play the role of an innocent friend whose only motive was to play 'hide and seek.' The suspicion was there, but we need all the information we can get."

"It is a dangerous game, and amateurs can easily get into trouble. I am glad you told me about this story," commented Marceau. "First, we must protect her. Secondly, I was the one who recommended her and we must know how she operates, and thirdly, we need to find out what she saw. We cannot and must not meet her in person. The Gestapo is on the look-out and we must lay low, very low for a number of days or weeks until the dark clouds dissipate beyond the horizon."

"Try to find out as much as you can via drops. She must curb her curiosity for some time, at least, until the officer has redeveloped trust in her. You have to communicate this to Jeanette. We will tell Jeanette how to behave in the future with the officer and prepare her for possible escape if it becomes necessary," replied Shaw.

"I am pleased overall with your operation and I am getting the same messages from OSS and MI6."

"We did not get enough vital information yet but we are slowly collecting the pieces of the puzzle," said Shaw.

"When all the pieces become available, plus the plan of the German defense strategies, we'll save thousands of lives during the invasion of Normandy," added Parker.

"One thing you must be careful of and that is conceitedness. We are always being watched by our enemies," warned Marceau.

Bridget's voice interrupted the conversation as she announced that a customer was waiting in the front. Marceau excused himself. A Gestapo man introduced himself as a new customer for a handmade boot. Parker peeked through the door and recognized the man who was walking in front of the shop earlier this morning.

"Look who is here," said Parker.

Shaw took a look and said softly, "Bloody bastard."

They both stepped out and greeted each other. The Gestapo man looked at both of them and with a sarcastic tone remarked how many diverse customers Marceau attracted since he opened his shop.

"I am Fritz Kohler from the Gestapo. Nice meeting you from Organization Todt. May I have your names, officers of the Organization Todt please?"

Shaw introduced Parker as Hans Dietrich and Parker introduced Shaw as Erik Krueger.

"I am delighted to meet you. What brought you here to this place?"

"We need new boots for our daily work," responded Parker.

"Ah so! You seem to speak wonderfully educated German."

"Thank you. We learned from our parents, school, Gymnasium, and University on how to express our thoughts and feelings," remarked Shaw.

"Do you think you will accomplish your goal of building our defense structure in light of the problems we have with the Allied bombings, saboteurs, Resistance spies, and forced laborers who have no spirit for the Reich?"

"All we can do is look at the master plan, do our very best, and ignite the spirit," replied Parker.

"I am so proud of you! You are well serving the Fatherland! You are intelligent, hard working citizens of the Reich!"

"Can I be of help to you?" Marceau interrupted.

"Oh yes, I would like a pair of custom made boots."

"No problem. We have to make a form and discuss the details. When would you like to come in?"

"But I'm already in. I had the impression that you are free now."

"I must have the material to make the form. I have to order it from Paris. Perhaps in about ten days I should have it."

"How come the generals can have it in one week?"

"I was told that they are very short in material. If you have a contact to get it sooner I can make the form next week at the same time."

"I will see you in ten days or less."

"Thank you, sir!" said Marceau.

"By the way," asked the Gestapo man, "Does that young man who was investigated by my deceased colleague still visit you?"

"I have not seen the young man since he was here."

"Marceau, you are a fine cobbler, and we want to be proud of you. You are helping us to carry out our task and that means heavy legwork. Please try to cooperate with us. Understand?"

"I will provide you with my very best service."

"Auf wiedersehen—I'll see you again!"

The Gestapo man left the place without the slightest hint about the participants. He did not get a morsel of knowledge about what had been going on. His approach was smart but Marceau, Shaw, and Parker were smarter.

The Gestapo man had hardly left the place when Michael Woerner entered the shop. Bridget gave him a big hello.

"How are you Michael? I haven't seen you for some time," said Bridget.

"I was away only for three weeks."

"Where were you?"

"I had to go to Paris on a special assignment, but I am back for now. I came to invite you for a concert if you are interested in classical music."

"Whose music are they playing?"

"It will be a mixture of Mozart, Beethoven, Chopin, and Liszt."

"I like the combination of the composers."

"It will be next Saturday evening at eight in Caen. May we have dinner together before the concert?"

"That will be fine."

"I will pick you up at five o'clock in the afternoon."

"Thank you and au revoir," said Bridget with a smile.

"Thank you and auf wiedersehen."

Michael arrived right on time, dressed in his freshly pressed dress uniform. Bridget had an elegant dark blue dress, low cut around the chest but covered by white lace, a white pair of shoes, and a short white jacket. Both of them looked stunning for the occasion.

They had dinner at six in a fine restaurant at the center of Caen. When they entered the place there was a reserved table waiting for them.

"Would you like wine or champagne?" asked Michael.

"White wine would be fine."

They both looked the menu, but the selection was limited. It was war time and people were used to the restaurants' limited offerings during the occupation.

"The fish looks good," suggested Michael.

"I agree. I like to eat fish too. It is good for you."

They looked at each other with smiles on their faces. There was a sense of peace and contentment in their looks. They set aside their nationalities and political differences for the duration of the evening. He extended his arm and touched her fingers without saying anything but feeling the warm pulsations of their hearts toward each other. They longed for these sentimental feelings in the middle of the war as if declaring ceasefire for a few hours and just enjoying the make-believe of a wonderful world of trust and love.

"What are you thinking?" asked Michael.

"About this evening, the wonderful dream we're having, and at the end we must wake up and face the opposite end of the spectrum. What an awful thought!"

"Do you have to?"

"Yes, I do. You are occupying our land with perverted philosophies of human existence. It is very hard to take. But you will never occupy our minds and hearts."

"I want a truce and no philosophies for this evening," replied Michael.

"I am sorry but you asked me something that is close to my heart. I am a free French woman even in your captivity."

"I respect your feelings. I know it is difficult to forget my uniform and where I come from."

The waiter brought the entrée and served the fish, potatoes, and vegetables. He put fresh napkins into their laps, filled the glasses with wine and wished that they enjoyed their meal.

"Bon appetite." Michael lifted the glass to touch her glass.

"May I offer the very same to you." Bridget lifted her glass and both glasses touched each others.

Both said "a ta ou votre sante-to your health, cheers" at the same time with their eyes wide open looking at each other.

"This fish tastes exquisite! What a wonderful preparation. The buttered sauce must be a house specialty," remarked Bridget.

"I am glad that you're enjoying the meal."

The entrée was followed by a homemade pastry and coffee. They left the restaurant and hurried to catch the concert on time. They arrived a few minutes before curtain time. Their seats were five rows behind center stage. Bridget and Michael sat down with the program in hand and waited for the performers to enter. There were a few minutes of eerie silence. The lights dimmed. The musicians came in first, followed by the conductor entering on stage. After the initial applause of greetings, the music began with Chopin which immediately captivated the audience.

During the first movement, Bridget and Michael moved closer and clutched each others fingers. The warm feelings they had for each other lasted during the entire performance. Certainly, there was a strong chemistry that permeated their bodies.

During intermission they were close together despite the various interruptions of pleasantries with his superior commanders and her friends. But they did not care what others thought or said about them, they were happy for the quiet moments of the evening. In the foyer of the concert hall, there were some offerings of homemade cookies and wine. Michael graciously offered Bridget both, but she only wanted the cookies. The music lasted for two hours with very beautiful renditions of each composer.

After the concert, they stopped the car at the seashore, and took a slow walk near the ocean. There was a half moon, and the wind caressed the surface of the water causing slight ripples on the surface.

"Did you enjoy the evening?" asked Michael.

"It was just delightful."

"I am very fond of you. I wish we would have met under different circumstances."

"The feeling is mutual."

They sat down on the sand facing the water, listening to the sounds of rumbling waves, and wishing that the moment could last forever.

"I hardly know you as a person, Michael. What did you do before the military?"

"I am an architect and engineer, specializing in commercial buildings and bridges. I have some pictures I could show you next time we meet."

"How about you, my darling, anything special you want to share?"

"I wanted to study theater in Paris."

"So why didn't you?"

"I couldn't, because I had to help Marceau."

Michael embraced Bridget and gave her a warm hug. Then they parted for a few seconds, looked at each other and then Michael kissed Bridget. She looked at him. And then they sat and embraced each other.

"It's getting late, Michael. I'm afraid Marceau will be worried about us."

"I think you are right. How inconsiderate of me!"

They walked back to the car and headed back home to Port-En-Bessin.

"May I call you, Bridget?"

"We have no telephone."

"But your father has a business, he should have a telephone. May I get you one?"

"Don't bother. Marceau does not care to have a phone. He thinks it is not necessary. So, just drop in and ask about me, leave a message with Marceau, or just drop a line in the mailbox. Tell me where and when, and I will contact you."

Marceau was waiting. He was impatient and paced up and down in the kitchen. "Bridget does not stay over midnight, but the dinner, concert, and getting back home takes time," were in his thoughts. But his fears began to dissipate as he spotted Michael's car through the shop window.

Michael thanked her for the evening and so did Bridget. She entered the house from a different entrance that directly leads to their home upstairs and apologized for being late.

"Oh I was not worried, but concerned," admitted Marceau. "You know our double life evokes concern all the time."

"I know it very well, and I try to be careful."

"Did you have a good time?"

"I had a wonderful time. He is such a gentleman. We both needed a diversion."

"That is true. It is very late. Two o'clock in the morning is not my bedtime."

"Nor mine, but occasionally it is good to splurge!"

"Let's go to bed! Good night. Oh by the way, Bridget, please contact Shaw or Parker to see me in the morning. Thank you."

Shaw and Parker got a message from cell 401 to meet as soon as they could. They agreed to meet in the afternoon at 1400 hour in the usual designated place in the country. After reading the drop, they went to see Marceau.

Marceau took them to the backroom with a pair of boots in hand, and they sat down without the presence of Bridget.

"Bonjour Good day. Thank you for coming. Oh! Just one minute. I forgot to close the curtains." Marceau got up and looked through the windows than pulled the curtains together.

"I don't like the Gestapo here, but he has the right to have new handmade boots. I wish to get rid of him, but not the same way as his partner was. I cannot afford that. So here is my plan. When he comes to try out his new boots, I'll have a small Normandy flag hanging on the door or window and you'll know he is here. I think it is better not to engage him. I have something more serious."

"One of our operatives, not in your cells, while working on casemates, cut into the connecting rods at critical points. When the cement was poured the structure collapsed. They are investigating now and a whole army of experts, Gestapo, and Herr Military Police are looking into the matter. If and when they find the culprit here there will be a bloodbath. This I can assure you. They will hang the person who worked on the iron rods upside down and cut them with razor blades until they bleed to death. In addition to increase their suffering, salt will be poured on his body. The worker will scream until he loses consciousness. We have to save him the best way that we can."

"It is a formidable task to defend and save his soul, but we can try," said Parker.

"We have to do it for the sake of our operatives and the infantry who will be coming in with the first wave of the invasion. Give us the directions and we'll be there in no time," added Shaw.

Shaw and Parker got into their car and drove toward the northeast. There were quite a number of people gathered around the collapsed concrete. Shaw and Parker requested the backhoe operator to dig deeper and began examining the rods which were covered with partially set concrete. Parker got out his pocket magnifier and began to examine the cuts. They were asked by one of the investigators to identify themselves, which they did. Parker studied the pieces and with eloquent German emphasized that the cuts were made by the manufacturer who provided the already damaged iron rods. Parker explained that the cuts were too fine to call it in situ sabotage.

"Besides" he continued, "who would commit such a suicidal act with so many guards around?" Parker invoked the German sabotage law which stated immediate execution of the perpetrators. "In a case like this, where so many lives are at stake and the defense/offense posture must be maintained, one must be suicidal to perpetrate this kind of structural damage," emphasized Parker. Then he further added, "In my entire engineering career I have seen many kinds of iron rod cuts, but never like this so imprecise."

"I don't quite agree with you," said a Gestapo investigator.

"Saboteurs are quite crafty and brave these days, especially the members of the resistance," he added.

"But you have no proof, only an assumption," replied Parker.

"What is your point, Officer Parker?"

"We must be more alert before we use any merchandise in the future. We do not construct first, then punish later. That is a waste of time and terribly demoralizing for the working crew. To execute on the assumption will create fear among the workers and slow down the building process. Every worker will be petrified to see the punishments. The Fuhrer gave us the order for so many casemates and bunkers to be erected within a short time. That is my point!" replied Parker.

Everybody became quiet and there was no further debate. Parker ordered the removal of the damaged structure and rebuilding the section of the bunker that collapsed. Shaw was extremely proud of Parker the way he handled himself and saved the lives of several people around the project.

Shaw and Parker stayed for awhile then left for the meeting with the cell. The meeting took place in a bombed-out farmhouse. The cell members were in one room and Parker and Shaw were in another room. Through the crack of the door the cell members were visible enough to see their fears on their faces. All three cell members were absolutely dismayed by the recently acquired news.

"We could use some help and instruction," said a pathetic voice.

"What is happening?" asked Shaw.

"We found out that a German mole is among the construction workers and he pretends to be a forced laborer from Paris. He has caused a serious uproar because several of our friends who supplied information have been arrested. Those friends in jail were severely tortured and confessed. We don't know how deeply we are compromised. We are still getting information through Resistance workers in jail via the most devious drops."

"We'll take care of the mole," said Parker.

"How about our safety?" asked one of the female operatives.

"Go to Paris and get lost for one week," suggested Shaw. Then he added, "As long as the Gestapo does not know your identity, don't worry. They are watching the drop and if nothing happens, they stop looking. Never give personal information to any supplier. Every message goes through drops which must be changed every time. Watch very carefully. The Germans are smart. Do not underestimate their investigative abilities. They are persistent and cruel in their interrogation methods."

"Have a good time in Paris. We'll see you next week," said Parker.

Shaw turned to Parker as they walked toward the car.

"We must get the mole tonight!"

"You have to ask Marceau to call the 'exterminator'. Let's drive back and talk to him. I know he doesn't want us to hang around, but in this case we have no alternatives. Do we?"

"We'll make it short and fast," replied Parker.

Shaw stayed in the car, and Parker talked to Marceau. He was told that the "exterminator" would do his job tonight. The whole conversation lasted five minute. Shaw and Parker were headed for home. It was enough stress for one day, but they had a sense of satisfaction. The cells must be saved to guarantee the flow of information.

Bridget drove to find the exterminator. He was in his usual bar drinking wine and flirting with women.

"How are you Bridget?" asked the exterminator.

"I came to see you."

He excused himself from the ladies and sat down with Bridget at a table. He was in his forties, bearded, tall, and an athletic man. The Germans respected his plumbing skills. He fixes all the toilets for the German army barracks, private homes, and the local sewer system. They don't know about his alliance with the Resistance and French patriotism. Whatever Marceau wants, Philip tries to satisfy the request. Bridget explained the situation to him that first he must find the mole. Philip did not waste time and left the bar in a hurry to the camp where the forced prisoners stayed. There he got in with the excuse that the major pipe was clogged and people in town were complaining about the stench. He talked with his

Resistance friends but it was difficult to find the mole with an adoptive French language among the thousands of workers.

By sheer coincidence he was talking to another Frenchman when he came to listen in on a conversation. As soon as he talked Philip became suspicious.

"Where are you from?" asked Philip.

"I was born in a small village between Germany and France."

"Why are you here in this forced labor camp?"

"I was a bad boy. I had worked for the Resistance."

"What did you do?"

"I sent radio messages to England."

"On what frequency and call letters did you talk?"

"I don't remember, it was some months ago and the Germans beat my head."

Philip knew then that he was lying. A real radio operator remembers those codes. When he found out that Philip was a loyal plumber for the German army and that he was there because he wanted to be, he confessed that he was providing information to the Germans. Then he asked Philip if he wanted to work with him on small things, like sending messages to a friend who was writing a book about the war.

Philip told him that it must be reciprocal. He was delighted. They talked about their favorite pieces of music and their trip around the world. Little by little he began to trust Philip. At one point he asked him if he wanted to visit the camp's sewer plant. He trusted Philip and they walked together to the plant. He was offered a mask of which he took with great pleasure. Philip waited a few minutes as he was busy gasping for air. The "medication" that was put into his mask was inhaled and minutes later he became very dizzy. At that point Philip suggested taking a walk for his dizzy spells from which he never really recovered and later expired on the sandy beach. The coroner's diagnosis was a heart attack.

Philip informed the camp's military that his mission was accomplished and the sewer was fixed. He drove home without a trace of guilt, as a matter of fact he was whistling a song all the way home about victory in Normandy.

He stopped in Marceau's place for a nightcap and talked about his encounter with the mole.

"Marceau, I am telling you, it was a piece of cake, no problem at all."

"I am glad, now I can sleep. Good night," said Marceau and he retired to his bedroom.

Bridget said, "Thank you in the name of Papa."

"Don't mention it. Au revoir!"

Days later when the Gestapo found out that one of their moles collapsed and died in the company of the plumber, they wanted to investigate the plumber. However, the plumber was more important to them than the mole. The Gestapo figured that there were a plethora of moles but very few skilled plumbers who are good workers for the Germans. The Gestapo dropped the case and agreed with the coroner. Marceau was satisfied with the plumber. Shaw and Parker received accolades from the cells. The Resistance was grateful for saving lives.

Despite all the Allied air photographs of the batteries, bunkers, casemates, and pill boxes there were a number of Atlantic Wall defense structures that had to be examined by human eyes. One of these was a bunker and casemate connected with underground tunnels.

In Marceau's last fishing trip he received an urgent order from Allied Intelligence asking Shaw and Parker about details of those hidden tunnels which served many purposes. Marceau indeed transmitted this inquiry to Shaw and Parker who were not quite ready to undertake this assignment.

It was a dreary morning, raining and foggy when Shaw and Parker set forth to determine the location of all the tunnels. They decided to cover the entire Atlantic Wall, starting from Cherbourg and ending at the Caen area. Some tunnels were complete and others were under construction. About twenty coastal artillery batteries had to be inspected for the tunnels.

The approach to visit the tunnels seemed to be routine, but the officers were difficult to handle at times.

"Why are you interested in the tunnel?" asked one of the German officers.

"We received complaints that the electric and plumbing materials were of inferior quality when they were constructed and that we should inspect them," said Shaw.

"We don't have any problems," said the officer.

"The problems will occur when you're experiencing heavy bombing or an internal explosion," said Parker.

"We did not receive any communication from our HQ about tunnel inspection."

"Why should you? It is not your expertise. You can call your HQ and ask them about a quality control inspection. You would make a real fool of yourself and betray your ignorance," said Parker.

The officer pondered for a few seconds, looked at Shaw and Parker, and yielded to their requests.

Shaw and Parker used foot measures, memorized locations, rooms, toilets, weapon and ammunition storages, ventilation, and exits.

Other inspections were less pleasant and more complicated. Storage facilities and bunker connection were said to be 'off limits' by senior German officers. They were accompanied by two German soldiers at all times. Fortunately, both agents had brilliant memories and they were able to store all necessary data in their minds until they got to the car.

In one situation, they had a difficult time gaining access to a particular tunnel system.

"I understand why you're here, but I will not let you inspect because we have classified materials in our interconnecting tunnel," said the German officer.

"It is up to you, but because you mentioned classified materials, we find it doubly important to inspect the tunnel. Should any bombs or explosions destroy your circuitry, you'll be in trouble," challenged Shaw.

"I am under orders. Nobody, except authorized personnel, can enter our tunnel."

"That is fine, but you must sign this paper that you have refused an inspection. This way our butts are covered," asserted Parker.

This was a brilliant gamble, but it served the purpose. He refused to sign the paper and allowed them to inspect every nook and cranny of the tunnel. There were astonishing revelations about the forthcoming V1 and V2 weapons. Shaw and Parker made every effort to note the intricacies of the tunnel.

They did not cover a fourth of the tunnels when the military police were greeting Shaw and Parker and asking for inspection authorization by the German Military Command.

"May we have your papers, please?" asked the officer of the military police.

"We have been verbally instructed to look into the possible electric fire hazards and sewage overflow in some of the tunnels. The final report, which incidentally is highly classified, must go directly to Commander in Chief West Gerd von Rundstedt. This is the only reason why the authorization is not in writing," said Parker.

"This makes sense if what you're telling me is the truth," said the Military Police Officer.

"You may call for verification, but if you do, you will be admonished and lose your rank. Don't blame us. We are warning you!" said Parker.

This bluff worked, but it too was risky. Parker was an excellent poker player in his younger years and with the same fervor he applied the same principles to bluffing. Shaw was absolutely flabbergasted by Parker's courage, but it had to be done.

Shaw and Parker called it a day and with smug satisfaction drove to Marceau shop to tell him about their accomplishments. They ate dinner there and drank wine until midnight.

The completion of the tunnel project, however, would have to wait, because other urgent issues had to be dealt with in the days ahead.

CHAPTER THREE

Shaw awoke quite early in the morning, looked at his clock on the night table and couldn't believe his eyes. It was five minutes past five. There was plenty of time to eat breakfast and get ready to visit his cells. He couldn't go back to sleep. He had to get up; there were too many things on his mind. He made a mug of tea and had some biscuits, turned on the radio, and listened to the BBC world service newscast. There was nothing extraordinary in the news, so he turned off the radio, decided to get dressed and took a leisurely walk on the cobblestone covered streets.

The fresh air of early spring was a sheer delight to Shaw and he really enjoyed the opportunity of solitude to think about the immensity of their next assignment in Normandy. They had to know minute details about the mines on the beaches and in the water surrounding the beaches. How do you get into the "prohibited zones," beaches, and water? The roads were checked by German military police, the beaches were patrolled by coastal military units, and the water was scanned by high powered telescopes from the bunkers.

Shaw was overwhelmed by the commanding task of carrying out the urgent assignment and sending the information that was badly needed by Allied Intelligence. There was no time to waste. The job had to be done! He walked back to the apartment and found Parker making breakfast.

"Would you like pancakes and eggs?" asked Parker.

"Yes, thank you, I'll join you."

"We have to think about the beach and underwater operations to help the cells before they do something stupid," said Shaw.

"Besides us, we need operatives with passes and skills acceptable to the military police and patrolling army. We need plumbers, electricians, nurses, cooks, carpenters, and whoever is needed to work in the 'forbidden land'." As for the underwater explorations, we need commandos from England to take soil samples for consistencies, make observations of underwater boat and tank obstacles, and mines," remarked Parker.

"Good thinking! But not good enough," said Shaw.

"What the heck are you talking about?" asked Parker.

"What's the matter with your logic? Those bloody craftsmen and women have no training in clandestine activities and we have no time to train them how to get out of a mess that they have created. In each unit there is a bloody squealer who reports to the commandant," remarked Shaw.

"My logic is fine, yours is messed up. We cannot explore those intricate structures that were already built in utmost secrecy. We need experts to get there. But before Marceau sends anybody into harm's way, we'll have a little talk with that person," replied Parker.

"That's not enough. That is absolute bullshit! It takes verbal skills and sophistication to explain why you are interested in the 'forbidden zone' of a highly classified bunker," said Shaw.

"So, what's the alternative?" asked Parker.

"We need some more agents with diverse training," replied Shaw.

"Why don't you propose this to OSS and MI6? They will love you for the suggestion," advised Parker.

"Captain Parker, don't you believe that some people have indigenous talent to survive?" asked Shaw.

"Some, but I still wonder about their behavior under stress," commented Parker.

"Look, I have all the respect for your training, but theory and lab training is not life. Life school is different. Some of these guys and dolls have had plenty of shit in their lives. They are swift to respond to situations," replied Shaw.

"So, what are you proposing?" asked Parker.

"Two weeks of intensive training for each cell member." suggested Shaw.

"Shaw, it is your game. By the way, do you have any idea how many hours are needed to train them each day?" questioned Parker.

"It'll depend on how fast they can learn," replied Shaw.

"I hope you're right. God be with you!" said Parker.

Shaw and Parker, having finished their meals and washed the dishes, drove to Marceau's to discuss the training plans and meet with their respective cell operatives.

Before either of them had a chance to discuss the issue of training and underwater exploration, Marceau presented an important message he received yesterday from Allied Intelligence.

"Two underwater commandos have been exploring the Normandy beaches to assess soil properties and German defense structures about one hundred miles north from here to deceive the enemy. This has been going on for sometime. There have been some successes and some failures. Now, according to the message, the two commandos will be in our area next week at about the same time. They need your help in case something goes wrong. If they are caught, the Gestapo will torture them into confessing their mission. Because the area has been considered as a possible landing site, we must protect them the best way we can, and that is where you come in to the picture."

"We need some time to figure out a plan to accomplish the task. Can we have a conference to discuss this and some others things tomorrow?" asked Parker.

"We certainly can. How about 0945 hour here at in my place?" replied Marceau.

"Very well, we'll see you tomorrow," said Shaw.

Shaw and Parker walked to the seaport and sat on two crab trap boxes facing the bay and inlet water. Both were quite pensive and circumspect about their role in the expeditionary assignment of underwater reconnaissance.

"So, my friend, what's on your mind?" asked Shaw.

"How are we going to save them without compromising our mission?"

"We go on a night watch duty looking for new and secret construction sites."

"But why at night in an area that has not been designated by Organization Todt?"

"Because, the secret nature of the project."

"The Gestapo could have some serious inquiries about us in the Organization Todt in Berlin."

"It can happen only if our story seems to be suspicious."

"How would you explain the 0200 hour exploration to a curious bunker officer?"

"We are having too many spies, commandos, and RAF reconnaissance during the day."

"Not too bad. I like the idea. It is a good alibi."

"Once we know the coordinates, we go there, lie low, and watch for the German sentries. Should they suspect activities in the water, flash their search lights, and move in with a patrol boat, we'll encounter them," said Shaw.

"To allay the sentry's suspicion, we could also say that one of us must observe the shore from a dinghy in the water," commented Parker.

"That is a plausible excuse for the rescue of the commandos."

"How about using our pistols with the silencers?" asked Parker.

"It would be the very last resort."

"I wholly agree with you."

"Good. We have some plans for our conference with Marceau," remarked Shaw.

"Now let's go, and meet with our cells," concluded Parker.

It was cell three meeting in a farm house near Carentan. There were two young women and one middle aged man waiting. Shaw and Parker stayed in the kitchen while the ladies and the gentleman were sitting in the dining room.

Parker spoke first with a kind but curious voice.

"Are you ready to tell us something important or are you waiting to hear from us?"

Jane responded with trepidation. "We have concerns for our safety since we have been followed for a week by two men wearing long, black, leather overcoats."

"Did these two men ever speak to you?" asked Parker.

"Not really. Just smiled a couple of times," answered Sarah.

"Did you do anything that provoked their behavior?" asked Shaw.

"We went out dancing with a Gestapo agent. We did not know who he was until we got into his place and had fun in bed," said Jane.

"Why the two of you?" asked Parker.

"It just happened."

"Go on," urged Parker.

"We went to a bar. He was a good looking man and spoke perfect French. He introduced himself as a tourist from Italy. We danced, drank, and had a fabulous time. He was witty, a good conversationalist, and a terrific dancer. We were invited to his hotel and he was very sensual. We just had fun with him. Then he asked us to play cards and the loser had to disrobe a garment. We were having a good time, laughed a lot, and somehow Sarah got turned on and passionately kissed the man. He became quite aroused and I was ready to exit, however, he asked me to stay and began to kiss me while fondling her."

"We all had a very passionate sexual play which ended in pleasure for all of us. It was just fun. We had never, ever been in a situation like that. We all slept together, and late in the morning while he was dressing, he accidentally dropped his Gestapo identification."

"Sarah and I almost fainted. He assured us that we were safe and nothing was going to happen to us. But, now we know better. We were vulnerable and believed him. He did not tell us the truth. We are paying the price."

"Were you followed to this house?" asked Shaw.

"No, absolutely not!" answered Jane.

She continued, "We know better than that. We were very careful in coming here. Sarah looked in the mirror the whole time while I drove. We stopped at three places on the way here and we were not followed by any men or women. We would never jeopardize you guys and our mission. We made a horrible mistake but we are not stupid."

"O.K. how about you Peter?" asked Parker.

"I am fine, but I have very little to report to you. I saw about five kilometers of mines being laid north of here which I can show on a map."

"This is good information," said Parker. He laid a map on the table where he had marked all the areas where mines were planted.

"How did you manage to get this information?"

"I was called by the German military to fix a water leak. Being a plumber I had the opportunity to make some observations. I was allowed to check the outside water pipe which gave me an opportunity to look around."

"You did a very good job."

"Thank you, sir."

"You're welcome."

"We are concerned about you ladies, however. We don't want either of you to make any observations for the time being. We do not trust the Gestapo. They will abandon you for a while, but they will return. So we have to suspend you. You will be contacted when to resume function. Please stay away from any bars, or public places until you hear from us. Do not connect with any members of the Resistance until further notice. Today, you will leave first and go straight home. If you are being watched again, just behave as you usually do. Nothing will happen to you unless you are careless and make contacts. The Gestapo is feeding on your mistakes. Watch out and don't be stupid!" warned Shaw.

Shaw and Parker left the house thirty minutes after the cell exited. They were very careful and looked with their binoculars before they walked toward their car, which was parked a half a mile away from the house, hidden among the tall hedges. They drove away fast to meet their fourth cell at midday in Insigny.

"We have to replace those two girls. They have little training in intelligence and self-protection," said Shaw while driving to Insigny.

"Those two girls are examples of amateurs and reflect our previous discussions."

"Everybody can make mistakes. Don't be so harsh. They were trapped by the agent's looks, his conversational French, and sensualities. Granted, they had very little training, but the plumber had not been prepared any better. He was just damned smart."

The meeting was held in a lawyer's place on the second floor. The lawyer and his secretary were on vacation and there were three rooms available for a secret conference. Shaw and Parker arrived twenty minutes early and settled into the lawyer's office. The three gentlemen of cell number four remained in the waiting room.

"Good afternoon Gentlemen. Please remain seated in the waiting room. My partner and I will conduct the conference, as usual, in incognito. You also, please, address yourself only by your first name or as you wish, 041, 042, or 043. For us, you can address us as 004 and 006. Thank you," said Shaw.

Parker began the questioning by saying "Hello there. I am 006. What information do you have for us?" 041 curtly replied, "We saw a lot and nothing."

"What do you mean?" asked Parker.

"Well, the three of us work for the railroad. We change and align the tracks and ties. We see a lot. We were assigned to fix the tracks around Pointe Du Hoc. There were two carloads of boxes labeled 'mines.' We saw them being unloaded but the trucks took them toward the cliffs and beaches and we were ordered to carry out our work. We couldn't have wandered away because we were watched by the German military guards. When we finished our job, the guards asked us to get back into the trucks and they shipped us back to Insigny," commented 041.

"At least we know what was in those boxes and the area where the mines were taken," said Shaw. Then he added, "since you have travel clearance for the prohibited area, wouldn't it be possible to revisit your work site and recheck the strength of the ties and rails for possible weakness? There is always a chance to see where the mines are being laid."

"We could do that. Tomorrow we are off and we don't need permission for a revisit. We will just go there pretending that we are rechecking the rails and ties. That way we are not being watched by others," said 042. The other two also agreed by nodding their heads.

"Splendid. Please drop us a line and tell us the whereabouts of the 'round chocolates', and don't forget the meeting next week," said Shaw.

"Thank you gentlemen, and good bye," said Parker.

Shaw and Parker drove home psychologically exhausted. They did not appreciate the agent's encounter with the Gestapo and were not looking forward to a very complicated assignment of rescuing commandoes, if the mission failed.

They stopped on the way home for groceries and beer. At home they made a fast dinner, looked over some papers, and hit the sack.

The next morning, Shaw and Parker rose early, had breakfast, and drove to Port-En-Bessin to meet with Marceau. They talked about the Gestapo, the two women operatives, and their possible replacements. "Don't you worry. We'll find you two replacements for cell three and let you know as soon as they accept the assignment. We run into these problems from time to time, but these things just happen to people. I will take care of this matter."

"We have another request. For an alibi, we will need surveying instruments, a rubber dinghy, first aid kit, blanket, and a large bag," said Shaw.

"I can arrange the purchases but you have to pick them up at various locations. I assume you are thinking of surveying and engineering explorations. You certainly could study the affects of tides, overnight building constructions for security purposes, air surveillance, and so forth. I am not a civil engineer, but it is a good excuse for studying the locations at night," said Marceau.

"You are so right, Marceau," said Parker.

"You are knowledgeable about these matters, so use it!" added Marceau.

"What would we do without you? You are such a wise man," commented Parker.

"Just a little older, and more experienced. Do we have another agenda for today?" asked Marceau.

"We need all the information you can provide us about the commandos," replied Shaw.

"All I can tell you is the essence of the mission. Two men will emerge from a mini-submarine, wearing frogmen's rubber suits, and swimming in shallow water. They will take soil samples, examine concrete, steel, or wood obstacles, look for mines, occasionally observe beach fortifications, searchlights, and count German sentries. At this point in time this is all you need to know. As time goes by, I will inform you on a need to know basis. Please be patient. You have a lot to accomplish yourselves."

"Thank you Marceau. Thank you for your time, help, and advice" said Shaw.

They both left for their next cell appointments. There was a great feeling of satisfaction and comfort in both of them. Shaw and Parker found Marceau a great guy to get along with and both adopted him as their "underground" mentor.

Michael came by to pay a short visit and to ask Bridget out for Saturday afternoon and evening.

"There will be a beautiful chamber concert Saturday, mostly Debussy, in Caen. Would you like to join me?"

"I have to ask Marceau, but I think it'll be OK"

"I also would like to invite you to dinner in a nice restaurant after the concert."

"Are you sure? I am costing you a lot of money"

"You are well worth it, my dear Bridget. You are working so hard and have no time for fun. Let me have the pleasure of providing you with a little relaxation."

"This is so nice of you, Michael, for thinking of me. I do accept both invitations, but I must ask Marceau about Saturday's schedule. Please wait a minute."

Bridget went to see Marceau and he had no objection for her Saturday outings.

"What time do you want me be ready for the afternoon?"

"I shall be waiting for you at four-thirty."

"Very well, I'm looking forward to seeing you Michael. Bye."

"Bye my dear, I'll see you Saturday."

Bridget felt really good about the invitation. She was working most of the time, hardly going out with a friend to dine or see a concert. Her role as a helper in the shop and as a Resistance operator has been overwhelming. These little pleasures have been the first break in a very long time.

Shaw and Parker went to see Marceau later that day. They received the date, time, and coordinates of the commandos' arrival. He read the top secret information from a deciphered note. Nothing else was said. It wasn't necessary. Shaw and Parker received training in aiding this type of commando operation and they were well prepared for all kinds of eventualities. They had multifaceted training. It is one thing to learn from books, but it is another to carry out what you have experienced. Both Shaw and Parker, performed superbly in military and civilian exercises.

"I think we better work out for a few days before the big event. We need some more physical exercise other than morning pushups. We can do a number of things. Why don't we start out slow and get into shape. Have a three mile fast walk tomorrow starting at 0600 hour, building it up to five miles?"

"I think that is a good start. In the afternoon we can swim for an hour," added Shaw.

"We must get into shape just in case the rescue becomes very difficult and strenuous."

"In the evening we can dine early and relax," said Parker.

"What a splendid program. I am so proud of your ideas. You're a fine chap," commented Shaw.

They spent the rest of the day looking at various stages of bunker constructions and making notes of them. Every bit of information was helping to solve Hitler's Atlantic Wall puzzle in terms of strengths and weaknesses. They went home late and tired, but they covered over fifty miles of bunker and casemate constructions.

It was 0530 when Bridget knocked on Shaw's door. He was sleepy when he opened the door, but Bridget unimpressed, and without social graces delivered an urgent message.

"Marceau wants to know if you're interested in a room of a villa overlooking the Channel, near where the commandos are supposed to explore the coast?"

Shaw promptly responded with "Yes."

After Bridget left he went back to sleep only to be awoken by Parker. He wanted to remind him to ask Marceau about lodging for the big event.

"You're late. Bridget was already here with an offer. Good deed!" replied Shaw.

Having had a good breakfast in a nearby cafe, they were about ready to visit some construction sites well north to Bayeux. But their three mile walk had to come first.

They began with a slow pace and gradually increased their speed. It was tiring but refreshing. This walk reminded them how much they were out of shape.

The next few days, Shaw and Parker spent time on physical exercises, rest, and entertainment. They had also visited the "secret commando site" at various times of the day to observe the number of sentries and possible escape routes in the area. As time went by, Shaw and Parker had gained knowledge of the terrain and of the military guarding the casemates, bunkers, beaches and the coast in general. They were quite fortunate in making all the observations without any military inquiries despite the fact that they were using optical land surveying instruments. Only one day before the designated day, an officer of a bunker asked questions of Shaw regarding the necessity of another fortification. Shaw's response was that the military was planning to have super secret fortifications that could not be observed by military over flights, expeditionary commandos, or spies. He further elaborated about the German military technology that would surprise the enemy, just in case they wanted to invade the French coast. Shaw was very circumspect not to reveal the nature of their study but informed the officer that Parker and he would be conducting day and night studies in utmost secrecy and help was not necessary. The officer promised to keep the information confidential, but let the others know about the survey Shaw and Parker were conducting in the area.

The night had finally arrived and Shaw and Parker spent most of the day going over the tasks that might be employed to save one or both commandos. Besides various physical exercises, they engaged in psychodrama and role playing. Before they realized it, it was eleven o'clock at night. Despite the fact that both received training in military rescue, there was always the unknown factor that raised their blood pressure. The anxiety, excitement, danger, and compromise accompanied them all the time. But these were the factors they lived for. They loved to walk on the edge of the cliff. These were their choices, except this time it was a double jeopardy.

The midnight breeze whipped up the waves into frenzied white caps. It was mad out there navigating any small boat, but the sentries kept looking with binoculars as ordered by their superior officers.

Shaw and Parker arrived thirty minutes after midnight and set up their little protective tent for their instruments, pretending to study the shores for possible defense construction. The sentries were informed by their commander about Shaw and Parker and their top secret explorations. Shaw handled the transit. He placed the tripods into various locations and Parker was walking at the edge of the shore with a long measuring rod.

The wind became stronger and the little tent collapsed over other instruments. One of the sentries volunteered to straighten out the tent and yelled into the direction of Shaw.

"Can we help you Herr Engineer? We have an awful wind tonight."

"Thank you for your offer, but we are used to working in these kinds of conditions," Shaw yelled back.

The wind started to pick up even more and the white caps of the Channel looked more and more ominous. The eerie silence was occasionally interrupted by the howling sounds of the wind, and the sentries' dogs, the mouthy German shepherds.

Shaw looked at his watch and told Parker to stand by; meaning the time frame of plus or minus thirty minutes arrived. There was no communication other than a very faint Morse codes by flash light pointing skyward from the commandos and similar returns of signals directed toward the water from the tent containing the instruments.

The submarine was about four-hundred and fifty yards from the beach when the captain lifted the periscope and had a good look of the shoreline, beach, sentries, and pillboxes that could easily decimate the commandos.

"Everything looks ok, but I'd like to get closer by about fifty yards. When I stop, one of you should signal and wait for the reply," said Commander Oliver Lancaster.

One of the commandos, Henry Dowell, sent the signal. Shaw picked it up and replied thirty second later. Dowell reported it to the commander and his partner, Scott Williams. The commander looked at his watch, and gave the orders.

"We have arrived. The time is 0225. Yes, we are late but strong underwater currents and German patrol boats slowed our scheduled arrival. Please be careful as you have approximately thirty to forty-five minutes to accomplish the mission. I will wait no longer than sixty minutes for your return. In case of emergency you'll have two agents to rescue you. Good luck."

The two commandos entered the water in their wetsuits. Their gear consisted of a flashlight, compass, fishing line, .45 colt automatic, hunting knife, and a small waterproof pouch. They were swimming noiselessly and fast underwater with snorkels in their mouths, making long breast strokes and leg kicks. This way they avoided splashing and recognition. As they got closer to the shore, Dowell and Williams studied the terrain and watched the motion of the sentries with the dogs.

Submerged again, they attached the fishing line to a curved steel rail. The rails served as an obstacle for landing boats and tanks. Dowell began extending the line and Williams counted the rails. As they gingerly swam about a mile, the passage became dangerous because of the mines attached to the lower and upper parts of the rails. Dowell decided to swim back following the fishing line. He avoided touching the ground as he noticed that at every fifth and seventh rail bottom there was a mine in the soil attached to the rail.

Dowell and Williams took soil samples in the water and when it looked safe they ventured to the shore to collect sand and soil samples.

In the meantime, Shaw and Parker tried very hard to masquerade their research and distract the sentries with all kinds of theatrical showmanship. They yelled at each other, argued over techniques, and used all kinds of German foul language as their exploratory studies heated up. Their eyes stayed focused on the water and beach. Suddenly, Parker noticed that one of the dogs started to pull the sentry in the direction of the water. This was followed by loud barks. He asked Shaw to signal danger. The other sentries joined with their dogs, and unclasped the leash from one of the dogs. The dog began to swim in the direction of the commandos. Parker started to intervene and asked the sentries to withdraw because they were interfering with the research. The dogs continued to bark and the commotion became unmanageable. Parker demanded the withdrawal of the sentries with the dogs, warning that any interference would be dealt with severe punishment.

Dowell and Williams heard the commotion and sat still in the cold water getting air only through the snorkel. They had only eighteen minutes to return to the sub. Dowell hand signaled to Williams, "I'm swimming back before the sentries use their powerboat."

Williams signaled back, "I agree, we should submerge and head toward the sub."

One of the German officers walked toward Parker and in an authoritarian voice said, "I find it strange that you are ordering my sentries to withdraw from their duties."

Parker was ready for a fight and snapped back with a warning. "I am carrying out the German High Command orders to construct defense positions that will be invisible to the enemy. If you wish to stop this, I have to report it and you will take the consequences. You don't know what is out there, you're assuming. It could be a large live or dead fish. We are not being attacked. There is no invasion. But we are undertaking the defense of a whole German army and you are saying that I am interfering with your sentries."

One sentry asked the officer for permission to use the powerboat.

"Can you wait a minute; I am talking with the Org. Todt engineer."

The German officer looked at Parker and said, "We will see who was right."

The officer ordered two powerboats to enter the water and follow the dogs' scents.

Shaw signaled emergency codes from the tent and watched the drama unfold. Parker tried to appear calm but his heart was beating heavily. Parker looked into the eye of the German officer and said: "I hope you know what you are doing, because the stakes are high. If you find nothing in the water and I am unable to report by tomorrow our findings, I will ask the High Command to court martial you. I hope they hang you. You and I come from different backgrounds. You want to be right. I on the other hand am trying to save the army who is defending the Normandy coast. There is a difference between the two."

The German officer looked at Parker and replied, "I swore that I would do my duty for the army, Reich, and the Fuhrer. I am not a philosopher as you are. I am a plain soldier who follows orders. You do what you have to do. I am not afraid of you or your warnings. Good night."

He turned around and went to the beach to watch the catch.

"Go to hell!" said Parker.

Dowell and Williams swam very fast in zigzag patterns toward the sub. Williams was slightly behind Dowell. The powerboats followed the dogs but they were confused by the zigzag pattern. This gave the commandos some lead time. Finally Dowell reached the sub and got inside fast. Williams, however, had fallen behind. He had an unfortunate cramp in his left calf and just didn't make it. The commander decided to submerge as the powerboats came very close to the sub. Fortunately turbulence and fog prevented the sentries from identifying the sub. Williams took a very deep breath and sank deep into the water. The powerboats were searching all over but found nothing. The sentries picked up the dogs and headed back to shore.

Williams swam to the surface and found no sub, no motorboats, and no sentries. He took his flashlight and signaled that he was alive. Shaw signaled back to wait for rescue.

The motorboats came back with the sentries and dogs, but without any commandos. Parker approached the German officer and asked sarcastically, "Are you satisfied with your catch? Now, can I continue my job? This time I have to use a rubber boat and measure the distance of deception from the shore. Would you tell your men to withdraw the dogs and let me be?"

"You can continue your work." He told his sentries to take the dogs back and allow the Organization Todt officer to finish his job. Then, the officer looked at Shaw and Parker and in a humble tone whispered, "We all have a job to do." He gave a salute and went back to his bunker.

Shaw sent a Morse light code of 'all clear, rescue on the way.' Parker inflated the rubber dinghy that they carried with them, dragged it into the water with emergency supplies, and began to row toward the direction of Williams. It took Parker a good twenty minutes to row against the waves and notice the faint signal that Williams' emergency light was emitting. Parker pulled Williams aboard under a small tent cover. Williams was totally exhausted, extremely cold, and dehydrated. Parker rubbed his body, gave him water, orange juice, and some sweets. Parker signaled o.k. to Shaw and that he was rowing back. Williams stayed under the cover until Parker rowed to shore, a good couple of miles north of the beach where Shaw was, and waited until they were picked up by car.

"I almost did not make it. My leg cramped in the cold water and I had a terrible time trying to stay afloat."

"But you made it!" replied Parker

"You guys are terrific. Risking your life for a lonely commando and sacrificing your mission was really something. God Bless you all!"

"You are part of our mission, a member of the team. We were more than happy to save your life. We need to get out of here quickly."

As Shaw was driving home he noticed a roadblock ahead and a car behind them. He made a quick turn to the right and stepped on the gas. He was going at least one hundred and twenty kilometers per hour. He quickly turned into a wooded area, stopped the car, and turned off the lights. Parker asked Williams to lie down in the back seat, put the tent and boat on top of him as a cover and then he piled all their equipment on the top of his back. He told him to stay put until they get home.

Shaw drove back to the road where he made the turn and stopped at the check point. The German Guard asked the men, "Where are you coming from in this late hour and what's in the backseat?"

"It is our equipment that we are using to survey the area of study," said Shaw.

As he said that, he noticed in his rear view mirror that the car that had been following them appeared again. Shaw quickly left the checkpoint making a left, then, a double right turn, a left again, and then he stopped, turned off the light s and waited. Williams offered his colt automatic, but Shaw always preferred diplomacy over a fight. The car behind them stopped a distance away and two men stepped out of the car. One was saying an MI6 code, the other an OSS code. Shaw and Parker waited until the two gentlemen were three feet away and then Parker asked for identification. Once the identification was exchanged, they shook hands and briefly talked about the ordeal and rescue. Shaw and Parker were tired and asked them to meet at 1600 hours at Marceau's place for a short debriefing. They agreed and both parties parted quickly. Shaw, Parker, and Williams were finally home by the early morning hours.

Marceau was delighted to hear that Williams was rescued and nobody was compromised. The Allied agents arrived promptly and a very brief discussion ensued. Williams was then debriefed and the agreement was to send him back England on the next available early morning departure by Lysander plane. The arrangement would be made by Marceau.

Shaw and Parker drove Williams back to their apartment and he was given all the comfort that was affordable for a few days. On the night before his departure, Bridget came with news. "Some members of the Resistance are flying tomorrow morning to England and Williams has to be at the airport by 0130 hour."

"This sounds great," said Shaw.

Parker suggested they have a brief celebration with Bridget. Shaw left for wine and groceries while the rest of them began to tell jokes, sing, and dance.

They ate a good dinner, had a wonderful time together, and promised to have a reunion. After dinner Bridget had to excuse herself. They had a few hours left before departure and they filled the time by sharing a few memories of their past experiences. After a short nap, they woke up at midnight to the local radio playing swing jazz. A few minutes later they departed for the airport.

The plane came in low at 0145 hour. Williams hugged Shaw and Parker and thanked them for his rescue and their wonderful hospitalities. There was a lady and a gentleman also in waiting. The pilot had to check one of the landing gears but there was little to do mechanically because of the lack of materials and time. He was able, however, to make a minor adjustment with his available tools, just enough to take off and land. He was ready to depart and asked everybody to come aboard. The plane took off without any problem and disappeared into the dark sky.

Shaw and Parker drove home and had a good night sleep. The agenda for the following day was the collection of information about the mines in the possible invasion areas along the beach. The precise location and the number of mines were difficult to determine because of the 'forbidden zones'. Those who had anything to do with the transportation or actual placements of the mines were selected people and loyal to the German cause.

It became more difficult to recruit people to collect information on strategic mine placements and numbers. The German High Command was becoming aware of the Allies spying on German defenses. The Gestapo became very busy and extremely suspicious. When they caught someone spying on German defenses, it was common knowledge that they tortured the people until they confessed their connections. Shaw and Parker, however, managed to tie together most of the information that was provided by the cells and what they had obtained as they inspected the construction of a myriad of batteries consisting of casemates, bunkers, pill boxes and surrounding mines.

Marceau's place was busy with German officers, waiting for their new boots to be made or old boots to be repaired. Shaw and Parker decided to take a walk at the edge of the 'prohibited zone' facing the water while they waited for Marceau.

"We have, at least, some preliminary information for Allied Intelligence," said Parker.

"True, but we have to be somewhat conclusive in our findings. There are several facts, replied Shaw that we can discuss with Marceau which could explain the locations and possible numbers of mines. Given the size of each battery, including the enclosed area, and the invasion beaches plus explosive distances of mines we could roughly estimate the number of mines already laid along the invasion beaches. The way it looks, we might overestimate the German defenses."

Parker was eager to state the facts.

"Fact number one, the German High Command Western section did not consider Normandy as a high risk area for a long time. It wasn't until Rommel took over the Western Front and Hitler sensed Normandy as a strong possibility of invasion, that the construction of the batteries and beach defenses were given great priority."

"Fact number two, the construction of batteries, and coastal defenses has increased considerably. As a matter of fact, the Normandy coast is being considered as a forward if not a main line defense. Whether they will be able to build their defenses within a given invasion time frame set by Eisenhower that remains to be seen."

"Fact number three, the mines are skirted around the batteries, anti-tank ditches, and the beaches. Fact four, we don't know the extent of the executions of all defenses at this point in time, but we have an educated guess."

"I accept your dissertation of facts, but isn't it true that we should never underestimate the enemy?"

"Precisely, and I am happy that you concur with me to make this presentation to Marceau."

When they returned, Marceau was free of customers and ready to talk.

"I am happy to see you, gentlemen," said Marceau. "Bridget just made some yummy desserts. You must have something to tell me."

"We have more than something, there is a lot to tell you," said Shaw.

"So, tell me. I am waiting eagerly to hear some good news," replied Marceau. "First, Williams."

"Williams arrived and he is at home in England. To save him, as you know, was a nightmare," said Shaw.

"But we are gaining. We have collected a lot of information," commented Marceau.

"Yes, we have. There are, however, only estimates about mines," offered Parker.

"That is better than nothing."

"We don't know what Allied Intelligence will accept even though we are talking about a preliminary report," commented Shaw.

Shaw and Parker continued the discussion, elucidating the facts they talked about prior to their visit, and emphasizing the increased Gestapo activities regarding information gathering of the Allied Intelligence and the Resistance.

"I am aware of what is happening. We gain and we lose, but, we are at war and must fight on all fronts. Our job is extremely risky. You must consider, however, that the first wave of the invading forces will be decimated if we don't prepare for the assault. We cannot afford very large casualties because we must establish a beachhead before the enemy becomes mobile. It is our job to soften the blow for our troops by providing advance knowledge regarding batteries, casemates, bunkers, firepower, killing zones, machine gun placements, and so forth. We have tremendous aerial, naval, and mechanized infantry power, not to mention our saboteurs, and they can inflict a serious blow on the enemy before and during the invasion. The German High Command Western section knows that we are up to something spectacular. That is why they are after us."

"The Resistance is very, very vulnerable. I am terribly concerned about the number of arrests by the Gestapo. Their suspicion, insecurity and fear are inspiring them to fight back as dirty as they can. The Germans know we do not want them here as an occupying force or people with their Nazi policies."

"Under these circumstances, we just have to tighten our belts and fight back just as brutally as they do. We have to be as brave as we have been and carry out difficult assignments."

"Speaking of difficult assignments, I must go now and visit a beautiful young lady whose husband passed away last year. He was one of the best Resistance operatives we ever had. He was young, energetic, and extremely brave because he died while he was saving another operative. He made a wrong turn and a Gestapo's bullet hit him during crossfire."

"Adieu and au revoir!"

Marceau exited the shop with a grin on his face like a professor who was satisfied with his own lecture. He shouted back to Bridget, "Au revoir Bridget, don't wait for me. I'll be coming home late."

Shaw and Parker followed, and left for home to find a little stray, starving kitten in front of their house crying for help. Fortunately, they had some leftover tuna and this took care of the feline's hunger. As for themselves, they made a delicious salmon dinner with French fries, garlic bread, and wine. They listened to music, read the news, and hit the sack around eleven o'clock.

Michael came a few minutes late. He arrived with roses in hand. With a smile on his face he extended his right hand and gave the roses to Bridget.

"My dear Bridget, I bring these roses to you as a symbol of my great affection."

"Thank you ever so much for thinking of me. It is very kind of you."

"You look absolutely stunning tonight."

"Well, thank you again. I have dressed for you. It is my symbol of affection."

"Madam, are you ready?"

"Would you allow me to say good-bye to Marceau?"

"Well, of course, my dear, by all means. Please, give my best to him."

"Thank you, it will be short, and I'll give him your greetings."

Bridget said good bye to Marceau and returned in a couple of minutes later. Her face looked joyous. She felt that Michael was only in a Nazi uniform in the outside but deep inside he was not. She had this instinctual feeling from their first rendezvous.

Michael drove pretty fast, as he didn't want to miss the concert. Bridget was looking at the landscape, houses, and military everywhere.

"I am driving fast because I was late. I am sorry for that, but really it was not my fault. I was called in to my superior's office to supervise the slave labor units which I respectfully declined. My superior officer started questioning me about my refusal and I just listened and did not change my mind. By the time he gave up on me it was rather late."

"I like your character. You have guts to say no to what you don't like. It must be very difficult in the military."

They arrived to the concert hall just in the nick of time. They sat in the seventh row from the stage. The music was beautiful and the violinists and cellist played each note with absolute perfection. But it was more than mechanics. It was real art as they emulated the composer's feelings. During the entire concert Michael was holding Bridget's hand and both were totally enthralled by the music.

After the concert they drove to a small but elegant place to have dinner. The owner was the chef and his wife attended the bar. They were in their late fifties. Michael ordered a bottle of white wine and some shrimp appetizer. This was followed by a tossed salad, marinated broiled steak with roasted potato and asparagus with a cream sauce. The food was excellent. The atmosphere was supreme. Thanks to the owner's brother, who had some physical handicap, he entertained the guests with his accordion and songs of the past.

Bridget and Michael sat in a booth next to each other and enjoyed every bite of the dinner. She occasionally put her head on Michael' shoulder and both felt the warmth toward each other. Before the dinner ended Bridget felt brave enough to ask a question that had been bugging her for sometime.

"Michael, something is telling me inside, it may be intuitive, that you would prefer to live in peace, under a different regime."

"You are right. I am not a good conformist. I have a difficult time fitting into the present regime, but I grew up in the German culture and it is difficult to change. Just the same way as you grew up as a French citizen."

"It is getting late, do you want to go home, walk along the beach, visit my place or go straight home to Marceau?"

"What would you like to do?"

"I would like to hold you in my arms at my place."

"I am going to be a gentleman."

"Do you promise?"

"I do. I will not do anything you don't want me to do. My feelings for you are very respectful."

"O.k. let's drive to your place."

Michael paid the bill and they left the restaurant arm in arm and walked slowly to the car. This time Michael drove a moderate speed taking into consideration that both had finished the bottle of wine and his right hand embraced Bridget. They had an excellent time and wished it would last forever.

"How far is your place from here?"

"Only five minute drive."

"That's good because I am thirsty."

"We are almost there. You see that house on the right facing the water?"

"Yes, I do. What a beautiful location."

Michael parked the car and helped Bridget to get out of the vehicle. He went ahead, opened the entrance door, turned on the foyer light and allowed Bridget to walk in first.

"What would you like to drink?"

"Just water, please. I had too much wine."

"Well, that is not a problem."

Michael let the water run to make it sure would be cold and handed the glass of chilled water to Bridget.

"This tastes good. Thank you. What a charming place."

"This was given to me by the military. This was an abandoned cottage. The owners live in Paris and did not want to participate in the frontline combat. The military converted it to a house with all the amenities."

"Well, of course. What makes you think this place will be in the frontline fighting?"

"The whole coast could be vulnerable, from Pas de Calais to Cherbourg."

"I hate war, the killing, atrocities, torture, forced labor and concentration camps- people are so cruel to each other."

"I would rather have peace too, than fighting a dirty war. But we are not making the decisions. Why don't we take a rain check on this topic of war?"

Bridget had a long look into his eyes, then wetted her lips and embraced him on his neck. Michael was standing with his back against the big picture window and Bridget was facing the water and the stars.

"You are so charming and beautiful."

"And you are so kind and handsome."

Michael opened his lips and touched her upper lip and Bridget opened her lips and touched his lower lip while they both embraced each other. This was followed by a deep kiss by Michael which was reciprocated by Bridget.

"I think we would be more comfortable embracing on the sofa," suggested Michael.

"That is fine my dear."

They both sat down on the sofa and Michael gave her a big hug and held her for seconds, then the kissing continued. Michael then touched her upper left leg and slowly moved his hand from her knee to her thigh and then stopped. The kissing became heavier, and both of their faces were flushed.

"I am getting warm," confessed Michael.

"Me too."

"So what do you suggesting? I am willing to suffer." Michael had a smile on his face.

"You are a charmer, kind man. If you behave, I will permit you to take off your shirt."

"But what about you, you must be also warm with your dress on?"

"We'll see, you just worry about yourself. When I get overheated you'll help me with my back zipper. Will you not?"

They continued with the kissing but only a short time. Bridget put his right hand on the zipper and let him pull it down. He began to undress her. Bridget removed her bra and Michael removed his shirt and under shirt. The two chests began to touch each other Michael kissed her nipples and breasts and all over her face and neck in a frenzy. Bridget did the same to his nipples and chest and face until both felt supercharged. Michael touched her upper thigh and moved his hand toward her panties but Bridget repositioned his hand and said, "Michael you have to stop now. I am very attracted to you, but I don't want an affair until we can trust each other."

"Whatever you wish my dear. I told you that I respect your feelings and desires."

"Michael. We have to talk. I am afraid of an affair that has no meaning other than sex. I am falling in love with you but I am strong and must stop if it means a casual affair. I do not want to get hurt and I don't want you to get hurt. I must know more about you as a person. You have to be honest and sincere."

"Ask me anything you want and I'll try to be frank, open, and straightforward as possible."

"I really would like to know more about your family and upbringing. These are the people who influenced your present thinking and behavior. I probably will never really know you, but I will try to understand you as much as I can. You mean a lot to me and my mind will rest better after I've talked with you, and I don't mean chitchat."

"I don't know where to begin, but I will go back as many years as I can," replied Michael. "I grew up in a middle class family with a caring mother and father. I was told to respect others and live according to our faith."

"My parents wanted me to study the piano. They said, 'learning to play the piano will teach me discipline.' I studied for years, but I was more interested in science and building things."

"Politics were never my interest. My father was a mathematics high school teacher and my mother an elementary school teacher. They were very conscious about the rise of Nazism and seldom talked about the new Germany. They were frightened by the unfolding events and possible repercussions for those who disagreed with Hitler's policies."

"Your intuition was absolutely correct about my early

affiliation with Nazism. I had not joined any Nazi youth organization. You were sensitive enough to judge that I don't belong to the Nazis in any shape or form. I am not a Nazi. I was drafted and I have to serve my country."

"I have problems, however, changing history. Hitler came to power because Germany was in bad shape. It is like someone having an operation, and after surgery the body is weak and vulnerable. The Germans believed that Hitler was the savior, the panacea for Germany. So the devil got into their souls and slowly transformed them into killing machines without feelings, thoughts, or a conscience. You know the rest. "I don't think that an evening is enough time for you to know about my character, but I tried to give it a shot."

"I understand where you're coming from and we'll talk about you more."

Bridget had an inner conflict. She realized that her revelation could be disastrous for everybody and that included Allied Intelligence, Resistance and over a million people who were preparing for the invasion. She did not have enough trust in Michael yet. On the other hand, she was very much attracted to him, both psychologically and physically. She decided to hold off her complete story, especially her real background and association with Marceau.

"My life had been simpler than yours. In my younger years I studied in Paris. Professionally, acting was my first choice. I always loved the theatre and movies. So, I had private acting lessons for a while. The war, Marceau's ennui in living alone and him needing assistance because of increased business, prompted me to come back and help him. And here I am. That's all I can tell you about myself at this point in time. Later, I hope, we'll have an opportunity to talk more."

"I should be going home, sweetheart."

"It is so difficult to be without you."

"I will give you a picture."

"I had hoped you would."

"But you must hide it. Remember we must be careful for your and my sake."

"I will hide it under my pillow."

"Good idea. Let's get dressed; you have to take me home."

Michael gave a hug and a kiss to her and they both started to dress. It was a cool evening but the half moon and stars made the trip back to Marceau's warm and romantic. She sat close to Michael holding on to his right arm and resting her head against it. For musical company, the radio was playing Debussy and Chopin.

"Thank you for the lovely evening, my dear Michael."

"It was my pleasure. Thank you for coming."

This time they stopped before Marceau's place. He got out first, looked around and told Bridget it was safe to exit. She got out of the car, gave a hug and kiss to Michael and rushed toward the house.

"Do I see you next Saturday?"

"Come midweek and I'll tell you"

"Love you."

"I love you too."

"Bye."

"Bye."

Michael drove home happily, and was singing to the jazz orchestra on the radio.

Shaw and Parker had an early breakfast, 0600, left to pick up messages, met with various cell groups, and investigated sites of their own. Carrying out assignments for Allied Intelligence of this magnitude meant little rest, total dedication and sacrifice. While they ate, they were always listened for hidden messages on the BBC radio, read the French papers, especially the advertisement section for additional hidden information and occasionally made a short trip to pick up prearranged communications from drop zones. This morning, something came up unexpectedly through the BBC radio world news that had to be investigated. One of the British MI6 agents discovered that the Gestapo was holding an important person. Since there was no other information it had to be checked out through Marceau. They hurriedly finished their eggs and toast and drove extremely fast to Marceau's.

"What is the problem?" asked Bridget.

"We had a message from the BBC and we have to get information," said Shaw.

"Just a minute, I will call Marceau."

"What can I do for you?" asked Marceau.

"The Gestapo is holding an important person," said Parker.

"It is a Spanish Diplomat who has an architectural engineering background and he is being questioned why he was accompanied by a lady in one of the batteries. The lady happens to be one of our operatives and belongs to your sixth cell. At this point, however, we have to sit tight, because the slightest move on our part evokes curiosity in the Gestapo and they go for smell. She is Chris Savignion, an attractive lady as you know and she knows how to turn on an older man. She is fluent in Spanish, intelligent, and has a lot of connections among the German Generals. I don't think the Gestapo will start a detailed investigation because she will call her General friend who will personally go to the Gestapo and ask them to release her in his custody. But there is a fanatic man in the Gestapo who would torture her and he would later apologize to the General. The question is whether she will be called or escorted to the Gestapo. If she is going to be escorted, Tibault must get in touch with his friend right away. I will give him his name and telephone number."

"Can we fly her to England tonight," asked Parker.

"That is an option."

"How about extending diplomatic courtesy?" asked Parker.

"The Spanish Consul was informed, but they are in a 'wait and see' situation. They have no idea about the connection between the lady and the Spanish diplomat," said Marceau.

"We hope they will never find out," said Shaw.

"Is the Gestapo on her tail? Because if they are we should definitely not meet her today," said Shaw.

"Bridget, please call Chris and tell her not to attend the meeting until further notice. Thank you. Well, gentlemen, this will take care of things for the time being. Should the diplomat be retained for two more hours, I think one of you should call her and offer a flight to England tonight, or she should get in touch with her General friend."

"I think, under the circumstances, we can't do anything more," said Shaw.

"The Gestapo is not embarrassed by her being protected by the Generals. The important thing is to win the war at any cost."

"We must go now and get some more information. We are trying to put the pieces together so we can have an idea as to what is going on. It is our hope that in a few weeks we can send a preliminary report of all the findings," said Shaw.

"Good. Have a nice day. Bye," said Marceau.

Shaw and Parker waved "goodbye" as they headed toward the car.

On the way to meet cells four and five, Shaw and Parker

stopped at various pre-arranged drop points but they did not find more than a page of information from each cell. Well, seven pages per week are not too bad, but it could be better. Over the months they had been given quite a bit of information, plus their own collections, it was enough to send an interim report. A sizeable number of batteries of various sizes were either complete or under construction. The exact numbers had to be tabulated which also included: machine gun positions, seventy-five millimeter and twenty millimeter anti-aircraft guns, various field guns, machine gun tobruks, casemates (houses guns of large caliber), troop quarters, ammunition magazine, various storage facilities, hospital facilities, water storage, and surrounding mines. These elaborate constructions had to be identified for above and underground sabotage operations. Various facilities were interconnected by underground passageways. It was paramount information for the Allied air force, glider and naval commando operations, mechanized military and infantry operations, and the invasion forces to know the entire German defense structure. The military reconnaissance, commandos and French resistance operatives did an absolutely fantastic job, but for the final analysis everything had to be checked and rechecked to assure that the enemy was not feeding misinformation. Mistakes can cost lives, time, money, strategic planning, and ultimately winning.

Parker and Shaw arrived to the Bayeux's cell rendezvous location and one of the cell members, a young, attractive lady, hurriedly approached both of them with a message to immediately return to Marceau for an urgent consultation. This request was delivered by Bridget fifteen minutes earlier.

"Thank you." We'll turn around and drive back. Please

watch your drop for the next meeting, which could be tomorrow or after."

Shaw and Parker sensed the trouble must be with Ms. Savignion. They drove back quickly and Marceau was at the door to greet and ushered them to the back room.

"This Gestapo man is causing us trouble. Chris was summoned to appear tomorrow for a hearing. In the meantime, the diplomat stirred up enough trouble and refused to cooperate until the Gestapo egomaniac apologizes. The Gestapo wants to prove that they were spying. He does not care that he has diplomatic immunity or if his artistic consult is valuable or not."

"It is our bad luck, however, that she is summoned," said Parker

"The Gestapo had problems with the diplomat's arrest. The Generals are very upset with the

Gestapo summoning Ms. Savignion. One more arrest and the shouting match will erupt into war between Hitler's friends and protectors and Generals of the Defense of France, namely, the Atlantic Wall. They both are mad as hell! We have to protect Chris who has superior qualities to make her intimate friends enjoy the ultimate pleasure of sex. I know she is good because her General friend, who happens to be my customer, raves about her. He says she is the goddess of sexual pleasure. She can transform a sixty-year-old General into a twenty-year-old tiger."

"So, there you are gentlemen. This is what we are facing in a time of life and death!

This whole situation is so tangled, convoluted, corrupt, and absurd that I feel like choking this idiot Gestapo man. He is the worst egomaniac, sadistic animal that does not care about anybody but himself, his reputation, his uniform, and his world of evil."

"We understand how you feeL. You have our support," said Parker.

"As we said earlier, one option is to ship her to England tonight," commented Shaw.

"How do you know what the Gestapo is up to? They could be watching her, listening to her phone, watching who is contacting her. She could easily be trapped. For all practical purposes, she is under house arrest."

"Marceau, you are absolutely right. We admire your intelligence, but we are not stupid either. I don't think that we are in check-mate yet," said Parker.

"Give me your proposal."

I think this egomaniac Gestapo man will not yield to the General. He is proud, wants to save his hide, and wants to prove that he is right. She will be threatened with all the fancy torture procedures if she hides the truth and if she refuses, this sadist will start with electrodes attached to her vagina to make her talk, and then we are in big trouble," said Shaw.

"You are assuming this scenario."

"Marceau, we cannot afford to think of anything less. We are planning an invasion and should not be influenced by the vanity of a madman," replied Shaw.

"So, what is your plan?"

"We are going to abduct her, if necessary, at night. The operation will be through the roofs. We'll have enough ropes, tapes, sac, medical emergency supplies, and an ambulance vehicle to transport her. We must get through at least one city block of rooftops. We will hide her if necessary," said Shaw.

"What if she is living in a one story house?"

"We will come in with a garbage truck and take her out in a garbage bag, switch her to an ambulance, and rush to the airport." commented Parker.

"Do garbage men work at night?"

"They don't know the French customs," continued Parker.

"How much violence do you envision?"

"Hopefully very little, but if Tibault has to he can use a sidearm Luger pistol, .45 Colt, or submachine gun if necessary. We are at war, Marceau, and we are tough!" continued Parker.

"We have to get the Lysander plane. We must contact the Resistance by radio. It is an emergency. It must be a coded message," suggested Shaw.

"I approve of your plans and will contact someone to radio for the plane. Good luck and let me know if there are any problems or how you made out. We will stand by."

Tibault was notified of the emergency nature of the rescue. He began to assemble the best help and was ready to carry out the rescue.

It was found out that she was living in a villa in the area of Port-En-Bessin, close to the main road but outside of the restricted zone. By early afternoon, Tibault visited the area and through telescopes he spotted two cars in a wooden area, one in the front and another in the back of the house. Tibault did not hesitate, but called her from a public phone as a friend. Chris was surprised and said very little other than she was fine. That was enough for Tibault to know, but the question was how to inform her about the trip. Tibault did not want to have any lengthy conversation because they were afraid that the line was bugged. So the only way to talk to her was through some means of subterfuge. Tibault, with the help of Bridget, got a mail truck and dressed up as a mail delivery clerk. Tibault created a bill that had to be paid or she would lose her credit. He drove over to her place, rang the bell, and she opened the door.

"Madam, I have a letter for you but this is only an excuse to talk to you. My partner and I are members of the Resistance. You are in great danger and your place is being watched by the Gestapo. They have summoned for you but you will never return to this house again. They will torture you and then send you to an extermination camp. We have arranged a dangerous but ingenious escape."

"Why shall I trust you?"

"You only have two choices."

"Do you have any identification with you?"

"Not for this assignment."

"You sound French."

"Yes, I am."

"Can you tell me more?"

"I'm sorry, but I can't. You just have to trust us."

"So what's the plan?"

"When it gets dark, we'll come with a large garbage dump truck, put you in a sack and take you with us for a short distance. Then you will transfer into an ambulance and you will be driven to a hidden airport. After midnight you'll be picked up by a British Lysander plane and it will take you to an undisclosed location in England. Please prepare a small suitcase of the most important and valuable things you have, including your identity papers."

"I guess I have little choice."

"Very little, Madam. There is a serious problem and you better leave France."

"Thank you. When shall I be ready?"

"Please be ready in a couple of hours."

With the help of Marceau, Tibault rented a huge garbage truck and drove it in the back of the villa surrounded with overgrown shrubs and trees. The ambulance had been parked about a mile away from the truck. Tibault and his assistants were dressed in black, black hats and blackened faces. Under the black overalls, they donned a white coat for the ambulance. All the other paraphernalia were in a bag to be easily transferable from one vehicle to the other.

During the late afternoon an urgent message was sent to MI6 to prepare a Lysander for an emergency pick-up in Normandy. The response came back one hour later with an affirmative answer of, 'flight is booked for 0130.' Everything was all set for the execution of the escape. Marceau also informed the Resistance flight security forces to stand by under operation of highest priority.

Bridget picked up Tibault and his associate and drove them to pick up the truck about 2230 hour. After changing the license plate, Tibault drove the truck and one of his assistants was standing in the back looking for any suspicious car that might be following them. They arrived at the villa at 2310 hour. One of the Gestapo cars moved closer to the truck and stopped. Tibault and his assistant men with blackened faces entered the house through the back door and started to take out boxes first, her small luggage, and finally a large sack. One of the Gestapo men got out of the car and started asking questions.

"Why are you taking garbage so late at night?"

"We had an engine and hydraulic problem."

"Yes, but I do not see other garbage being collected."

"The truck broke down at her collection point. She asked us to remove the garbage as soon as the truck was fixed. She has a bad allergy to garbage. Others don't care if we collect their garbage until tomorrow."

"Did you guys talk to the lady?"

"Oh, yes. She was very happy to see us!"

"Go! Do what you have to do."

At that point Tibault got into the truck, stepped on the gas, his associates jumped on the back step and they off drove meet the ambulance. Marceau prearranged the return of the truck by armed resistance operatives. They put their black overalls in the truck, helped the lady to get out of the sack, gave her the luggage, and put her on the ambulance stretcher with an oxygen mask. Tibault took over the wheel, turned on the flashing lights and whisked her away to the airport.

They all got out and were surrounded by half a dozen armed Resistance fighters. It was close to departure time so they gave a quick hug to Chris as the plane was taxing in. The propeller was whirling, while the pilot helped her to climb the steps with her luggage. He asked if there was anything else to take care of, then stepped in the cockpit, waved good-bye and took off into the dark sky.

There was a sigh of relief on everybody's face. The ambulance was returned by a Resistance operative; Tibault and one of his assistants were picked up by Bridget and taken home for a good night's sleep.

"Marceau had asked for a debriefing at 0830 sharp," said Bridget.

"I'll be there," said Tibault.

He stepped out of the car and walked toward his front door. Bridget then took his assistant home. A few hours of sleep weren't a hardship for these guys. Both arrived on time for the debriefing and were ready to talk.

"You had some day yesterday," said Marceau.

"Oh, we are used to it, but it was fun. We made those Gestapo guys a little excited when we showed up, but things happened too fast for them to investigate. I'm sure they will be knocking on her door today. When they find out that she skipped the summons they will be infuriated. Those guys don't like disobedience. The trip to the airport and flight arrival and departure were uneventful. Mission accomplished," said Tibault.

"Not quite. There is something else that we had to prepare for. The Gestapo will investigate the origin of the garbage truck, hopefully without success. Nothing was recorded. But the owner of the truck is a problem. We had to send him away, which I have been working on since yesterday. For all practical purposes, I asked him to disappear in Paris and fly to Spain. I gave him enough money for food and travel. He must live in Barcelona with our organization until the liberation of Normandy. He'll be reimbursed by Allied Intelligence, they will take care of all his expenses," said Marceau.

"The Gestapo will be a problem until the invasion. As soon as the beachhead is established they will disappear in thin air because they know that we'll be looking for them and they'll be meeting their Maker. I recommend a little rest for everybody until the Gestapo madman quiets down. Enjoy life, whatever that means to you," suggested Marceau.

"To begin our little vacation, we would like to go home now, and have a good sleep and we'll see you next week," said Tibault.

A young lady entered the shop crying because her sister was taken to the Gestapo for interrogation. She was sobbing relentlessly and it was impossible to question her. A few minutes passed by before Tibault was able to ask her, "What is your sister's name."

"Her name is Rebecca Flaubert."

"She is our Resistance agent. She is very good," commented Marceau.

"We must help her before she spills the beans," said Tibault.

"It looks like another rescue," remarked his assistant.

"Tell us what happened," asked Tibault in a calm voice.

"She was one of the cell members and had been working in a bunker kitchen. She became friendly with a German officer who was supervising the mine laying process around the perimeter of the bunker. One of the officers accidentally stepped on a mine. The mine exploded and threw the officer in the air. When he hit the ground, he was a bloody mess and lost both of his legs."

"He was alive and taken by ambulance to the hospital. There in the emergency room they removed his garments and a piece of paper fell out. A German soldier took the paper and kept it for evidence. He was furiously jealous of the officer and mad at my sister."

"So, what happened?"

"We don't know. The next thing we heard was that my sister was taken to the Gestapo."

"We'll have a talk with the soldier about the paper before going home, and we'll take it from there. We have to ask Parker or Shaw to help us."

"Good-bye my boys, you did a swell job," said Marceau.

"Don't worry young lady we'll get your sister out from the Gestapo today," said Tibault.

"Have a great week, so long," said Tibault.

Just as Tibault and his associate left, Shaw and Parker showed up to find out how things worked out with Ms. Savignion.

Marceau informed them about the rescue and praised Tibault and his associate for their daring job. He then disclosed to them the incident that recently occurred with one of the cell members and a soldier.

"We have to get to the bunker and straighten out the mess," continued Shaw.

"Aren't we compromising our professional status?"

"Not if we are smart."

"So, what's the plan?"

"I will ask a soldier how the officer is doing. If he directs me to the soldier who was with him in the hospital, that's just fine. If he does not, I will ask where I could meet him. Once I get to know him and what was written on the paper, it'll be smooth sailing."

"You hope. I like your enthusiasm, but you may have to curb it if he does not want to cooperate with you."

"I will use the girl as an incentive."

"Good luck. You're on."

Shaw and Parker drove to the gate of the bunker and received permission to check the latest repairs. The captain in charge was summoned to assist and show Shaw and Parker where the repairs were done.

"We had a minor structural problem in the left wing but they did a very good job repairing the problem."

"How do you know that it was minor and the job was well done?"

"We no longer have problems with the wall. It does not shift or leak rain."

"Good. May we inspect this repair?" asked Shaw.

"Go ahead as you please. I will come back for you in a half an hour."

"That would be super."

Shaw and Parker were looking for soldiers and found a young man of seventeen who was very cooperative. He was a recent inductee from Austria.

"I understand you had a mine accident quite recently," asked Shaw.

"Oh yes, Herr Officer."

"Were there any casualties?"

"Fortunately, only one officer was hurt."

"How badly was he hurt," asked Parker.

"He lost both legs."

"Was there anyone near him who saw the accident?"

"Yes, do you want to talk with him? He just came back from the hospital."

"That would be lovely," said Shaw.

The soldier walked to the mess hall and asked the "accompanying soldier" to see a couple of officers. He was surprised but willing to talk.

"I am Private Hirsch, Ludwig Hirsch. What can I do for you, Officers?"

"This is Officer Dietrich and I am Officer Krueger. We were quite shocked to hear about the mine accident," said Shaw.

"When you lay mines and you fail to see where you are going, accidents are prone to happen."

"Did you know the victim?" asked Parker.

"I used to play soccer with him during our military training."

"How is he doing?" asked Shaw.

"He is not well. He lost a lot of blood."

"How is his mood?" asked Parker.

"He is rather sad."

"Does he have a girlfriend somewhere?"

"He used to go out with our kitchen help, a French girl."

"Would it help if she could visit him?"

"She is in the custody of the Gestapo."

"But why, what did she do?"

"She was to receive some paper from the victim which had numbers and coordinates on it."

"How did this happen?" asked Shaw.

"After the accident, he was brought here to receive emergency aid in the infirmary. A piece of paper fell out of his pocket. I saw it, picked it up and reported it to the military police. The police informed the Gestapo."

"What did those numbers and coordinates represent?" asked Parker.

"He was told to note the location of the mines."

"So, the paper was supposed to be given to her to forward it to the Commandant?" asked Parker.

"You know we could clear up this whole mess and get her out from the Gestapo by telling what happened."

"I really don't want to get involved."

"Why not?"

"I do not want to help him. He stole the girl from me."

"I tell you what. If you save her neck, she'll be very grateful to you," said Parker in an affirmative voice.

"How would she know that?"

"We'll tell her."

"It is not such a bad idea."

"I will ask the bunker commandant to relieve you for half a day and we'll take you to Caen."

The officer came back and saw Shaw and Parker talking to the soldier.

"Did you have enough time to carry out the inspection?"

"Everything seems to be in order," said Shaw.

"I would like to talk with the Commandant."

"He left for Paris, but I am in charge until he comes back."

"May we take private Hirsh to the Gestapo HQ in Caen as a material witness?"

"I do not see why not if he could be of some help."

"Thank you and see you again," said Shaw.

If was difficult to enter the Gestapo and even more problematic to talk to the agent in charge of Rebecca. After waiting for forty-five minutes, two agents accompanied Shaw, Parker and Hirsch to his office. He was sitting at a large desk and looking with his icy eyes at the officers and the private. He had a large picture of Hitler on the wall behind him. The desk was neatly organized.

After the initial and superficial greetings and introductions the Gestapo agent did not hesitate to inquire point-blank the nature of their visit.

"You must have something important to discuss with me, because my time is precious."

"That is correct."

"So get on with it!"

"You are holding an innocent French girl who was assumed to be the bearer of the piece of paper that was written at the request of the bunker commandant," said Parker. "That piece of paper contained the updated coordinates of the newly laid mines that had to be compared to the original plan."

"Are you assuming this or is there definite truth to this assertion?"

"Private Hirsch under oath will testify as a material witness," said Shaw.

"Before I hear his testimony, I am curious, how and

why did you get involved in the fate of this French girl? We are trying to establish a Resistance connection and you are interfering with our investigation."

"Everything has a reason," said Parker.

"Are you lecturing a Gestapo officer?"

"No sir. That was not my intention. I simply started to elucidate the nature of this matter. We are technical employees and battery advisors for the construction of the Atlantic Wall. If we fail, so will you!"

"Don't threaten me, Officer!"

"Please hear me out, out of courtesy. Please."

"Go ahead. Continue talking. So far you've said nothing."

"It is our job to investigate even the most insignificant accident to construct better batteries. That is how we got involved."

"That makes sense to me."

"So let me hear what the private has to say and I will make a decision about the fate of the French girl."

He described in vivid detail what actually happened and how the paper ended up in the wrong hands. The Gestapo agent listened very carefully to every word what the private told him.

"We started with the interrogation procedures, but I can stop it. I will, however, keep an eye on Rebecca in the future and hope none of this will happen again. She'll be released in two hours. Don't thank me. I am just doing my job. Heil Hitler!"

Rebecca was taken by a Gestapo agent to the exit room where she received her garments and other belongings. She looked absolutely terrible. Parker, in front of the private, told her that he saved her from further torture and asked for her release. Rebecca thanked Hirsch for doing this and gave him a brief hug. Then Parker and the private drove back to the bunker. Rebecca was first examined by a Resistance physician in Caen.

"How is Rebecca?" asked Shaw.

"She has several lacerations. Those monsters put electrodes in her and sent the current into her vagina, but she'll be all right. Please, don't ask questions about her torture because she is very upset and embarrassed to talk about it."

"Thank you. Can we take her to Marceau?"

"Oh yes, drive carefully."

"I'll be careful."

CHAPTER FOUR

The Gestapo was absolutely furious when they found out about her disappearance. The chief, Herr Siegenthal, wanted to know every detail and ordered his men to investigate the circumstances of Ms. Savignion's escape and whereabouts. He asked that the four Schutstaffel (SS) elite guard, protection squad men who were guarding the house to appear in his office at 1400 hours sharp.

"I want to know what you saw and heard the night when you were watching," demanded the chief.

Officer Burger, as being operation chief for the surveillance of Ms. Savignion, began the story with the mail truck then the garbage truck.

"Was there anything unusual?" questioned Siegenthal.

"We didn't find anything suspicious with the mail truck."

"Didn't you find it strange to collect garbage at night?"

"Yes, we found it very unusual to come at night and take the garbage. So we asked the men why they were collecting garbage at such a late hour of the night."

"How many men were involved?"

"We were not sure, but it seemed to be three."

"What do you mean by, 'there seemed to be'?"

"One guy came out from the driver's seat, the second one, from the left rear, and as he was collecting the garbage and walking back and forth, he returned to the left rear, but someone appeared to come from the right rear. It was confusing to determine the exact number of people involved because they were dressed in black and it was night."

"Were there any large packages?"

"The only large package, as compared with other items, was a sack. It was not very big and was thrown in to the back."

"Do any of you have different observations to report?" asked Siegenthal of the other officers.

"Some of us had doubts about the number of people involved," said officer Krieg.

"Did you inspect the packages?"

"No. We did not suspect a human would be dumped in a garbage truck in a carton or a small sack," said Burger.

"I am terribly surprised by your lack of suspicion." You'll all be transferred to Germany. That is all for today. Heil Hitler!"

All the Gestapo men left the chief's office with surprise and sadness—surprised at the transfer and sadness for their serious mistakes.

The chief ordered that the mail and garbage trucks be found and their routes investigated.

As the orders went out, the chief received a note that a huge explosion occurred about fifty miles north from his HQ in a corn field. According to the farmers, there were two totally demolished trucks. The chief immediately ordered his Gestapo officers to investigate the explosion and take pictures.

The General, who befriended Ms. Savignion, entered the chief's office in the afternoon and in an angry voice demanded to know why he targeted her when there were thousand of saboteurs roaming Normandy and relatively little was being accomplished to find them.

"I am sorry, Herr General, but we don't have enough people to carry out our duties," said the chief.

"But you have enough men to watch, without success, Ms. Savignion?" asked the General.

"There was an oversight, and I take the blame for the selection of men who were assigned to watch her."

The General, without the usual salute, left the office slamming the door shut. This incident between the General and the Gestapo chief, however, did not go unnoticed, and it slowly became a topic of gossip among the officers.

Marceau, who had ears through the maintenance people in the Gestapo, heard about the incident and cautioned all operatives to be on guard for a loose tiger. That meant he could strike any person who had the slightest connection with Ms. Savignion. His method was to arrest a person and torture him until he names the culprit.

The file on Ms. Savignion was never closed and the fear of arresting the culprits just lingered on until the end of the war. Shaw, Parker, Marceau, and Bridget were all relatively immune to the episode. They had become used to living under fear and threat. It was Marceau's philosophy to involve people on a need to know basis. The Gestapo cannot get to the bottom of a case in case one is arrested and tortured.

The truck was stolen and had false registration and plates. It was found in a Parisian junkyard so the owner could sell it as damaged merchandise. It required mechanical work that the Resistance operatives had to take care of before it could be delivered to a drop place in Normandy. Afterwards, they were totally destroyed. The whole thing was executed with surgical precision. However, one always had to be careful of the Nazi sympathizers and the Gestapo who always welcomed spies to crack a difficult case. These spies were among the forced laborers and tried to infiltrate the Resistance. Marceau was very selective in assigning cell members to work for Shaw and Parker. They were all handpicked and had a thorough background checks.

Although the case of Chris Savignion remained open, the Gestapo's revenge policy was placed on hold. Her disappearance certainly remained an enigma. Stories were floating around about the Gestapo and his chief. Among the gossip, people asserted that her disappearance could have been a failure of the Gestapo, a suicide, homicide, abduction, or voluntary departure. These assumptions sometimes helped or hurt Chief Siegenthal.

He became sick over the failure to catch Ms. Savignion. He was like a wounded tiger. Marceau's assessment of his future behavior was absolutely correct. All Resistance operatives were warned to be doubly careful in every endeavor.

Agents Shaw and Parker also proceeded with caution and sent notes to all seven cells to operate with extra caution. The seventh cell from Caen placed an urgent message in the drop box. They were calling for an immediate meeting. Shaw responded to the request by asking Bridget to contact one of the cell members and arrange a meeting for the same day at 1600 hours in a wine cellar that Marceau's friend reserved for emergencies.

The cellar consisted of two sections. The rear section was for the vintage and the front for recent wine. The place was over a hundred fifty years old, but was kept in a very good condition. The stone walls were scrubbed clean; the floors mopped, and it had adequate ventilation by means of vent pipes. Shaw and Parker arrived earlier and stayed in the old wine cellar, deep inside. The cell members, Maurice, Carl, and Andre, were asked to stay in the forward section, close to the entrance. Their greetings sounded jubilant but actually they were apprehensive.

"What can we do for you, gentlemen?" asked Shaw.

Andre began with his story that sounded like a dream. "We found a pure treasure. Being an electrician, I was asked yesterday by the German military HQ if I would have some time to fix the wiring in one of the officer's houses who complained to about it being in almost total darkness. I had an hour free between two jobs, so I accepted the request. I was given the key to the house, and went there during the afternoon. There was no one home. Finding the problem required a room to room search. As I was tracing the faulty wire, I entered the office, and to my surprise I found a large map spread across his desk with all kinds of military markings on it. I did not know what to do within a short time. I called Carl and Maurice to get a camera because I was afraid to take the map. Unfortunately, they did not have a camera, and in my desperation I began to copy the markings. Another officer came in who was sharing the house, picked up some clothing and told me that they were driving to Cherbourg to check on an installation of a big gun. They would not be back until tomorrow evening and that I could work in the house as my time permitted for that day and the whole day tomorrow."

"What you're telling me sounds very promising. Before we celebrate however, the map must be obtained and photographed. We must exercise caution, which means being absolutely silent about it. You cannot tell this to anyone, wives, girlfriends, parents, or best friends. The next step is to get the map for a short time, photograph it and return it. We will meet at this same location. I will have lights and a camera. Andre, you, should have a long two tier toolbox and put the map in there. Upon your return if somebody enters the house and will look for the map, you can tell the person very calmly that you put the map away to protect it just in case you have a fiery short circuit," said Shaw.

"The map should be rolled and lying on the bottom tier of the toolbox," added Parker.

"What time will we be meeting here again," asked Carl.

"2100 hours sharp. If there is a problem, communicate with the same drop box in the same location," replied Parker.

Before they parted, Shaw put money in an envelope and tossed it to Andre to purchase a larger toolbox than he owns and wished everybody the best of luck.

Shaw and Parker drove back to Bayeux to meet with other cell members. It was a short meeting and not much was reported. They decided to have dinner there in one of the restaurants and rested for an hour in their car before they returned to Caen. Parker checked their camera and lighting equipment which had been left in the trunk of their car from the rescue operation. They left Bayeaux after 2000 hours and leisurely drove to Caen.

Andre returned to the house with the new toolbox and to his surprise he found another officer with a girlfriend making love in the bedroom. He had enough time to continue with his repair which was actually a simple wiring problem that shorted out the electric in the rooms. The officer and his girlfriend, upon hearing the electrician working in the room, started dressing and excused themselves to leave. Andre rolled the map and placed it in the bottom of the toolbox and walked slowly toward the door. As he was descending from the second floor staircase to the street, his heart was racing, while he tried to maintain a calm attitude. He entered the waiting car and Carl and Maurice drove him to the wine cellar without incident.

It was exactly twenty-one hours when all parties met at the wine cellar. Shaw did not waste any time setting up the tripod, camera, and lights. He took five dozen pictures from many angles and asked the cell to return the map in a hurry and they did. Andre unrolled the map from the toolbox, and tried to return it as it was. He succeeded without the slightest suspicion that it was taken and photographed.

Shaw and Parker rushed to Marceau's and asked him to develop the film.

"You're late. What do you have here?" asked Marceau.

"A pure, undiluted, treasure was found where one of the German officers lives. One of our cell members saw this map on the table as he was repairing a wiring problem," replied Parker.

"Great. Let me work on it and I will let you know tomorrow what we find."

Shaw and Parker exchanged a few pleasantries and left for home.

The next day, after visiting some construction sites and making mental notes of the new defenses, they drove to Marceau's. It was after 1400 hours and his place was filled with German officers. They decided to walk around a little bit and return in a half hour. When they returned Marceau was elated because what the photos revealed was priceless.

"These pictures will be microfilmed for my next fishing trip."

Shaw and Parker were amazed that the pictures provided a clear plan of what the German defenses of the coastline and well beyond were.

"Well, the question is whether the German High Command will be able to implement what is on this map," stated Shaw.

"Only time, money, and material will tell," remarked Marceau.

"But at least we have some idea how many batteries, bunkers, casemates, big guns, pillboxes, tobruks and mines we are facing should implementation take place, especially in the invasion area," commented Parker.

"Well said. We now have a better idea what we should be looking for," added Marceau.

"A word of caution, however. The Germans can be just as deceptive in their literature, propaganda and construction as we are. Although we can now authenticate some of their projects and make sense of their defensive posture, we have to be careful what we are sending to the home office," suggested Shaw.

"That is very true, but we now know the difference between a coastal villa and a casemate. Some of them are painted to look just like a house to deceive the Allied air force but in reality they are dangerous defense casemates facing the water and waiting for the incoming infantry to decimate them during the invasion. So, now we have the map and the next job is to authenticate what is drawn on the map," said Marceau.

"We agree with you," Parker replied.

"OK, let's go to work. Thank you very much for your comments and bye," concluded Shaw.

Shaw and Parker left to pick up messages from the seven drop boxes. Because there was no information or requests in any of the seven drop boxes, they decided to spend the afternoon learning about one or two existing batteries facing the invasion coast. The plan was to visit as many coastal batteries as possible within a year or less, memorize the defense structures, reproduce and send them to Allied Intelligence. Only through combined efforts would the intelligence community paint a true picture of the strengths and weaknesses of each coastal terrain and surrounding territory. To coordinate all incoming information and disinformation was a formidable task. Each Allied operative had a distinctive role to play in the process of defeating the enemy. Andre had been an intelligent, observant and cautious operator who had passed on invaluable information that would have taken immeasurable amount of time to accomplish, even by a very experienced and skillful agent. But without the help of Shaw's and Parker's mentorship and Marceau's grit, superbly wise intellect and reputation, their operation would hardly have been successful.

Shaw and Parker had been visiting many of the batteries but some were under construction and did not provide sufficient information to be transmitted. As time went by, they needed to revisit some of the coastal defenses and found considerably more sophisticated weaponries and ordnances than before. As they were looking around, one of the German officers questioned their presence at La Grande Dune which was later to be designated as the Utah for the invasion forces.

"What are you looking for, gentlemen? Maybe we can help you."

"We are inspecting bunkers and casemates for cracks in the concrete," explained Parker.

"You must be careful where you are walking because we are surrounded with minefields. The direction where you're going will not lead to the casemates and bunkers."

"Thank you for telling us. We were just admiring your defenses you have taken to defeat the enemy," said Shaw.

"If you want, I can be your tour guide and escort you around so you won't accidentally be blown up."

"Well, you lead and we will follow," suggested Parker.

"How are the bunkers holding up?" asked Shaw.

"We had some problems, but they seem to be all right now."

"Wait a minute. Let's walk a little slower, Captain. You see this entrance wall to the bunker. Now if you just get a little closer, you'll see a hairline crack right at the door," said Parker.

"So, what does that mean?"

"Nothing now, but may be tomorrow," replied Parker.

"Do you plan to do something about it?"

"Depends on what happens a month from now. We'll be back," responded Shaw.

"We have a similar situation in another bunker, but we don't worry too much about hairline cracks. One of the casemates, however, has a structural problem and there are several people working on it. Officer Hauptman, a construction engineer from Organization Todt, you probably know him, happens to be here now directing the work."

"What kind of problem do you have?" asked Parker.

"When we tested the antitank gun, the explosion ripped the upper wall of the casement gun open. They are reinforcing and rebuilding the whole opening."

"Can we see it?" Shaw inquired.

"Of course you can. Just come along and I take you there, but please, do not wander around because we have mines all over."

They walked about a quarter of a mile in the direction of the coast and met Herr Engineer Burgholzer. He was five feet three inches tall. A very thin, gray haired man with a sour humor that was impossible to understand.

"I am pleased to make your acquaintance," said Burgholzer, and he shook everybody's hands.

"We feel the same," said Shaw.

"What are you doing in this 'condemned' battery?" continued Burgholzer with a grin on his face.

"We were told that in this particular region the water has a damaging effect on the mixture of concrete," said Parker wryly.

"I never heard such a thing."

"We never did either, but we must investigate every rumor," responded Parker.

"Waste of time. There are more important issues."

"Like what?"

"We don't have an adequate number of supplies. I had to wait two weeks for reinforcing rods to reconstruct this casement opening, but let's talk about something more pleasant."

"Are you going to the Organization Todt Recognition Dinner?"

"I'm sorry but I forgot to make a reservation. What day, time, and place?" asked Shaw.

"The meeting will be held next Saturday, 1900 hours at the Grand Ball Room of the German Military HQ. Only officers of the Organization Todt, Military, and Gestapo will be allowed by reservation only."

"Thank you for your kind reminder. We will make our reservations as soon as possible," said Shaw.

"What do you think about our batteries?"

"I have been inspecting the various stages of construction and in all honesty we are doing a fine job," commented Parker.

"I am glad that you are satisfied, because from a military point of view we may not be ready with our defense structures when the Allies come knocking on our doors. We lack steel, heavy loaders, excavating equipment and skilled people to build each battery."

"All in good time," said Parker.

"There is no time. The Allies are preparing for the invasion and we are nowhere near ready to defend our shores."

"You are pessimistic. We are doing what the Military High Command West is telling us to do, and they know what is going on," commented Parker.

Shaw was absolute taciturn and had a difficult time holding back his laughter. He was amazed at how Parker managed to create a 'make believe,' nationalistic spirit and sell it to a man who was absolutely right in his assessment of the military situation.

"I admire you, young man, but your optimism sickens me."

"I must have faith in winning this war to be able to continue my work," said Parker.

"Good luck to both of you and keep up the good work."

Shaw and Parker excused themselves to the German 'tour guide' officer and headed for their cars. It was around 1830 and they were hungry and needed some rest.

"You missed your calling," said Shaw.

"I was involved in acting during my high school years. It was o.k. for fun but it was not for me. I need more than acting. I like to solve problems."

"Anyway, I liked the way you performed."

"Thank you for the compliment."

"You deserve it! Now, what would you like to have for dinner?"

"I am not very hungry. Some cold cuts, vegetables, bread, fruit, and a couple of glasses of wine."

"Let's go shop on the way home."

Parker was preparing the table and Shaw was sitting at the kitchen table, deep in thought.

"What are you musing about?" asked Parker.

"How many things you can remember?"

"Why don't you test me and if I can't remember you help me out."

"Let's start with the machinegun positions. How many did you count?"

"I believe they were three."

"I think you're right. What about anti-tank guns?"

"I counted two fifty millimeter guns."

"That seems to be right."

"Let me ask you about the personnel bunkers," asked Parker.

"I recall five, but there were different types."

"You are o.k., buddy."

"There was an ammunition bunker also," Shaw added.

"There were other ordnances, antitank guns and machine guns encased in concrete pits," said Parker.

"We'll tell Marceau to send this mental picture along with the coordinates and dimensions to England. I don't know if our present bombs can smash the bunkers and casemates the first time, but even if they miss, the RAF and USAF can create such havoc by hitting the mines and everything else that they will not forget it for a long time," said Shaw.

There was a silence again. Parker asked what was wrong and Shaw's response was simple and brief, "Thinking about home."

They are not supposed to reveal their home lives for security purposes. Therefore, any type of questioning was forbidden. No voluntary revelation. If it happened, the agent had to go home and was replaced by somebody else. No letters and no calling home. This mission was not for the faint-hearted.

Shaw was married with one child. He missed his family terribly, but he was strong and committed. Parker had a girlfriend and a mother whom he deeply adored. He was also very devoted, committed, and had great strength to overcome adversities and home sickness. They were well matched for this engagement.

After their little talk, both retired to their flats.

The next morning Shaw found a note under the door. It was from Bridget. She asked them to see the local cell at noon in Port-En-Bessin. They met at the usual meeting place, in an old ship. The operatives were sitting below in the cabin waiting for Shaw and Parker.

"Hello there, anyone at home?" greeted Parker.

"We have been waiting for you guys," said Corinne.

"We have problems," added Genevieve.

"What kind of problems?" Shaw asked.

"The Gestapo wants Genevieve to meet one of their agents in a small café where she works tomorrow afternoon at 1350," said Philip.

"Do you have any idea what it is all about?"

"I don't have the faintest idea," said Genevieve.

Shaw asked Parker to get the binoculars from the car and look around to see if she was followed. Parker slowly walked toward the car, sat inside, took the binoculars and panned around. In the far distance there was a car with two people. One was looking with a pair of binoculars in the direction of the boat. Parker started the engine and drove near the car with the two guys watching. He walked to the car and asked both of them to get out because he wanted to talk to them.

"Are you with the German secret police?" one of the guys asked.

"What business is it of yours? I belong to the Organization Todt."

"This is a restricted area for civilians, unless you have a permit from the German Military or Organization Todt. I want your identification papers with the restricted zone permit," said Parker.

"I don't think you have the authority to ask for the papers," challenged the other guy.

Parker took out his service pistol, and took their pistols away. Then he asked them to turn around, walk to the trunk of their car, open the lid and then he hit both of them with a chop on the neck so hard that both of them fell in the trunk. He grabbed their legs and tossed them inside. Then he drove back to the ship, asked Shaw to assist, and told the cell to meet them in a couple of hours in the same place.

Parker drove their car to an isolated hedgerow, took the two guys out, tied their hands behind their backs and the interrogation began.

"Who are you working for?" Shaw asked.

"I will tell you nothing," hissed one of the guys as he spit in Shaw's face.

Shaw did not want physical violence, but this time there was no alternative and he punched the guy in his stomach so hard that he began to vomit. Then he punched him in his face.

"So, you don't want to talk?" asked Parker, and he punched the other guy in the stomach, chest, and face so hard he started to bleed.

"We are working for the French secret police. We are collaborators, and we know that the three of them were up to something so we followed them," said the first guy.

"Why do you do this? Money, Fascism, Nazism?" asked Shaw.

"For the three reasons that have you mentioned. We believe in Hitler," said the first guy.

Shaw turned to Parker and asked him to step back. He whispered in his ear, "We have to terminate and burn them in their car otherwise we will be implicated and compromised. Let's fake an accident," said Shaw.

Parker hit both of them on the head so hard that they fell instantaneously. Shaw took their identification papers from their wallets.

They were put into the front seat. Then Parker and Shaw rocked the car until it turned over, removed the gas line and with their matches ignited the gasoline. In minutes the whole car was engulfed in flames. They waited until their bodies charred into ashes. It was an unpleasant scene but it had to be done.

Since they had no car, they started to walk and they did not want to be questioned by others. They were in good shape, so a little hiking did not bother them. There was a military truck going in the direction where they had left their car and they asked for a lift. Parker told the driver that his car had an ignition problem and they would appreciate a ride to his friend's house. The driver of the truck gladly obliged to take them to their destination.

Shaw and Parker picked up their car and drove back to the boat. They were twenty minutes late, exhausted, and briefly explained that these people were not from the Gestapo, but were collaborators, and wanted to blackmail Genevieve. Parker said only that they took care of them and they would never bother them again. He refused to elaborate, but Shaw summed it up by saying, "It's them or us. We are at war. Thank you for telling us. We would have been in a terrible situation if you had remained silent. Thank you again!"

Shaw and Parker made another appointment with the cell and drove to Marceau's. It was the first incident where they had to use force of this magnitude. Marceau had to know about it. This was another face of the enemy which they had to deal with.

Marceau was not surprised at all when he was told what had happened. There was nothing new about these kinds of incidents. Unfortunately, betrayal for whatever reasons did cost a number of lives of the members of the Resistance.

"You made the right decision," said Marceau.

"How about the aftermath?" questioned Shaw.

"We'll play it by ear," replied Marceau.

"Lay low or go on with our daily activities?" inquired Parker

"Just go on with your daily schedule. In this day and age a couple of lives do not matter as long as they are not German."

"Thank you, Marceau. We are on our way to Cherbourg to meet with the first cell members," said Shaw.

"Have a good day, gentlemen."

Shaw and Parker drove away with a new dimension of awareness. Knowledge of French treachery is one thing, experiencing it is another. The combat has been extended on several fronts: Allied Intelligence, The Gestapo, French treachery, German counter-intelligence, German intelligence, and Allied counter- intelligence.

The German spy network has been providing information of the increased Allied preparedness for the invasion but the sources have been unable to pinpoint where and when. Allied Intelligence needs to know what kind of defenses the German High Command West has planned for the invasion. The stakes are high. Shaw and Parker have been feeling the increased concerns of both sides and they are between a rock and a hard place. They have been getting messages from Allied

Intelligence to provide more and more information and the Gestapo is making their investigation increasingly difficult.

The morning after was different. The RAF and USAF bombers flew over and dropped their bombs all over the beaches. It was a deafening experience. The Germans responded with the full force of their antiaircraft guns and this went on for an hour. The Allied aircrafts bombed in waves. Shaw and Parker decided to wait until the situation calmed down and they could travel without being stopped. But their curiosity about the damage made them leave the house and they started to drive around the coast. They were stopped a few times but were allowed to pass under the pretext of repair assessment of the damages.

The bomb holes around the bunkers showed the mistaken trajectories but at least there were some hits of the mines, pill boxes, casemates, and antiaircraft guns. They went to a small store and bought the daily paper to see if there was any mention of the car fire. They found a brief mention that two passengers were burned in a car accident and that they probably had consumed too much liqueur which caused them to speed and crash.

"Good article," Shaw said after reading about the car fire to Parker.

"At least until they start to investigate the accident," replied Parker.

"Time will tell, so why worry about it? No Germans were involved."

"Not directly, but who knows," said Parker.

"Why don't we drive to the neighborhood of Bayeux? There is some bunker and casement construction going on," recommended Shaw.

"That's fine with me."

They drove to the construction site to find a large commotion. One of the workers had an argument with an Organization Todt building supervisor. The yelling got out of control, the worker punched the supervisor, he hit him back, then the worker slugged the supervisor with a pick who died at the scene a bit later. A German guard tried to separate the two but the worker kicked the guard hard. The guard then shot the worker to death.

A German military officer arrived at the site and asked Shaw and Parker to help out until the day was over. The workers needed help with the pouring of concrete and aligning the reinforcing rods. Shaw and Parker looked at each other and without any hesitation offered their help. This gave them another opportunity to study the terrain and make notes about the defense structures.

Around seven o'clock, the work was partially completed and they let the workers go home. Shaw and Parker said good bye to one of the OT officers and drove home to find a note from Bridget that Marceau wanted to see them tonight. They were not happy about this, but it must have been important if he wanted to talk to them twice in the same day.

This particular drive back to Marceau's felt longer than any other before, perhaps because they had a long, exhausting day.

"What's up, Marceau?" asked Parker.

"One of our operatives was arrested by the Gestapo in connection with the death of the two French guys who burned in the car," said Marceau.

"Does this operative belong to our cells?" Shaw questioned.

"Yes. She is a sweetheart and she can't take the torture."

At that moment someone was knocking at the door. Marceau asked Shaw and Parker to go inside in the area of the waiting room. Marceau opened the door and to his surprise Genevieve was there. They embraced each other.

"What happened? We were just talking about you," said Marceau.

"They wanted to know where I was at the time of the car accident and ensuing fire."

"Why were you implicated?"

"I met one of the passengers once and had rejected his Nazi fanaticism and sexual advances."

"Can you elaborate on this?"

"He made up a story about me to the Gestapo for money and revenge."

"Did they interrogate you?"

"No. They only wanted to know where I was when he had the accident."

"Did they follow you here?"

"I don't know."

"If they did follow, you what would you say?"

"I was frightened and went to see Bridget who is a good friend of mine."

"That's good."

"I want you to stay here and relax. Here is a little brandy. I'll be back."

Marceau went to see Shaw and Parker and told them about Genevieve. He also said that she must leave town tonight and be replaced.

"Genevieve, you better leave town for a year or more because the Gestapo will follow you and you will have no peace. I will take care of your expenses. Since you were not asked to return to the Gestapo, you can leave tonight for Paris. Later you can go to Cannes. Change your name and hair color. I will give you documents and money for now. Here are names of people in Paris and Cannes who will look after you. You can trust them," said Marceau and continued, "You'll make friends in Paris and Cannes. Paris is an exciting city and Cannes is for the celebrities. You can meet interesting people. I will know how you are faring from others that you're connected with. You must not write to me directly because the Gestapo will find out where you are. I'll go to Paris or Cannes and we'll meet there."

"The rest will be explained by Bridget and she'll take care of the money and ticket. You can buy all you need in Paris, so don't worry about your clothes and cosmetics. Upon your arrival in Paris and Cannes, it is important that contact be made with the people I recommended. They will contact me right away. Thank you and good luck. Bye darling, I must go now."

Marceau returned to Shaw and Parker.

"Everything will be all right. She'll be in Paris tonight. She can stay there under an assumed name, work, have fun, get an education, and she can also go to Cannes and look at the movie stars."

"This is very nice of you, Marceau, "said Shaw.

"Well, we are glad that this had a happy ending," commented Parker.

"Marceau, we've had a long day and we must go home. Will you please excuse us?" said Shaw.

"I know my friends, but we are in a twenty-four hour business and the war is not ending tomorrow. I'm sorry to ask you to come here after a hard day, but as the French say, C'est la vie."

Shaw and Parker tipped their hats and left the place. Parker drove and Shaw just stretched out and closed his eyes.

"Are you going to sleep on me?" asked Parker.

"Would you mind?" replied Shaw.

"Go ahead, but only if you don't snore"

"Right, if I snore, wake me up."

"I will. Have a good rest."

As Parker was about to park the car, he saw a black Citroen in front of the house with two guys sitting in the front. Parker woke up Shaw and asked, "Do you see those two guys in the Citroen. What do you think?"

"Drive away. Let's go to the next street on your right, make a turn, and come back to this street but park at the corner so we are facing the Citroen and let's wait."

A girl exited the front door, entered the car, and three of them drove away.

"Cautious, paranoid, or simply mistaken about the Gestapo," asked Parker.

"Maybe not. It could have been French Nazi sympathizers, who knows."

Shaw and Parker went upstairs, took a shower, and got some shut eye.

The next morning they slept an hour longer than usual and did practically nothing but listen to the BBC News Service, music, and caught up with their readings. This was the day of leisure and a banquet in the evening. It was the annual Recognition dinner. They made sure to dress up properly, which meant the dress uniform that was worn only for special occasions. The shirts, cufflinks, and ties were brand new, and so were the armbands. Shaw and Parker looked like actors on a movie set ready for the next shoot.

They arrived at eight o'clock sharp. The hall was decorated with flags and flowers. The center wall had a beautiful horizontal red and white Organization Todt flag hanging down majestically and was lit with four flood lights. Below was the stage which was set up for the orchestra and speaker. To the right was a lectern with a microphone. The tables were round and could seat ten people. The center of each table had beautiful flowers and number displays. The napkins were folded on the plate and there was a plethora of silver. Three crystal glasses were at each place setting for the water, wine, and champagne.

The waiters and waitresses were dressed in black and white uniforms. The lady ushers wore long red evening dresses with carnations on the upper right shoulder. The atmosphere and decorations were remarkably festive, totally ignoring the hard times at home and the losses on the fronts including the number of casualties.

When Shaw and Parker arrived, the orchestra was playing waltzes from Strauss. In the lobby, people introduced themselves or the ushers helped them to get acquainted with each other. Parker was holding a glass of wine when a pretty, brunette, blue eyed girl in her twenties took his arm and asked whether he was alone or with somebody.

"I am with my colleague. You see that good looking Todt officer, that's him.

"Do you dance?"

"Sometimes, depending on how I feel."

"You have to be in the right mood."

"Yes, how did you know that?"

"Perhaps I have an instinct or sixth sense, who knows."

"You are very perceptive."

"Well, that is very nice of you. So tell me, what would put you in the right mood?"

"You. You could ignite my flame."

"Are you flirting?"

"You asked me a question, and I answered it."

She blushed, and he never sensed that she was an American. He had fantastic training in how to behave in these kinds of situations. Well trained agents do not fall into traps easily.

She let go of his arm and looked into his eyes. It was a passionate look of desire.

"I must go now. If you feel up to it, I am here to dance with you. Bye."

It was definitely a temptation for Parker. His girlfriend, however, is his true friend whom he loves, adores, and respects. She has been a terrific girl, and does not forgive. He did not want to take a chance and lose her. It was not the distance, war, loneliness, or sexual desire, but cheating was not his style and commitment meant a lot to him. He had to live with himself. Social dancing is one thing, kissing and arousal is something else. His inner conflict between temptation and commitment became quite serious over time since he had not heard from his friend in the States for quite sometime.

Shaw was involved in a discussion with a Todt engineer about a specific construction material that required his background in chemistry. Although the conversation required his full attention, he couldn't help but seeing Parker as he was chatting with the usher lady at length. It did cross his mind to tease him, but out of respect, he kept silent.

The music stopped and the ushers announced that dinner was being served. The menu was Crab bisque soup, chicken or fish with sauce, asparagus, potatoes, salad, and for dessert chocolate cake topped with whipped cream.

The seating was arranged randomly except for requested reservations. Shaw and Parker were sandwiched between a Gestapo Kommissar and Inspektor. These were high ranking officers. The rest of the table consisted of Todt engineers and construction supervisors. The ushers did the name and rank introductions. During dinner, a few pleasantries were exchanged, but Shaw and Parker were careful not to open any discussions that could have led to controversial topics. After dinner, several short speeches were in order. Then special awards were given to Todt officers and building supervisors who, according to the General's and Todt's management team, performed superbly during the last year. Many of the reward recipients were friends of high ranking Nazi party members. After dinner, the Gestapo Kommissar started to ask questions of Shaw and Parker. The Inspektor was rather funny and lightheartedly defused the Kommissar's interrogative questions. Parker didn't mind having a little verbal play with the Gestapo. He turned the questions around and became the detective, for the fun of role playing. The Gestapo did not like the defendant role and became the prosecutor again.

"You should have been a lawyer, a prosecutor," said the Kommissar.

"No, thank you. I like to solve problems and sometimes create new things. This is the future," replied Parker.

"Where did you study engineering? Your German is refined, highly educated, and may I compliment your well articulated discourse."

"I studied in Berlin at the University and Architectural School."

"I would like to see some of your drawings," said the Inspektor.

"Unfortunately, they are on loan now, and I must get them back first."

"No problem. Where is your home?" asked the Kommissar.

"I grew up in Munich, Dresden, and finally we settled in Berlin."

"How come you lived in so many places?"

"My father was a plumber. You know how hard it was to get a job after the first war."

"And where did you grow up and go to school?" The Kommissar turned to Shaw.

"I was born, raised and studied in Berlin. I went to the University there."

Parker took over the questioning and asked them about their backgrounds, but they did not have too much to say and the subject was dropped quickly. They mostly referred to 'life school' and low ranking policemen in small villages. But they did emphasize early Nazi party affiliations. They were proud of their achievements and their careers in the Gestapo.

Shaw and Parker had all they could tolerate of listening about Hitler and the Nazi Party. They politely excused themselves and headed for their car. It was late and they had to get up early to meet with the number one cell in Cherbourg.

Michael came to the store and said hello to Bridget. She was quite busy with customers who had been waiting for their shoes and ordering new boots. Marceau had more customers than he was able to take care of and his backlog was horrendous. He had to reschedule some of the customers for new boots and repairs.

Bridget asked Michael to return in an hour because it was impossible for her to take a break. Michael threw a kiss and left for an hour. The backlog had occurred because of multiple reasons. First, new reinforcements came to relieve some of the old timers who wanted to go home to visit their families. Secondly, a shoemaker in Bayeux passed away, and lastly, everybody preferred to have new handmade boots by Marceau.

The supplies to make the forms, the plaster of Paris, had to be ordered from Paris and the shipment could take at least two weeks. Because of the war situation, Marceau couldn't order large quantities. There was a shortage of heavy paper to make the cartons and there was a limit of one large carton per order once a month for each customer. Marceau could have used two or three cartons per month.

Bridget was so busy taking small repair orders that she just couldn't get away. In addition, she spent a minimum of two to three hours a day running various errands, including work for the Resistance. As the telephone was unavailable for security reasons, everything had to be personally delivered. Marceau had to spend three hours a day for the Resistance which included deciphering messages, microfilming pictures and messages, coding highly confidential and personal information, organizing, having conferences, and keeping a payroll for Resistance members in and outside Normandy. Marceau's payroll was several thousands of Francs a month and the money was deposited in various banks in Normandy and Paris.

Michael returned an hour and a half later and the shoe repair shop was still very busy. Bridget offered a seat in the back room but Michael preferred to go. Bridget told him that she would close the shop in fifteen minutes for sure. He promised to return.

When he returned the third time, Bridget fell into his arms and asked for a date Saturday evening at his place. She offered to cook a sumptuous dinner for which she would purchase the groceries and prepare the ingredients. He was allowed to purchase the wine. Saturday was only two days away but it seemed to be an eternity for them to be in each others arms. They were counting the hours and minutes until they would meet again.

Bridget was praying for an uneventful evening, that she will not be summoned for an emergency by the Resistance or Marceau. The prayer was heard and fulfilled. She was free to leave at five o'clock. Michael arrived on time. He was very happy to see and be with Bridget. It was a spirited feeling of longing for someone you love. Before they drove to Michael's place they did a little shopping, because she hardly had time to prepare for the evening meal. Everything had to be done impromptu, but by seven- thirty they were ready to start their festive meal. She made sure that the candles were lit, the wine was poured, and the music was playing. Bridget was dressed casually. She had on a nice dark blue skirt, white blouse, and a cream colored knit cardigan. Her hair was down, lipstick hardly visible, and a lightly sprayed seductive perfume scented her upper body.

The menu was simple but nourishing. She made a crab casserole in cream sauce, sliced potatoes with butter and parsley, tossed salad with spinach, tomatoes, mushrooms, and croutons and French bread with whipped butter. For dessert they had a multilayer éclair with whipped cream and mint candy. She was an excellent gourmet cook and a delightful hostess.

Michael picked up fresh mixed flowers on the way home, and made a centerpiece for the table. He was preparing the best white wine for the occasion. He took off his military jacket and sat at the table. His face was lit with joy and was waiting to lift the glass and toast Bridget. When she sat down, he took her hands, looked into her eyes and said, "Thank you, my dear. Thank you for coming and preparing our dinner. Thank you for making my life so happy. Thank you for fulfilling my dream."

"To my sweetheart, you're very welcome. You make my life very happy and meaningful. Thank you for inviting me and giving the best of yourself. You bring sunshine to my life."

He lifted the glass and said, "We should drink to that and salute each other."

To which she added, "And to our health, happiness, and future. God Bless!"

They started their dinner by Bridget serving the casserole. Michael cut the bread and served the salad from the salad bowl.

"This is casserole is just delightful. I never had such a tasty crab casserole before. Where did you learn to cook so well?"

"I watched my mother and she taught me how to make many things. She ran a fabulous kitchen."

"Everything is so tasty and delicious."

"It is a labor of love. I love to cook for you, to see your happy, contend face. I love to excite your senses and see how you react."

"Bridget darling, you are the love of my life. I could not imagine life without you."

"That is very nice of you to say. Thank you."

They were about to finish their meal when Bridget asked about the dessert.

"I am fine now. Can we have dessert later?"

"Sure."

"What would you like to drink? Coffee or tea?" asked Bridget.

"Coffee please, my dear."

Bridget collected the plates and started to wash the dishes. Michael took a towel and dried the plates, silverware, and glasses. They were about to finish when Michael gave Bridget a big hug and said twice, "Thank you!"

"You're welcome. my dear."

"Michael please, let's sit down on the sofa. We must talk about something very serious, something that has been touching our lives."

They both sat down on the sofa, facing each other, and looked into each other's eyes.

"Michael, don't interrupt me. Listen to me very carefully and try to answer my questions honestly, sincerely, the best way you can."

"I have told you about some of my past and present. We have a world situation where millions of lives are at stake. Whatever our understanding is about the war, what we are fighting for, the causes and consequences of the conflicts are issues that we must talk about, to crystallize what is happening, because they stand in our way, disrupt our love, and can destroy our lives."

"So, let me ask you, do you believe in Nazism as a viable political system for the future not only for the Germans but for other nations also, including all the ideological, economical, political, and racial issues?"

"This is a complex question. You must understand I was raised in the German culture and had few opportunities to experience other cultures, governments, policies, economics, and how their ideologies relate to practice, the everyday life of the average person."

"Let me dissect the question. According to the Nazi theory, the Aryan race is the 'master race,' 'superior race' to other races. This is exactly what Hitler elaborated in his book, 'Mein Kampf.' Do you agree with this statement?"

"Although there are exceptions to every ideology, I do not."

"Economics were a primary factor for going to war. Unemployment and the increased public consumption were managed through the work projects, expansion of war-fighting machines and initiation of the military draft. Do you seriously believe that the German economic program would have been viable without confiscating the wealth from the 'enemies of the Reich?'"

"I am not an economist however, what you are saying makes sense. But one must see the whole issue from a historical context."

"It was alleged, that international banking organizations managed by wealthy Jews were exerting influence on the German state, namely the Weimar republic, by withholding credit, thus creating unemployment in Germany. It was an excuse to inflame hatred toward the enemies of Germany, and justify the economic problems in Germany."

"Again, I have to agree with you that Hitler needed a scapegoat to justify his racial hatred, horrible policies, and atrocities."

"Hitler regarded America as a 'mongrel' nation, but his racist ideology does not measure up to what

America has achieved ideologically, economically, politically, and racially in a relatively short time in comparison with European history. True, they fought a civil war. The North wanted to abolish slavery, and it took quite a bit of time to accept the Negro race, but the American Constitution and democracy will win the race issue. Economically, products of war will help the depression, and I'll bet it'll be the strongest nation on earth."

"You are giving a good example. But the power is still in Nazi hands. The leaders and the people are still fanatic about Hitler, and in his policies."

"Michael, do you believe in freedom?"

"Yes, I do. But, with certain limitations."

"What are those limitations?"

"Take the case of a young baby or a child. How can a mother or father allow a baby to put anything in his mouth or when a toddler plays with fire? One has to attend school."

"But given maturity and understanding, the child will understand that choice is freedom. Understanding the choice between good and bad, the child will respect the parents for allowing him to make choices. Likewise, giving the Germans the opportunity to choose would have far greater positive consequences than telling them what to do. Freedom and democracy go hand in hand. Likewise, racism and Nazism belong together. But you cannot coerce people forever. It will not work!"

"I understand. But Germany is going through a process of transformation."

"Yes, but, at the expense of enslaving and killing innocent people."

"I understand how you feel, and I also have reservations about Hitler's policy."

"You are aware that there are dissidents. They are Germans who see that the evil will not win and the war is going to be lost. You have a choice and should bail out before is too late!"

"How do you want me to do that? I just can't walk out. I'm an officer of the German army. If I am going to desert, I'll be shot. I love you too much to lose you!"

"Michael darling, listen to me. You could stay in the army and help the Allies to win. It is not physically deserting but spiritually bailing out! You are badly needed to defend freedom and democracy!"

"Just how do you envision me doing this?"

"We can talk about this some other time. I want you to think about what has been said."

"Thank you. I must admit, you are very convincing."

"I just wanted you to think about the importance of freedom! I know we should not engage in these intellectual exercises but I would love to remove the barrier between us."

Michael embraced Bridget and they started to kiss each other's lips very gently and slowly. The kissing became more and more passionate. Bridget then offered her tongue and Michael accepted it. Then they reversed the offer. Michael's flame of passion rose higher and higher and he started to kiss Bridget's neck and began to unbutton her blouse.

"Let me take over now," said Bridget.

She unbuttoned her blouse and removed her bra. Michael also removed his shirt and undershirt. Michael kissed her breasts all over, while his hands were stroking her thighs.

"Wait a minute, Michael. We'll be more comfortable if I remove my skirt and you drop your pants."

By this time both were drunk with passion and neither of them were able to articulate a sound other than an occasional sigh. The heavy kissing continued, and Michael started to kiss her thighs. Bridget allowed him to remove her panties. He also dropped his underpants. They were motionless for seconds and he gently entered her body while they passionately kissed each other. As they united, each felt an unbelievable sensation of warmth, the feeling of oneness. It was more than sex. Their physical togetherness was the culmination of love and affection for each other. As they achieved the crescendo of their love making, they both cried with happiness.

Michael's and Bridget's bodies slowly parted and rested for a few seconds then they turned sideways facing each other.

"Happy, darling?" asked Bridget.

"I'm very happy, darling? What time is it" asked Bridget.

"Five minutes past one."

"I'll stay a little while, but I must go in half an hour."

"You should have a piece of éclair before you go home."

"Good idea, let's have more sweets," said Bridget with a smile.

They sat down in the kitchen when the telephone rang. The HQ wanted him to supervise a gun and ammunition shipment at 0700 hour.

"This éclair is very good. Anything to drink?" asked Bridget.

"Just a cup of black coffee, it'll help me to stay awake while I drive."

"Good, I will have some too but with milk."

Within a half an hour both finished the dessert and drank the coffee. They were about to leave, when the telephone rang again, but this time it was the Gestapo.

"It is the Gestapo. We received information that you are going to receive a very large shipment of guns and ammunition. We have arrested a saboteur yesterday and under interrogation he confessed that the Resistance is planning to derail the tracks and explode the ammunition cars. You need extra military protection and we will help you as much as we can."

"Thank you for your information. I received word from the HQ about the shipment. I'll be waiting for the train at 0700. I'll appreciate the extra military protection."

"I hope this is the last call," said Michael.

Bridget and Michael walked toward the car hand in hand and drove home to Port-En-Bessin. On the way home, they hardly talked. Michael held her hand in silence, but both communicated their deep love for each other.

Marceau was still up and repairing shoes when Bridget came home. She was surprised to have Marceau greeting her in the early morning hours.

"My dear Marceau, you should be in bed at this early hour in the morning."

"Did you have a good time, Bridget?"

"It was just a great evening. He was very nice and kind."

"Let's go to sleep. You have a lot of customers tomorrow. I am going to bed."

"I'm going to sleep too. Have pleasant dreams, Bridget."

"Thank you. Good night. I'll see you in the morning."

It was eight o'clock in the morning when one of the cell members knocked on the door. Bridget opened the door and asked about the nature of the visit.

"It is highly confidential. Please keep it a secret until we find out the details."

Marceau couldn't help to overhear the words and took over the conversation.

"What is the matter, Philip?"

"I couldn't sleep the whole night. I found out that we have a traitor in the Resistance who delivers our brothers and sisters to the Gestapo to be tortured and killed for money and sympathy. We must find him; otherwise we'll all go under."

"Bridget, please get Shaw and Parker to come here now. Thank you."

"I want you to tell me in detail what happened and why you are suspecting one of our Resistance operatives as a traitor. This is a very serious charge and if we find out that you are right, the penalty will be death," said Marceau.

"You know Girard? He is the carpenter who works for the German officers, Gestapo, police, private homes, public civil centers, and business places. He spends money on women, drinks, jewelry, automobiles, and buys clothing as never before. Well, the man who makes money working like a horse cannot be accused for spending money when somebody earns that money."

"Last weekend, I was sitting at the local bar and Girard came in with two women. They were sitting at the bar and drinking quite heavily. Another operative, Charles, the dentist technician, came in and sat down close by to the two girls and Girard."

"Girard started to have small talk with him, and but he kept bragging to Girard about his braveries. The two girls left for the powder room and did not return for at least twenty minutes. Charles was telling Girard that he heard about a new shipment of guns and ammunitions coming to town at seven in the morning. I don't know where this information was coming from, but he asked Girard to join him in removing some railroad ties. Girard told him he would."

"The next thing I heard was that Charles was arrested by the Gestapo. He was badly beaten and received a dozen electroshocks to his testicles to confess his circle of operatives who were going to blow up the German supply train. He did confess about two operatives. Charles, for good behavior and cooperation, had his head removed by chainsaw and his body was dropped near the railroad as a future reminder."

"We should authenticate this story before we accuse anybody," said Marceau.

"Isn't it possible that Girard told the two girls about the story that Charles revealed to him.? One of the girls could be a traitor. Another assumption is that one or two girls are working for a traitor who collects information and gets paid for it."

"In any case, we are in trouble. The Gestapo is doing everything to stop sabotaging the supply lines for the Atlantic Wall. They have devious information collecting methods that are guaranteed to produce the most dramatic results without any scruples, ethics, or conscience as long as they have results. The Gestapo will penetrate any obstacle to find the enemy."

"But we know that. We are prepared. Our losses are inevitable. But as long as we are able to function and prepare for the invasion, it is worth the risk. Of course we want to minimize our losses. This is the reason why we deal with the best people, who are devoted to the cause, and loyal to the Resistance. I commend you for your honesty, sincerity, and cooperation. We will not forget you after our victory," promised Marceau.

Shaw and Parker arrived about noon after having various meetings with cell members.

"Why so late?" asked Marceau.

"We had important conferences with cell members who were terribly concerned about the disappearances of other Resistance operatives," said Shaw.

"That is why I called you. We have a traitor and we must flush him or her out. It will not be an easy job. We have to use the best investigative knowledge we have and when the culprit is found, we must terminate that person. In a way, it does involve you because you work with the Resistance. There is due process, of course, but it has to be brief. We must find the traitor as fast as we can, otherwise we all go under."

Shaw and Parker headed for Caen. On the way they stopped for lunch in a café and tried to assess the whole situation that was getting out of hand.

"What do you make of this whole mess/" questioned Parker.

"We have a mole and we have to flush it out, otherwise our whole operation will be jeopardized," replied Shaw.

"But why do we have to do the investigative work when it is within the Resistance?"

"First, we are just helping and secondly, the Resistance lacks a trained investigative body. We have three alternatives.

First, is to pack up and return to England. Second, is to stay and be arrested and shot as spies by the Gestapo. The third is to flush out the mole, kill him with the help of the exterminator, and continue our mission."

"If we choose the third one, what is your plan?"

"I propose to bait him or her."

"I accept that. When do we start and what kind of bait are we talking about?"

"We start now, as soon as you drink your coffee. For bait we use sex."

"What gender?"

"I don't really know at this point in time. It could be a male, female, homo or bisexual. I am not fussy. However I want the best. I don't want a cheap prostitute. The bait must be the best. Someone who is able to lure, catch, and perform. I am talking about a professional."

"Do you want to start with Philip or Girard and the two ladies with him at the bar?"

"Are you suggesting in that order?" asked Shaw.

"Do you have a better suggestion?" replied Parker.

"Honestly, I don't know, but let's start with Philip," said Shaw.

"Do you have all the addresses and phone numbers?" asked Parker.

"Yes, I do. Let's contact Philip."

They called Philip and he was told to meet them in one hour at the same place they met the last time and not to tell anybody where he was going and whom he was meeting. "Do not tell the other two cell members that you are meeting with me," instructed Shaw.

They met at the designated place, sat down at a table and began to talk.

"Hello Philip, how are things working out for you?" asked Shaw.

"Not too well. We have a traitor who works for the Gestapo and we are very scared to do any observation."

"You must have some idea who could be the culprit," Shaw probed.

"I don't know. There are four people involved as I told Marceau."

"Tell us something about each person in as much detail as possible," prompted Parker.

"Girard is a lady's man. He adores women. He makes money any way he can. He is a carpenter, but he sells drugs and has women for rent. You know kinky, perverted hetero, homo and bisexual encounters, and he'll hire people to beat up somebody. He appears to be a good hearted fellow. He is strange sometimes. He said that he is French, but I don't know. His French is not educated. He uses German words when he can not express himself in French. The two girls who were with him are hardly known. I saw them together once or twice at the bar with or without an escort. They could be bisexuals, lesbians, or straight. Only Girard could tell you."

"The others are plain prostitutes. There are two males and one female. They drift from drugs to stoolpigeon. If there is money, they'll sell their own mothers. The Gestapo uses them but very sparingly. They know that they will easily become double agents. The Allies will outbid the Gestapo and get what they want."

"What are their names?" asked Shaw.

"They are Margaret, Paul, and Patrick."

"Well, thank you very much for your information. Again, please don't talk about this conversation with anybody. I mean *anybody*. We have to find the person who is trying to destroy the Resistance. We'll let you know about the time and location of our next meeting. Now, please call Girard and tell him that your friends would like to talk with him," said Shaw.

Before they parted, Parker asked Philip to wait a few minutes before he exited. Parker had to make sure that he was not followed. He took his binoculars and scanned the whole area. There were no cars or humans within a mile distance. Parker gave Philip a scarf and a wig that had to be returned later. After fifteen minutes Philip left. Thirty minutes later Shaw and Parker left the place.

"Girard is next. He could be the mole. But this is only an assumption. One can never tell. It could be one of the girls who were trained by the Gestapo's special school," said Parker.

"My guess is as good as yours. Let's find out."

CHAPTER FIVE

Shaw called Girard at 0700 at his home which was an ungodly hour for him. He was expecting the call, but not so early.

"Hello. What do you want?"

"This is 004."

"So, I don't care if you are the king of England. Nobody calls me at this time in the morning. This is a civilized house. Call me back."

"I can't call you back. I don't have the time! I must leave town. If you don't talk to us your life will be worth less than a franc. Don't be stupid. The assassination squad is on the way to kill you."

"Why should anybody kill me when I give away millions of francs for good causes? I support the Resistance, The Century underground, The Free French Intelligence Service, the wineries, the bars, whores, and beggars on the streets."

"Please meet us at noon."

"Do you have a place where we are safe to talk?"

"There is a barn less than five miles from Caen. It is off the main road. It was built in the seventeenth century. It is two stories high and has five entrances. It is on Rue de la Sade 342. We, my partner, 006 and I, are going to be on the second floor, you stay on the first floor."

"How do I know that it is you, whatever the numbers?"

"I'll give you a code."

"I will say France in reverse, Ecnarf."

"You must be alone and not be followed. Be very careful!"

"How do I know whether I'll be followed by the Gestapo?"

"Watch! Watch your rear view mirror every two seconds. If a car follows you, try to be evasive. Go in circles then break out. Speed and go around small streets. You'll eventually lose those Gestapo guys. Give yourself enough time to shake off the tail."

"How much lead time would be necessary to Caen?"

"To be safe and comfortable, about one hour should be sufficient, including diversion. If you have to wait for us, get something to read."

"What if I get arrested?"

"Just tell them that you are meeting a married woman and are trying to avoid the husband who is a crazy man. With your reputation, they'll believe you. If you can't shake the tail and he continues to follow you, don't worry. We will be watching you. If you have a tail, just wait in the car for thirty minutes. Park the car on the right side to the entrance. If you park on the left side, we know you are alone. You get out of the car, but you must wait for fifteen minutes while we check out the area. Then you enter the barn and the rest you know."

"I will meet you guys at noon. Bye."

"Have pleasant dreams. See you later. Bye."

Shaw and Parker headed to a restaurant for breakfast. They found a small café on the way to Caen.

"Well, one less to catch. I hope we'll get a lead," said Shaw. They stopped at Marceau's place for a while to discuss the situation.

"What's the good news?" asked Marceau.

"No good news yet, but we are working on it," assured Parker.

"We want you to know that all cell meetings are on hold until further notice," added Parker.

"That's a wise precautionary decision. Whom did you talk to so far?"

"We talked with Philip, and this afternoon we'll be meeting with Girard," replied Shaw.

"It looks to me that the mole has been operating for sometime because we are losing people especially those who are placing explosives under the tracks," remarked Marceau.

"We'll flush him out," said Parker.

"We'll be back tomorrow. Take care. Bye," said Shaw.

Shaw and Parker continued their trip to Caen. There was an identity check by the military police and it held up the traffic for thirty minutes. They were at the outskirts of the city at 1130. Parker suggested driving around the barn before they parked the car. He was always cautious and didn't like surprises. They entered the barn at about 1150. Shaw and Parker separated upstairs. Shaw concentrated on the barn below, while Parker was looking out the window with his binoculars.

Twenty minutes later, Girard arrived. He entered the barn and the conversation began with the Ecnarf identification.

"You are fine there. We found a stool for you, just grab it to your right and sit down," said Shaw.

"How are you? Did you experience any tail coming here? If you need water, we placed a bottle of mineral water with the stool," said Shaw.

"I am fine. I was not followed. The Gestapo leaves me alone, because if they don't, they will not get their candies, you know, those perverted girls."

"Do you know why we called you?"

"I assume you are concerned about the mole. Well, that is not me! My reputation as a business man is very important for the future. The future is a free France. I could not talk to any Frenchman if I would be labeled as a traitor. I would never, and I mean never, betray my fellow Frenchman. There is not enough money for giving names to the Gestapo. In my book those guys who want to liberate France from this Nazi dictatorship are the best."

"How about the girls who were with you when Charles asked you to help?" asked Shaw.

"Those girls did not hear anything. They had left for the powder room. I don't discuss private matters with those girls. They are with me for making money. We talk about all kinds of sex business, but that is all. I'll give you their names."

"One is Lorraine and the blonde one is Carla. They are in the Venus bar till one o'clock in the morning. After that, they go home, or visit a client. They are smart. They treat everybody kindly and do not get into politics. They are there to satisfy men's desire for sex."

"Since you know Charlie's demolition friends, do you remember their names?"

"I can only recall a few names: Louis, Georges, Alex, Richard, Arthur and Thomas."

"Where do we find them?"

"That is a problem. Perhaps you can find out where they work and live. Why don't you try in Caen by visiting the barbershops, bars, and even some prostitutes in some private homes?"

"Did he have any women friends who helped him with explosives, sex, alcohol or drugs?"

"He was married, but had many girlfriends. He liked to watch his friends make love. He paid for it, and sometimes joined the party. He was a guy of pleasure."

"Well, would you leave a message with the local bartender, at the place where you met Charlie the last time?"

"You mean at the Chez L'Amour?"

"Yes."

"Thank you for coming and all the information. Philip will call you if we need to talk to you again. Look around before you get into the car and drive around for fifteen minutes before you hit the main road to see if somebody is tailing you back home. Bye."

Shaw and Parker waited twenty minutes in the car with drawn pistols in their hands. In the backseat they had two automatic rifles, just in case things became dangerous.

Fortunately nothing happened. Girard was gone and Shaw and Parker decided to go home, but before that, they had to visit a bar and drink a little bit of cognac. After two jiggers Parker stopped and told Shaw to stop too before they were going to be disciplined.

"This is the best cognac I ever tasted."

"Good, I am happy for you," said Parker.

"It is a pity to leave such a fine cognac in the bottle."

"I know, we'll come back tomorrow and have some more."

Parker actually had to pull Shaw away from the bar. He had a rough day. Parker suggested finding a place to relax. They drove near the coastline and stopped in an area which looked calm and peaceful. They sat down first, but Shaw stretched out and fell asleep on his back. Parker was watching and allowed Shaw to have a good nap. About an hour later, Shaw woke up and thanked Parker for being a guardian.

"What's next Parker?"

"You tell me."

"We have options. We can interview, do an observation by ourselves, or by somebody else, or an interrogation under duress. Pick your choice."

"Time is of the essence in this cat and mouse game, Shaw."

"I know. I am suggesting getting all the addresses and observe first. We may be able to narrow the suspects," said Parker.

"We can start the process right now if you wish. Let's find out the addresses."

"I recommend next to use baits. This would allow us to identify the suspect," added Parker.

"Why don't we call Philip? He can probably give us some addresses and phone numbers," suggested Shaw.

Shaw called Philip who was unavailable but left a message with his wife to locate as many names as possible and later in the day they would contact him.

In the meantime, they visited Chez L'Amour in Caen for a drink and connect with some girls. Investigating a mole was a very time consuming process, time they didn't have.

As they entered the bar, there was a welcome hostess who offered them all kinds of seating, but Parker insisted on staying at the bar. Within minutes they were surrounded by a couple of girls who offered companionship while they were drinking and after that in one of the girl's apartment.

"I want all the girls to have fun," said Parker.

"We have five girls here, and two at my place. Can you afford us?" Yvonne was asking.

"Yes we can," was Shaw's reply.

Yvonne became quite curious, and continued by asking, "What do you want us to do?"

"Do you have an idea? We are open to suggestions," said Parker.

"We can put on a show, or change partners in the middle of your excitement, or we can simply meditate nude," said Corinne.

"How about just talk, just pure human companionship?" Shaw's question was totally unexpected.

The barmaid became involved with the idea to booster business and bluntly asked Shaw and Parker, "Officers, how about a drink for the ladies?"

"Oh, yeah, give them food and drink on our behalf," said Parker.

The barmaid suggested a table so everybody could eat and drink comfortably. Shaw and Parker followed the hostess to a semi private place and they all sat around three tables. They had all kinds of food and drinks. Parker suggested that one of the girls should invite the other two girls, so they could have fun here with everybody.

The girls very seldom had such an upbeat situation and they just couldn't understand what was going on.

Corrine bravely asked, "Is this a public relations affair to boost the German soldiers' image?"

"No, this has nothing to do with that. We are just very lonely and need human relationship. I believe you can differentiate between sex and companionship," replied Shaw.

"Yes we can, but this is very unusual for us. We are not accustomed to this kind of behavior from you guys," said by Louise.

"Well, we are all different. We had parents who valued the feelings, emotions and expressions which could be symbolized by words, music, paintings, sculpture, dance, and other forms of art. We learned this at home, and now we are offering to you what we have experienced," said Shaw.

"Oh, this is beautiful. I could listen to you for hours. You are really different, so well educated," said Jeanne.

"What would you like to talk about?" asked Parker.

Everybody became silent. They had deep feelings to express, but they were told not to do it because it could lead to trouble and they were not allowed to mix business with their personal feelings. This axiom prevented them from having deep seeded discussions about anything.

"You must have something we can talk about. Like the best lovers or the best paying customers. You don't have to identify the guys by family name, you can just call them Bud, Charles, Georges, Peter, any way you feel comfortable. We don't know them and it would not matter to us," said Shaw.

"We can talk about Charles; he was killed by the Gestapo. We don't know what happened, but he was always nice to us. He liked sex very much, but always with two girls. Most of the guys, however, have been regulars," said Yvonne.

"Not Arthur, he was a very strange guy. He used to come in with two German officers and the only way he was able to have pleasure is if he slapped us on our buttocks. He had a filthy mouth and never spoke a kind word," said Alice.

"You speak about him in the past tense. Doesn't he come here anymore?" asked Parker.

"We haven't seen him in the last three weeks. He is weird. Arthur is French but always hangs around with Germans," continued Alice.

"Who was the nicest guy so far?" asked Parker.

"You guys are the real old time classical gentlemen," said Odette.

"Well, thank you. You must think we are weird because we don't want sex," said Parker.

"We understand. We are not as stupid as others think we are. Maybe one or both of you are married or engaged and don't want to cheat on your wife or lover. We know that there is more to sex. But some guys just want stimulation and pleasure and no emotional involvement. They don't want to be committed," commented Jeanne.

"How about you girls? Do you ever enjoy a guy and have pleasure?" asked Shaw.

"Let me answer this question," said Yvonne. "If somebody is socially nice to us, and treats us like you do, we get easily stimulated. But we also need physical stimulation, because we have been giving a lot of energy to please you guys. We also have to desire the person, the scent and taste are significant to us. We want the same things we give. No restrictions. With us it is a whole night affair, including dinner and talk. Not the number, but the quality of pleasure that's important. Some men cannot hold it back and must have pleasure in a very short time. We don't like that. We want a long, extended time of pleasure which comes with experience and the desire of giving."

"Well, thank you ever so much for your entertaining time. I will discuss the charge with Yvonne and pay the waiter for the drinks and food," said Shaw.

"You guys are very nice. It will be our pleasure to please you in the future. Any time you need us just let us know," said Yvonne.

It was late afternoon. Parker made another call to Philip. This time Philip was home but terribly disappointed and discouraged. Half of the people were not home and he couldn't confirm the addresses. He requested another call back.

"What's on your mind?" Parker curiously looked at Shaw while he asked the question.

"The same as what you're thinking."

"It must be Arthur."

"We have to track him down. Let's find out who he is, if he is married or single and who his relatives and friends are," said Parker.

"I'm going to call Philip again," replied Shaw.

"Be my guest. The hunt is on," said Parker.

Shaw called Philip and he was told by his girlfriend to call back every fifteen minutes. Shaw had called six times and nothing yet. The seventh time, his girlfriend gave Shaw the bad news. Philip just received a phone call from Paris, and he has to go to visit one of his friends who is dying from lung cancer. He'll be home in a couple of weeks.

Parker did not like hearing this kind of news. "We have to get word to Philip somehow that the Resistance is planning another bombing. Philip has to tell Arthur of the plan so he can inform the Gestapo to stand by, and then we'll have our man."

Before Philip was able to leave for Paris he received a telephone call informing him that he has a 'cousin' in Port-En-Bessin- meaning there is a military shipment under way. Philip then called Shaw to inform him that "spring was in the air." Philip gave his cousin's phone number to Shaw in case they needed to reach him. Parker suggested that before they make the call about the shipment, they should authenticate the data.

"All ordnance shipments have a military escort, but we can certainly nail Arthur," said Parker.

"The Gestapo will check Arthur's information, and then will round up as many of the suspected operatives. The trap has to be set," commented Shaw.

"Then, we need to fabricate a fall guy and watch the Gestapo catch him," replied Parker.

"But, if they can't find him they will grab others, and torture them until they confess or die of pain. It is not easy. The Gestapo is not stupid. They can smell a trap and they will protect their source," said Shaw.

"How about giving the name of a guy who passed away a few days ago? When the Gestapo arrives to arrest him he will already be dead. This way we would not compromise any living operative."

"Good idea. Where do you intend on finding find a body?" asked Shaw.

"I think the best place would be a cemetery. We just have to find out who was cremated a few days ago. Change the name in the register. That way the Gestapo cannot trace through the hospital morgues or open the caskets."

"Let's put this in sequential order. First, you have to know about the shipment of ordnance in terms of time and place. Second, you have to inquire about who, when, why, where somebody passed away, and time and location of cremation. Third, you will call Arthur and tell him that such and such a person is working by himself to blow up the tracks. Fourth, you wait for the Gestapo to show up and learn that the saboteur was fatally wounded by an explosion while he was preparing the explosives to be put on the railroad tracks and was taken by a hearse to the funeral home to be cremated. Fifth, someone from the Resistance actually blows up the railroad tracks. Sixth, Arthur is determined to be the mole and is killed."

"Shaw, you are a mind reader, a born genius. I didn't know what a great partner I picked."

"You didn't pick me, you had no choice. I was given to you, probably by mistake."

"Now that we are stuck together, let's try to do our very best!"

They both laughed. They usually don't tease each other, especially when operations are getting serious, but laughter is good medicine, and right now they certainly could use it. To synchronize the suggested exercises means more than intelligence. It requires a stroke of luck.

To get German ordnance transportation information they had to see Marceau. Since his place was on the way home, they stopped by and Parker found the place closed. He knocked on the door and Bridget answered.

"Sorry, we don't want to intrude, but something came up and we need his help."

"Marceau wasn't feeling well this afternoon and decided to close early and go to bed. May I help you guys if it can't wait until tomorrow?"

"First, and foremost we want to express our heartfelt concerns and wish Marceau the very best. He is our guide, help, friend, and mentor in our lives and if there is anything we can do please do not hesitate to ask. You are alone, without a telephone, we would be more than happy to help you out."

"Our problem is time. We have suspended all operations until we catch the mole. The mole is not only harming the Resistance but our entire operations. Bridget darling, we need the ordnance transportation schedule to catch this mole. We could use some form of a timetable," said Parker.

"I don't know who can help you in these hours, but I'll go across the street to make a call to the café. I'll be back in ten minutes. Wait for me in the car, this way nobody will be suspicious."

Bridget went to call her friend, a village clerk. Bridget was told that she had a town meeting and would not be home before ten o'clock. She returned to where Shaw and Parker were waiting and informed them of the news.

"I'm sorry, but I was not able to make contact. Can you wait for a couple of hours and she'll be home by then?"

"Well, we can have a drink, walk a little bit, and meet you little after ten o'clock. But isn't that too late for you, my dear?" asked Shaw.

"Honestly, I don't mind being up. I have tons of work to do, and I love reading before I go to bed."

"When you do come back just flash the headlights three times at the store, and I will come out. Please don't blow the horn or knock on the door. I'll be waiting for your signal. Bye."

"We'll see you at about ten o'clock. Bye."

Shaw and Parker left the car there and started to walk toward the bay. On one of the side streets they found a little café, walked in, and sat down at a small round table close to the window. The owner, a pudgy man in his middle fifties, approached the table, introduced himself, and welcomed the guests.

"May I serve you, officers?"

"Do you have any dinner left?" asked Parker.

"Of course, we serve dinner until eleven o'clock."

"Fish, potatoes, vegetables, and salad for me," said Shaw.

"That sounds very good. I will have the same," ordered Parker.

While they were waiting for the fish to be cooked, Parker expressed concern about the trap.

"I hope her friend will help us."

"There are daily military shipments to Normandy, the question is what kind. We know that ordnance transportation requires military escort. We'll know better in a couple of hours or by tomorrow," said Shaw.

"I don't know if she can talk in front of her roommate."

"Well, all good things come to those who wait. Tomorrow is not too late to find out when and where. Don't forget, we have a lot of hurdles that must be overcome. A day or two will not change the situation. I am just as eager to get this mole as you are, but this is a serious waiting game," commented Shaw.

Fried fish with golden brown potatoes, salads, and mixed vegetables were served.

"This looks good and tastes good," remarked Parker.

"Good fish fry, the potatoes are crisp and the salad has a special flavored dressing. Probably a French specialty," said Shaw.

They skipped the dessert but had coffee. After paying the bill, they left toward the bay and had a good mile walk along the seashore. It was close to ten o'clock at night when they returned to Marceau's place. Five minutes after ten, Shaw blinked the head lights three times. Within minutes, Bridget walked toward their car and told them that she was about to make the call in the nearby bar.

"Hello?" questioned Bridget.

"Hello," another officer answered.

"May I speak with Michael please?" asks Bridget.

"How are you darling?" this is Michael. "What can I do for you at this late hour?"

"I must talk to you about something."

"It is not a good idea to talk over the phone. Can you wait until tomorrow morning."

"I can. What time will you be here?"

"I'll see you at 0730."

"Thank you, Michael. I'll be waiting for you. I love you. Bye."

"Please go to sleep sweetheart, I love you too, very much. Bye."

Bridget walked to the car and let them know that these conversations were highly confidential and her friend will visit her early in the morning.

"I think, by 0830 I will have some answers for you," said Bridget.

"Thank you. Please give our very best to Marceau," offered Shaw.

Bridget walked back to the shop to work for a while. Shaw and Parker, a little bit disappointed drove home and called it a day. They intellectually understood the difficulties they had encountered during the day's events, but still they had missed the actions and forward movement of the case.

"Too bad, but better days are coming. Good night, Parker."

The next morning Michael arrived at the shop and Bridget greeted him with a big hello and hug. Michael returned the hug with a kiss and asked with concern, "Why did you call me so late last night? Are you alright?"

"We are fine, but we have a little problem. Our material shipment did not arrive and we don't know what the problem is," said Bridget.

"I shouldn't give you an explanation, because I could be court-martialed for this, but your shipment will be late. The incoming rail track is under heavy patrol. There is a big military shipment coming in to replace the one that was blown up. Your shipment will be a day or two late."

"How do you know?"

"You just have to trust me."

"Tomorrow night at 0100 a train is coming in to Port-En Bessin with thousands of rounds of ammunitions for all caliber guns. The next train will go to Caen ten days from now, and the third one to Cherbourg three weeks from now."

"Thank you, Michael. Marceau will explain to the generals that he has not received a shipment of the necessary supplies so he is unable to make their boots."

Michael hugged and kissed Bridget again and left in a hurry.

Shaw and Parker arrived at 0845 and Bridget happily informed them about the arrival times of the three trains.

"Michael was here and he told us that a military transport is coming here tomorrow night 0100. I promised we'd seal our lips about it."

"How did this conversation came about?"

"I complained that Marceau cannot deliver the boots on time, because his shipment is late," said Bridget.

"I'm glad he trusts you guys," said Shaw.

Shaw and Parker discussed the details of their plan with Marceau and they asked him if he has some connection to find out about any cremations in the last two days of a male between twenty and sixty years of age. Marceau reminded Parker and Shaw that they are not supposed to be directly involved in determining who the mole is and that it is the job of Philip. Parker told Marceau that Philip has gone to Paris to be with his dying friend and will not be back for two weeks. Shaw responded that there is no one else who can be trusted to carry out such a dangerous mission.

"I have to get in touch with a number of people, preferably undertakers, from the Resistance, which will take a few hours," said Marceau.

"A few hours will be fine," said Shaw.

"We must have an explosion, a mock hearse delivery certificate, and cremation. All these things must take place within a day. So by the time Arthur calls the Gestapo, the make believe culprit will be dead and cremated. All the false identifications and official papers will be ready and waiting to be processed," said Parker.

"But what if you can't get in touch with Arthur on time?" Marceau questioned.

"We are then in big trouble and we'll have to cancel the project," said Parker.

"Why don't you call Arthur and find out his schedule? You can always come up with some story why you want to know his whereabouts," suggested Marceau.

"I guess we can do that. Splendid idea," remarked Shaw.

"Well, I am going to make some calls to find out who was cremated and who is going to be created," said Marceau.

Shaw and Parker decided to have some inspections in the meantime in the nearby construction sites. As they were watching the steel mesh layouts for the casemate construction, Parker thought of a story that might work for Arthur. Arthur hangs wall paper for a living. Parker called Shaw aside and whispered what he had in mind.

"We call from Cherbourg to find out if he would be interested in wall papering my restaurant/bar/nightclub that is 45 by 75 meters. We say that he comes highly recommended by people who have watched his work and asked him where we can call him later to confirm the offer. So what do you think?"

"It might work. Why don't you try calling him?"

"I will call him now. First, I must find a public phone."

"Let me go with you. Do you mind?"

"Be my guest."

They both went to a restaurant and Parker called his Paris apartment and found him there. He made the inquiry as the owner of a future establishment and he was very appreciative that he was given the opportunity to decorate the establishment.

Arthur wanted to know the name but was told that the name had not been chosen. Everything, he said, was in the planning stages to find out how much start up capital would be needed. Parker said that he would call back later today to find out if Arthur wanted the job. Arthur became a little excited since he had not had such a big contract in a long time. Money and fame played a significant role in this preliminary call. Parker did a good job and Shaw told him he should become an actor in the future. Parker just loved his vanity to be massaged, but this was another form of teasing for "poor" Parker.

The next step was to find out about the cremated body. When they arrived at Marceau's place, they found him in excellent spirits, feeling much better than the day before.

"You are very lucky this time. A member of the Resistance, who is a very fine undertaker, cremated a man of twenty-nine from a heart attack, this morning at 10. Here is the name of the person and the urn is placed at the Avignon cemetery."

"It's your turn now to call Arthur," said Parker.

"But you are a much better actor than I am."

"But you studied voice; you are better at the accent than I am, I can't do that."

"You can always change your voice, you are a born actor."

"I may be a born actor, but you can improvise."

"Do you want to flip a coin?"

"Nope, you make the call, and I'll just stand by."

"Good deed chap, it's my turn to call."

"Before you call, we must first choose a collapsed farmhouse where he stores his explosives and operates from. If Arthur is the mole, he'll call the Gestapo and we have little time to complete the job," said Parker.

Next Shaw had to call Arthur.

They went to a bar. Shaw asked for a double brandy and cold water. He gave the bartender paper money and asked for extra change. Then he went to the call box.

"Hello, this is one of your buddies from Chez L'Amour, Olivier, do you remember me? We used to fool around with the girls. I'm calling you about something that you might be interested in."

"I'm looking for the best wallpaper hanger and I was told you're the best. If you want to join me and to talk about the details you must take the first express train to Port-En-Bessin tomorrow morning. A German ammunition train is coming in from Paris at one in the morning, and you'll probably be delayed a couple of hours for security."

"How do you know all these details?"

"I'm blowing up the train before it gets to the station. You know I am a Maquis."

"Are you going to wait for me at the railroad station?"

"I have no time for that, but you can join me at the address below."

"Give me your name, address, and phone number."

"Gladly, you're my buddy. My name is Olivier Couriz, address 3023 Rue de Maison, Port-En-Bessin. I have no telephone. The Gestapo likes to listen in to my conversations. I am calling from a public telephone."

"All right Olivier, I'll meet you at your home. Thank you for thinking of me."

There was no au revoir, Arthur just hung up. So did Shaw.

Parker couldn't wait to ask, "Well, how was it?"

"I don't know if he took the bait."

"Well, let's find out," said Parker.

Both got in the car and drove fast to the farm house. Parker placed a live grenade underneath the collapsed beams and removed the safety pin. Then he threw another grenade and there was a double explosion. They had to hide the car, which was no problem with all the hedgerows and woods. They found a perfect spot to observe the Gestapo. Parker took out his special light sensitive binoculars and began to scan the entrance area. They waited for over an hour in the dark and nobody showed up. Both of them began to feel discouraged. Parker took another look and in the distance a couple of faint lights began to appear. As the lights became brighter Parker focused his binoculars and saw the outline of a car. The car stopped at the entrance and two men in dark trench coats looked at the still smoldering house. This went on for a few minutes. Then one of the Gestapo detectives called out, "This is the Gestapo, open the door." This order was repeated three times. Then they focused the car's high beam on the building. "We are walking into the building; put your weapon down."

There was an eerie silence.

Both agents with automatic rifles entered the ruins but found nothing. They heard another car stopping. The agents went to the car and the occupant looked at the agents with disdain.

"We are from the Gestapo, who are you?" asked agent Munster.

"I am a farmer from two miles away. I heard an explosion earlier this evening; I rushed here and saw a hearse taking somebody away. That is all I can tell you. I have never seen this man before. After this explosion, I didn't think anyone would come back. It was structurally unsafe even before the explosion but now it is dangerous to walk inside."

"Thank you for the information. Do you have any papers?"

"Not with me, they are in the house."

"What is your name?" asked agent Hochstein.

"I am Charles Berzerac."

"Good farming!" said Hochstein to the farmer as he left.

"What do you want to do?" asked Munster.

"Since he is dead, we don't have to worry about the saboteur," said Hochstein.

"We have to know the name of the deceased and find out what happened to the body," said agent Munster.

"This could have been an accident or one of our sympathizers finished him off in behalf of the Reich. But we'll make some calls to verify what happened," said agent Hochstein.

"Then the mission is accomplished and we can go home," remarked Munster.

They walked back to their Citroen car and drove away.

Parker triumphantly said, "The bait was taken. Arthur is the mole."

Shaw and Parker had another full day of accomplishments. They decided to dress up in the O.T. uniform and go out to celebrate in a fine restaurant in Bayeux.

The next morning, Shaw and Parker returned the hearse and visited Marceau in the afternoon. While Marceau was sewing a new boot together, Shaw and Parker gave an account of all that was happening.

Now comes the fun part. The hunt is about to begin. The Gestapo will find out that this was a trap. Arthur is going to disappear because he'll be afraid of being killed by the Resistance as a mole, or by the Gestapo for making a fool out of them. He is now between a rock and a hard place. However, the exterminator must find him because he is now a monster and will viciously kill all our operatives. He will not reveal his new address to anyone and it will take a long shot to find him."

"We'll catch him but at what price?" said Marceau.

Shaw, along with Parker, was seriously listening to his dissertation. There was no dispute but concern about the lives of the Resistance.

"Any suggestions, Marceau?" asked Shaw.

"It will entail a lot of experimentation, meaning leg work and sweat. The exterminator, Philip, must develop a profile of him, where he lives in Paris, his habits, the places he visits, check the brothels, restaurants and banks. He must be very careful not to leave any trace of himself."

"If the Gestapo finds out that somebody is after him and smells any connection between the exterminator and the Resistance it will be catastrophic. We'll all perish. It must be smokeless. Shaw, since you have Philip's number, you call him and give him the go ahead. Go, my friends, and let me work. Come back with some good news. Goodbye!" said Marceau.

Shaw and Parker were impressed by Marceau. Here is a man with tremendous talent making hand made quality boots, running a courier and recruiting service for the Allies, advising the agents who work for Allied intelligence and he is worried about finding and killing the mole.

"Sometimes Marceau makes me wonder," said Shaw.

"We should be thankful to have him as a mentor," commented Parker.

"This mission is much more involved than I ever thought it would be. Even in my wildest dreams I couldn't have imagined the intrigues that we are experiencing—helping the commandos, saving the lives of so many people and finding traitors and eliminating them. The average person on the street thinks that the work of Intelligence consists of only gathering facts. These people don't have the foggiest notion what it entails to secure our invasion forces and prepare them for the worst. We have our own battle, but this one is different. We have to fight the enemy and the moles. Good luck agent Shaw, be brave, be smart, and keep your eyes open!" said Parker.

"I love your philosophical mood. It gives me more energy and spirit to fight and show the Armed Forces that there is more to war than shooting. You have it right my friend and we'll show them what hell is, and what we have done to save more sons and daughters, husbands and wives, and children of the future. I am proud of you. You are a great partner, fighter, companion, and friend. God Bless you!" beamed Shaw.

Shaw and Parker got in the car and drove to their apartment to get ready for their trip, to visit a few bunkers along the Atlantic Wall. Then on the way to Cherbourg, they stopped to eat in a small restaurant. While they were waiting to be served Shaw was curious to find out if Arthur's telephone was still ringing in Paris. He had Arthur's old address and phone number but the chances of finding him there was very small. He called from a public phone. His phone was ringing, but nobody picked it up. They communicated this to Philip.

"Now that we have an idea who the culprit is, what is your recommendation?" asked Parker.

"From a judicial point of view, he is entitled to a due process. Unfortunately, we are at war with Germany and we don't have the luxury to guard him until the end of this war. So we have to find him and terminate him to save the Resistance, our souls, and the Allied Invasion Forces," said Shaw.

"How do you intend to find him?" asked Parker.

"It is not our job."

"But we can suggest," offered Parker.

"Well, we can," said Shaw.

"How about putting an ad in the classified section under personal. 'Well endowed woman in her 30's, available for buttock-slapping pleasure. Pay in advance, call between 6-8pm. Phone number——,' suggested Parker.

"Very interesting," said Shaw with a smile.

"Don't be cynical," said Parker.

"I'm not. I was just fascinated how you use sex as bait."

"We have to hire a personal confidant who will lure him into Philip's place. Maybe Marceau knows someone in Paris who can impersonate or is a prostitute who is willing to take a chance."

"What if Arthur left Paris and lives in a small town?" asked Parker.

"He is not stupid. He cannot hide in a small place. The Resistance will get him. He is in Paris. It is easier to get lost in a big city. He also needs money. The Gestapo dropped him from the payroll. We'll get him."

"You must have self-confidence. I think with the right approach we'll be able to get him into Philip's net," added Shaw.

"I admire your positive and logical thinking."

"Now, come on Parker. You know better. This guy is a loser. He knows we trapped him, and we'll get him. It is only a matter of time. We are strong and determined; Arthur is weak and without a backbone. He knows he messed it up and he is paying for this with his life," said Shaw.

Having visited and checked on the progress of the bunkers in the area they drove home, and packed their belongings for the trip to Paris. Shaw and Parker decided not to change their appearance for this trip. When they left their apartments, both looked like officers of the Organization Todt. Their objective was to be available to consult with Philip, collect additional information about the Atlantic Wall construction, connect with other Allied Intelligence agents, and if some time was left enjoy what Paris has to offer. On the way to Paris they stopped at Marceau's.

"Hello Marceau, hello Bridget. We are on our way to Paris and we need an address of a smart, good looking prostitute from the Resistance whom we can trust to become a lure for Arthur," said Parker.

"We'll help Philip if he needs help," said Parker.

"I have a surprise for you, Philip knows more women in Paris than you think. Sex is a powerful lure and I agree with you. But don't be disappointed if Arthur will not show any interest," said Marceau.

"Why do you say that when you believe in the power of sex?" asked Shaw.

"Because now he is emotional, fearful and I suspect his sexual desires will be crushed by being hunted. He is fighting for his life. But of course, I could be wrong. Some men use sex as a stress relief. In that case, you may hit the jackpot. Just in case Philip can use it. Here is her address, phone, and workplace. Keep me informed. I give you my friend's name and phone; she calls my other friend here. Tell her that Marceau is sending a thousand kisses."

Shaw and Parker left Marceau in a jolly good mood and drove to Paris without having to stop for too many checkpoints. Finding the Hotel Lorraine, that Marceau recommended required asking for directions. But driving on the Parisian streets was refreshing from the Atlantic Wall scene. The German military, however, was a constant reminder that Paris was not free.

Shaw had driven in Paris several times before the war and was familiar with the lay out of the streets. After making many wrong turns he found the hotel on Rue de Rennes. From the outside, the hotel looked like an ordinary building, with a double door entrance. There was no doorman waiting for them to open the car doors as was the custom in the more classy hotels. No bellhops were taking their luggage. Having placed their own luggage in the lobby, Shaw and Parker found a parking place on the nearby street. The reception desk was jammed with German officers and OT personnel. After waiting half an hour, Shaw and Parker were given the registration form to fill out and the keys to their room on the third floor.

Unfortunately, the elevator had broken down a day before their arrival, and they were told they had to walk up and down the stairs for a couple of days until the mechanic could locate the necessary parts for the elevator. The dining room was located across from the reception area. In the foyer there was a telephone, bathroom, and a storage space for the luggage carriers.

The reception personnel were polite but reserved. However, a young lady receptionist who registered Shaw and Parker was quite different. She, with her friendly attitude, immediately charmed Shaw and Parker and made their entire stay comfortable. She was blonde, blue eyed, about twenty-five years of age, had a small waistline, medium size bosom and being five foot seven made her a very attractive looking lady. But it was more her personality than the physical appearance that people noticed. Her name tag on her uniform jacket read Christen.

Shaw and Parker had a nice dinner in one of the restaurants on Boulevard du Montparnasse. After dinner and a long walk they decided to go shopping and then see a good cinema.

Following a tip, Philip was busy looking for Arthur, hoping to find Arthur at home and terminate him without too much of a problem. But, as he found out, it was not that easy.

Philip did not have all the instruments he needed opening the apartment door, but he had the basic door opener. He drove to the Latin Quarter. The house was an early 1900 apartment building on Rue de Poisse. The address called for number 32, third floor, and number 5. He checked his pistol and left his holster open. When he reached the third floor, Philip looked for an emergency escape on the other side of the corridor. He found one and was ready to enter the apartment.

Philip knocked on the door, but there was no answer. He listened for a few minutes, then he knocked again and again. There was no response. Then Philip took his lock opener put it in the keyhole and tried to loosen the spring. Within seconds the lock jumped open and he opened the door. What he found was a remarkable mess of papers on the table and a few garments on the sofa. The bedroom showed a couple of unmade beds, the blankets touching the floor. Philip opened one of the night tables and found a bunch of papers. One of them was a carte d'indentite, identification card, with the name of Arthur Renoir, professional painter and paperhanger, and a stamped picture on the lower left.

Philip to his surprise yelled out with a strong voice, "I found a picture of him."

"Good job, keep looking," he said to himself.

He found some additional clues as to his whereabouts, but nothing definite. He just lives in this mess, Philip thought. Philip found a picture of Arthur with another guy and three other girls on the beach.

"Could this be his roommate?"

"That is possible, or a friend to one of the girls," Philip said to himself again.

Philip took both pictures and headed down the staircase when he saw a man with two girls walking up, laughing and betting about who will climax first. As they passed each other, Philip recognized the guy from the picture turned around and walked up the staircase and started asking questions of him:

"Are you sharing the apartment with Arthur?"

"That is not your business. Who the hell are you?"

"I am a restaurateur, and somebody recommended Arthur as one of the best painters and wallpaper hangers around this area. We really need to find him for our business."

"He used to live here, but moved to another flat."

"Do you have his address? I'll give you a retainer for the information."

"He left in a hurry, and he did not leave his forwarding address."

"Thank you," said Philip with a small grin on his face.

Philip sensed the man was lying but he kept his cool. He walked slowly downstairs hoping the man would change his mind for the money, but it did not happen.

Philip felt this guy was being evasive; he knew where Arthur lived but was afraid to give his address. He pondered, "Maybe I could find out from one of those girls or from the girl Marceau recommended."

Shaw and Parker returned to the hotel to check for possible messages. When they returned to the hotel Christen told them that there were two gentlemen looking for them.

"Do you remember how they were dressed?" asked Parker.

"Yes, I do. They had brown jackets with kind of beige trousers, open shirts, no ties, but had black caps."

"Did they leave any message?" asked Shaw.

"Yes, they left an envelope."

Shaw opened the envelope and read the contents. It said 'the flowers are blooming.' He gave it to Parker, who read it with a smile. He knew what it meant. They thanked Christen. Shaw and Parker then went outside, and Parker jokingly remarked that even here in Paris they couldn't get away from the home office.

The message was delivered by two Resistance operatives. The OSS and MI6 were watching them and they should not be afraid whatever they were planning to do in the next few weeks. Since they did not tell anybody where they were staying, Shaw and Parker were almost convinced that it had to be Marceau who gave the information to Allied Intelligence.

Both returned to the lobby and Parker fleetingly looked at Christen sensing something but not quite sure what to make of it. He approached the front desk and asked Christen about the weather, not that he really cared about it, but it was his way to start a conversation.

"We are going to have sunshine but moderately on the cool side Mr. Dietrich. Are you planning to go somewhere?" asked Christen.

"Not yet. We are staying in Paris for a while."

"That's good. We will try to make your stay as comfortable as possible."

Shaw moved closer to listen in on the conversation and out of the blue asked her if she could recommend some fine restaurants.

"I'll be more than happy, but we have different ideas of what 'fine' is."

"Something that tastes good, pleasant atmosphere, and good service," said Parker.

She took out a small brochure of restaurants and circled a few places.

"You know, we are fussy, and careful about what we eat, just the same as where we stay," said Parker.

"You mean this hotel?"

"Yes, this is the first time we have visited here," commented Shaw.

"You're in a good hotel. It is my job to see that you're comfortable and safe."

Christen looked at Parker, and with a smile added, "I was informed about your stay with us."

"Who told you about us?" asked Shaw.

"If you step outside, I'll be happy to talk."

They walked outside and Parker asked her to join them for coffee and dessert.

"My break is in fifteen minutes and I can join you then for only half an hour."

"We'll be waiting for you across the street," said Shaw.

"I'll see you soon, but if I'm late, please wait for me. There is always something unexpected."

"Don't you worry; we'll be waiting for you. A little fresh air is good for us," replied

Shaw.

Christen returned in twenty minutes, and they walked to a nearby café. They found a table far away from the entrance in one of the corners. All three ordered coffee and assorted French pastries. When the waitress left, Christen began to talk with a low voice.

"I might surprise you, but my partner, Howard, and I have been keeping an eye on you guys. I am with OSS and he is an MI6. I have been employed here since the Germans occupied Paris and Howard works as an anesthetist associate with the surgeons in two hospitals."

"We received a full description of you guys. It was a comprehensive document of your physical and personality characteristics."

"Well, thank you for telling us," said Shaw.

"This is good. I feel much better. I didn't know why but I had this feeling of somehow being connected with you. Honestly, I did," added Parker.

"Have you been told why we are here?" asked Shaw.

"You are here as a consultant seeking information about the Atlantic Wall construction and as time permits have as much fun in Paris as you can."

"It's partly correct. You left out the meeting with the Resistance and Allied Intelligence agents."

"Well, you met me."

"Your first assertion was correct. The guy who is the trouble maker has betrayed a number of Resistance operatives to the Gestapo. They were all interrogated, tortured, and killed. Philip, the guy we call 'the exterminator' is trying to flush him out. He is one of the best men of the Resistance."

"We must get the perpetrator otherwise our mission will be compromised. It won't be easy because he is crafty, elusive, and hiding in his friend's apartments. But Philip will flush him out sooner or later," said Parker.

"Can we be of any help to you in your hunt?"

"We are not actually involved in the hunt. We are here to advise Philip if and when he needs our assistance. Thank you for your offer, we'll certainly let you know if the need arises for your help," replied Shaw.

Parker looked at Christen and said, "Thank you for being with us. We appreciate your honesty and sincerity, and hope to see you in private very soon," said Parker.

"You will. But now, I must get back. Thank you for your hospitality. Please don't bother to accompany me, it is not necessary. It is better if we are not seen together. Bye."

Shaw paid the bill, and they decided to contact Philip to suggest that he place an ad in the paper. They went to find a phone booth and did a little window shopping while enjoying the Parisian sceneries. On the way back to the hotel they decided to hire a taxi.

Shaw and Parker sat on their beds contemplating their next move. There was no specific agenda in their minds.

"What's the next move?" asked Parker.

"We could visit a few museums, libraries, or whatever strikes our fancy."

"That's smart Shaw, but where do we start?"

"We can begin with the Musee du Louvre."

"That's fine with me."

"What is Philip's next move?" asked Shaw.

"I think he is following some lead that Marceau suggested."

"He could visit an old girlfriend of Arthur, or the neighborhood bars at his old address. Perhaps he is at some nearby brothels. It occurred to me that Philip should revisit his place and see if he left some pictures there that could reveal something or somebody."

Philip, however, drove to the old address. He walked upstairs again and listened for any sounds coming from the apartment. The place was silent. Philip delicately engaged his gadget into the lock and with a little maneuvering opened the lock. He entered the apartment and started to look for papers, but there was nothing to indicate his whereabouts.

As he walked downstairs, one of the neighbors, an elderly lady in her late seventies, opened her door and asked if Philip could help to take down a little shopping carriage.

"I'll help you. You look like a nice lady," said Philip. They walked down gingerly together, Philip holding the lady's arm and taking the carriage.

"Do you remember Arthur living here Madam?" asked Philip.

"Yes, I do very well. He was a rough fellow with a dirty mouth. I heard screaming every time he had a lady guest. I don't know what he did with those ladies."

"Do you know where he moved to?" asked Philip.

"I honestly do not know where he is now."

"Well, thank you for your information," added Philip.

"Thank you for helping me out with the carriage. I would not been able to carry it down. You are a very kind gentleman."

Next, Philip went to neighboring bars but no one knew of Arthur's whereabouts. Philip was not surprised; he was a clever fellow and knew how these kinds of people hide. The chances of finding him in a large city became more and more difficult but not daunting. Philip was hungry and decided to eat something before he continued the hunt.

He found a little café in the neighborhood. It was a very small place, only nine tables and two waitresses. The inside décor resembled a small vessel's cabin, oval walls with portholes, low, indirect lights, and pleasant light blue wallpaper. Philip sat opposite the entrance. He noticed that one waitress, dressed in a sailor's uniform had an eye on him.

She was rather young looking, between twenty and twenty-three. Her face looked like a doll on display in a toy store. She had brown hair and eyes. Her height was 5 feet 7 inches and had a well proportioned body. As he sat down, she came over and read what was available on the menu. It was rather late in the afternoon to eat lunch, but it was quite early for dinner.

"I highly recommend mussels in butter and fried potatoes," said the waitress.

"That sounds good to me," said Philip. "May I have a dark beer on tap," he asked.

"Oh, what's your name?" asked Philip.

"Reba, it's my nickname from Rebecca," answered the waitress with a smile on her face as she left for the kitchen.

"I wonder what kind of eating habits Arthur has," pondered Philip.

The waitress came back with a tall glass of dark beer and a small baguette.

"Can I have some butter with it? By the way, who did this beautiful wallpapering?" asked Philip.

"There is a guy by the name of Arthur. My boss knows how to get in touch with him."

"I heard of him. Can you ask your boss what's his address and phone number?"

"I will ask him and give it to you."

Reba returned to the kitchen and prepared her tray. She served the mussels and asked him for his patience because her boss stepped outside.

"Well, when is he coming back," asked Philip rather impatiently.

"It's hard to tell. He sometimes visits his lady friend for an hour or two." She excused herself and left for the kitchen for some more butter.

"I thought I had a winner."

Reba came back with some more hot butter and said, "The boss called and he will come back later. He also said that he does not know where Arthur moved, because his business number was disconnected. This means that we cannot leave a message for him."

"I thank you for your help and effort. I'll give you my phone number and you can call me. Maybe I can help you find him," said Reba. She gave Philip her phone number.

"When is the best time to call you?" Philip inquired.

"Call me at 10:30 this evening. I will try to get his address. I know a girl who sometimes goes out with him," said Reba.

"Thank you very much, it is kind of you. I had a wonderful meal. Please give me the bill, I must go now."

Philip felt that Reba had a crush on him. But in this business one never knows. He decided to give her a call.

At 10:40 PM Philip called her and she was absolutely delighted.

"Hello. You told me to call you tonight."

"Yes, I did. I just got out of the tub, soaking wet, and I prefer to talk to you in person. My address is 90 Rue de Vaugirard, second floor, number 4."

Phil drove there with a little trepidation. He entered the apartment after the second knock on the door.

"How are you, handsome?"

"I am fine, thank you."

Reba had only a robe on, and her hair was combed by the time Philip arrived.

"Make yourself comfortable. Relax. I'll be with you in a minute."

Philip surveyed his surroundings. It was a small flat with one bedroom, a living room, and small sized kitchen. The walls were wallpapered with a beige background and silver graphic design paper. The furniture was comfortably arranged and everything looked very nice and clean.

She had her robe loosely tied, so her breasts were easily noticeable. She looked very happy and salacious.

"Do you want some good wine?" asked Reba.

"Yes, I would like some wine."

Reba poured the wine into two crystal glasses for both of them.

"You have an exquisite taste. You should be an interior decorator."

"I will be after the war. As soon as we kick the Germans out of France, I'll enroll in the finest school."

"Let's talk about you," said Reba.

"What do you want to know?"

"I don't even know your name."

Philip hesitated a moment, and decided to give her an assumed name.

"Just call me Pierre."

"Sit down next to me. I don't bite. As a matter of fact, I am very gentle," said Reba.

Philip took off his coat, and sat next to her. She removed his tie and looked into his eyes, and smiled.

"You act like a boy who is sixteen-years-old and never kissed a girl or had sexual pleasure."

"Do I?"

"How about your sexual experience, my darling?"

"Only with guys I really liked. I like to enjoy life. I don't like to rush. I savor every bit of a kiss, the stroke of his fingers, and the man who is very excited to please me."

"So, you are a gourmet of sex."

"Yes. At times my body and my soul need it. How do you feel about pleasuring a lady?"

"I like it. I enjoy it even more with someone I love."

"I find it very difficult to find the right person to love. Love means to me total surrender."

Philip looked at Reba and gave her a very gentle kiss

which was returned. Philip and Reba just looked at each other and he gave her a French kiss. She reciprocated. Philip touched her breast and kissed her. Reba began to sigh and became very passionate toward Philip. While he alternated kissing her breasts and mouth, she unbuttoned his trousers and began to touch him all over. Philip tried to maintain his composure, but he couldn't. She aroused him to the point where he came under her spell and both reclined on the bed facing each other.

"Why don't you make yourself more comfortable?"

Philip removed his garments and shoes and faced her naked. She also slipped out from her robe and both united in a heavy embrace. They snuggled and kissed. She caressed him. Philip in his ecstasy kissed her all over and so did she. This passion culminated in an explosive climax that was a surprise for both of them.

He poured some more wine for both of them and looked at Reba. She returned the look with her seductive eyes and said, "I needed it badly."

"We needed it, "corrected Philip." You are some sex kitten. You must have a good mentor."

"It is instinctive. I have no mentor. You brought out the passion in me. It was a very natural reaction to please you while I was in heavenly pleasure. I wanted you to climax, I longed for your scent, and thank you." Philip spent a little more time with her. He excused himself and started to dress.

"Reba."

"Yes."

"I need the address of Arthur. Do you have it?"

"I told you, I'll get it from my friend. But it will cost you."

"What's the price?"

"We'll figure it out."

"When will I see you again, I need you. You gave me such pleasure and vitality."

"I will contact you in a couple of days, but I need Arthur's address. Please do not forget!"

"Bye and she gave Philip a big kiss.

"Bye sweetheart. I'll contact you at your place."

Philip contacted Shaw and Parker at their hotel and bragged about the wonderful time he had with Reba.

"How about Arthur's address?" asked Parker in a curious voice.

"Sorry chaps, but she was not forthcoming this time. But she promised to find out the places where Arthur has his ultimate pleasure."

"Maybe we should visit a few more bars and after that brothels," Philip suggested.

"That is fine, you do it my boy," Parker responded.

Philip returned to his hotel and called Reba to find out how she was doing. No sooner had he began talking to her when Reba, in a hysterical and screaming voice yelled, "Pierre, Pierre, I've got it! I have Arthur's address for you."

Philip was in a total daze for a minute, like some one who is momentarily blinded by the sun while driving.

Philip drove over to her place and in a heightened emotion embraced Reba. He took the paper, kissed Reba and the other girl in the room jokingly said, "I brought the paper, I deserve a kiss too."

"Thank you, my dear, thank you very much."

Philip embraced the other girl and her perfume almost anesthetized him. He gave her an open mouth kiss and she kissed him back with her mouth open. Reba was just standing there totally mesmerized by the scene.

"Ladies, I must really go now. See you in a few days."

He rushed to Shaw and Parker and ran to their room.

He opened the door and Shaw teasingly greeted him, "Hello Philip! I did not know that you turned out to be a Romeo. You became a charmer, lover, and heartbreaker."

"I didn't know that you were envious!"

"Well, I did not learn how to romance in spy school."

"It was not in my curriculum either. I don't know what some women like in me."

"So, did you receive Arthur's new address?"

"Let's drive to the Latin Quarter again. Rue Rollin 7, 2nd floor, number 3," said Philip.

They drove with little hope but every place had to be investigated. Shaw stopped the car opposite the building. Philip got his pistol ready, and proceeded to the apartment. He knocked three times but no answer. He opened the door by picking the lock. The place was completely empty. Not a sign of occupancy. Philip went to the bathroom, opened the cabinet and found an empty bottle of medication written for Arthur Renoir. He took the bottle and was looking for other signs in the wastepaper basket.

There was a note scribbled in a rush for a lady named Vivian. "Try to contact me next door." Philip knocked on the door to the right. The door opened and a young girl and boy in their early teens answered.

"Can we help you?" said the girl.

"I am looking for Arthur?" asked Philip.

"We met Arthur, but he only stayed here one day."

"Do you know where I can find him?" inquired Philip.

The boy hesitatingly said, "I heard him saying to my mom that he is moving back to the empty apartment next door with a friend."

"Did he say when?" asked Philip.

The girl answered, "I think, he said tonight."

"How does your mother know Arthur?" Philip was curious to ask.

"I don't know. He slept here with mom. I think something happened, because my mother cried when he left and she had to see a doctor," complained the little girl.

"Thank you. Here, take a few francs for your information. It is not necessary to tell anybody that I was looking for Arthur, except your mother," said Philip.

Shaw and Parker moved the car a certain distance from the building where they would be able to observe what was happening. At darkness, a moving van arrived and stopped in front of the house. Two men jumped out and started unloading the van. An hour later a car stopped across from the house and a young looking man started to talk to the movers.

Philip approached him and asked him point blank where Arthur was now because he had to start wallpapering a new restaurant tonight.

"Oh, he would be happy to live up to his contract because the guy is hungry for money. I think, he is at the Cabaret bar here in the Latin Quarter," said the young man.

"Thank you," said Philip.

Shaw drove around and asked people on the street how to get to Cabaret bar and he found it in twenty minutes. There were a myriad of girls at the bar keeping guys and German soldiers company. Shaw and Parker ordered two glasses of white wine at the bar and waited to be approached by a couple of girls. They didn't have to wait too long. Two nice looking girls politely asked if they would accept companions.

Shaw answered, "By all means you are welcome to join us."

Parker ordered drinks for the girls and they began talking about everything but politics. Shaw very skillfully directed the conversation to asking the girls about customers that they had some problems with in the past. The girls were very circumspect but Shaw sensed that they were better off talking farther away from the bar.

"Do you girls feel more comfortable chatting in private?" asked Shaw.

One of the girls said, "Oh yeah, let's sit in the back room."

The back room was dimly lit and each table was partitioned to insure utmost privacy.

The chairs were velvety cushioned, extremely comfortable. Parker led the party to a corner table. The waitress was asked to bring a bottle wine and some hors d'oeuvres and bread.

"I know that you prefer to talk about sensuous things, but we need some information from you girls."

"Before we chat about confidential things, let me introduce ourselves. I am Carrie and she is Ruby. We'll gladly spend time with you and provide you with some gossip, but it will cost you money."

Parker did not ask the girls about the retainer. He took out a few thousand francs and divided them between the girls.

"Oh, my, this is a lot of money for gossip! Can we give you pleasure?" asked Ruby.

"No my dear, all we want is information about Arthur. Who are the girls he has sex with, where does he go to have sex, and where does he live?" asked Shaw.

"This is a tall order, but we'll see what we can do for you," said Carrie.

"Before we start talking, we have to know who you are talking about," said Ruby.

"Arthur is a sadist, who likes to slap girls on their buttocks until it really hurts, and hangs around with German soldiers, mostly officers, or sometimes with the Gestapo," described Shaw.

"Now we know who you are talking about. He was here earlier and picked up a girl by the name of Janine. She is about twenty-three, very pretty, and sexy. Janine has been having a lot of money problems, and when somebody offers her money, she becomes very vulnerable. Janine lives not too far from here. She has a little girl and her mother watches the kid while she is having sex with guys like Arthur," explained Ruby.

"Can you give us the address?" asked Parker.

"No, but we can show you the place," added Carrie.

Shaw paid the bill and the four of them headed for the car. Ruby told them where to go to get to Janine's place. Philip drove right behind them. Parker flagged down a taxi and sent the girls back to the restaurant. Philip walked upstairs to open the door.

He very quietly walked inside. Philip found Arthur semi-conscious as he lay naked with a woman who looked unresponsive. There were several empty liquor bottles on the floor. She was badly beaten with black and blue eyes and vomit on the floor. Philip had a difficult time lifting and dressing Arthur.

Why not continue with the cognac to finish him off, was the thought that crossed Philips' mind. Good idea. He found a douche bag and tubing in the bathroom. He carefully inserted the tube down Arthur's throat into his stomach and slowly began pouring the cognac down the tube. He emptied one bottle. Then he opened another bottle and slowly poured a quarter of that bottle. He waited for his pulse to start to skip and his breathing to become shallow. Philip removed the tube, cleaned the bottle to remove any fingerprints and put the douche into a bag for disposal. Then he sat down and waited.

Arthur's face and fingers became blue then white as he passed away. Philip put the half empty bottle of cognac in Arthur's hand for fingerprints.

Janine was breathing normally, but she was knocked out from the beating and cognac.

When she wakes up she'll be all right. The police will see what happened to her but she will not be implicated. The autopsy will show that Arthur died of alcoholic intoxication.

Philip called the ambulance and the police.

"I think we can leave now and go back to the hotel to check out," said Shaw.

"I am glad that we gave fake names and addresses," commented Parker.

Christen was at the desk when Shaw and Parker arrived. Parker asked her to step outside for a few minutes.

"What is happening?" asked Christen.

"We have to check out. Our job is done."

"Can I drive behind you with my colleague?"

"How much time do we have?"

"Twenty minutes. I am checking out now with another receptionist."

Shaw and Parker went upstairs to get their luggage and checked out in fifteen minutes. They waited five more minutes on the street for Christen, who was able to convince her manager that she had a family emergency and had to leave immediately.

Philip called Reba before he checked out of the hotel.

"Darling, I must go away. Something came up and it is very important for me to participate."

"But Pierre, I will miss you terribly. I will not sleep or eat until you come back! May I come along? I'll be a good girl and help you to relieve your stress!"

"That is impossible, my sweetheart. But I'll be back in a jiffy. If not, you will come to see me. I will send you train tickets. Bye, sweetheart!"

Philip checked out of the hotel and followed Shaw and Parker.

They left Paris as fast as it was possible. When they were in the outskirts of the city they stepped on the gas and without stopping anywhere, except at the military checkpoints, they arrived to Normandy in no time. The first stop was, of course, at Marceau's. He was introduced to agents Christen and Howard.

"Hello, Christen and Howard. On behalf of the Resistance I want to thank you for all the protection you provided for agents Shaw and Parker. They are outstanding agents for the Allied Intelligence. May I introduce another outstanding operative of the Resistance and supporter of Allied Intelligence, my adopted daughter, Bridget, and, of course, Philip, who is brave and resourceful and who carried out an almost impossible mission," said Marceau.

"I hope you realize that this saga is not over yet. We can expect some consequences. The Paris homicide detective branch is one of the best. The hope is that when they learn the details of the case including his background they will drop the investigation. The Gestapo has lost a valuable mole. They will be interested in all the details concerning his death. They will search for all his previous contacts and all the people who pursued Arthur to question them. Where this will lead is a good guess."

"We have a job to do and we must protect the fact finding

mission of the Atlantic Wall. Hopefully the invasion will be victorious and we can talk about it after the war. Arthur was a casualty just like we have lost a number of good people who were executed by the Gestapo," said Marceau.

"I couldn't agree with you more. You stated the facts very eloquently. We have a very short time to complete the picture of the German defense plan. We are trying to complete the puzzle, but there are a number of pieces that are missing," said Shaw.

"The Resistance is helping Shaw and Parker, but they are not perfect. They are not professionals and they lack the education, training, and experience. But what they are doing is heroic. The losses of the Allied Forces would be much greater if it were not for them. We must do the preliminaries prior to the invasion. We can not afford moles to destroy our invisible army. I am saluting Philip and everybody who helped him by risking their lives every minute of the day," praised Marceau.

"May I offer you a little hospitality by presenting Bridget's outstanding homemade cookies with some vintage wine?" offered Marceau.

"May we also thank Christen and Howard for all their support which was hardly realized until we returned to Normandy. They looked after us during the entire operation. OSS and MI6 should be proud to have women like Christen and men like Howard," said Parker.

"There are few accolades I would like to offer that have not been said yet. Upon arrival in Paris we didn't have the foggiest notion that we had a blanket protection, just in case something went wrong. We thought that we were on our own but we weren't. It is a bloody good feeling to know that somebody cares in an unfamiliar environment. Thank you, Christen and Howard," said Shaw.

Bridget offered a second round. Everybody felt like celebrating and had another drink. Marceau suggested that Bridget, Philip, Shaw, and Parker take Christen and Howard for a ride and introduce them to Port-En-Bessin. Then come back for a hot snack and brandy.

"By the way, how did Christen and Howard manage to get here with all the identification checks?" asked Marceau.

"We had all papers prepared in advance. Christen is a nursing assistant for me and was sent to Normandy to give influenza vaccines to the population and military if necessary," replied Howard.

"That is very smart. I really admire you guys, you think of everything," said Marceau.

Everybody stepped out and started to walk toward the shore. Parker suggested not crossing the forbidden zone, even with Shaw being present. Shaw described some of the military alertness and Bridget pointed out the existing businesses. They walked all over, covering a great portion of the port. At one point, Christen and Parker separated from the others and a very delicate theme began to emerge.

"You seem to be reserved and quiet. Are you homesick? Committed?" asked Christen.

"Why are you asking?"

"I am just wondering."

"You must know?"

"Committed? Yes. Etched in stone? No."

"What does that mean?"

"Things can happen. We are at war."

They were on a different street and far away from the rest of the group. She stopped walking and leaned against the wall of a street corner. She looked straight into his eyes, and he returned the look. They were silent and searching into each others soul. She wet her lips with her tongue. Parker gently touched her lips, then he kissed her passionately and she kissed him back. The whole passion ended in a warm embrace.

"I needed that," whispered Christen.

"I know the feeling. I needed it too."

Bridget started to look for both of them and found them far away from the group. In their privacy she interrupted the two and said, "We were looking for you. So this is where you are hiding. We are walking back to have Marceau's cooking. Coming along?"

They all got back in time. Marceau was ready to carve the duck and serve the rest of the meal.

"You got back just in time. Please sit down and have a glass of wine." Marceau said.

He surprised them with a delicious bowl of mixed salad with croutons and homemade cheese dressing. The table was pulled out to seat seven people and he had some folding chairs in the basement. He decorated the table with white tablecloth, napkins and two large candles sitting on silver candleholders. Bridget said a prayer and the dinner began in a festive atmosphere. Everybody was quiet and eating the well prepared food.

"Marceau, I'm just nosy, where on earth did you get this duck?" asked Parker.

"I was waiting for this question. I have a customer, who has a farm, and he surprised me."

There were occasional praises of the various dishes and wine. Christen sat opposite of Parker and their eyes were filled with joy and happiness. It was about ten o'clock when Howard excused himself and asked Christen to join him at the hotel. They had to start back to Paris early in the morning. Parker accompanied Christen to the car.

Christen and Parker exchanged addresses and phone numbers. They embraced each other and she whispered into his ear, "Let me hear from you, keep in touch. I need your hugs."

Parker also embraced Howard and said, "Thank you! I'll never forget all the support you gave to me and my partner. God be with you."

Shaw came out with Marceau and Bridget to wave goodbye and Christen and Howard slowly walked toward the car, turning around only once and waving back.

"It is time for us to go home too," said Shaw.

"Wait a couple of minutes, Bridget is preparing some tea, coffee and cookies. Also, I'm not finished with you guys yet. Please sit down, we have to talk about Arthur's demise," said Marceau.

"The thing that bothers us the most is the forthcoming Gestapo investigation," commented Shaw.

"I was the most exposed person, but I gave the name Pierre," said Philip.

"The fact that two Organization Todt officers mingled with some bar girls is acceptable, but inquiring about Arthur could arouse suspicion," suggested Marceau.

"We have the right to ask about a person whose reputation as a wall paper hanger is outstanding," replied Parker.

"Hopefully this whole case will quiet down, but the Gestapo will keep their eyes open and will not forget that one of their valuable confidants passed away because of an alcohol overdose. Arthur was known to them as a ladies man and a heavy drinker. It had cost him 0dearly for all the damages caused by drinking and abusing women.

"So, I have a recommendation. Philip, you must disappear at least for three months. Go to Spain," suggested Marceau.

"Shaw and Parker stay on course and concentrate on the Atlantic Wall construction for the coming weeks without the input of the cells. We'll know from my Resistance operatives how deeply the Gestapo is involved in Arthur's case," said Marceau.

"This is a very sound idea," sounded Shaw with an approving voice.

"I also agree with you and will leave tomorrow for Madrid," said Philip.

"I hope we'll have some good news for you guys," said Parker.

"You can come any time and don't hesitate to ask for help," offered Bridget.

"We will. But now we must go home, because we are exhausted. Goodbye, have a nice trip, Philip. And thanks for the delicious food, cookies and drinks. Marceau, I don't know what we would do without you!" said Shaw.

Parker drove fast at first, but some memories of the events occupied his mind and he began to slow down a bit. He thought that Christen stirred some feelings of romance in him. Being committed to a nice girl at home, he tried not to think about Christen, but it did not work. Christen was on his mind, but there was another factor. One of Parker's colleagues had a short assignment in Paris and visited Parker while he was there. He had a chance to talk with Parker's girlfriend back at home before his departure to Paris. She told him that she was seeing another guy. It was impossible for Parker to verify the truth and depth of her relationship. He had to wait until his liberty in the US.

"Penny for your thoughts. You are driving very slowly and pensively," said Shaw.

"I was just wondering about things at home and Christen."

"War produces strange feelings in a person's life. Sometimes we feel that we live for moments only and we must have everything that we can have. It is very hard to live a one-hundred percent ethical life."

"I guess you're right."

"I try very hard not to let my memories influence me, otherwise, I cannot do my present job."

"I just can't help to neutralize my feelings and cut out some recent episodes in my life."

"I think you can. You are a very strong willed person. Have faith in yourself."

Both arrived to home and without any discussion they walked upstairs and were about to enter their flats.

"Have a good rest," said Shaw.

"I wish you the same. Good night."

CHAPTER SIX

S haw and Parker rested a couple of weeks before they resumed meeting with their cells. Bridget had already notified each cell person of the resumption of operations and meeting places.

Back in Paris, the police had completed the preliminary investigation and the hospital pathology department forensic section determined that Arthur died of alcohol intoxication. Because another mole happened to visit Arthur a day after he was found dead, the Gestapo received a complete police and forensic report. The Gestapo found the police's investigation adequate and decided to wait for further developments before getting themselves involved. They had quite a number of moles all over France. The chief of Normandy Gestapo replaced Arthur in one hour. He could not match Arthur in his skill and experience, but the Gestapo did not have a great selection of stooges from which to choose. The successor was also asked to look into Arthur's demise.

Shaw and Parker were meeting all the cells the third day after their return. They instructed the cells concerning the increased German surveillance of the Normandy defenses. The Gestapo was especially watching for Allied informants. German foreign agents had infiltrated Allied intelligence abroad and sent back messages to Berlin about the Allies' knowledge of the Atlantic Wall and beyond.

For Allied aerial reconnaissance the Germans increased their firepower with guns and the Luftwaffe, but their aircraft became less effective as the USAF and RAF bombed the hell out of them at the hangars and airfields. Also the Allied bombing targeted special areas of the seacoast of Normandy and knocked out a large number of anti aircraft guns. The German military became very strict about who could enter the coastal region. They sent a number of special military intelligence agents in addition to the Gestapo to watch for foreign agents who were mixed with the general population or who worked on the construction of the Atlantic Wall.

They were trained to watch the German speaking engineers, building foremen, and all the military personnel who directed the construction. When someone's speech, grammar, and vocabulary indicated imperfections, the agent would begin talking with that person to trap the individual and then give him to the Gestapo for further questioning. Under these terrifying circumstances collecting information for Allied Intelligence became difficult.

Shaw and Parker, however, used all their craftsmanship and training to assist the cells in what they could and could not do. To get caught and interrogated was not only dangerous for themselves and other cell members, not to mention Shaw and Parker, but catastrophic for the whole mission.

Parker and Shaw visited the cell in Cherbourg region and the discussion began with the emphasis on German alertness. The reasoning behind that had to do with the cell's personal security.

The very first question was: "How can we collect information without exposure and how can we expose ourselves without danger?"

Parker responded to the question first. "Isn't it that danger is part of the risk we are taking every day?"

"The question is true and valid, but you must listen to me as an expert in these matters. You can execute an observation by acute or insidious exposure. You don't have to make yourself noticeable if you are not asking another person a question, if there isn't a change in your body posture and if your general demeanor is not conspicuously different than others. Danger is part of life. You don't have to do anything and you can be killed because a German soldier accidentally drops a mine and you are in the vicinity of the explosion. You don't think about the danger when you are working on a project. But you are careful! Yes you are taking risks when you're in this business. The most important thing is called foresight! A Latin proverb states, 'quid quid agis prudenter agas et respice finem—whatever you do, do it cautiously, and look at the end.' We will win this war if you live and act by this proverb," said Shaw.

"I will need a comprehensive report of all your findings in your designated area. In addition, we would appreciate your recommendation for further information gathering. You have a week to work on it. Good luck! Cheerio. We'll be meeting next week in our usual designated location for Monday at 0800 hour. Have a good day and start!" said Shaw.

Shaw and Parker delivered the same message to all seven cells and made appointments for the following week. The rest of the day was spent traveling, checking various construction sites and dining. While Allied Intelligence was collecting information about the Atlantic Wall, the German High Command West was totally puzzled where the landing would take place. The belief that the landing would be at Pas-de-Calais was indicated by the amount of cement allocations in 1942, 1943, and 1944. There had been four to one cement allocations in the Pas-de-Calais region than in Normandy. There were less casemates built in Normandy than Pas-de-Calais, and two and a half times fewer troops stationed in the former than in the latter region.

Shaw, on the way home, stopped the car in front of a construction site and declared, "I don't think that the reporting from all the cells will be accurate. Although, I hope that next week will provide a better picture of the Atlantic Wall so far. I think the OKW (Oberkommando West; German High Command West) is putting most of their eggs in the Pas-de-Calais basket."

"You're right. I understand that Allied Intelligence wants a complete picture so they can compare the reports from the other Resistance spies and the aerial photographs to determine which the fake ones are, but we can do only so much before we compromise our mission. The Atlantic Wall construction started slowly and at times we had to wait for materials because of the allocation and shortage of materials, but now that High Command West feels that the invasion is getting closer and wants to complete the Wall in a short time. We are doing fine under the present increased surveillance circumstances," added Parker.

They joined the construction workers and the foreman and made some suggestions to accelerate certain aspects of the casemate construction. As they were conversing with the foreman, a military police officer approached them and asked Shaw and Parker for their identification papers.

"I am sorry, but I have to ask you some questions for security. What is your business here?"

"We are supervising various construction sites because of our expertise in engineering and material science," answered Shaw.

"You speak a beautiful German with a very slight dialect. Where did you learn your language?"

"My mother and my father read to me, and of course I was in elementary and high school in Berlin and later I attended the University of Heidelberg," answered Parker.

"I want to thank you for your cooperation," said the officer.

No sooner had the military police ended the inquiry when a military intelligence officer approached Shaw and Parker and continued to probe into their past education.

"Mr. Dietrich, I wonder if you remember the names of your teachers in Berlin?"

"Of course," responded Parker. "How many names do you want?"

"As many as you can remember." The officer took out a notebook and was ready to write the names.

Parker purposely named those teachers who passed away during the war. Allied Intelligence had managed to enter his name into the class roster.

About the University of Heidelberg the officer was rather curt. He only wanted to know the name of the Dean of the University. Parker responded without hesitation.

"Mr. Dietrich, you are doing very well and I don't think I have to go on with Mr. Krueger.

But what is so fascinating to me is your superb articulation of German. I guess some people are better than others."

Parker did not say any more than he had to. He just politely grinned and saluted the officer.

Shaw and Parker felt intimidated and their heartbeats increased with each word they uttered. Their training paid off. The intelligence officer never suspected that their calmness was only a facade. They stayed and helped the workers with the iron rods and showed them how to mesh faster. After an hour and a half Parker signaled Shaw to leave. They left with a handshake and salute. The intelligence officer, foreman and the military police officer saluted back.

On the way home, they stopped at Marceau's. He was busy as usual, but Bridget asked them to wait because Marceau had something to say.

"Oh, welcome. You smell the spring in the air? I always recognize a new year not from the calendar but from the smell coming from the fields, nature's awakening. Time flies, it's hard to believe, but we are writing 1944. Of course, we don't think of seasons, we are at war. Oh well, this is not what I wanted to talk about."

Marceau took a few seconds of respite. He lit his pipe with a matchstick that burned out without lighting his tobacco. He tried another stick, and the third one finally lit the tobacco. He drew a couple of puffs, looked them in their eyes and said, "I had Christen, from MI6, looking for you guys this morning. The news is that the preparation for the invasion is moving fast. Allied Intelligence must make an assessment of the strength of the Atlantic Wall. The deception named 'Fortitude' must be embedded in the minds of the German Generals. They have to believe that the invasion will be in the Pas-de-Calais region. She was sorry to miss you, but her itinerary called for three more stops before returning to Paris. This is all the news I have to tell you."

"Thank you. We have asked our cells for an updated report that we expect to receive next week. It looks like the German High Command West is concentrating most of the strength of defense on the Pas-de-Calais region. To a certain extent this would give an advantage to the first and second wave invasion forces, unless there is a plan to have a mobile tank force in between the two regions. But since Hitler was convinced that Pas-de-Calais region will be the deciding battleground, he will concentrate all his forces, including the panzer reserve, in that area. This is fine with us, and we'll certainly do our best that he should be absolutely right," said Shaw.

Shaw and Parker excused themselves because it was time to go home. They were driving at a leisurely pace. Just before they turned onto their street, a terrible accident occurred at the intersection. The driver of a German military vehicle lost control of the steering and hit the electric pole on his right. Shaw stopped the car at the curb and tried to help the passengers. The driver was slightly injured, but the passenger had serious breathing problems besides other injuries. Shaw and Parker put the passenger and the driver into the back seat and drove to the nearest hospital emergency room. Both patients received immediate attention and the passenger was taken into surgery for broken ribs, lacerations, and breathing difficulties. There were preliminary questions of the accident by the police and Shaw and Parker went home to have some peace and quiet after a day of conferences and work on the wall.

The next evening when they were having dinner, two gentlemen knocked on the door and identified themselves as being from the Gestapo.

"We came to thank you for your help and saving the life of one of our Gestapo officers.

It was very gallant, kind, brave, and heroic what you have done as fellow officers of Organization Todt. We would like to recommend you for an award and salute you," said one of the Gestapo officers.

"But that is absolutely unnecessary!" said Parker with an emotional voice. "We Germans must take care of each other and we do these things for humanitarian reasons. We could not accept any award that we consider as a natural behavior of a civilized man. But we want to thank you for coming over and thanking us for our deeds and making the offer," replied Parker.

"Your German is so perfect. It is a pleasure listening to you," said the other Gestapo man. "We must go now, but we'll never forget your deed. Heil Hitler!" With that salute both men left the apartment.

The next few days for Shaw and Parker were routine tasks: collecting updated reports and new information, collating all information from the seven cells, random supervision of casemates and bunkers, and promoting 'fortitude' among military officers. The workload became about ninety hours per week, but the job had to be done. The collection of information, although it was preliminary, revealed an overwhelming amount of data concerning the Atlantic Wall. It included: information relating to the pounds of cement and steel mesh, armor plate thickness, howitzer turret; mortar turret; machine-gun; tobruk-circular concrete pit for one man. Some tobruks had machine guns, others mortars, and still others tank turrets, number of 35, 47, 50, 75 and 88 mm antitank guns, open emplacement for 150mm gun, enfiladed beaches—where guns fire from two directions toward the same target, camouflaged houses which served as gun emplacements, fire control posts or command posts, underground tunnels for personnel, ammunition storage, and the list of information goes on. The final collating required clerical help and Bridget volunteered to help in the evenings. The report had to be microfilmed and sent in pieces.

Three days after the car accident, Shaw and Parker received an invitation from the Caen Gestapo Chief. It'll be a testimonial dinner, on the third Saturday of the month. This was an unwanted and unavoidable situation.

"I feel like I am between a rock and a hard place," lamented Parker.

"The show must go on in any circumstance," was Shaw's reply. By the way, don't you ever forget we are spies masquerading in a German uniform. We'll be shot if we are discovered. At least there will be mercy on our souls, and we'll be spared to be tortured and hanged by a piano wire," added Shaw.

"I find that very encouraging. We will be tested for our artistry of acting, lying, and, most of all, controlling our emotions," assessed Parker.

"Touché," said Shaw.

"These qualities are exactly what make a good spy, and boy, we are good at it. We terminated in cold blood a guy who could have ruined us, the mission, and perhaps thousands of lives. Not to mention the beachhead that must be fought for and won, for the invasion to occur. To think, we have three million men and women involved in 'Overlord' and over a million in the actual preparation of the landing. And because we were brave, bold, and swift in our action we are still alive."

"Some people would have little respect for what we are doing and they think that the Ultra, the secret German code machine, is the only intelligence that the OSS and MI6 can provide. They want proof of our work. For now it is super secret and will be kept secret for a long time."

"What we are doing and what we have accomplished so far is an achievement. Yes, we are going through the whole masquerade and performing again, but this time as saviors and celebrities. Yes, you'll be all right," said Shaw with a tiny grin on his face.

"If you say so, I believe you."

Although the overall picture of the information from the cells looked awesome, new data was pouring in from other sources. Shaw and Parker decided that the preliminary report should wait a few more days. Cell members were still getting information from their friends, members of the 'Century', a French Resistance Organization, physicians who had access to work in strictly prohibited zones, and some girls who were smuggled in to batteries as play girls or nurses aides to take care of high ranking German officers. Even if they provided tidbits of data, it all added up at the end of the day.

Michael began to see Bridget at regular intervals and they went all over in Normandy having a good time. On very rare occasions, they drove to Paris to see a show or listen to a concert. They were busy with their own lives. Not necessarily by choice, but because of obligations. The weekend that was coming up had to be special. It was Bridget's birthday. Michael wanted to make sure that she would have nothing but the best that evening—dining out, birthday cake at home, a beautiful gift, not to mention flowers and champagne. It was all planned with love and care.

Around six-thirty that Saturday afternoon Michael was waiting for Bridget in front of the shop. Bridget met him in a stunning outfit and a smiling face. She gave a kiss to Michael as he handed her a beautiful bouquet of flowers.

"Thank you, handsome. You're a charmer."

"For you darling, it's a starter for your birthday!"

"Where are we going?"

"Not too far. There is a little restaurant in Bayeux, and I hope you'll like it."

"I'm sure, I will. But the most important thing is that we are together in these turbulent times."

"How was your week?"

"Mine was fine, no troubles or complications. Just the usual. Everybody is in a hurry to have their shoes or boots fixed or have new ones. What is happening in your life, Michael?"

"We are under tremendous pressure to complete the Wall, at least in certain sections. Although the emphasis is on the Pas-de-Calais, there is a debate going on if the invasion site is between the Pas-de-Calais and Normandy. The Central Command is driving us crazy."

As they entered the street where the restaurant was located, the military police stopped the car and asked for identification and prohibited zone permit papers. Michael had no problem but Bridget left her prohibited zone permit home. Michael vouched for her and when the police officer heard that she was Marceau's daughter, there was no problem to let her through. The officer said facetiously, "It will cost your father a pair of boots."

They had a nice reserved table, decorated with flowers, and champagne glasses. The owner greeted them, and wished Bridget a very happy birthday. For appetizers, they had escargot, snails in butter along with a mixed salad with croutons. Michael ordered her favorite entrée in advance, roasted chicken, which was cooked to her satisfaction. She liked the skin crisp and the meat medium, surrounded with slices of baked apple. For Michael, it was duck with fried skinned potatoes and asparagus. For dessert, of course, they had a specially prepared small birthday cake. For drinks, they had champagne and after dinner liquor. Bridget was absolutely awed by Michael's thoughtfulness.

"I have a little gift for you." Michael presented a little box, wrapped in silver paper.

"You didn't have to." She unwrapped the paper, opened the box, and there was a gold necklace with a dainty heart on it.

"Thank you." She embraced him. "It is beautiful. I shall wear it for the rest of my life." Michael helped her to attach the necklace around her neck and gave her another hug. She put her head down and both were silent for a couple of seconds.

"Michael, I want to clarify something for myself. I need to know that you understand the inner conflict I have about you and me. Please hear me out and when I have finished, you can respond and comment about it."

"Why don't we discuss this somewhere outside sitting on a bench, away from people?" suggested Michael.

"I agree."

They walked a short distance and found a bench in a little park. Both sat down facing each other and Michael waited for Bridget to begin talking.

"It may be inappropriate to talk about the issues tonight, but we have an extremely short time before we are going to face the thundering masses. I sincerely hope we are going to survive and be together for the rest of our lives. However, our future is interwoven by forces that can help or hinder our future."

"We understand the antecedent conditions that helped Hitler and Nazism come to power. It is the underlying premise, the entire foundation of Nazism, however, that must be brought to light and examined. The whole Nazi ideology has been based on racist doctrines that place the pure Aryan race on the top and everybody else below. The master race must control the mongrel and/or subservient. The master race is strong and the subservient is weak. Hitler tried to show the world that Nazism is the future, by winning, enslaving, and humiliating the subservient. The faulty logic that followed the ideological premise and the military defeat of nations gave Hitler an edge to prove that he was right and everybody else who was against him and the Nazi dogma was wrong. If you look at the total execution of his belief, you'll find nothing but terrible brutality."

"Yes, he gave the German people bread and butter, an opportunity to redress the losses, and to his party members extra benefits, but at what price? To achieve his objectives, he has been robbing people from their existence, humiliating, torturing, and gassing them. He has killed millions of Jews and his enemies in the concentration camps. The suffering of people, the destruction of human existence, the inhumane treatment of political and combat prisoners cannot be described with ordinary words, because there is no language that can express the pain that he has caused."

"Michael, this is madness. It is below human existence. It is a hell that he created. We must fight with every ounce of blood to destroy him and his evil regime. I hope that you will think about what I have said and help us. Help not for me but for us, for the future of the people of Germany and others."

"Darling, I am really astonished at what you are asking. You are asking me to help the Allies. That means treason! You want me to commit acts for which I can face the firing squad. I do not understand why you are asking me to betray my country."

"Helping to win freedom and democracy is not betraying your country. To the contrary, you are helping your country by preventing total destruction. Look, Hitler is a madman. He is possessed with the notion that by eliminating all his enemies, Germany will flourish like never before. Then, he will dictate with absolute power how to live your life, who you can marry, and what to believe in. Hitler is a pathological case, a homicidal maniac; he is going to destroy Germany."

"I still have difficulties following your logic. I am trying to understand you, but I don't know where you're coming from. Your perception may be shared by some German people, but Hitler is still the Leader, despite some opposing forces within the German Army."

"Yes, there is an awakening in Germany and in other parts of the fascist world. One Leader, one party, one philosophy cannot and will not rule the world."

Both looked into each other's and kept silent for a minute. Bridget broke the silence and said in an admonishing voice, "You have to know who I am, because you can get into trouble by associating with me. Now listen very carefully."

"I am not Marceau's daughter. I was placed in his protective custody because my parents were Jewish Resistance operatives. They were caught by the Gestapo during an assignment and sent to a concentration camp in Germany. When I came to live with Marceau, I joined the Resistance. I am an operative. At worst, we are at opposite ends of the spectrum; at best, we are damned honest with each other and we know where we stand. But, we are playing with fire. The question is where we're going from here and will we be able to save our relationship?"

Both remained quiet. Michael tried to absorb what Bridget had said. It was a very complex situation. Michael was torn between his love for Bridget and his country.

"I am trying to understand where you are coming from and put everything into a proper perspective. It is difficult my dear, my love, to join your side. But, I am beginning to see your point. How are we going to justify all the murders and destruction? Can we do it in behalf of the German losses in World War One? Two wrongs don't make one right. I will have a difficult time to living with my conscience. I am not on the side that kills innocent people."

Michael looked at her for a few seconds, then embraced her and whispered in her ear,

"I will help you, my darling."

"Thank you, Michael."

"You're welcome, my love."

"It is getting late. I must go home, sweetheart."

"I need to know what kind of information you want me to provide you?"

"Everything you can muster up about the defensive preparations, maps, mobile panzer units, aircrafts, divisions, and the latest V one and V two weapons."

"I will try to get some documents copied. I will bring to you what I can find, but you must be careful. Try to hide things the best you can because the Gestapo will dig until they find a shred of evidence and then we'll all perish."

"Thank you, Michael. We are very careful."

"I'm sorry about mixing politics with my birthday celebration, but I had to tell you about my inner conflict that has been tearing me apart. I had to confide in you my feelings and I had to know where you stand. Our love and our future are at stake."

"I understand."

Michael and Bridget slowly walked hand in hand toward the car.

"What's next, other than the papers? Anything special you want to do?"

"Yes, I want to go to your place and snuggle with you."

"That's not a problem."

Michael was holding Bridget's hand while holding the steering wheel in the other hand.

Both felt the aftermath of their emotional catharsis and the depth of their commitment. Bridget worried about Michael and vice versa. When they reached the house, Michael held Bridget in his arms and said: "Darling, my love, don't worry. Everything will be all right."

"I hope so. You mean a lot to me Michael. Please be very, very careful."

Parker and Shaw cleaned and pressed their uniforms for the special occasion in Caen. They were dressed with immaculate tidiness. Fresh white shirt, black tie, shiny black shoes, and even their faces and hair had been cared for like performers on the stage.

They arrived on time and were seated among the dignitaries. Allied Intelligence would have found it so comical to have two of their agents masquerading as Organization Todt engineers being honored for bravery by the enemy that they would have exploded with roaring laughter.

The place was a medium sized dining hall which held fifty-five people, including some ladies, packed to capacity. These people were covering not only Normandy but some of the western regions in France. All were dressed in Gestapo uniform, short jacket with belt, black pants and shoes. The Gestapo officers sat at circular tables for six except the head table which was a rectangular table which sat eight. Shaw and Parker were seated at the far right of the head table with six Gestapo officers.

The dinner lasted for about an hour. The speeches began after the lights dimmed and the focus centered on the head table. Everybody congratulated Shaw and Parker, but the most raving presentation was made by the chief of Gestapo in Normandy. He not only congratulated Shaw and Parker, but to everybody's surprise he decorated them with the life saving distinguished medals which he himself placed around their necks. Everybody got up from their seats and there was a standing ovation for saving the life of one of their comrades. Only one Gestapo man failed to applaud and he was noticed by Parker.

Shaw and Parker were the last to speak. Their German was so perfect and erudite that they practically mesmerized the audience. They not only used rare words but their general vocabulary and sentence structure were more for scholars than Gestapo personnel. Both gave perfect ad lib deliverances based on what others said and what actually happened. Shaw and Parker tried to be modest but accepted the accolades of a deed well earned. There were three standing ovations and long applauses for Shaw and Parker's speeches.

After the presentations, there was social mingling among the Gestapo men and women and between Shaw and Parker. It was an unbelievable mockery to have the presence of Shaw and Parker there, receiving medals from brutal torturers and killers. But the show had to go on to operate, collect and transmit information while creating the amount of least suspicion.

On the way home Parker remarked, "I recognized the agent as the one who was suspicious of the young man who delivered the news of the arrival of the British commando to U.K."

"I agree with you. I noticed him when they were applauding because he failed to do so. He still smells something, but he can't put his finger on it. I would watch him, because we are a big prize for him. He is certainly after us. He is patient and waits for our mistake to catch us."

"In war many things can happen. We certainly cannot afford to be arrested by him. He can have an accident, but we will not save him."

"Be careful, Parker, he is very dangerous."

"But he lacks our training. We are better than he is. We will also wait. I would like to confront him on the day of the invasion."

"It can only happen if you really luck out. Those guys are cowards and if they hear the first gunshots of the paratroopers they will flee so fast to the east they will look like rockets."

Shaw and Parker drove directly home without stopping. It was late and they had to get up early to meet with the cells and later with Bridget.

All cells submitted their reports and Bridget was collating them. There was no new information and because of the caveat of extra precaution, the cells became careful not to arouse suspicion by the Gestapo.

The preliminary reports turned out to be a very useful map of intelligence for comparative purposes. Most port areas were heavily defended especially Cherbourg and the fifty square miles around it. Apart from Cherbourg, Pas-de-Calais, Le Havre, other ports, like Carentan, Ouistrehem, and Port-en-Bessin were extremely vital for the German defense. The number of batteries, bunkers, casemates, underground connecting tunnels, troops and vigilances were remarkably well documented. Bridget held the reports to be sent to UK a few more days, hoping to add Michael's latest secret military documents. Bridget requested Marceau to limit her participation in the store and various courier services while she readied the first comprehensive report to be sent.

Those were very tense days. The slightest discovery by the Gestapo could be fatal for everybody, not to mention all the work that was waiting for shipment. Marceau took care of the customers, repaired the shoes, and made new boots, but there was a two week delay making new boots.

He suspended all Resistance matters and only dealt with emergencies. The generals complained about the extra two weeks of waiting but Marceau blamed everything on the transportation and the new security measures.

Michael showed up in the latter part of the week. He was upset that the Gestapo was stopping everybody entering Port-En-Bessin. There was practically a ring around the port city.

Everybody had to show what business they had to enter the port. Michael told the Gestapo that his left boot was uncomfortable and he had to see Marceau. He had blueprints of various battery and defense plans with him. He was scared of being searched but was lucky. As he handed over the documents to Bridget, he warned that the plans were subject to change. He did not stay longer than ten minutes. He told Bridget to hide all the documents and stop working for the time being because the Gestapo was after something. He kissed her and left the store.

Bridget took all the documents to a special safe place which opened from the repair room. Marceau constructed the room from steel, concrete, wood, and double sheetrock. It is like a bank's vault: burglar, fire, sound, water, and demolition proof. Inside the room the walls and floor was covered with double layer of Styrofoam and in between there was air trapped in plastic. When one bangs the wall it does not echo or indicate that there is another room behind it. The entrance is operated by a hidden lever that is connected to a hydraulic lift. The lever is embedded into a sewing machine and you must know how to operate the machine in order to get to the lever, which takes five steps.

It was complicated to enter the room and once you were inside, it was not easy to get out either. You had to signal that you were ready to get out and hope that the place was not being searched. There were safety features to get out just in case the hydraulic system failed. Special hand lifters overrode the hydraulic system.

Bridget spent hours inside to type, microfilm and develop pictures. She had a small bed, blankets, toilet, sink, refrigerator, drinks and canned food. The only way Marceau and Bridget were able to communicate was through a circuit breaker that connected with the repair room inside. They used Morse code to communicate.

After Michael left, there was a knock on the door. It was a Gestapo agent with three soldiers.

"Open up," the agent yelled.

Marceau opened the door and all entered the premises. It was the same agent who had failed to salute and applaud Shaw and Parker during the recognition dinner. This intrusion was the very first one by the Gestapo. Marceau was absolutely surprised by his tone of voice and arrogant behavior.

"Are you hiding anybody in this place?" asked the agent.

"Why should I hide anybody? This is a place to make and repair shoes and boots"

"It was reported to me that you have frequent visitors from the German Army and officers of the Organization Todt."

"Yes, we have customer who are German Generals, officers, Gestapo officers, and OT officers. They come to see me because I perform a good service for them."

"Do you mind if my men will search your premises?"

"You do what you have to do. But please be careful because some of the boots belong to Generals."

"Are you teaching me how to search, you French swine?"

The agent ordered the soldiers to search everything, take apart what was necessary, kick the walls, look at the floor, and confiscate any valuable documents or radio transmitters. He told Marceau to sit and shut up.

The soldiers searched the rooms everywhere, hit the walls and the floors, looked at the billing papers, and tore some of the boots apart that belonged to two Generals. When Marceau saw what was happening, he asked how is he going to explain what happened to the Generals' boots.

"You are a swine," the agent said, and hit Marceau with his fist. His nose started to bleed.

"You tell them that we searched you because we had good reason. We suspect that you and your whore daughter are collaborators of the French Resistance." He took the broom and with the handle hit the walls so hard that the handle broke but there was no sound of an echo from the hidden room.

The agent was mad as hell. He asked the soldiers to leave the premises. Before slamming the door he yelled, "I will be back!"

It took several minutes for Marceau to collect himself and signal Bridget that all was clear. Marceau discussed every detail with Bridget. She was furious and immediately called Michael but he had not arrived home yet. She got into her car and drove to Shaw and Parker's apartments and waited for them to come home. Meantime, a kind German General arrived and saw Marceau depressed, bleeding and shaking.

"What happened to you?"

"I was searched, harassed, and beaten by a Gestapo officer."

"But why? What was the reason?"

"He made all kinds of accusations, hearsay, but no proof."

"When did this happen?"

"They came two and a half hours ago, and stayed for one hour."

"I am going to the Gestapo headquarters and demand proof! We are not barbarians!"

The General left the place and told the chauffeur to drive in a hurry to the Gestapo HQ in Caen. The agent who was responsible for the raid had not come back yet and the General asked the radio dispatcher to send an urgent message to the Gestapo officer to return to the HQ immediately.

The Gestapo officer arrived a half an hour later and apologized for his lateness. They were both standing and facing each other. The General, in a demanding voice, ordered him to sit down and hear him out.

"We are German soldiers and not barbarians! We belong to a civilized society that produced Goethe, Kant, Hegel, Wagner, Beethoven, and I don't want to give you a lecture because I think you are lacking the intelligence, the education, and the home environment to understand what I am talking about when it comes to literature, philosophy, and music. You have not earned my respect to acknowledge you as a security officer because of the way you behaved this afternoon.

"How dare you hit Marceau?"

"He was disrespectful."

"You are disrespectful now and I did not hit you!" You're supposed to say Herr General at the end of the answer. Your behavior is a disgrace to the German Gestapo and I will request your transfer to become a foot soldier!"

"I am sorry, but I was ordered to secure the area."

"I wrote the order. But you have to have proof before you hit a man like Marceau. He helps us to walk and carry out our duties. What schooling and experience did you have before you entered the Gestapo?"

"I went to high school and worked as a prison guard."

"And you called him swine!?"

"I did because of the way he looked at me, Herr General."

"You should apologize to him before all Frenchmen and women and German soldiers."

"I will not do that. That is humiliating and I am a German Security Officer of the Gestapo! Heil Hitler, Herr General. I will appeal if you order me, because I am not under your jurisdiction, Herr General."

"I don't know why I waste my time with you. I will make my recommendation to your superior and I hope we can transfer you somewhere in the front line and there you can prove your strength and arrogance. Our conversation is over."

The General walked out of the room without a salute in total amazement, shaking his head and deeply pensive, asking himself how the Gestapo could ever assign him for any duty.

It was raining hard but Shaw recognized Bridget's car parked in the dark. As he approached the car and saw the contours of her face, he knocked on the window. She got out the car.

"I can't waste time. Something bad happened. The Gestapo searched Marceau's place and the officer hit him. Please come right now. It is urgent. He needs your help."

Shaw and Parker got back in their car and drove with lightning speed to Marceau. The three of them went to the backroom and had an emergency conference.

"I think the Gestapo man has collaborators watching my store," said Marceau.

"That is quite possible," said Parker. "I am going to take a walk in the rain and check the cars nearby."

"I am going with you," said Shaw.

They walked less than five minutes when they found a car just opposite of Marceau's entrance. As they approached the car, they saw a man trying to start the car, but Parker was fast, and opened the door, grabbed the guy, and pulled him out of the car. Shaw handcuffed him and put his gun against his head and said, "You have two choices and seconds: talk or die."

"What do you want to know?"

"Who you working for?" asked Parker.

"I cannot tell you. My wife and kid will go to the concentration camp."

"Are you being blackmailed?" questioned Parker

"Why are you blackmailed?" asked Shaw.

"My wife is Jewish."

"Where do you work?" questioned Parker.

"For the Organization Todt building bunkers as a forced laborer.

"If we let you go, what will you tell the Gestapo man?" asked Shaw.

"I don't know."

"Yes, you do," said Shaw.

"I cannot lie."

"Why can't you lie?" asked Parker.

"There is another car, two cars behind. A guy with a beard is watching me."

"Thank you for telling me," said Parker.

"You'll sit in the car with me until my partner takes care of the other guy."

Shaw walked over to the other car, put his gun against the side window and asked him to open the door. He opened the door and looked for a weapon while holding the gun against his head. He found nothing. He asked him to move over and handcuffed him.

"Are you working for the Gestapo?"

"That is not your business."

Shaw took out the silencer, screwed it to the barrel and asked him again.

"Are you with the German Secret Service?"

"Why should I tell you?"

"Because you have to. Your life is at stake."

"You are just bluffing."

Shaw shot him in his stomach, and then said, "I don't like traitors. I was not bluffing."

"You'll pay for this when the Germans find out that you killed me. If you take me to the hospital you'll have a chance to live."

Shaw shot him again in his head and drove him to the pier where he set the car on fire with gasoline and drove it over the pier. Parker saw the fire and the explosion and drove the other guy's car closer to the pier to pick up Shaw.

"What do you want to do with him?"

"He cannot be released, the Gestapo will question him."

"The Resistance must take care of him and his family. They must leave the country.

I will call Tibault to take care of the transport. You watch him until I come back," said Parker.

Parker called the rescuer.

"Hello, this Parker."

"What can I do for you?"

"Nothing over the phone, but we would appreciate it if you could meet me and Shaw as soon as possible."

"But I have a commitment tonight."

"This is a great emergency."

"All right. I will meet you, just tell me where."

Parker told him the location and asked him to hurry up.

Tibault arrived twenty minutes later and started to ask questions.

"I will smuggle him out with his family, but it'll cost a lot of francs."

"We are not interested in the cost, we want to smuggle them out of France," said Shaw.

"I need the money in advance."

"Why don't you take care of him and his family while I'm getting money from Marceau? We'll meet in an hour at the railroad station. We'll dump his car later," said Shaw.

"We have to stop for picture taking, identity and travel papers at my place," said Tibault.

"I'll give you two hours before we meet. How much money do you want?"

"Marceau knows my smuggle fees."

Shaw went to Marceau and secured the money for the trip. Tibault asked for two Resistance operatives to assist him. The Frenchman was handcuffed during the entire trip. In Spain, he and his family was given to another operative and kept under the protection of the French Resistance in exile.

Shaw and Parker drove the two cars to Marceau's. They informed him about the whole episode. Bridget called the Maquis to take the Frenchman's car.

It was around two in the morning when Marceau, Shaw, and Parker resumed their talk.

In essence, there was little Shaw and Parker were able to do but change the locations for the meetings. Should the Gestapo post twenty-four hour surveillance at Marceau's place, he could manage to escape without anybody knowing where and how. When he built the secret room, he also made a single pass tunnel to another building that was purchased by the MI6. The building is occupied by retired people of the MI6 who speak fluent French and have permits to live in the area as senior citizens. Some still work in the post office and others in the local hospital as aides.

Shaw made the suggestion to use the car and go somewhere or discuss issues right in the car. If there is an emergency, Shaw and Parker can always call someone in the MI6 building who can deliver the message in the morning. Should the Gestapo or their henchmen follow Shaw and Parker while Marceau is with them that could complicate matters, but Shaw and Parker have been trained for this type of confrontation.

"I think we have managed pretty well up to now, and these kinds of irritations are expected to happen. So we have little ups and downs for the time being, but it will not last long because the invasion is in the air. I certainly can smell it," said Marceau.

"We are getting to the second phase of our mission, which we call 'confrontation'," responded Shaw.

"You may call it as you wish, but it will be bloody. The Germans feel the pressure and they know the Allies are coming. This is their last hurrah! I must go to sleep now. Adieu my friends and Viva la France!" said Marceau.

"Have a good night and sweet dreams. Bye." said Parker.

Shaw and Parker drove home exhausted but reasonably satisfied with their accomplishments. As they checked their mail, they found another Gestapo invitation for the coming Saturday in Caen. The Head of the Paris Gestapo waned to express his gratitude again for saving the life of their comrade.

"Another dinner, smile, and boredom," said Parker.

"Don't be so sure. There may be something more this time. They are very shrewd.

The top is educated and smart, but we have to play the game to the end. We know how because we are better educated and trained. So, don't you worry, we'll outsmart them," responded Shaw. Both went to bed in the early morning hours.

They slept till eleven, had brunch at noon, and hit the road at one in the afternoon.

The cells for some reason turned out to be quite productive. The Germans worked feverishly to complete their defenses, but not everywhere. To find out the weak points in the defense was crucially important for landing the waves of small crafts. The beachhead had to be established during the first day before the

German reinforcements could arrive. Shaw and Parker received good information despite the increased security, but everything had a price. The contributors were taken into custody by the Gestapo and cell members had to disappear before they could be arrested. Each time a cell mate did not show up it became evident that somebody was interrogated and punished. Cell members were supplied with false identity papers, transport money, and names of safe places in Paris and in the south of France.

Shaw and Parker spent the week with new cell members and very little on OT construction. In every cell, one or two members resigned because of illness, assignment problems, safety failures that would have jeopardized others in the cells or they were just burned out. In addition, there was fear among the cell members because of the Gestapo's increased scare of arrests. Although the arrests had a short lived lull, the Gestapo surveillance continued. The scare among the Resistance operatives was intense. Their methods of interrogation by torture and cruelty were well known in the Resistance. The Gestapo knew that losing the war meant payback. Their fear, however, was ominous. The fear of invasion made them paranoid and their job was to stop the leaks of information from France to UK by all means and measures. They were like wounded animals. Retreat in the Eastern, African, and Italian fronts, daily poundings of bombs in Germany, constant explosions by sabotage in France made them mad and dangerous. The Gestapo had an absolute fanaticism to win the war by all means.

"I think we are getting a good picture where the invasion should take place in terms of batteries and pillboxes," said Shaw sitting in their car and looking at the Channel.

"I tend to agree with you, but there are geographical strong points that the Allies must master and it could be very costly.

Some areas are devastatingly steep to climb and the Germans could practically obliterate the climbers, platoon by platoon," responded Parker.

"But, we have the Royal Air Force, United States Air Force, and Navy big guns that could decimate those pillboxes before the climbers start taking the cliffs."

"Yes, the word could does not mean that they can or will execute their task on demand. We have to give a better picture of those hills and cliffs. We have to know where the hidden machine guns are located, the number and kind of other portable guns, where mortars and rocket propelled grenades are stored, and the number of soldiers occupying those hills before our boys leave their boats," replied Parker.

"I agree with you. We did not get information concerning those areas because they lack big construction sites and provided very few sources for our cells to obtain information."

"Then we have to do it! It is a must because our boys will bleed to death there," said Parker.

"OK, we'll start today," suggested Shaw.

The cell in Caen had two carpenters and a nurse from the local hospital. Although she was relatively new, only three months in the Resistance, she was able to supply considerable information. Colleen replaced a veteran plumber who was ill with cancer. The other two were carpenters and worked in a German Headquarters remodeling project.

Shaw and Parker met them in an empty store. They stayed in the front pretending to work on the moldings and the nurse was cleaning the walls while Shaw and Parker stayed in the back room.

"We have little time to wrap-up our work. The first report was an excellent summation of the overall German defenses, but we need more details. Should paratroopers land in the

Canal and Orne Bridge vicinity, they must know what they are up against in terms of panzer units, infantry, pill boxes, hidden machine guns, antiaircraft guns, mortar stations, medium and heavy guns. We need this information very soon," said Shaw.

One of the carpenters, Rafael, looked in Shaw's direction, and in a sad voice replied, "It is very difficult these days to obtain information, lest in a short time with the existing German military security. However, there is a possibility. We are scheduled to do some work in one of the General's homes next week who is undergoing colon surgery. If he could stay a little longer in the hospital we could perhaps dig out a map. That means giving him less painkillers."

"Splendid opportunity," commented Shaw.

"But, be careful. There are French nurses and doctors who are moles who work for the Gestapo. You cannot trust anybody who is present while you are injecting the painkillers. You must plan ahead and if there is the slightest danger, don't do it. We have no room for error in the last stages of information gathering," said Parker.

"We are careful. When it comes to safety, I will not risk our cell to be exposed to the Gestapo. Those creeps would torture me to death until I confess something. No, I would rather lack information than suffer," said the nurse.

"Is there anything else that we did not cover?" asked Shaw.

"There is," said the nurse. "We have some access to obtain vital information through home visits. One of my colleagues and I visited an officer's home who had major surgery. There were secret maps of batteries spread all over the floor. She asked me to bring one map closer to his bed. I was astonished to see all the markings of gun emplacements."

"So what was your response?" asked Shaw.

"I kept quiet. But I looked her in the eyes and searched for some answers."

"It was a smart move. You have to be careful. These moles love to test your curiosity," said Shaw.

"Anything else?" asked Parker.

"Yes. I meant to ask you about the underground tunnels," said the second carpenter.

"We were called out to check some structural problems last week in one of the batteries. I had seen some structural problems in the past, so we figured it had to do with German engineering. There were some structural failures, but we could only go down to a certain point. Then we had to stop our investigation. The officer offered his assistance and went into the super secret area to find water leak. He returned and said that he found the leak, but we couldn't repair it. He would have to have German engineering specialists with plumbing background to fix the problem."

"Thank you for telling us this important observation. We can certainly use some more information about the battery. See you next week. Should something happen to anyone in the cell, don't try to contact us directly. If we don't hear from you, it means that something bad happened. But, we hope nothing will happen. Remember, all information should be posted in the drop box. Always look around before you place anything there. One watches, another drives in circles, and the third one makes the drop. The Gestapo has paid informants and the idea is to confuse them. The best time to place a drop is between 0200 and 0300."

"When you see a car in the distance with an occupant, don't do it. Rainy nights are better. Try to enjoy life, au revoir," said Shaw.

"Be brave, but exercise extra caution. Bye," added Parker.

Both Shaw and Parker worried about these three. They had been good suppliers of information. Their new data was urgent and strategically extremely vital. There was nothing, however, that the two allied agents could do, but wait. The secret tunnels and the hidden water supply suggested that the German engineering prepared the promised secret weapon, the unmanned rocket. In addition, they had logistical limitations that prevented them from looking into every significant report. Patience became an important virtue.

Michael rushed to Bridget to warn her about the impending invasion, anxiety among the German military and unprecedented security precautions. He did not stay too long, but promised to see her during the upcoming weekend. He left a very important package of documents in her trust which he needed to return as soon as she could microfilm it. He kissed her and left with a pair of boots in his hand as a decoy to justify his visit.

When Marceau and Bridget had a chance to look at the documents, they were dumbfounded. They were military defense preparation maps including Orne Bridge region. Marceau studied the maps and made copies of them. Bridget was happy and asked Marceau to allow her to see Shaw and Parker and give them a copy.

"I think you better take a copy to them so they have an insight concerning the German strategic preparations."

Having copied the maps, she was ready to go. "I am going Marceau. Take care, and be sure you are going to bed early. Tomorrow, you are having a rendezvous with the crabs and I hope you'll catch some for dinner."

She drove fast and detoured to watch for any car, truck, or motorcycle following her. She was ready to turn around, drive back home, or play a cat and mouse game. The maps were well hidden in the passenger floor, sandwiched between two panels. Bridget was well trained in courier service and knew how to avoid trouble. In the worst case scenario, she was ready to face her enemy. Bridget always had a gun in her glove box with five extra clips of ammunition. Fortunately, there was little traffic and she arrived to their apartments without any complications. However, they had not come home yet and she had to wait, which reluctantly she did for twenty-five minutes. She did not park or leave the car, but circled the various streets in the neighborhood. In her last circle, she recognized their car. She parked her car, placed the maps in her bra and ran upstairs with the gun in her purse. She knocked in a trice, followed by two knocks and one knock afterwards.

"Give me your name," asked Shaw.

"You know my name."

"Yes, I do now."

"What brings you here so late at night?"

"I am desperate for a hug, kiss, and some kind words."

"You must be kidding."

Parker embraced her, kissed her, and told her that she was the sweetest gal in France.

She looked at both of them and said thank you. There was a moment of silence and then Bridget undid a couple of buttons on her blouse, loosened her bra, and took out the maps that she had hidden there.

"These are the defense preparations in the Caen area including the bridges."

Parker looked at the maps and was totally fascinated. "Where did you get these?" asked Shaw.

"Michael gave them to me this afternoon."

"This is absolutely fantastic. We asked our cell to rush and provide something similar and you have it this evening, it is unbelievable," said Shaw

"Marceau is going to carry the maps on microfilm with him and stuff them into the baits tomorrow."

"Good deed, they will be elated. General Montgomery is going to open a bottle of champagne," said Shaw.

"All we need is a little luck, a few more maps, and we can prepare the soldiers for the landing," commented Parker.

"Security is so tight that we can prepare for casualties," said Bridget.

"We are aware of the possible casualties, but the job must be done. My dear Bridget, we are with you in mind and spirit. But you must be tough, wipe your tears, and continue to fight. Think that even when we are losing those brave men and women, we are winning. We are preparing a better life for the future, for those who want to live in a democratic free society. Each person's sacrifice is another's gain of life. You cannot get bogged down and feel sorry for yourself or others. I know it hurts to see a relative, friend, or compatriot fall, but it hurts even more to live in bondage," commented Parker.

The time had arrived to dress up again for another the recognition dinner. Shaw and Parker had to play the role to the very end, but the end did not seem to be in sight. They had forcibly managed to put on their freshly starched shirts, silk black ties, and swastika arm bands. They looked sharp and classy. With all the fanfare, the banquet hall had an ominous aura which did not matter at to all to the Gestapo agents a few military officers and generals inside. But it certainly elevated the trepidation already felt by Shaw and Parker.

The main speech was delivered by the Paris Gestapo Chief with thundering emphasis on security, patriotism, sacrifice, and the German's final victory. He was interrupted several times by standing ovations. The strength of the applause completely covered the sounds of his last words and he had to wait until the room became quiet before he started his next sentence. Shaw and Parker were sick to their stomachs listening to the achievements of the Gestapo in France. He talked about the number of arrests, methods of interrogations that produced the most remarkable confessions and information. He was proud to stop the enemies of Germany by all means as it was necessary. At the end of his speech he asked Shaw and Parker to come to the head table, and as he was flanked by them, he lifted his glass of wine and paid tribute to their heroic actions. He praised them for fifteen minutes and offered two special Letters of Recognition from the Gestapo High Command in Germany.

After dinner the Gestapo Chief had a little chat with both of them and then the Normandy Gestapo Chief took over the conversation. He picked a table in the back of the room. He invited them to join him for a bottle of wine, cheese, and crackers.

"You must be very proud of yourselves?" asked the Chief.

"I did not know that we have to pride ourselves by saving the lives of two human beings," replied Shaw.

"Oh, you are very modest. A Gestapo agent is not just an ordinary human being, but an officer of the German Security Service."

"Both of you are special people. Your German is extraordinary, you are well educated and certainly the best in your specialties. We hear nothing but the best about you. The carpenters, masons, foremen, and engineers speak highly of you. You are well liked in all circles and men like you could be a great asset for the Gestapo," commented the Chief.

"We are very people oriented, but our profession comes first. We are overseeing every construction, and as you know, our mission is to build the best defense structures, so we can repel the enemy. We cannot mix our profession with politics. We have to deal with all kinds of people and they must feel trusted to perform their best. If they sense that we are watching them, they'll become suspicious, fearful and paranoid. If that happens they can make mistakes, and there is no room for error if we want to win the war," responded Parker.

"What you are saying is a very interesting concept and I find it quite logical. You have convinced me about your mission and I can respect that. Let me show you how we are contributing to the war and defending the Reich."

The chief got up and asked them to follow him to various places in the building.

They stopped at the staircase and he put his key in the lock of a large door that opened to the file room.

"This is where our defense structure begins. Each office deals with either suspected or convicted agents of the enemy. We have all kinds. Spies, commandos, saboteurs, Resistance operatives, Jewish nationals, forced laborers, foreign nationals, homosexuals, lesbians, and just plain insurgents. In some rare cases we have files on our own nationals. Some of these people are government officials, secretaries, diplomatic representatives and military personnel. We have files also on French government officials and their personnel, foreign nationals and diplomats.

"As you can see, we have a very elaborate and comprehensive documentation on those who don't like us. Nobody, but the Fuhrer, is above us. We have the power to arrest German Generals, French officials and foreign diplomats. We are the security system of Germany."

"You may ask questions as we go on, but I am not sure that I can or will answer them."

"This door opens to special offices that have double doors and the walls. All these offices are sound proof. It is impossible to hear any sound coming through those walls. We call them the interrogation rooms. We start with the subject in a simply furnished room. It consists of a table and three chairs. If he is cooperative, we end there. If he is not, we put him in a cell and wake him up in every ninety minutes. If this does not work, we take him next door."

The Chief unlocked every door and led them to the infamous rooms. Shaw and Parker watched carefully and noticed every detail. They had no visible emotional reaction, which were inculcated in their training, but their inner feelings were of repulsiveness and hostility.

"This room is set up for forced confessions," continued the Chief. "We don't like to do it, but we have to know who the real culprit is. The subject is asked to undress completely and he is told what could happen if he keeps silent. All instruments are visible and shown to the subject. As you see the floor is cemented and has five drain holes to let the fluid down."

"How do you start the physical interrogation?" asked Parker.

"We usually begin by beating the subject. Then we put him in the tub and hose him with hot and cold water. Then we hang him upside down and attach electrodes to his penis or her vagina. If this does not work, we let him hang, without water and heat up the room to hundred-twenty-five degrees. Two hours later we hose him down with cold water. At this point, we make an assessment and wait for a day. He is put into solitary confinement, naked, without food, and very little water. We wake him up every hour. Sometimes, we deal with a very stubborn subject and other methods are being applied."

"What other methods do you use to break the subject?" asked Shaw.

"We have a metal helmet with several turning restrictors. Each turn will cause pain on the skull until it becomes unbearable. Another method is removing finger and toe nails.

Sometimes electric charges mixed with other methods produce confessions. Chemical irritants or sodium pentothal injections can be quite effective. Each person has a breaking point and we are careful not to make the subject unconscious, but suffer long enough to talk. In my experience, all subjects confess at the end of interrogation given the proper method."

"What do you do with them after the confession?" asked Parker.

"It depends on the seriousness of the offense. Most of them are sent to a specific concentration or work camps. Others are executed by hanging. We Germans demand unconditional order. It is our job to enforce internal security whether it is in Germany or a foreign land. We rule by decree."

"The upper floors are for agents of the Gestapo. Radio and telegraph rooms are on the second floor. We have a projection room on the third floor. Each floor has a lavatory for men and women. The basement has holding cells. Which rooms are you interested in?"

"I think we better go home because we must supervise some projects tomorrow. But we want to thank you for your kind hospitality and the grand tour. By the way, what are your plans for after the war?" asked Shaw.

"That's an interesting question I never thought of that. I'll probably stay with the government and teach the young folk how to secure the fatherland."

"Goodbye and thank you again," said Parker.

"How do you feel? You look pale," said Shaw as they left the building and walked to their car.

"I'm sick to my stomach. I wonder how much he know about us and what was behind the showing of the Gestapo building. These guys are not stupid. They know how to instill fear into the mind. It can't be much otherwise we wouldn't be driving home. We are so close to the completion of our work, they will not deter us. Still I am worried about Marceau and my cell members, not to mention Michael who saved us a lot of headaches," replied Parker.

"You would make a good actor, because your face looked normal and your cheeks were rosy. As soon we left the building you turned snow white."

"I had a good trainer in the OSS. I was thinking of a good lay with a terrific gal all the time, which made me flush my cheeks. Why don't you pull over to the right, stop at the bar, and let's have a drink."

"If that is what you want, it's fine with me."

Shaw parked the car and they walked toward the bar when a series of explosions, one after another, ripped buildings apart. Shaw went into the bar first followed by Parker and both ordered fine scotch whiskey. The barmaid had none, but offered French brandy. She looked frightened from a nearby blast. Parker reassured her that it was an accident, probably ammunition storage blew up.

She smiled at him and asked, "How do you know these things?"

"I smell it in the air," said Parker.

"Do you want another drink?" asked the barmaid.

"How did you know?" asked Parker.

"It's written on your lips, besides your eyes are talking. Plus, we are closing in fifteen minutes."

"You have another place to recommend," asked Parker.

"You want to come up to my place? I mean to drink?"

"How about having companionship?"

"You don't want my companionship, you want something else?"

"How do you know? You hardly know me. You are a very attractive blonde with blue eyes, a fantastic smile, gorgeous figure, and sound mind, but you're an interesting person. I would like to talk to you. I'm sure you're mentally very stimulating," continued Parker.

"This is all very nice, but it won't take me to bed."

"Well, that is too bad. OK, let's go home then." Parker put money on the bar and started to walk out when she grabbed his arm, and asked "What are you going to do with your friend?"

"I'll take him home and come back."

"Are you sure?"

"Shall I come back here or to your place?"

"How long will it take you?"

"About an hour or you can come with us and then you don't have to wait. Just follow our car. We have our own apartments," said Parker.

"If I come with you and bring a bottle of cognac will you bring me back tomorrow?"

"Of course, I'll bring you back. That's my girl, don't forget the cognac. I like you because you know how to live!"

The three of them had a happy hour in the car, singing, cracking jokes, and talking about the future after the war. They went to Shaw's place first and had some snacks and drinks.

"Where are you from?" she asked Shaw.

"You guess, and I will say yes or no."

"I say that you are from the UK and he is from the US."

"And how did you figure that out?" asked Parker.

"I watched your manners in public at the bar and in semi private while riding in your car. You dropped your masks fast and acted quite differently. You're o.k. when you want to be. Women can have an affect on you Parker and you fell for my sensuous behavior. We graduated from the same OSS school and I distinctly remember, our teacher, Dr. Peterson emphasized to watch out for changes in our mannerism."

"I am Brian Parker and he is Matt Shaw from MI6. May we know what you are doing here," asked Parker.

"I am Genevieve, and I'm trying to find a suitable terrain for the first wave parachute drop. We have serious topographical problems because the Germans are flooding the possible drop zones."

"Can we help you find the proper drop location or direct you where to look for possible sites," asked Shaw.

"I would appreciate that. I have great trouble with the German security and you certainly get around much better with your uniforms than I do. However, you have other business to attend to and I certainly don't want to interfere with your schedule."

"Are you disappointed in me Brian? You seem to avoid looking at me."

"You were a nice illusion, a wonderful French dream. I don't know what to say at this point," said Parker.

"Say nothing. Just enjoy our acquaintance. It is getting late. May I find respite in your place, Brian?"

"By all means. I was about to ask you if you want to retire, my dear."

The two of them went to Brian's apartment.

"I'm sorry if I put a damper on your impromptu sexual adventure. Can I make it up?"

"Things did not change. You are still a knock-out."

"So what changed the tiger?"

"We are now under different circumstances. I don't know if I should fraternize without possible repercussions. I did not have anything serious in mind but a one night stand. I don't want you to resent me. I had to be blunt and tell the truth."

"You know something, Brian? I like you more now the way you are. I can't think of the tomorrow in these turbulent times. What is given today, I'll make the best of it.

Right now, time is moments, and this is one. I can't think of fraternizing when we are facing death."

She looked deep into his eyes and Brian reciprocated the look. He inched closer to her and both felt the passion to embrace each other.

"Let's stop now. I want to talk to you. You are more than a sex kitten. What my experience and the OSS education are telling me is that you are a very smart and intelligent person."

"You got it, Brian, but not completely. I am very passionate. You missed that!"

She moved her head back and he caressed her hair and very slowly both lips touched each other in a wide open kiss that lasted several minutes.

"Genevieve, I like you a lot and I respect you. Do you mind if we just have an intellectual discourse? I don't want to make you feel cheap; I don't want a one night stand. Our lives are so uncertain and you and I are going in so many directions that it would be much better to leave everything to fate."

"Are you saying that you don't want to feel me despite the fact that our chemistry is telling us otherwise?"

"My darling, I don't want flesh to meet flesh without having a relationship."

"O.K., what do you want to talk about?"

"I want to know everything about you."

"You know I cannot reveal information about myself, my home, and my friends."

"I will limit my questions. What did you do before you joined the OSS?"

"I was a medical doctor. I have an MD in cardiology. How about you? What was your profession before?"

"I was an engineer. My degrees are in Civil and Mechanical Engineering."

"What made you decide to join the OSS?"

"I wanted to serve my country. I thought that I had something to offer. I thought my medical background, being fluent in German and French, reasonably athletic, adventurous in spirit, and being people oriented would be valuable."

Genevieve looked at him and her body language, her posture and eyes told him that it was his turn.

"I was very much like you. A different profession but for very similar reasons I chose to join the OSS."

Tear drops were falling from Genevieve's eyes and Parker touched her hand, embraced her, and kept her in his arms for a few minutes.

"What's the matter?"

She answered with silence and a passionate look.

"Maybe we can dream about what could have physically happened between us," said Parker in a soft voice.

"Good idea. We can talk about it in the morning, said Genevieve.

"I am going to bed. Now about you?" asked Parker.

"I am going to do the same. Do you snore, turn a lot, or are you a restless sleeper?" asked Genevieve."

"Is this a medical question?" asked Parker.

"No, but I don't remember when I last slept in the same bed with a stranger," said Genevieve.

"You will enjoy me as a partner in bed, but only to sleep." remarked Parker.

"You like to tease me, don't you?"

"I want you to think of me as a gentleman."

Both laid down in the same bed and turned toward each other. She faced him with seductive eyes and he reciprocated the look.

"Brian, you should have a degree in 'how to break hearts.' We should be partners. As a cardiologist we would have a booming business."

Parker gave her a passionate kiss and she did not let him go.

"Your French kissing is absolutely divine," said Genevieve.

"Yours is just the same, but darling we really must stop. We would end up in an affair and I don't want that to happen. Good night sweetheart."

"Good night, Brian, 'the heartbreak kid.' "

It was eight o'clock when Shaw knocked on the door. Parker partly opened the door and said, "She is still sleeping."

"I'll see you in an hour. Please make some breakfast for us, Agent Shaw."

"Who was that, and what's happening? I'm somewhat disoriented. What happened to me? I must have had too much to drink. You were a gentleman that I remember. You did not take advantage of my good nature. Are you engaged, married, or what? I never had a man like you! You're smart, educated, and kind."

"Thank you, you're very kind. I have a girlfriend back at home. But, I have not heard from her in several months. I heard, though, that she has a toy boy, but who knows. I have been away for sometime, and honestly, I am not faithful and

I can't expect her to be. But, as far as she is concerned, this is only my assumption."

Both entered Shaw's apartment. He was still preparing the food and asked them to wait a few minutes until he was ready.

"I do not love easily. A man has to earn my love. I am a tough cookie," said Genevieve.

"What does love mean to you?"

"I don't know. I have never been in love. Perhaps you could tell me?"

"What you're willing to give up for it."

"Not bad. I like that."

"Who introduced you to the birds and the bees?"

"I had a mature divorced woman who was the most experienced lover in my younger years. She taught me everything. I was with her two days at a time, because she had an unbelievable manipulating hand and mouth that totally captivated my sexual feelings. She had the most wide lipped juicy mouth I ever had."

"So what happened?"

"She got married to a wealthy man and we had to break it off."

"Did you love her?"

"I don't think so. She was forty and I was a freshman in college. I had what she wanted and I was happy with her, but our futures headed into different directions."

There was little time left for more chatting. The breakfast was ready and they had to eat fast because Shaw and Parker had an appointment with cell members six and they had to drive Genevieve back home. There was an agreement between the two of them to meet again next week.

Parker accompanied her to the apartment. She went through the mail and found a letter from a girlfriend who works for MI6. She was in trouble with the Gestapo and asked her to come urgently to Paris to help her out. Parker offered his help, but she knew how to handle the situation. Consequently, their meeting had to be postponed for two weeks. Parker and Genevieve had a long embrace and kiss. Then with tears in her eyes she said, "Thank you. I had a lovely time. Please call me. Don't forget!"

"I'll try not to. God speed!"

Shaw and Parker went to talk with cell members six which was strategically a very important meeting. Marceau suddenly became busy with his new customers who were mostly German generals and officers. The Gestapo left him alone for the time being. Bridget was planning to go to Paris for the weekend to enjoy a cabaret, concert, night club, and restaurants with Michael.

Life became different for a number of people. It was like the calm before the storm. There was too much pressure in Normandy. The impending invasion rattled too many nerves and people needed some rest to collect their strength and refresh their minds. Bridget had to get out of Normandy to escape the inevitable repression and listening to the daily bad news of arrests and executions. These things were happening in other places, but Normandy was unique because of the German military investments in the Atlantic Wall. They did not know where the Allies would land and that drove them crazy. The time had come for Shaw and Parker to devote all their energies to the demands of Allied Intelligence and produce the necessary details for each invasion site.

One of the cell members in cell six was absolutely jubilant. He was working as an electrician in the nearby battery and witnessed that two casemates had problems with their guns that faced the sea. Those guns were captured in the eastern front and sometimes the firing mechanism failed to function. Other times the ammunition was the wrong caliber. The width of the casemate did not allow the guns to rotate in the prescribed manner so the openings had to be reengineered to meet the firing directions. The test firings were disheartening to the generals.

There were additional antitank obstacles built from concrete and steel that was recorded by the woman operative. She was hired as a nurse and had the opportunity to observe how the force laborers poured the concrete into the forms. She was called out to the field because a soldier was hurt in the cement mixing process.

Shaw and Parker were satisfied with the information received especially because there were no complications in obtaining the data.

"We are happy to learn all this information, but sad at how much our forces have to cope with to demolish these concrete beach obstacles to advance the beachhead," said Shaw.

"We are in on a new discovery," said the male operative.

"What kind of discovery?" asked Parker.

"We are hearing things that is hard to believe."

"What kind of things?" questioned Shaw.

"Hitler's super bomb," said the nurse operative.

"Could you find out more detail about the bomb? asked Parker.

"I'll try. What I heard so far was fragments. That it will destroy a lot of people and structures," said the operative.

"Thank you, see you next week," said Parker.

Shaw and Parker decided to visit one of the casemates under construction. They were specifically interested in the steel-cement construction. The 1: 2: 3 ratios of cement, gravel, and sand was the ideal concrete pouring. Added water plays an important role to insure satisfactory chemical processes, which creates heat, and eventually leads to extremely hard concrete. The concrete is poured over the steel mesh and is slowly cured to form a bunker wall that is virtually indestructible. The Germans perfected battery building and became extremely conceded over the Organization Todt production methods.

It was Shaw's and Parker's intention to buck the system but that was not their directed objective. They knew that, but couldn't help wanting to see the system fail. The cement was delivered from French sources. The quality of German cement was better but because of the Allied bombing it became undeliverable in full loads.

In visiting one of the casemates, Shaw complained about the cracks and durability of the casemate.

"I don't understand why on earth these engineers allowed continuing the construction when they saw basic errors in building these casemates," said one of the German officers.

"This is something I don't want to get into in great detail. I assume the orders had to be completed in a certain time. The drying process must have been compromised. Also the cement quality had to be tested before mixing with gravel and sand," said Shaw.

"Thank you for your inspection. We could certainly use your talent to make the casemates stronger."

"We don't want to interfere with the improvement of these casemates which are highly specialized engineering projects. But we can make our recommendations upon request," said Parker.

Shaw and Parker returned to Marceau's to report some of the findings and discuss future operations.

"Well hello, my comrades! What good news are you bringing to this blessed house?"

"We'll tell you if you first introduce us to this beautiful lady," said Parker.

"I intended to do that, but you did not give me a chance. She is a good friend of Bridget's. She is a tough Resistance fighter. She wants to be called Renee. She is very young, only nineteen years old. Renee is studying modeling and cinema photography. She is beautiful because first, her parents are good looking people. Her mother is on the front pages of several beauty magazines, and her father is a successful stage and movie actor. Second, she does not use any cosmetics. Third, she does not allow herself to be stressed. She tries to avoid stressful situations. Even as a Resistance operative, she works alone, and does not share or communicate her assignment. She is terribly secretive. God Bless her. She is one of the most productive operatives."

"Well, hello. We shall remain anonymous to you. You can call me or my partner any name you want," said Parker.

"I really like that. You're in incognito? It is a wonderful idea," said Renee.

"Since we cannot talk about what contributions you're making to the Resistance, we would love to hear about your experiences as a cinema photographer," continued Parker.

"If I tell you, will you get mad?"

"You go ahead, please tell us," asked Shaw.

"I photograph German generals. Selectively, as they wish, I make portraits of the photography."

"Is it in their privacy?" questioned Parker.

"Of course, it is done in absolute privacy."

"Do they like what they see?" asked Shaw.

"They love it! They pay me quite well."

"Are they decent to you? Do they propose sex?" asked Parker.

"This is where I become discreet."

"We understand, but we must congratulate you for your work and achievement," said Parker.

"Marceau, your recruiting technique and selection of the candidates is absolutely fantastic," said Parker.

"I am glad you like it. For your information, many candidates come to me for a job and it takes several weeks before I hire them. They must come with high recommendations. They are checked and rechecked. As you know, I am a fanatic about security. There are no moles in my personnel garden."

"We came to see you about what we have learned from cell six. Also, we would like to talk about cement deliveries to the batteries," said Shaw.

"I'll be with you guys in a few minutes."

Bridget came in and took Renee by the hand and directed her to the customers waiting and fitting room for a long chat, pastries and tea. They talked about her vocational aspirations after the war, romance, and various aspects of life. They had a nice time together and Bridget was impressed by her mature and philosophical answers.

"She'll be here for a long time, so we'll not say adieu, until you finish your business with Marceau and then you'll join us for a little snack," said Bridget.

The three of them went to the living room and Shaw presented the findings. Later,

Parker talked about the cement issue.

"I am very glad about all the information but not so happy about the cement barricades. The commandos have to blast them before the tanks come in. We have had problems with the cement. When it is manufactured, we have operatives in the plant trying to alter the mixture but the security is tremendous and they can't do anything. They are watching them like hawks. There are hidden agents all over the plant. Some are native French turncoats and others are paid agents. The management has its own security people all over. The Gestapo told the management that if the plant sabotages the cement production, meaning produces inferior quality, the Gestapo will make the management responsible and they will pay the price as traitors, which means death."

"The only way to diminish the quality of the cement is exchanging the bags by the Maquis. This is sabotage. They can do it. The problem is where to manufacture inferior cement. The other issue is delivery at the point of exchange. We had this discussion before with the Maquis. We may succeed or may not. It is a risky business. The penalty is death for those who get caught. Even if we succeed, should the Gestapo smell dirty business, they will order a quality check before the water is added."

"Your recommendation?" asked Parker.

"Stay with your assignment and report to me all the cracks in the cement."

All three joined Renee and Bridget and they had a wonderful afternoon. Parker was flirting with Renee. Parker liked to tease Renee and she liked to reciprocate. Marceau was telling love stories from the past. Shaw and Bridget told funny jokes. They had such a good time that they all stayed for a cold beer and had cold cuts for dinner.

CHAPTER SEVEN

Marceau usually had an early morning stroll to enjoy the fresh cool spring air and the seagulls landing on the cobblestone streets. He needed the walk for his circulation and metabolism. Occasionally, he stopped to take a sip of coffee from his mug, but more importantly, he wanted to check using the store windows to see who was following him by foot or car.

When he found the streets safe enough to join Shaw and Parker, Marceau turned toward the designated street where their car was parked. The three of them took a ride and found serenity in the countryside.

Shaw parked the car off the road in an area surrounded by growing hay. Marceau began to talk about the latest messages from Allied Intelligence and about the possible Gestapo naval surveillance that could vent him from continuing his work.

"In the last message, Allied Intelligence requested information regarding the latest beach and water obstacles, including mines and overhead pill boxes between Quineville in the Cotentin region and Trouville in the Le Havre area. It was marked urgent. Apparently they are trying to finalize all incoming reports from the commandos, air reconnaissance, Resistance, and your cell's observations. In my estimation, the invasion will be between Quineville and Trouville, give or take a few miles in both directions. Of course, we have to deceive the Germans that the invasion will be at Pas-de-Calais and North from there up to Norway."

"If and when my privilege of crab fishing is revoked, I must find an alternate route to send the messages. Radio could be a viable possibility, but not from my house. The German radio direction finders are very good and in no time I'll be arrested. I must change the location every time I'll send a message. Of course, it will never be as good as a picture, map, or written document, but we have to deal with what we have. We are also slowly winding down our operation and will only concentrate on extremely vital and urgent messages. Well, in a nutshell, these are some of the important facts that I needed to tell you."

"Our situation is getting more and more difficult as the Germans sense the inevitability of the invasion and the battle of Western Europe. The German Military have become very alert concerning the leaks about the Atlantic Wall, which they had hoped to keep it a secret and surprise."

"It was the German General's dream to throw the Allied forces back into the sea and beat them so badly that it would be many years before they would attack again. Of course, in the meantime, they would develop their secret weapons and hit the UK and US with missiles that would torch the continents," continued Marceau.

"That could happen if we don't finish them off in time," said Parker.

"We have, however, quite a bit of work ahead to complete the Allied Intelligence request, and we must replace the operatives who left us," commented Shaw.

"This is another problem, and I am glad that you brought it up. We are having a difficult time when it comes to replacing cell members. We must be sure that the person is trustworthy and capable to carry out the assignments. With all the arrests and threats, I have had a hard time to recruit operatives. As you know we have lost quite a number of leaders and operatives among the Resistance. You kill a Gestapo agent and the whole village will be massacred. Their retaliation is absolutely brutal. You may have to work with two operatives until I find the third person. I will not compromise quality with quantity."

"That is fine. We'll be able to manage. In some cases, when it is necessary, one of us may have to substitute," replied Shaw.

"I wanted to send Bridget to England, but she would not go. She wants to take care of me and Michael who is very dear to her. He is risking his life by supplying vital information to the Allies. War is a terrible thing, but my hope is that good prevails over evil," said Marceau.

"The good will win, Marceau. That's what we're fighting for," said Parker.

"We must go," said Shaw.

They left to meet with cell number six. Only two women showed up in a dilapidated apartment house. One had considerable difficulty collecting information because the German officer who befriended her two weeks ago was transferred to southern France and took all the valuable maps with him. What she saw and remembered was rather sketchy, but she was able to give some outline of the overall water obstructions, but nothing about the beaches. She had made, however, some sketches which did not mean too much for her.

The other woman had some interesting information about the shortage of medical supplies. They lacked morphine, bandages, and IV bottles for the seriously wounded.

"That is not very surprising given all the problems of transportation and supplies from occupied territories and Germany. Thank you. But, can you find out about the beach defenses?" asked Parker.

"I don't know. He left no specific address other than the military HQ in Nice. The guy is crazy for me and I hope he will call tonight asking me to come visit him," said the first woman.

"What happened to the third operative?" questioned Shaw.

"We don't personally know the other guy, but one of my Resistance friends told me that he is in big trouble with the Gestapo and he is hiding. He probably left a message in the drop box," said the other girl.

"If you leave for Nice, please leave a message in the drop box. How long do you plan to stay?" asked Shaw.

"Not longer than it is necessary."

"What do you mean?" asked Parker.

"He is sexually addicted to me and he must get a 'shot' to calm himself down. I will probably stay a couple of days."

Parker and Shaw were laughing. Parker had to comment, "I understand. I'm very empathetic. Concerning the other operative, we will try to rescue him. Thanks for telling us," said Parker.

"While working in the nearby pharmacy," said the nurse, "I had the privilege to deliver medication and a condom to a General who was taking a bath. He asked me if I could massage his shoulder that he claimed was aching and he would generously reimburse me for my effort and time. As I was massaging him he gave a sigh and fell asleep. Since he left his bathroom door ajar, I tiptoed out of the bathroom and started to look around. He could not see me because he was asleep.

"I looked around and found two folders on the table that I quickly glanced through and found that one of them contained the military mapping of the Port-En-Bessin area, approximately seven kilometers to the northern and southern direction. I returned to the bathroom just to be sure that he was still sleeping and found him snoring loudly. I walked back to the table and began to trace the outline of the area on paper with on his desk. I noted whatever was on the map. Because it was in German, I just copied fast. Here it is and I hope you'll be able to make something out of my very fast drawings," said the woman in an anxious tone of voice.

She threw the drawings from the other room and Shaw picked them up from the floor.

Shaw and Parker looked at the drawings and they were astonished at what they were looking at.

"This is very good. These drawings will be a great help for the infantry. You have copied what we needed, the area, machine-gun positions, mine locations, howitzer like guns, rocket propelled grenade launcher positions, and tank defenses. Excellent work," said Shaw.

"How much time did you have for all these drawings?" asked Parker.

"About twenty minutes."

"What happened when he woke up?" Shaw queried.

"He invited me to join him in the tub. I hesitated first to give an answer, but I thought this was an opportunity to get protection in case I got in trouble. I told him that I had to ask my supervisor for additional time and then I would join him. This allowed me to put the papers in a secure place. I returned to him five minutes later. He asked me to give him massage, before taking the bath together. Then he requested an erotic massage with my fingers. He was getting aroused and began to undress me bit by bit. Then I joined him. The rest is up to your fantasy," said the woman.

"You ladies must play the game to get information and secure safety," commented Shaw. "We are very proud of you," added Parker.

They ended the meeting and the women left first. Shaw and Parker waited about twenty minutes, then looked around with telescopes until there were no cars or people who would possibly spy on them. They circled around to see if they had followers, then disappeared on the winding roads of the countryside.

Shaw had informed all cell members at the beginning of their operation of three safe houses in France, one in Northern region, one in the Middle, and one in the Southwest area. Hopefully the missing operative would be found in one of the safe houses. In their search, which took four hours, they found the guy. He was terribly frightened and it took Parker a good hour to convince him that he was safe and that he did not have to continue working for the Resistance.

Shaw and Parker left with disgust about the whole situation but it was expected to have casualties.

They drove to a small café in Cherbourg and they had a bite before going home.

"I would like to do something about this ambitious Gestapo guy who has caused us so much damage, but I am aware of the consequences. If we kill Fritz Kohler, a Gestapo officer, the whole town will pay for it and they will do everything to find the perpetrators. There will be no rest and it will interfere with our operation," said Parker.

"He could have an accident," replied Shaw.

"Takes too long to develop a scheme and they are too smart to fall into a trap," said Parker.

"What about his personal life? How much do we know about his weakness, passions, and interests?" asked Shaw.

"That takes time to figure out, and we can't go around asking questions," responded Parker.

"But somebody can. There must be somebody who hates him," said Shaw.

"To find that person is complicated, costly, and could be dangerous."

"So what do you want to do that will have no or minimum risk?" asked Shaw.

"This is precisely the problem, my friend Shaw. We have multiple problems: time, trust and retribution. Whom can we trust when the Gestapo has tons of paid collaborators who don't give a damn about tomorrow and will sell their mothers for liqueur, sex, drugs, or for the thrill of being a Nazi?"

"So that I know our options, what do you want to do?"

"Do I have to give you my choice right now Shaw, or can I sleep on it? We cannot cut him out right now. I know he is a growing cancer, but we can contain him for a little while."

"That is a sound choice Parker. Some cancers can wait if they are not too aggressive and invasive. Kohler is a slow type. He knows that killing Marceau requires a lot of investigation and the same applies for us. He does not want to create problems for himself and the Gestapo in terms of military relations until he can sufficiently prove that he is guilty of espionage."

"He has an optimal sense of smell which I am afraid of. It is a chess game and he is a good player, but, we are better players because of our keen perception and foresight. However, having said that, we must watch him, tacitly collect information about his personal life, and move in to kill, as an accident, when the coast is clear."

"I am with you on that Shaw, without any reservation. What's next?"

"We go home and have a good night sleep."

"That's it my friend, you got it!"

They left the café and drove home in a positive attitude.

The Gestapo had a special meeting to discuss security matters concerning Normandy's defenses. It was conducted in utmost secrecy and all the assisting personnel had to be German nationals. They were brought in from all over for this special occasion. One of the nationals, named Greta Richter, was actually an MI6 agent from Bristol, who had been in France for two decades. She was a perfect sleeper when her relationship began with her Gestapo friend. She was a pretty faced, conservatively dressed, blonde haired secretary. Her tall slender figure, beautiful smile and Bavarian dialect instantly charmed her future employer and she was hired within three days of her application.

He was absolutely hypnotized by her loyalty, sex, and compulsiveness. All her work in the office had to be perfect and her love-making never deviated from his likes. She had to masturbate and climax first in front of him, even if it was an act. It aroused him into a passionate love making. After pleasuring they ate cake which she had baked just to his taste.

Their relationship has been thriving for years and he has been so mesmerized by her that she was able to collect all the advanced planning of the Gestapo and inform the targets in advance. He has never suspected that she was a spy of the first order. She was present during the whole conference and memorized all the essentials to be passed on to the Resistance.

Greta had a chance to inform Marceau about the Gestapo meeting by taking her friend's boot in for repair. It was a perfect alibi to warn the Resistance of the impending danger that was coming in the months ahead. Marceau knew about Greta but they were seldom in touch because of the nature of her position.

"I am delighted to see you," said Marceau.

"Is it safe to talk to you now?"

"I will call Bridget to help me out with the customers and we can talk in the back where I'm repairing the boots. You can always say that you were waiting for the repair. So what brought you here?"

"The Gestapo had a meeting yesterday and you ought to know certain things that not only concern you but Shaw and Parker too. The meeting had to do with defense security in and around Normandy. The Gestapo is convinced that there are definite leaks about the Atlantic Wall, installations above and underground including radar, batteries, bunkers, casemates, pill boxes, mortar positions, beach obstacles, mines, big and medium size guns, fortifications beyond the Wall, and the flooding of low level areas to drown enemy parachutists."

"What is their logic in coming to these assumptions?"

"Heavy aerial surveillance, increased shoreline bombing, findings abroad by various spy agencies, confessions of Resistance operators, paid observers, increased sabotage activities by the Maquis, and the Gestapo instincts that they trust, as reliable sources to make decisions."

"How do all these assumptions affect us, Bridget, Shaw, Parker and me?"

"Your name came up during the discussions. Kohler has been after you for sometime."

"What proof do they have to accuse us?"

"They have nothing at this point, but they are getting reports about the visitors and the frequencies that they enter your shop."

"Will they arrest many of the field generals, officers and customers who visit my place more than they figure is appropriate?"

"They will arrest anybody whom they consider as a possible informant. They are above all generals and officers. It was conceived by Hitler to have everybody, except himself, a subordinate of the Gestapo."

"What else happened during the discussions?"

"You also have friends among the generals who defended you and called Kohler a sadistic robot without having any human considerations."

Kohler responded by saying, "I cannot have human considerations when our lives are at stake. We are fighting for the survival of our Fatherland, the Fuhrer, and the future of National Socialism. I do my job the best way I can. If you think I am harsh and inhuman, please transfer me to some desk job."

A high ranking Gestapo officer who wields considerable influence and power replied, "I want you to be patient with Marceau, who has been caring for our welfare and do not accuse him without having definite proof. You come to me with the proof and I will personally arrest him, but I am warning you, we are still at war and we did not win yet. If we lose you'll have to face the enemy bearing total responsibility."

"I am concerned about you and Bridget. You must lay low for a while, at least until the hunting season is over."

"When do you think Kohler's hunting will be over?"

"Soon, the invasion planning is in the last stages."

"But we have a lot of information to transmit and Allied Intelligence is counting on us."

"I know. You will have to devise some new plans to avoid detection."

"I will work on it. I will limit all Resistance and other operatives from contacting me at the shop. The observers can sit in their cars twenty-four hours a day and they will not be able to identify one single operative or AI agents entering my shop. My fishing trips will also be reduced or totally eliminated. I will contact AI by radio from various locations, virtually undetectable. By the time they discover the location, I'll be gone."

"They can follow your car, and search the car at will."

"The radio will not be in my car. It will be in possession of Shaw and Parker."

"We must communicate with Allied Intelligence even at the risk of being caught. We must pass on vital information that can save the lives of many foot soldiers in the first wave."

"I know, but you are not the only source. Remy and other Resistance operators are in touch with Colonel Passy, the head of Free French Intelligence. The OSS and MI6 are getting daily reports from other agents too."

"I am aware of that, but Shaw's and Parker's mission is different. They are at the scene. I do not minimize the heroisms of our operatives who have an opportunity to obtain written materials, plans, etc. but those maps and written orders are subject to change, sometimes at the very last minute. The top German Military planners have no idea what is going on, first, because of Allied misinformation, and secondly because Hitler runs the show."

"Marceau, you are right and wrong. Because the German Military is so terribly confused they try to plug every hole. The Gestapo is willing to do anything to prove to the German Military that they are protecting the Atlantic Wall. I know them. They will destroy you just for the sake of it. They are maniacs! And some are dangerous paranoids."

"We will be careful, that I can promise you. We are not, and I repeat, not foolish risk takers."

"Thank you, Marceau for your time. Be careful! I would like to meet with you after the invasion and open a bottle of champagne to celebrate the victory."

"I will meet with you if I make it."

"What do you mean if you'll make it?"

"I just found that I have terminal leukemia."

"I am terribly sorry."

"The doctors are not optimistic, but I am in the hands of the dear Lord. I want to thank you for your concern. I will repair the boot in a couple of days. Bye."

The warning of the Gestapo's new security measures was evident from the number of arrests in Port-En-Bessin. You just couldn't trust anyone. Even Michael had to be careful meeting Bridget. He was careful to watch for anyone following him and observers sitting in their cars on the street in front of the shop. Before the German Military intelligence began enforcing the new security measures, they had planned to spend the weekend in Paris. They decided to continue with their get-away plans.

Michael arrived at the shop at nine o'clock at night.

"Did anybody follow your car, Michael?" asked Bridget.

"I don't think so. I stopped the car three times and saw nobody following me. I even circled for ten minutes before I stopped. I believe we are safe to travel."

He placed her luggage into his car and they were on their way to Paris. The roadblocks were annoying and dangerous at times, but Michael's officer status helped to overcome the unpleasant questioning. He drove very fast to make up for the lost time at the check-points.

"Hello, my darling. I did not have time to greet you. Everything seemed to be so technical. Please forgive me."

"I understand. We are living under stress, but it shall pass. This war will end and we'll resume our normal lives. Honey, where are we staying in Paris?"

"A friend of mine is going back to Germany for a week and he offered his apartment."

"Well, that is wonderful. We can enjoy total privacy."

"That is one of the reasons why I was glad to accept the invitation. I've really had it with Kohler sniffing into our affair and trying to cause problems. He is one of the worst trouble-makers I have ever known. He has made some inquiries into our relationship. I have a good mind to erase him from my life. I also think that he is trying to instigate trouble, so he can justify any of his retaliatory action."

"I will not let him ruin our weekend. He is in Normandy and we'll be in Paris."

"Unless he's sending somebody to watch what we are doing and who we contact."

"Well, did you check the mirror? Is there anybody following us? Let's take the next exit, and stop at the next light. Look to see if there is a car behind us. Identify the car. We resume driving but with an increased speed make two right turns and then once to the left, we'll slow down and watch for the same car to reappear. If it is the same car then we are being followed. Then we just have to shake him off by speeding and several detours."

"I like your idea, so let's do it."

Michael's feeling was right. Indeed they were followed by a car or two. They took the evasive action as Bridget suggested. It was a dark Citroen car that followed them. Michael drove extremely fast and made the turns like a racecar driver. They were able to lose the tail but they were not sure. The idea that there may be another car, suggested another shake down. Michael exited again at the next town where he stopped the car in a desolated area. They waited fifteen minutes, but nobody followed. Bridget even got out of the car and watched carefully but she saw and heard nothing.

Michael took a deep breath and said, "It is not what I envisioned about the nature of National Socialism. Yes the Germans were without jobs and money after World War I, poverty was rampart, but we never had a police state where Germans were spying on Germans."

"I am a German Army Officer. I have rights and privileges. This is outrageous what's happening. I think I must have a word with Kohler when I get back."

"Darling, I am so sorry to get you into trouble, but I don't think it is a good idea to get in touch with Kohler. He is a dangerous man. You must ignore him the best way you can. He is desperately looking for some link between Marceau and the Resistance, so he can arrest him and show some of the Generals that his suspicion was correct. This man's vanity and pride have no limits. Let's enjoy our lives together this weekend in Paris. Darling, it will not be long before he'll disappear from our lives."

"I hope you're right. I am very angry with him."

"This is exactly what he wants. He wants to provoke you, so he can prove his point. Even if you kill him, he'll win. Don't you see his strategy? It is a game. It is a hunt. It is the excitement. So let's beat him in his own game. Let's make him angry, so he'll make a stupid mistake that will accidentally kill him."

Because of having to stop at the roadblocks and losing the tail, they arrived to the outskirts of Paris in the early morning hours. They were tired and hungry. Michael suggested having a hearty breakfast. They stopped at a roadside diner and had some goodies to refresh themselves. They ate and drank coffee like two hungry wanderers who had gotten lost in the wilderness.

"This was good," remarked Bridget.

"I am glad you liked it."

"I love to eat with you, Michael. You are such good company."

"Thank you sweetheart. I feel the same about you."

They drove to his friend's apartment. Michael embraced Bridget but they were too weary to make love. Both decided to go to sleep.

It was in the morning hours when the phone rang and his friend asked if the accommodation was satisfactory. Michael's conversation was short because they needed more time to sleep. That never happened because Michael began kissing Bridget which culminated in passionate love making.

Having rested, bathed, and dressed, they began exploring the streets on the Rue de Montparnasse. They were holding hands as they went window shopping, visited some stores, and then decided to get tickets to the opera. Puccini's La Boheme was playing that night but most of the tickets were sold. They took a taxi to the opera and tried to get two seats next to each other when someone returned two pricy tickets. Michael grabbed the opportunity and paid for them in the hurry. Then they visited a couple of bookstores and went to an elegant restaurant to have a leisurely dinner.

"They really know how to cook and present the food in an appetizing way," said Bridget.

"These chefs are exceptionally well trained and getting a premium salary. Of course, the guests are paying for it. The sauces are superb and are well guarded secrets."

"Occasionally one must cultivate new tastes and I believe it is well worth it."

"Yes, my dear Bridget, and you are well worth it too!"

"That is very kind what you just have said. Your love, my darling, extends in all directions."

"I found a girl whose heart and mind are exceptional in the universe. I feel that you have been the greatest gift of my life and I want to treasure you forever."

"The feeling is mutual, my darling. I hope our lives will be bound together now and in eternity."

"Amen, my sweetheart. You know, that I will never abandon you and only the good Lord will separate us."

Michael held her hand while he spoke the last sentence and bent over across the table and gave her a gentle kiss on her mouth. There were two German generals across the table and both applauded the kiss.

"Thank you, Herr Generals," said Michael. The Generals, in an unusual manner, ordered the waiter to bring a bottle of champagne for Bridget and Michael. Michael, then, asked the waiter to bring four glasses with it. The champagne was served and all four got up and saluted each other. It was a beautiful gesture to ease the pain of the forces of evil, hatred, and death. But nothing, absolutely nothing was able to help Bridget to forget her parent's fate and Marceu's beating. Her forced smile did not suggest forgiveness.

Bridget and Michael skipped dessert and asked the waiter for the bill. They rushed to the opera by taxi. They were seated on the right side of the first balcony. The view of the stage and the acoustics were just right. Both of them were delighted to have such wonderful seats, but something had to spoil the evening. During intermission, out of nowhere, Kohler appeared with a number of Gestapo agents and their ladies. They were having fun, offering cheers to the Reich with the wine glasses in their hands and laughing loudly. Bridget and Michael turned their backs and ignored them.

The good thing was that Kohler left Normandy. That evening, Shaw and Parker had planned to catch the two turncoats who had been watching Marceau's place day and night. They planned to lure them into a perverted sexual encounter with special Resistance agents who would drug them with chemicals that would cause memory loss. The chemicals needed twenty-four hours to take full effect which was the exact time that Kohler would be absent.

"One never knows when bad is good and good is bad," said Bridget "Why are you saying that?"

"Oh it is a Chinese philosopher's adage."

"In what reference do you say this?"

"In connection with Gestapo Kohler. I hope his watchdogs will pay a price."

"What's going to happen to them?"

"I don't know yet, but I have a premonition something will happen and my instincts are always good. But one never can tell."

"You know something that you don't want to share with me."

"I can't share with you what I don't know. The only thing I can tell you is that there are agents who hate French collaborators and are willing to sacrifice their lives for Marceau. I was not privileged to know the details. They operate on the need to know basis."

Michael and Bridget had a wonderful evening together enjoying the exquisite meal and beautiful sounds of the opera. They cuddled together in the taxi and shed their clothes as soon as they entered the apartment. They had a tremendous craving for each other and didn't want to stop kissing.

"You make me so wanted, you are so erotically tempestuous, my sweetheart. Your desire of me is just so overwhelming, that I just cannot hold back to wait for you, come darling and pleasure with me."

Michael did let go and pleasured with Bridget together in total synchrony.

"I love you Michael, you're so considerate of my feelings and sexuality. Thank you, my love."

"I am totally responding to your wants and needs so we can have a beautiful and harmonious togetherness. Your body rhythm is so alluring that I have a difficult time of holding back, but I love waiting for you so we can enjoy the culmination of our excitement together. You are so beautiful when you let go with all your body movements and sounds."

"So are you, my handsome. I love it when you are pleasuring. You have this irresistible aroma that can be so arousing. I just crave for your fragrance."

Both fell asleep in each other's arms. It was late Sunday morning when they woke up. They decided to clean up and have a luscious breakfast in a nearby restaurant. Both wanted fresh pastries, bread, eggs, and lots of jam. They walked down the stairs arm-in-arm and walked toward the main boulevard to find a restaurant. They found one just around the corner, sat down near the window, and ordered food they desired.

After breakfast they drove to Champs-Elysees and parked the car. They went for a walk and enjoyed the window shopping. Bridget felt it was time to get back home to Port-En-Bessin. She had a number of errands to do for Marceau. Michael understood her predicament but he did not want to return to Normandy before nightfall. He felt this was a rare occasion to be away from home, and that she deserved a little vacation. It was a hard decision for both of them. The issue to stay longer or leave was easily resolved by a phone call. Bridget called her friend who usually looked after Marceau whenever she was away more than a day. To her surprise, Marceau had been admitted to the hospital with pneumonia. There was no further discussion about the stay.

They got back to Port-En-Bessin in mid afternoon. They went to see Marceau in the hospital, but he was sound asleep. The doctors told them that he was doing well and that he could return home provided he had no fever. Bridget and Michael waited until Marceau awakened, and the doctor allowed him to leave. They took Marceau home and called it a day.

Shaw and Parker took care of the watchdogs and the Gestapo didn't even know what happened. They just could not report any significant observation. First, Marceau was not in the shop, and second, both lost their memories. When the Gestapo did not hear from them, they were escorted to the Gestapo for questioning.

"What do you want us to do?" asked one of the collaborators.

"Are you crazy?" shouted Kohler. "Are you insulting my intelligence? Watch and note every person who is visiting Marceau day and night."

When they left they totally forgot what they had to do and of course there was no surveillance at all. Again, their reporting failed to materialize, and they were arrested again. Kohler noticed their unusual behavior but did not make anything of it. In his frustration he ordered them to be locked up in the hospital as crazies and asked the medical staff for a comprehensive examination regarding their blood chemistry and memories. Since the medical staff had no neuropsychiatry specialist and the lab did not have any sophisticated testing apparatus, both tests were ordered to be sent to Paris.

It took two months to get a report which did not identify the cause of their sudden memory loss. According to the report, it was a severe stress reaction to their assignment.

Kohler was devastated with the report and in his frustration asked the military to assist him. One of the generals got so angry at his request that a serious altercation ensued and the military police had to be called out for a conditional arrest of Kohler for disorderly conduct and insulting a general without cause. Kohler was taken to appear in front of the head of the Gestapo for disciplining.

The head of the Gestapo was terribly embarrassed by Kohler's behavior and ordered him to take a two weeks vacation outside Normandy. Kohler was informed that when he returned from his vacation he would be reassigned to office work only. All this filtered through the military officers and Michael was absolutely delighted to hear the good news. He shared the news with Bridget who in turn told this to Marceau, Shaw, and Parker.

Of course, there was a celebration, but it was short lived. The recreational fishing was suspended by the Kriegsmarine military police. Marceau had to find alternate means to send messages to AI. Shaw and Parker were in a bind and AI had been alerted of the new German regulation by radio. The flow of communication between Marceau and Allied Intelligence however did not stop; it just became more cumbersome and dangerous. The AI mini submarine sent one agent at two o'clock in the morning to a designated beach and removed the message box that was magnetically attached to a curved rail obstruction placed at the waters edge and replaced it with AI messages. The box was sealed and watertight, and the opening side was welded. There was a low level electronic signal that was emitted from the box that only the commandos were able to pick up. At first glance the box appeared as part of the curved rail. To place and remove the message box on the rail was a dangerous operation. Shaw and Parker's skills were tested to the limits. They pretended to inspect the rails and while one looked at the rails, the other placed or picked up the box below the waterline in the sand during low tide. The pick up by the commando was only during high tide. The German sentries were watching from their bunkers and casemates with high powered telescopes while the inspections took place. They did not have the foggiest notion that Shaw and Parker were never assigned to inspect the rails. Shaw and Parker informed the officers in charge of the beaches that the inspections were necessary because of the force of the currents was creating pressure on the curved rails and possibly weakening them. Shaw and Parker made a scientific enterprise of the whole operation. Parker pointed out the specific posts that needed strengthening by an additional pounding into the ground. In addition, they inspected other beach defense installations to allay possible suspicions of their focus on the rails.

"You must have a permit to inspect these rails," said one German sentry.

"I know, but we must secure these beach defenses, so the enemy tanks will have a hard time to climb," responded Parker.

"These defenses are a waste of time and money. They will blow them up or bomb them before the tanks arrive."

"Don't be so sure. The German artillery barrage will scare them."

"Not the British or Americans. They are vicious fighters."

"How do you know this?"

"I go to the movies. I watch those cowboys. They are tough cookies."

Parker smiled, but did not engage in a lengthy talk. He was just testing the sentry.

"Do you know where your superior officer is?" asked Shaw.

"Yes sir! I will ask him to meet you."

"Thank you, that is very nice of you."

"Oh, I do it anytime for guys like you. You seem to care."

The officer in charge came and looked right into Parker's eyes.

"I am in charge. What can I do for you, officers?"

"Well, we are in charge of the Organization Todt construction inspection, but because we are engineers we have been asked to look at the beach defenses for possible structural weaknesses due to water pressure, erosion, and metallurgical defects. May we ask your permission to inspect some of the structures under your leadership?" said Shaw.

"What specifically are you interested in?"

"We are looking at batteries, bunkers, casemates, underground tunnels, beach defense rails and other obstacles, and anything that you are concerned might need to be inspected," replied Parker.

"Do you need any assistance?" asked the commanding officer.

"Not at this point. But we will ask you questions as we go along with the inspections."

"Are there any restricted areas we should know about? We will honor your restricted zones," said Shaw.

"You may inspect some of those areas only in my presence."

"As you wish" responded Shaw.

"I like your attitude and consideration. You are the kind of officers I like to deal with. When I say stop looking, you will obey me."

"We will respect your orders at all times," said Parker.

"Good. Where do you want to start?"

"We would like to study the foundations and chemical decompositions of rails."

"You can inspect the rail defenses, but no other structures on the beach. We have mines all over and those areas are strictly prohibited to you."

"Thank you, we will be careful not to trespass into your prohibited zones."

Parker took out a shovel and the message box from his instrument case and Shaw covered him with his back while he dug six inches into the sand and placed the box onto the rail. The magnet of the box held it tight to the rail like it was part of it. Then they repeated the same in two other places. Having done that, they walked toward the casemate and later the bunker and meticulously inspected both of them. Before they left, they spoke with the commanding officer and expressed their satisfaction with the findings.

The next thing was to notify AI that the message box was in place and ready to be monitored day and night. Once they picked up a signal the directional finder told the area of the box location and the hunt began. They could narrow down the signal to a bench, car, or house.

The Germans mastered how to detect and locate radio signals of the Resistance but not the special box signal that was prepared by MI6 for the commandos. However, the operation of transceivers by Shaw and Parker varied by region and time. A small but powerful transceiver radio, prepared by MI6, was hidden in their car. They seldom used it. The time had come, however, to send short coded signals to Bletchley Park, 50 miles north of London. They had left Normandy and headed to the countryside where nature's beauty was the pre-dominance.

There were no German defenses, soldiers, barns, and homes, just overgrown trees, hedges, and grass.

"I think we can send the signals from here," said Shaw.

"It is hard to believe in this tranquil atmosphere that we are at war and where we are standing will become a killing field. Yes, we could send the coordinates and wait for the response."

Shaw looked around and sent the messages. Within five minutes the response came. Parker placed the radio back to the car and they drove away as fast as they could. As soon as they hit the main road, however, a German patrol car stopped them for identification and asked them where they had just come from. The German radio finders had already picked up the cryptic signal but not the location.

"Could you tell us if you saw a car or truck with a large antenna?" asked the patrol.

"We saw many cars on the road but nothing with a huge antenna," said Parker.

"Well, I thank you for your cooperation, but before you leave, please open your trunk."

Parker nonchalantly opened the trunk and then stepped aside.

"What is this case?"

"It is where we keep our engineering instruments."

"Thank you for your cooperation. You may proceed."

Shaw and Parker were nauseated and felt like vomiting. They left the sentry slowly with a smile on their faces. When they entered the road Shaw sped away from the scene.

"Close call. We picked the right location though" said Shaw.

"It is getting more and more challenging," replied Parker.

They did not travel more than five miles when another patrol car stopped them.

"What are you doing in this part of the country? The Organization Todt is not building around here. May we have your identification please," said one of the military patrolmen.

"You are right. We are engineers surveying new locations for possible defensive construction," Parker said in an authoritative voice.

"Why have constructions in the middle of nowhere?" asked the other patrol man.

"Because it would be a strategic surprise, just in case the invasion succeeds," replied Shaw.

"That makes sense. It is a smart thought," said the first patrol man.

"You may proceed, and thank you for your cooperation," said the second patrol man.

"I wonder where the next stop will be?" asked Parker.

"The orders are to look for spies and the search will be more drastic," replied Shaw.

They drove to Port-En-Bessin to meet with Marceau and Bridget in a park. Shaw got out of the car and looked for Marceau who was sitting on a bench and feeding the seagulls. He looked around while Parker was circling and watching for a tail. Nobody seemed to look suspicious, so after fifteen minutes of chatting Shaw asked both of them to join them in their car and go for a ride. Shaw drove in a southerly direction away from Normandy to the open country. There was a guest house there where they could sit down, have some refreshments, and even eat something if they so desired. Parker accidentally discovered the place sometime ago and thought it would be a good place to meet. Bridget was happy to see the guys since it was now unwise for Shaw and Parker to visit Marceau's place.

"So, gentlemen, what is the latest news?" asked Marceau.

"That is your department," replied Parker.

"Well, we hope that Kohler is staying put for a while," remarked Marceau.

"Don't be so sure. Just because he has been reassigned does not mean he will stay there after hours or weekends. He will not rest until he can prove a connection between Marceau and someone in the Resistance or Allied agents. He is absolutely fanatic about it. His pride, vanity, and reputation will not let him stop," commented Shaw.

"There is nothing that we can do to stop him short of incapacitating him," said Marceau.

"He must have others to help him by now," suggested Bridget.

"We must be very careful and all future meetings are no longer in my shop except in case of an emergency."

"We know that Marceau and he knows it too. He has nothing on you at this point in time. Kohler is compulsively crazy and he will fabricate something if his paranoia takes over his sanity," commented Shaw.

"There is nothing that we can do about the crazies. He and Hitler would make good friends. I will do my job as a courier and recruiter as long as I have to and am able to carry out my duties."

"If and when he becomes a threat to your life, we will trap him and it will be a homicidal death," said Parker.

"I don't want to implicate you guys. Your mission is more important than worrying about Kohler's intentions."

"You are part of our mission. Without you Marceau, we could not have accomplished what we did," said Shaw.

"I think we are all right now, but as the invasion is coming closer, I would like to find a safer place for Marceau," suggested Bridget.

"South of France would be an excellent place for him," added Parker.

"Let's talk about something more serious," said Marceau, "I think we are all needed when the invasion comes. I cannot foresee the beachhead without the cooperation of the Resistance."

"Yes, we all have to help as much as we can. Special instructions will be arriving soon regarding our role during the invasion. I believe the Resistances role will be quite different from the roles of OSS and MI6 agents," said Shaw.

"I am worried about Michael. He'll be supplying information until the last minute, but until a secure beachhead is formed, it will be difficult for him to flee," said Bridget.

"If we know where he would be we could alert the Military Intelligence, but during the fighting I don't think we can do anything to help him. It all depends on his location at the time of the invasion. At this point it is impossible to do anything unless he is in a safe place as a deserter and waiting to be liberated, but that is not his character," replied Shaw.

"I think we have quite a job informing Allied Intelligence about the last minute German defenses which are being strengthened every day," said Marceau.

"We covered cells six and seven, and are still waiting to hear from the rest. I think we are getting as much information as the cell members can possibly provide. Parker and I will make some inspections just before the invasion time," said Shaw.

"We do not have enough time. You must get the information in the next two to three weeks. Allied Intelligence is very concerned about the strategic bombing, commando raids, Special Operations Executive, OSS, MI6 operations and the Maquis sabotage and subversive activities prior to the landing. There is a lot to be done before the invasion and any last minute activities can be construed by the German High Command as confirming that the invasion indeed will be in Normandy. They don't want to give it away!" emphasized Marceau.

"All cell reports will be completed within two weeks and we will make additional inspections in one week. This I can promise you, but there are always unforeseen problems," replied Shaw.

"I think we better go," said Bridget. "We have a long day tomorrow with all the boots you have to start and then repair a dozen or more shoes."

"Let's check the neighborhood. There are a number of ways we can discourage the tails that might be watching us. When we arrived, we did not see anyone watching us, but we would like to make their acquaintance and discourage them from their activities. We don't like stool pigeons," said Parker.

"We can wait a few minutes. That is not a problem," said Marceau.

Everyone got into the car and they made a few circles around the area. Parker spotted two men walked toward the area where they had just been. Marceau looked closely at one of the men and recognized him as a member of the Maquis. Marceau said that he was one of them and to leave him alone. Parker drove Marceau and Bridget back to the park. They planned the next meeting for the same place and time the following week.

Shaw and Parker decided to call it a day because there was little left to do for the remaining time. They pick up some groceries on the way home and had dinner at Shaw's apartment.

The next day they met with only two cell operatives that not only covered the Bayeux region but Pointe du Hoc as well. From the moment they met it was nothing but a disaster. The meeting place was in a cellar of an old house that was occupied by two elderly ladies who created more trouble than they helped. They constantly complained about their lack of money, medications, food, and the danger they had been facing with picture taking and meeting with people who were spying on the German defenses. They demanded money for the short meetings between the agents. On top of that, one of the operatives was betrayed and arrested by the military for inquiring about the possibility to visit the top of the cliff at Pointe du Hoc.

"He was working as a plumber in the nearby bunker and wanted to open another sewer to ease the flow of waste material. He asked a legitimate question about opening up another line for the sewer. This question was reported to a safety officer and he was arrested by the military intelligence," said one of the cell operatives.

"How do you know these things in such detail?" asked Shaw.

"I worked with Andre when this happened."

"Where is he now?" asked Parker.

"The last I heard he was taken to the military holding place for interrogation."

"I want to stop the meeting now. We have to save Andre. We'll be meeting here this afternoon at 1300. Bye," said Parker.

Shaw and Parker drove to the Military Headquarters holding place and asked the officer in charge for permission to enter the building to speak with the interrogating officer in charge. This was a highly unusual situation, but for courtesy it was granted. They, however, only allowed one of them to enter. Shaw suggested that Parker should go in and try to save Andre.

"What is your name officer?" asked the holding and interrogating officer.

"My name is Hans Dietrich. Here are my papers. What is your name officer?"

"I am Carl Hoffbauer. What business is it of yours to talk about Andre, the plumber?"

"I am an engineer by training and he asked me what to do to find some other outlet for the waste products."

"It is very interesting that a seasoned plumber has to ask an engineer what to do to ease the flow of waste in one outlet. I personally think what you are telling me is nothing but pure garbage."

"I learned in my officer training school that there is a certain manner of discussion between two German officers. I think that your language and insulting behavior is totally unacceptable in the German Army, Herr Hoffbauer."

"And what are you going to do about it?"

"First, I will report you to the General in charge of this region whom I met during my award dinner in the Gestapo Headquarters. Then I will request that he remove you from your duty because of interference with the health of the bunker officers and soldiers who are going to defend the Reich."

"What kind of award dinner are you talking about Herr Dietrich?"

"My partner, Herr Krueger and I saved the lives of two Gestapo officers."

"Very nice, congratulations! This time, however, you are not going to save anybody. As a matter of fact, you have no business to interfere in our investigation."

"I did not come to argue with you. You do what you have to do, but everything in life has consequences. The fact is that you are torturing a man who has not committed an act of espionage; he simply asked questions to help you guys. If the sewage backs up, there will be bacterial consequences. It will not be his fault but your negligence by not allowing him to build another outlet. It was a reasonable inquiry, which I suggest that you follow up before continuing to torture Andre. You are having a power play over the whole incident. Let me give you a warning. Should anything happen to this man, I will do my best to take you to the military court and if I don't succeed, the French will if we lose the war. We are the occupants of France and after the war they will hunt you down and hang you. Think about it."

"I am not afraid of you or the French. We will win the war and you can go to hell with your threats. As a matter of fact, I could arrest you here and now as a material witness. I think our conversation is over and you better get the hell out of here before I get real angry."

"Herr Hoffbauer, I am asking you very nicely for the last time to release the plumber and have an amicable end to this matter. My partner is waiting outside, and he is not a very patient man. If I am not out in five minutes with the plumber, he will not care about your rights and privileges, but drive to Caen to the Military Headquarters, present the seriousness of the situation regarding the bacterial contamination, and you'll be arrested. Knowing him, he will make serious charges against you in the Military, and in the end you will lose. It is your choice."

"I cannot release the man in his condition. He was beaten and tortured. I promise you, however, that if I find any espionage attempt in his part, I will surely make you responsible for his release. He can go tomorrow afternoon. I am doing this because you put him up to the inquiry and the bacterial issue makes sense."

"Thank you. I am glad that we resolved this matter. Bye."

Parker and Hoffbauer shook hands and Parker existed quietly from the room. He joined Shaw and both drove away in a happy mood.

"Was he difficult?"

"That is a polite question. He was quite obnoxious. As our conversation got more serious he warned me that he could arrest me."

"So, what did you do?"

"I let him have it. I warned him of the consequences of his action. He is not stupid but feels extremely inferior. He made a fast calculation and gave up the man. He'll be out tomorrow."

"How about the Military? How is he going to justify his release?"

"I am sure he'll handle it at this point. He does not want to complicate matters. He did not want to gamble and lose. It was too sticky. He sensed from my voice that he had no justification and he knew that he was on a fishing expedition. The Military Intelligence will understand the legitimacy of his suspicion."

"So what is the next step?"

"We are going to continue with cell five after one o'clock."

"I have a hypothetical question. What if he retains the guy and tortures him to confess the connection between him and the Resistance?"

"I will kill him."

"Oh boy, don't do that. We'll have the whole German Army on our tail. We'll just have to step aside. We'll have one more war casualty."

"To be sure that such an idiotic action will not happen, I will revisit him this afternoon and make an inquiry about Andre."

"Isn't that too risky and he may change his mind because of your concern?"

"Shaw, you certainly enjoy getting me going. I am too wound up to think straight. Let me rest for awhile, say twenty minutes, and I will get back to you."

"Let me think for you, Parker. Shit does happen, and we have managed to solve problems in the past."

"The way we can get him out this afternoon is by bluffing we tell him that the Generals were in the bunkers and the stench was unbearable. We were ordered to remedy the situation on the double. We told the Generals that the plumber was not available now. We were told to make him available even if he had to be brought in on a stretcher. It is your turn Shaw and I'll be waiting for you in the car."

"I think we can pull it off, but let's hear what the other two cell members have to say."

They met just after one o'clock. The two guys complained that there was not enough to report. What they saw so far was only small arms fire, machine guns and light cannons. Because of the strategic significance of Pointe du Hoc, the hidden pill boxes and casemates were well camouflaged and needed a closer surveillance.

"Yes, this is precisely what I'm talking about! If we can't get in closer, our boys will be massacred in the water and on the beach," said Parker.

Shaw and Parker cut the meeting short but told them to meet in three days from now at the same time.

"I hope we can have your partner out today and the plumbing project can start tomorrow. In the meantime, please be careful, and do not talk about our project. Pointe du Hoc will be difficult to climb without heavy casualties unless we can silence those guns. We must know where the fire is coming from. Bye for now. We'll be seeing you in three days."

Shaw opened the trunk and under the sub floor he had a small attaché case where he hid his makeup, beard, mustache, and facial changeovers. He transformed his appearance into a very respectable looking officer, with glasses, beard and mustache, just in case he is asked to take the custody of the plumber which requires him to hide his true identity.

Shaw and Parker drove back to the military holding place and asked for Officer Hoffbauer. It did not take more than five minutes and Shaw was escorted to his office.

"I am Officer Dietrich's partner and I would like to have a word with you."

"I am listening, please state your case because I am a very busy man and have no time for a meaningless chit-chat. You may sit down if you wish; I can give you ten minutes."

"I only need five minutes."

"Good. I am waiting to hear what you have to say."

"It came to my attention this morning that the Generals who visited the bunker bitterly complained about the stench that permeated the entire place. They ordered that the plumbers must open another pipe for the waste on the double. When they found out that one of the plumbers was unavailable, they ordered to bring him, if necessary, on a stretcher. How can I tell the Generals that you are holding the plumber?"

"It is a problem, isn't it, Officer Krueger? I am absolutely fed up with guys like you from the Organization Todt. We are the muscle of the German Army. You just provide the blueprints, cement, rods, and nails. We have to take all the crap from you guys. I have really had it. Well, I respect the General's order and we will release the man into your custody right now. I really couldn't give a damn what he looks like, but you must sign him out."

"Well, thank you. You are a good man of the Reich! I will be waiting outside for the plumber."

"You can sit here while they are preparing Andre to exit. You look like a frail man. Are you sick? Do you want some cognac?"

"I just want to get the hell out of here and start the waste project before the Generals put me in jail."

"He'll be out in a few minutes. Here is some cognac. You really look sick."

Andre came out with the help of two soldiers. He looked horrible. Shaw with one hand covering his face with a handkerchief and with the other hand took his arm and helped him out of the room.

"Thank you again. Bye."

They slowly walked toward the car. Parker sat in the back and hid his face with a black cloth and only his eyes and mouth were showing.

"I got him out of custody, didn't I? He is a real son of a bitch bastard. I hope he will pay for what he did to Andre when the Allies will take Normandy."

"What did Hoffbauer do to you?" asked Parker.

"He did very little personally, but his henchmen followed the Military Intelligence officer and Hoffbauer's instructions. From the start they had very little to go on. They asked stupid questions I knew that they did not know anything. After an hour of questioning, they started to threaten me to confess otherwise I will not bear the physical torture. I told them that I can only tell what I know, what I have experienced, the people I work with, and the friends I meet on weekends."

"Then they asked me to get naked and bend down. Then somebody started hitting my buttocks with a stick. After that they turned me around and hit my face until I bled. They stopped hitting me for ten minutes."

"Hoffbauer was watching and asked me in French why I am so stubborn and hiding what I know. I told him I would be more than happy to confess but I have no knowledge of any wrongdoing. They asked me to turn around and the soldiers started to hose me with cold water. Nothing worked and Hoffbauer decided to use psychological torture and asked me to walk to a small room and stand until I talked. This did not work either. He realized that they had nothing on me and left me naked in the room. I sat down later and fell asleep."

"They are brutal people who will pay later," said Parker.

"We want you to rest for a couple of days, but the new pipe for the waste material must be constructed. During the construction you and your colleague will have the opportunity to study the German defenses. We must report to Allied Intelligence what is going on. Point du Hoc is a dangerous cliff and the casualties could be heavy. Pay attention to all the details and hidden places where machineguns, cannons, mortar launchers, and medium sized guns are stored. Count and memorize them. When you go home write it down and next time we meet you can hand it over. The next meeting is in three days, same time and place," instructed Shaw.

They stopped before a food market and bought all kinds of goodies for him. He was told to stay at home and a nurse would take care of his wounds and give him some pain killers and other healing ointments. He was taken home and Parker helped him with the packages. They put him to bed and Andre fell asleep in no time.

Shaw and Parker had a feeling of accomplishment. To ease their stress, they went to a restaurant, had double cognacs, ordered fine food, and met a couple of nice people at the next table. Both were from Sweden and had lived in France for the last twenty-five years. They were artists, and made living painting Normandy's landscapes. It was a delightful evening for all of them and they had a difficult time breaking up the conversation.

Shaw and Parker drove home around midnight to find out that one of the cell members from cell four had an automobile accident and requested immediate help. Since little information was given for security reasons, Shaw had to contact Bridget through an intermediate person by phone. In ten minutes he called again and Bridget came to the phone and told him that she had vital information to reveal but only to him.

She was facing surgery in the morning at the Caen's hospital and it would be important for them to talk to her before she was given anesthesia. Shaw agreed to see her and they left immediately to go to Caen. It looked like a whole night affair, but it was part of their jobs. First, they had to change from their uniforms to civilian clothing and camouflage their faces so they would not be recognizable. With makeup and wigs, it took them thirty minutes to transform themselves into two old ugly relatives.

Each had two cups of strong coffee while they were dressing. They were tired, but the news of vital information gave them the spirit to drive in the middle of the night.

It was no problem visiting the girl who at first was reluctant to talk. Shaw explained that they were using theatrical masks to cover their identities. She understood the subterfuge but she recognized their voices and revealed her secret information.

"You have to excuse me if I am incoherent at times, but I am under sedation. What we saw was incredible. I worked as a nurse and at times as a lover in the bunkers. Isigny and Pointe du Hoc are insidiously defended. I have a map that I sketched hidden in my purse between the outer and inner layers of leather and you can have it by tearing it open. It's an old bag, and I don't mind you ripping the seams," said Rebecca.

Shaw tore it open at the seams and there was the map. She explained the meaning of the symbols and it looked fantastic.

"This map provides the best information about their hidden defenses that could become catastrophic for the infantry. The question is how to neutralize these defenses before landing," said Shaw.

"How did you manage to get such an accurate picture?" asked Parker.

"It was not easy to get all that information, but I collected it piece by piece. One of the officers had some sexual problems and I helped him for months to get better."

"During those months I was privileged to hear some of his instructions to the soldiers to prepare the defense posture on the top of the cliffs, and dig all kinds of hidden machine-gun nests. Mortars and medium sized guns are practically invisible, because they are covered by nets, and vegetation. To flush them out you need carpet bombing and heavy explosives that can penetrate those holes. The best way would be blasting them by navy guns."

"I don't know how to thank you, but we'll be thinking of you. When you get better, I'm sure you will have a lot to tell about your experiences," said Parker.

"I must have some rest now before the surgery, but I wanted you to have these markings because one never knows how anesthetics can affect you. Thanks for coming and have a safe trip back home. Bye."

It was sunrise when Shaw and Parker left her room. They decided to stay put for a while. The waiting room was empty and Parker suggested a short nap before driving home. Shaw agreed, and both sat at each end of the sofa putting their feet up on the table. It did not take them long before they were sound asleep. They slept until one of the nurses woke them up around eight o'clock in the morning. Since Rebecca's operation started about that time, they decided to wait and find out the outcome of her operation. In the meantime, they had breakfast in the hospital's cafeteria.

About 0930, they were told that the operation was successful and that she could not have visitors that day. Shaw and Parker were extremely happy and jovial when they drove home from Caen.

This time there was no message at the door and they were able to rest until midday. Shaw and Parker still had to meet the two other members of the cell to find out if there was additional information. Collette and Georges were waiting for them and it was a happy reunion. They were glad to know that Rebecca was doing fine after the operation, but it would take some time before she could join the cell. The two other members did not provide any more information than what Shaw and Parker had already received, but there was one tiny bit of information that was significant. It was an underground tunnel that provided passage for the ordnance. The location of the tunnel, however, required further study because it branched out in other directions. That remained for Shaw and Parker to explore.

"We find the German defenses pose a significant danger for the invading forces and requires very elaborate demolition methods to smash the existing structures," said Colette.

"Did you find the military large enough to defend the shores?" asked Shaw.

"Not that large that the Allies cannot break through, but large enough to inflict heavy casualties," replied Georges.

"Colette works with Rebecca as a nurse and I am an electrician. We have access to various areas and we hear some stories from French speaking German officers," explained Georges.

Shaw and Parker found their information verified Rebecca's findings and so for the information gathering was adequate enough to start destroying the existing defenses before the invasion began. Under the new German security measures Shaw and Parker lowered their expectations as to what each cell could possibly provide. The rest was up to them to penetrate under the inspection subterfuge.

"I think we can go on the next cell area, Carentan, tomorrow," said Shaw.

"It looks to me like we are making some headway for the air and possibly commando attacks. We have to be careful not to jeopardize the Fortitude deception by heavy bombardments of Normandy," remarked Parker.

"Well stated. Let's go on and inspect the structures where the tunnels might be. We may learn something," responded Shaw.

Marceau had a bad night. In the morning, he was feeling weak and Bridget drove him to the hospital in Cherbourg. His specialist ordered lab work and suggested that they wait for the results. By late afternoon, his physician told him that he did not like his white cell count and he should return for another test in a couple of days. His medication was increased by a half a dose. He was also given some additional suggestions on how to overcome his tiredness by diet, rest, special herbs, and reduced stress.

"My dear doctor, I can follow your suggestions, but up to a certain point. I have no control over my stress. My business, like yours, is dealing with people and situations," offered Marceau.

"I understand, but you must reduce your hours of work and you should do that for the sake of your wellbeing."

"I will try, but there is always something. Some of my customers are generals and they demand perfection. They come sometimes after hours and complain about little things, but I thank you for your concern."

Bridget drove to a market place to shop for certain food items that were supposed to give him strength and vitality. Marceau in the meantime was waiting in the hospital's reception room and was reading the newspaper. He was asleep when Bridget came back and the short rest gave him strength to return home.

They were halfway home when Marceau suggested having dinner in a restaurant. Bridget was happy to hear that because lately he had no appetite. Marceau ordered fried chicken, roasted potatoes, spinach and a tall glass of milk. Bridget was surprised because Marceau does not drink milk for dinner and seldom eats spinach. Bridget ordered the same, except she wanted a glass of red wine for her beverage.

There was a positive mood change for Marceau and he said a number of cheerful things that made Bridget mighty happy. He predicted that Michael would be captured but later released with accolades by the American Army and she would find him and they would be happy after that.

"This is wonderful what you're saying, Marceau. God should bless you for it!"

"I am just having premonitions without any basis."

"I wish Michael would be able to fly to England with the help of the Resistance."

"Not at this stage, my dear. The Germans are watching the night sky and the radar screens to identify any invasion mission."

"Would you have room for dessert, Marceau?"

"Yes, they have a luscious whipped cream éclair!"

"I'll have the same. Thank you for suggesting it."

"You're welcome, my dear, but after that we should go home."

"We shall definitely do that."

No sooner they had entered the home, the neighbor knocked on the door. It was the usual neighborly gesture to call Bridget to the phone, but this time she had an anxious voice, "Telephone for Bridget."

Bridget rushed to the phone and asked, "Hello, this is Bridget, whom am I speaking with?"

"This is a friend and you may recognize my voice," said Parker.

"How can I help you?"

"We must see Marceau tomorrow morning before he starts working in the shop," said Parker

"We cannot make it before eight."

"Eight is fine."

"We'll be having our morning stroll toward the beach."

"Watch the other strollers and cars following you."

"Please do not worry. As usual, when you see me embracing Marceau with my left hand, please stay away. Give us a call an hour later."

"We will do that. Bye."

Bridget returned home and discussed the message from Parker with Marceau. His reply was simple.

"They must have something urgent."

"I believe so judging from the tone of his voice."

Bridget and Marceau retired early and hoped for a restful night and pleasant dreams.

The next morning, Bridget and Marceau had an early breakfast and by seven-thirty they were ready to walk to the beach. The weather was rather unpleasant. It was cloudy, windy, humid, and warm. Marceau loved the cool mornings. It had a refreshing effect on his body and soul, but now he endured the weather change for the sake of the meeting.

The streets were clean and there was a variety of pedestrian and vehicular traffic. A few French pedestrians' walked briskly by and German soldiers in groups of twos and threes bunched together standing around on the street corners. There were few civilian cars, mostly German military vehicles moving in all directions.

Marceau and Bridget cautiously continued walking and looking around for followers.

They saw absolutely nothing. They were no cars or people following them. Just to be sure, they changed their prescribed routine and entered a side street which was rather short and narrow. It was impossible for any followers to hide. There were no cars parked on the street.

It was comforting to know that there was no visible tail. Out of nowhere Shaw's car was approaching them and Marceau and Bridget quickly got into the car.

Shaw sped toward the outskirts of Port-En-Bessin and except for pleasantries; they hardly talked to each other. Parker watched the mirror for a tail, and Shaw looked for a desolate spot, where it was relatively safe to have a conference. They were prepared for eventualities, like German patrol cars. If a German patrol car were to inquire what they were doing in the middle of nowhere, Shaw and Parker were ready to invoke the so called 'first aid mission.' Since Marceau was having a condition, it would be natural to administer first aid to endure the trip as they headed to the hospital.

Shaw parked the car in the corner of an open field near a tall hedgerow where their car was hardly visible but they could still watch for an approaching vehicle.

"Let's talk. What was the urgency for this meeting?" asked Marceau.

"Rebecca, from our cell, presented us a fairly detailed map of the gun positions of Pointe du Hoc that we must get to the Allied Military Command before the invasion starts," said Shaw.

"How do you know this map is accurate?" questioned Marceau.

We don't know that, but this is the only map we have," replied Shaw.

"If this is inaccurate we have a problem and so will the Allied Military Landing Forces," said Marceau.

"We realize that. This is partly the reason why we had to meet you," said Parker.

"So we need justification before we consider sending the message," remarked Marceau.

"The question is do we have the resources and opportunities to verify these markings. I don't know how we can pull it off. The present German surveillance will totally prohibit any excursion to the area. Even with your uniform and engineering sophistication I don't think that you'll be able to get close enough to verify the map," continued Marceau.

"We have very little time, Marceau," said Shaw.

"Suppose you can manage to check all the markings, how could we send the map across the Channel?" asked Marceau.

"That is our next question," said Parker.

"We have a dilemma here, don't we?" surmised Marceau.

"We certainly have one and that is why we need your expertise," replied Shaw.

"Well, we cannot put the carriage before the horse. First, we must verify these findings on the map and then worry about the transportation of the message," declared Shaw.

"It looks like you are in another difficult situation, but you are good at inventing new stories and convincing the commandant that you must survey the area."

"Thank you Marceau for your confidence. But the area is absolutely restricted for any outsiders. We tried to enter two weeks ago for an inspection and we were told that we need a special permit from the Military Headquarters," said Shaw.

"Good luck, Gentlemen. Please let us know when you're ready to send the message."

Parker returned to the street where Bridget and Marceau had their leisurely stroll and after a careful inspection they stepped out of the car. Shaw and Parker decided to give it another try to inspect the Pointe du Hoc defenses.

Both were stopped at the entrance of the military perimeter leading to the various gun emplacements.

"May we speak to the commandant?" asked Shaw.

"May I ask why you need to speak to the commandant?" asked the soldier in charge.

"We have an assignment to study the feasibility of a new structure," replied Shaw.

"Thank you. I shall inform the commandant of your presence and the nature of your study."

Shaw and Parker were asked to wait for the commandant who took thirty minutes until he finished training the new soldiers. The commandant was a big man. He was tall, 6 feet 3 inches, and heavy, 250 lbs. He had broad shoulders and a big face with thick eyebrows. His mouth was wide with protruding lips. He arrived from his meeting with a disappointed manner.

"I just cannot understand how I can train these young men when they are still in diapers. They have no understanding of guns, ammunitions, and maintaining of ordnance, but we have no mature soldiers left and must take whoever we get," said the commander.

"So, what brought you gentlemen here?"

"We are here on a secret mission. We must study the feasibility of a casemate that can be rotated 180 degrees to face the sea and the shoreline. It would be embedded in the cliff and completely camouflaged," said Shaw.

"Do you have the papers for this study?"

"Because of the nature of this ultra secret construction, we do not have any papers," replied Shaw.

"I must have a written request to let you study this strategically important cliff; otherwise you are not permitted to enter this garrison. I can, however, make a call to the military headquarters in Caen to ask for a permit."

"Yes, but you will violate the confidentiality of the project," responded Shaw.

"I have already stated my position. I cannot allow anybody to enter without authorization."

Parker asked the commandant for a short conference with his partner.

"We could ask Michael to give us a paper," said Parker.

"Good idea, why don't we try?" said Shaw.

"We could try to get permission, but we must implicate your name," said Shaw to the commandant.

"How long would this construction take place?" asked the commandant.

"We don't know, but we would get all the manpower that is available," said Shaw.

"I just wonder, because the invasion is expected pretty soon. I don't think that you will be able to finish the project. The Allied reconnaissance planes will notice the material supply and the RAF and US bombers will bomb the hell out of your cement, reinforcing rods and other equipment," said the commandant.

"We will use all the deception. The supply trucks will bear the Red Cross emblem. We will be careful with the supply materials. We will package them as medicine and medical supplies," said Parker.

"Well, I thought it over. I will let you survey the cliff and the area in general, under the following circumstances. You will be accompanied by two sentries. All your notations will be inspected by me before you leave. You must submit to being searched at any time when my soldiers ask you. You cannot have a camera and take pictures. You cannot ask questions concerning our defense structures and strategies."

"Thank you. We will respect your wishes. May we start tomorrow morning?" asked Parker.

"Yes. You may start at five o'clock in the morning."

Shaw and Parker were absolutely delighted to pull off this assignment without much difficulty. They spent the rest of the day at home, listening to music and reading. Shaw and Parker awakened to their alarm clock at three o'clock in the morning. It was rather early for them, but they were used to working at different hours of the day. Shaw and Parker prepared a nutritious meal because they did not know when they would complete their study.

"I think we must make a mental note of everything that we see and use the musical lyrics to remember the information. This is the only way we can protect our findings. "For the 'alleged' survey we use numbers. The commandant will have no idea what the numbers represent. If he will ask us, we'll tell him that the figures are compass numbers," said Shaw.

They arrived at the designated place and time. The commandant was waiting for them and the introduction to each other began. Name, serial number, rank, and unit was exchanged and noted. Shaw and Parker showed their identification cards and everything seemed to be in order. The commandant assigned the two soldiers and the tour began.

Shaw and Parker were overwhelmed by the elaborate defense structures, from machine guns to 88mm anti-tank guns. They carefully set up their survey kits, transit, and other instruments. While one was busy with the metering, the other, made mental notations of the machine gun, tobruk, and other gun positions. Since there were so many, it was cumbersome to remember all the placements above the cliff and embedded into the rocks.

The commandant came to see both of them and brought some liqueur along. He was fascinated by their surveying method and asked a few questions to satisfy his curiosity and justify his permission to do the study.

"I hope you found what you wanted."

"I am afraid we found the project to be more difficult than it was originally conceived," said Shaw.

"I told you, this is a very complex project, and it would be very difficult to hide."

"Well, we are glad to study it, and who knows, we may succeed without being destroyed by the enemy," said Parker.

"I really like your optimism and spirit. I must return now

to my post, but if you have any problems, just call on me, and I will help you out."

Shaw and Parker were exhausted by early afternoon. They tried to remember all the important sites by using the music lyrics method, but by three o'clock both had run out of music and lyrics. At four o'clock, they were about to leave when they had two military intelligence visitors.

"I was informed that you are on a secret mission," said one of the officers.

"Yes, we are and we hope we have all the necessary data," said Parker.

"Who gave you the authorization to study this particular site?" asked the other officer.

"That is top military secret," said Parker.

"We were not informed in advance about your secret survey," said the first officer.

"That is not our problem. But remember, it is in the military regulations, that a top secret project must not to be announced to any agency," bluffed Parker.

"You may be correct, but I failed to read this military regulation," replied the first officer.

"Learning is a lifelong process," remarked Shaw.

"You are very right. We will read the secret section of the military regulation. Thank you," said the second officer.

Shaw and Parker had enough data to pack up their instruments and call it a day. They stopped at the commandant office and exchanged a few pleasantries.

It was close to five o'clock when Shaw and Parker returned to their cars and headed to a nearby restaurant to have a meal. Shaw called Bridget and told her that the fishing trip was successful and that they would call tomorrow to discuss it.

Shaw was getting really tired and skipped the dessert. Parker felt the same way and drove home to have a good night's sleep.

The next morning, they put down their coded lyrics on a piece of paper and compared the findings with Rebecca's papers.

"I find some sections coincide with Rebecca markings, but there are some discrepancies in terms of locations and weapons," said Parker.

"I have the same results in terms of ordnances and the respective locations," replied Shaw.

"We have a problem with authenticity," remarked Parker.

"We can send the map with some areas as 'verified' and the others as 'questionable,' " said Shaw.

"We better discuss this with Marceau," suggested Shaw.

"I will call Bridget's friend to contact Bridget and ask for an urgent meeting," said Parker.

"Please do that, thank you."

"Hello, hello. Please ask Bridget to come to the phone." The neighbor went to get Bridget.

"Hello, this is Bridget."

"I would like to meet with you at the same place at five o'clock tomorrow."

"I'll meet you there. Bye."

Bridget and Marceau were ten minutes late. Both were walking slowly toward the designated meeting place. Parker started the car but saw another car trailing after Marceau.

He gave a parking 'red light' signal twice and zoomed away. Marceau and Bridget turned around and headed back toward the shop. The other car stopped. Parker drove around the block and returned to the same street. He stopped the car behind one car that had been following Marceau.

Parker got out of the car and approached the driver. He bluntly asked him why he was following Bridget and Marceau.

"I was not following those people. I was looking for an address," said the driver.

"You are in a security zone; may I see your identification paper?"

"Who are you to ask me for my identification paper?"

"I am a German Security and Intelligence officer."

"But you have an Organization Todt jacket on."

"That is just to camouflage my intelligence mission."

"Well, in that case, we are deputy Gestapo agents working for German Intelligence."

"Good. Why don't you leave your car here and join us in our car so we can share some secrets with you."

"What kind of secrets?"

"I cannot tell you while you are in your car."

"Why? What is wrong with sitting in our car?"

"I am not going to stand and bend down to talk to you. It is impolite," said Parker.

Both agents got out of their car and started to walk toward Shaw and Parker's car. Parker pulled out the service revolver and Shaw tied their hands together and taped their mouths shut to keep them from yelling. Shaw and Parker drove with the two guys to the nearest restaurant to call Philip.

"Hello, Philip, this is Brian."

"How are you? What's happening?"

"We have two Gestapo traitors to exterminate and a car to incinerate."

"Does Marceau know about it?"

"We had no time to tell him. The two were following him and Bridget and we caught them."

"It will cost you a few francs."

"We don't worry about money."

"How many men do you need?"

"At least three but four would be better."

"You give me the pickup address and I will tell you our arrival time."

"We are at Pierre's café."

"It will take us thirty to forty minutes to meet you there. Of course, it all depends on how long the street patrols examine our garbage truck."

"Thank you. We are waiting for you. Please hurry if you can. Bye."

Shaw made another call to Bridget and told her what was happening. Both agreed to meet after dinner, at seven o'clock at the same location.

Philip was on time with four strong armed men. One went to pick up the traitor's car and the other three took the gagged traitors and tossed them inside the garbage truck. They were taken to be incinerated along with their automobile. Both were given cyanide pills before they were burned in a 1371 Celsius degree fire. The car was melted beyond recognition so the Gestapo had no chance to trace their demise and the car. The deputy Gestapo agents just simply disappeared.

Shaw and Parker went back to meet with Marceau and Bridget. Marceau and Bridget quickly climbed into the car. The earlier events shook them a little bit.

"I can't believe that this Gestapo snake is still after me," snapped Marceau.

"He will chase you until something happens to him," replied Shaw.

"So, gentlemen, what is happening? What was so urgent that we had to meet again?"

"We have two versions of the Pointe du Hoc. One is authentic, but the other one is not. Rebecca's map does not match with many of our findings. Further study is required by air and commandos," said Parker.

"I don't know how I can send these maps electronically," said Marceau.

"You have fabulous connections," said Shaw.

"I do, but circumstances have changed. I will not jeopardize the people for maps that have partially authentic findings. I have, however, a small chance to smuggle the microfilm with a diplomatic courier to England. One of my Resistance operative's boyfriend is a Spanish diplomat. He will be in Port-En-Bessin tomorrow and I can ask him to accept a nice gold ring for a trip to England. Of course, I will tell him about the contents of the ring. He will take it to MI6 and wait until they disassemble the ring and solder it back like new."

"It is an expensive gift," said Shaw.

"Can you attach money to save lives?"

"Thank you, Marceau. Here are the papers and we hope for the best," said Parker. Bridget hid the papers inside her bra. Shaw and Parker carefully looked around and let Marceau and Bridget exit from the car. Bridget held on to Marceau's arm and they briskly walked in the direction of the shop.

CHAPTER EIGHT

Shaw and Parker met with only two Carentan cell members, Jeanne and Edith. The other member, Georges, was ill with pneumonia. The place was in old barn with a leaky roof and the torrential rain was beating heavily on the cobblestone floor. The operatives, who were in their late twenties, were soaking wet and shivering when the agents greeted them. Parker suggested that they enter the farmhouse that was empty for the day. While they had a chance to shed their clothes and dry them, Shaw found a couple of blankets and tossed them into the living room for the two cell members to wrap their bodies in while they talked. Parker put some water on the stove which was still hot from the morning fire. He made some coffee for everybody. Shaw and Parker moved into the adjacent bedroom so that they could discuss their findings.

"We had a difficult time collecting information," said Jeanne. "As hairdressers we were lucky to enter the bunkers under strict supervision. Cutting hair for the officers and soldiers did not give us much opportunity to look around. We only had two occasions to study the forbidden military zones and that was rather limited in scope. In both situations we were having intimate affairs with the officers and what we noticed appeared to be very unusual to us. We saw toward the south westerly direction water inundating the terrain, making an artificial lake toward the Channel. I asked the officer, while he was trying to undress me what was going on, and he said it was a trap for the invading parachute jumpers. In his excitement to make love to me on the ground, I had a chance to see the vastness of the flood. It was immense, but I can't describe the measurements in kilometers."

"I had a similar experience with my lover," said Edith, "with the exception that my eager beaver took his sweet time to unbutton my blouse and skirt. It took him forever to unhook my bra which gave me plenty of time to observe the area. I saw the lakes in the same directions, gun emplacements in terms of pill boxes, mortar launches, and anti-tank guns, all surrounding the flood zones. It was an eerie sight. After his big excitement, we talked about the swampy defenses and he said that as soon as the air born drops begin, they will be shot either in their descent or in the water. In the flood lights, they will be blinded and unable to distinguish between land and water. I felt like puking as he uttered his words. I could have had pleasure with him had he kept his mouth shut."

"We want to thank you for your observations. This is important information that you have provided, and it will be difficult to avoid the water traps if they miss the target," said Shaw.

Shaw and Parker left the farm for the next meeting at St. Mere Eglise. The cell members, unfortunately, did not provide any information that Shaw and Parker did not already know. They left disappointed, but under the increased security circumstances their expectations were considerably lower than six months ago. The German infantry was all over town waiting for the invading forces by air and ground, but the Allies were confident to take the town according to the reports available at that time. Shaw and Parker had one more visit with the Cherbourg cell before they made their own Normandy assessment and submitted the report to Allied Intelligence.

The next day they had to return to Cherbourg again to meet with another cell, which replaced the previous one because of Gestapo surveillance. There were two females and one male operative present in an apartment that was for sex demonstrations and practices. They were recruited by Marceau as independent operators about four months ago and proved to be very skilled in intelligence collection. They had superior connections and put German officers into twilight zones during their pleasuring highs using drugs and liqueur combinations. They were able to extract some information during the sexual encounters, but most facts and figures came from personal contacts with German soldiers, skilled workers, and specialists who worked in bunkers and coastal shipping.

These operators practiced highly skilled sexual therapy for those who had sexual difficulties and were addicted to sexual pleasures. Their fees were expensive but they gave deep discounts to German officers to extract information.

Vivienne, Sera, and Charles were very well endowed in every respect. They were pretty and intelligent girls in their early thirties. They had a well kept shapely bodies and seductive behavior. Charles was a handsome, tall and slender young man in his late twenties and had a wonderful effect on people. He was kind, informative, and a good teacher.

According to the reports, the city had three ridge lines for the German outer defense.

Most of the defense concentration was focused on the attacks from the sea. The ground defense had some weak points. The further examination of classified information and the continuing search for relevant details was part of Shaw and Parker's assignment.

"Thank you for the information, your personal sacrifice, and volunteering for this difficult and dangerous assignment," said Shaw.

They left with some satisfaction, but again given the circumstances, they had to be satisfied with generalities. For the next few days Shaw and Parker were mostly occupied with filling in all the details that the operatives could not provide.

Marceau had an unusually difficult day at the shop. Customers were crabby and complained about the materials that were somewhat of poorer quality than before the war. The heels and soles did not last as long as they had experienced before. It was just one of those things, crazy irritating things that Marceau could not do anything about.

Marceau finished the day with certain sadness. He closed the shop and prepared for dinner, which meant washing his hands and assisting Bridget who was cooking a fine meal. They loved to chat whenever time permitted and shared a few jokes with a glass of good wine in hand. It was a way to relieve the stress before they sat down to eat their evening meal.

"What's new?" asked Marceau.

"Not much today. You have a lot of mail."

"Junk mail, bills to pay, or excuses for the delays of needed materials."

"Well, well, just don't be so pessimistic. There may be some good news."

"How is your friend, Michael?"

"He is fine, working hard to lose the war. How is your girlfriend? I have not seen her for sometime?"

"She is well and lovely as ever. I am delighted to have such a wonderful companion."

"You don't talk too much about her. Why is that?"

"I don't know. We are just keeping things to ourselves."

"Dinner is ready. Let's sit down and enjoy it."

Marceau cut two fresh pieces of the bread and began to eat his favorite cauliflower soup.

"Good soup. You made it just the way I like it."

"Thank you. I try to please you, but sometimes I am not always able to get what you like."

"Don't worry about it. It is not your fault. Besides I love whatever you're making."

"That is nice of you to say, but I can read your body language and it tells me what you don't like."

"You can make mistakes sometimes, especially when the meaning gets lost in translation."

"It can happen, of course. How is the veal?"

"It is excellent. The sauce is out of this world. The potato is crisp. The salad is just right. You are a fine cook."

"What did you bake for dessert?"

"Wonderful. Just add a fresh cup of coffee and you made my day."

"And you made my day too. I just love to cook for you. You appreciate my cooking."

"What would really make me happy is to see you sitting down with me and having a little chat. I have not had a good conversation with you in some time, but before we do that, I would like to read my mail, if you don't mind."

"Go ahead; I'll clean the dishes in the meantime."

Marceau went to his desk and opened his mail one by one. As he read one letter, he became motionless.

"What's the matter Marceau? You look totally transfixed."

"Yes I am shocked. Here read this."

Bridget read the letter and she was surprised also. "Well, you are being appreciated for your outstanding work and services you rendered."

"It is quite unusual, to invite me for a testimonial dinner by a number of Nazis and their sympathizers. I am to bring along a companion, meaning you."

"How about Colleen, they never met her?"

"She would not go. She hates them, just forget her! Colleen is very loyal to France and the Resistance.

Will you join me, Bridget, for this special occasion?"

"Of course, I want to share your happy moments of celebration."

"Well, let's sit down and chat a while. You were about to finish, weren't you?"

"Just give me five minutes more. Let me go to the bathroom, and then I'm all yours." While she was in the bathroom, Marceau read the rest of his mail and scribbled some notes on each envelope.

"I'm all yours, Marceau. I want to talk about Colleen. You are a very private couple, and I seldom hear anything about her."

"She is just fine, a very kind, warm-hearted, sensuous lady, who makes me happy. She is pretty as always and taking very good care of herself. Twice a week she gets massage therapy, goes to the gym and exercises with a few ladies and gentlemen, studies world economics, and snuggles with me in bed. She has a balanced life."

"Is she still working?"

"Oh yes, she is still with the same company. Colleen is an excellent bookkeeper. She works long hours, but her weekends are free. Her work day starts at six in the morning, and ends at, four sometimes five in the afternoon."

"You're really enjoying her company. Is she a good cook?"

"She is a marvelous cook and her dishes are exotic. Colleen's first husband was a continental chef on a cruise ship. She learned a great deal from her late husband."

"And sex, where did she learn that? I heard from your previous girlfriend, Darlene, that it is not easy to please you."

"Yes, I have an artistic pleasure to make love. It has to be creative, romantic, passionate, and long-lasting, and Colleen has a knack for it. It is in her genes. She can have a different sex play every week. And she goes for total exhaustion."

"I am glad that you can talk about it. Most men don't like to talk about their sexuality."

"But, my dear, it is so natural, creative, and a part of life."

"What are you going to say at your testimonial?"

"I don't know. May be you could help me."

"Why don't you talk about how you learned your craft, repairing and making footwear?"

"It is a good idea, but I don't know if they would be interested in it."

"Well, you could always talk about an interesting story from your learning years."

"Maybe that will work. I remember Madam Toulouse back from many years ago, who demanded an absolutely perfect boot that had to be done over and over again. Each time I touched her precious calf, she got terribly excited, and couldn't breathe."

"Well, if it is funny, tell it to them."

"I think that my working free for the poor might be another topic."

"I think they would be impressed by your philanthropy."

"You could talk about sports. You have had some interesting hiking adventures."

"Perhaps, you are absolutely right about my hiking stories. Each story has a message."

"You must find some time to collect your memories and put them on a piece of paper."

"May be you and I could sit down again and I would retell the stories and you would jot down what I have said."

"That is a good idea Marceau. We could work together on your speech!"

"What is happening in your life, Bridget? How is Michael doing? You're seldom talking about your relationship. He comes, you leave with him and you come home late and too tired to talk about the evening."

"It is very true Marceau, but we are having a busy life. Between the customers, you're repairing and making boots, courier and recruiting assignments, we have very little time to chat about Michael and me. My feelings have hardly changed about him, and he feels the same. We are deeply in love with each other. He is a good man, who understands my life and devotion to the Resistance. He has seen the light at the end of the tunnel. Michael joined our cause and believes in freedom and democracy."

"Bridget, what you just said warms my heart. I like that young man and wish you the very best for the future."

"Well, thank you, Marceau. Your approval means a lot to me!"

They got into a pensive mood and were silent for a few moments, when a couple of hard knocks broke the silence. There were two guys in terribly wet garments asking permission to enter.

"What can I do for you, gentlemen?" asked Marceau.

"We are British commandos," said one of them with a heavy Scottish accent, "and your name was mentioned for an emergency hide-out."

"Please come in and dry up first."

"This is Scott Peterson, and I am Andrew Lang, officers of the British Army Commando Unit. We have our identity numbers and that is all we can tell you. We need food and temporary accommodation until we are going to be picked up, hopefully within twenty-four hours."

"We'll help you, but you cannot stay here. This house is occasionally under strict surveillance by the Gestapo, and we don't know if somebody reported you tonight. You can stay here for a while until I can find a place for you."

"Thank you, much appreciated," said Lang.

"This is Bridget, and she'll prepare some food for you."

Lang and Peterson shed their garments and tried to dry up in the repair room. Both were tall and muscular, handsome looking chaps, and had only one thing in mind, and that was to survive.

Bridget left the house and went to her friend to make a few calls. She also called Shaw and Parker to come over because of this unusual situation and the need for their authentication. One of her friends offered a small room with two beds.

Bridget came back with the good news.

"I'll guess you'll be fine for tonight. But what were you looking for gentlemen?" asked Marceau.

"We cannot tell you," said Peterson, "but since you are one of us fighters, I can give you a hint. We need to know what is going on in the water and the beaches as we get closer to the invasion time table."

"But I was under the impression that the French, British and American agents had supplied you with all the necessary information."

"Up to a certain point," said Lang. "We cannot tell you what was missing in their reports because it's a military secret, but we need more information."

"What happened that you got all wet?"

"We missed the boat. The Germans must have spotted the periscope because the sub went down fast."

"Did you get what you were looking for?"

"Yes," said Peterson. "We know now what we are up against."

"Do you want to send a cryptic message home?"

"We'd love to. Do you have a radio?" asked Peterson.

"You give me the message and I'll send it."

"We can do it. It's not a big deal," said Lang.

"Nobody goes to my secret radio room. My transmitter is not here. I transmit in a burst of signals from different locations, but I use it only in an emergency. Since this is vital information, I want to let them know that you are alive, and you found what you were looking for."

Bridget cooked up some beans with meat and eggs. She had an extra loaf of bread and some wine. The meal was served in thirty minutes and they were absolutely delighted to receive such a prompt and kind reception.

There was another knock on the door. Shaw and Parker came in. They were introduced to each other.

"What is the name of your outfit and where do you have your HQ" asked Shaw.

"I cannot tell you. It is a military secret," said Lang.

"My foot, you are talking to a British agent," said Shaw.

Parker smelled trouble and took out his military pistol. He put it against Lang's temple.

"You'll talk or I blow your head off," said Parker. "What is your military code?"

"I will not tell you. It is a secret."

"Yes you will or you can say good bye to this world." Shaw tied the hands of the two commandos and asked them one last time to identify their military units they belonged to, but they refused. There was nothing else to do but to get rid of them for good. Shaw gagged both of them, took out his service pistol, and with two pistols to their heads ordered them outside and into their car.

Petersen raised his hand and wanted to talk. Shaw pulled out the cloth from his mouth and he asked for mercy.

"Talk you son of a bitch," said Shaw.

"We were hired by Kohler, the Gestapo agent, to find out everything about Marceau."

"I suspected that you were German agents," said Shaw.

Shaw put the gag back in his mouth.

"We'll see what we can do with you. Come on, move your stinky body," ordered Shaw.

Before they left, Shaw whispered into Bridget's ears to find Philip and meet them at the Chez Capri Café with the garbage truck.

Philip was there waiting for them outside with his truck.

"Follow me," said Shaw as he drove to a brushy desolate country road. He stopped the car and ordered them out.

"They are all yours. These bastards are working for Kohler in the Gestapo and were impersonating commandos. They are lackeys of the worst kind," said Shaw.

Philip shot both of them in the head and they died instantly.

He threw both of them into the truck and left for the dump site. There he covered their bodies with twigs and poured gasoline all over their bodies. He lit a couple of matches and created a small inferno. When their faces burned into an unidentifiable charcoal mass and the rest of the body was glowing into an ember, he put some more wood over to complete the cremation process.

When Shaw and Parker arrived at Marceau's place, they began to look for a car that had been parked near his shop. In a nearby side street they found an old banged up vehicle that was easy to unlock. It took less than a couple of minutes for Parker to open the trunk and to their amazement, they found dry clothes, shoes, socks, underwear, pails, ropes, and black skin markers tossed all over the place. The next job was to remove the car. Luckily Parker had removed the keys from one of the "commandos" pockets before he was incinerated. Parker started the ignition and they drove the car to one of the cliffs overlooking the Channel. With a little maneuvering they pushed the car over the cliff. The impact exploded the gas tank and the flames engulfed the whole vehicle. It looked like a mass of twisted and broken burned parts.

Shaw and Parker returned to Marceau's with a sense of satisfaction.

"This time we were lucky. You and Bridget and the whole operation could have been compromised. Kohler is a sneaky animal, and he will not rest until he can prove that we are all Allied agents," said Parker.

"I'm truly sorry. We have to be more careful in the future," replied Marceau.

"There will be no repetition. Kohler is not a fool. He will not play the same game twice, especially if he lost the first time," commented Shaw.

"How did you suspect that these people were not genuine?" asked Bridget.

"I saw there was something wrong the moment I laid eyes on them. Their clothes were the give away. Commandos do not come to shore like that. They are dressed either in a long woolen underpants greased all over or a rubberized suit, but not the way they presented themselves," replied Shaw.

"It is all over. We killed both of them and drove their car over the cliff. Both chaps were incinerated and left unrecognizable in the countryside and were covered with brushes. Unfortunately we had no other alternative. In war, sometimes, we have no time to adjudicate matters, especially when it comes to life or death. This time, ours and perhaps thousands of other lives were at stake. A quick decision was the only answer. Shaw and I acted in behalf of the OSS, MI6, and the Resistance. We'll take the consequences for our action," said Parker.

"Wouldn't it be a better idea to place their charred bodies close to their burned car so it would look more like an accident?" inquired Marceau.

"We are not finished with our assassination plan. Logistics required us to act fast and worry about explanations later. It will be no problem to make the disappearance of these Gestapo agents look like they were victims of an automobile incident. We'll go back in a few minutes and hopefully the bodies will have cooled off so that we can transport them to the wreckage."

"We came to see you to let you know that we are not ready yet to send a comprehensive report to Allied Intelligence. We need a little more time to complete the details that our operatives were unable to find out," said Shaw.

"How much time do you need?"

"Give or take, two weeks," said Shaw.

"That is satisfactory for me but I don't know about the urgency of the AI."

"Given the extraordinary security of the German Army and Gestapo these days we have to proceed with extra caution," said Parker.

"We may run into some new construction, casemates, gun emplacements, or 'secret weapons' which could delay our comprehensive reporting, but we'll let you know," said Shaw.

"Thank you for your patience and cooperation. We are sorry about what happened, but when we are at war anything can happen. We must go now and we'll check back next week. Bye, and have a wonderful evening together," said Parker.

"We will, and adieu, my friends!" said Marceau.

Shaw and Parker returned to the charred bodies and carefully placed them into the trunk of their car. They covered them with blankets and some old newspapers. The site of the broken-up automobile was fortunately poorly lit and they had no problems throwing the bodies toward the front seat without being seen. Shaw and Parker rushed back to their car and sped away without a second look.

Marceau expressed his sorrow about the incident and asked Bridget to continue their chat. Bridget put on some hot water for tea and served some freshly baked cookies with it.

"I will try to make my speech short and witty," said Marceau.

"By the way, how is Michael? I haven't seen him in quite a while."

"He is busy trying to make plans for the invasion. It is a very difficult time for him.

He has no spirit to fight the Allies, nor does he have the military support he asked for. He hopes to survive as a prisoner and go to the other side."

"I hope he'll be lucky and be captured unscathed."

"What is your assessment of the information we were able to provide to the Allies?"

"I think we did a splendid job within the means of our knowledge. There are some areas we cannot touch because Hitler has the upper hand. The Germans are good fighters and have the best panzer divisions. The best panzers are prepared to fight in the Pas de Calais region and they will not be released to move until Hitler is convinced that the invasion will be in Normandy. It did not happen so far. The Allies will have a formidable force, equipment, and supplies when they hit the beaches, but they will not lose their shirts if things do not go well. They are cautious and have the best strategic brains to establish a solid beachhead."

"You are encouraging to listen to Marceau. I wish I had your assessment of the situation."

"You have, because you live this war every day. You know what is going on. It is not too difficult to understand the nature of power. The Germans want to keep it. The Allies want to take it back. You also understand the historical antecedents. The methodology, however, has been different to gain, exercise, and keep power. The German inhumanity has been rationalized and defended as a result of the suffering of the German people after World War One. But what the Germans call inhumanity by the Allies does not come close to what they have been doing to their enemies since Hitler came to power. This war is more than a fight for power. Political ideologies play an important role that fuels the soul. The war will not be over after the Allies win this war. Political, religious and ethnic differences will exist for a long time."

"You have an early appointment tomorrow."

"I know Bridget, we should go to sleep, but I just love talking with you. Good night my dear I'll see you at seven."

"By the way, what's with the house sitters for the testimonial dinner?"

"A couple of guys volunteered to watch the place just in case the Gestapo's Kohler sends some curious hooligans. You'll never know. These days you can't be cautious enough."

"Pleasant dreams Marceau; it was nice talking with you again."

Two nights later, they were both ready to attend the testimonial dinner. She was dressed in a long, black evening gown with a white corsage, and Marceau wore a tuxedo. They looked stunning for the occasion. Both were seated at the head table and were honored with fresh flowers. There was a lot of chitchat before and during dinner. Before the dessert was served there was a short introduction of the coming events for the evening.

The master of ceremony called Marceau to take the center stage. He was squeamish concerning the whole appearance and it took him forever to rise and walk to the center of the table. He did not, however, present himself as a skittish fellow, but rather as one who was well prepared. He thanked the Generals and Officers for the invitation and the recognition. His entire speech was brief, not more than four minutes. He received a standing ovation. He was followed by a couple of generals who expressed their admiration for his art and workmanship.

After the speeches and dessert, there was a short meeting of the minds at the bar, but most of them began to disperse and leave the place. Marceau and Bridget only stayed for a very brief period, just long enough to again thank the Generals for their generosities. As they left the building, Bridget was curious and asked Marceau, "What happened to your childhood and witty remarks?"

"I must have had stage fright."

"Marceau. I can't believe you. You had stage fright?"

"You are right. I did not want to bore them. Plus, I was not in the mood. You know, I am not a hypocrite. I went because I found it unusual to be recognized by the German Generals. But who knows? Maybe there are some good people left among the German military."

"It's all right to say little. You received an accolade, and that is important for our cause. Let's go home happy and have a good night sleep."

The place was pitch dark, not a sound was heard. Marceau opened the door, turned on the light and to his surprise there were two bodies gagged, hands and feet tied with ropes, and their faces beaten black and blue.

"What happened?" asked Marceau of the two Resistance operatives who were house-sitting.

"These guys broke in and started to look around so we beat and tied them up and here they are," said one of the operatives named Pierre.

Marceau removed the gags and asked for their names, occupations, and several identification questions, and then he began to interrogate them. Bridget sat next to Marceau and stared at them with contempt.

"I could call the police and have them arrest you, but I don't think it is the wisest thing to do. You must tell us the truth because your life depends on it. You lie and you die! And I mean it! So, who sent you here?"

"The Gestapo," said one of the guys.

"What was his name in the Gestapo?"

"Agent Kohler," was the answer from the other person.

"What did he tell you to do and what was his offer or reward to you?"

"He told me to break in to your place and look for documents, hidden closets, and places where we can find intelligence materials that you are collecting and sending to the Allies. He offered me a million francs and promised to release my daughter from prison who was caught stealing documents from a German officer," said the first guy.

"Was she working for the Resistance?"

"She was one of the Maquis," said the same guy.

"We will hand you over to the Resistance for detention and they will determine your future. You will not return home until the end of the war. You are a traitor. The Maquis will verify your story."

"Please take them to Mr. Buchard. He will find a place for them," said Marceau. Pierre gagged them again, tied both of them together, put his pistol to the one guy's head and ordered them to get into Pierre's car. They were clubbed unconscious and the two operatives drove in the Cherbourg direction.

"Kohler cannot rest. He must do everything to prove that he is onto something," said Bridget.

"You are right my dear. But time is on our side and we'll get Kohler."

"Michael promised that he will club him personally."

"It is not soon enough."

"I hope the guys will deliver them to Mr. Buchard."

"They will. These operatives are smart and tough guys. If anything goes wrong they will kill them first before the Germans take them. They will come back early in the morning with the report."

"Good night, Marceau. See you in the morning."

The two operatives knocked on the door at 0730. The sun rays almost blinded Bridget's eyes as she opened the shop door and allowed them to enter the store.

"How was the trip to Buchard's gentlemen?"

"We had a little trouble with security, but we delivered the two burglars to Buchard," said Pierre.

"What kind of trouble?" asked Bridget.

"Oh, they asked about the two guys and we told them that they were drunk, belligerent, and obnoxious," said Maurice, the other operative."

"What did Buchard say? What is going to happen with them?" asked Bridget.

"A ship is sailing to Portugal tomorrow and hopefully they will be crated and delivered along with other zoo animals.

They will stay in Lisbon and then be shipped to Puerto Rico until the end of the war. After the war, they'll come back to France and will face trial for treachery and burglary. This way the Gestapo will never know what happened to them. We have quite a number of people jailed overseas and waiting for trial. Gestapo collaborators are either killed or sent overseas," said Pierre.

"How do you keep them quiet?" Bridget inquired.

"We drug them, and they sleep until they are permanently jailed. Among the crew there is a Resistance operative, who takes care of them. We don't take any risks," said Maurice.

"How many are in the waiting?" asked Bridget.

"We ship about a dozen or two from France and other parts of Europe. These captains are well paid. Some charge three times the cost of a one way trip, but they deliver and that is very important to us," said Pierre.

"Now I can sleep better," said Bridget jokingly.

"Thank you gentlemen," said Marceau.

"For you, Marceau, we do anything. You have done more for the Resistance than any of the guys I know."

"There are some very deserving operatives like me who risk their life for freedom and France, which in a way is, synonymous," said Marceau.

"We know that, but you are very special to us!" said Maurice.

"Well, thank you for your compliments, for house-sitting and capturing those burglars," said Marceau.

It had been a long day for Marceau and Bridget. By early afternoon they were ready to call it a day.

There were too many problems with repairs and new boot orders. During the lunch break Marceau listened to MI6 messages and there were a few requests. On the top of it all, there was a sudden emergency.

Fleur, the daughter of his best friend, came in panic, to ask for Marceau's help.

"Dad was shot by the Germans. He escaped, but needs surgery. The bullet is lodged in his back and he is bleeding badly. We cannot take him to the hospital under his real name. He must be admitted under an assumed name."

Marceau ran across the street and made a call to the hospital administrator in Caen. He had no problem admitting his friend but he was told that there was a shortage of blood. His friend, Roger, who was lying in the car and waiting for the transport, was taken by Fleur and Marceau to Caen. They drove quickly but safely. Bridget followed Marceau. When they arrived, the surgeon was waiting for him and he was prepared for surgery in the emergency room. The administrator had already taken care of the paperwork and they were waiting for the lab results. Bridget volunteered to give blood if there was a match. The results showed that Bridget's blood was compatible with Roger's and he was taken immediately to the operating room. He had lost a lot of blood but fortunately was saved by Bridget's blood. The operation lasted for three hours and there were moments of crises when the Gestapo entered the hospital and looked at the registration papers. Fortunately, nothing looked suspicious and the agents left without looking around. During the second hour of surgery, Roger had some heart rhythm problems but it was corrected and he survived the operation without any further problems.

When he was taken to the recovery room, the surgeon informed Fleur that he was very close to death when he arrived to the hospital. His loss of blood and the lung damage caused by the bullet made his survival very critical. But because they were lucky to find a matching donor, the blood loss was stabilized. The operation was a success thanks in part to his strength and bodily constitution.

"What happened to Roger?" asked Marceau.

"He was asked to assist in a sabotage operation. The Maquis planned to blow up a train transporting ammunition to the batteries. They succeeded, but the last cars had a number of accompanying soldiers who survived and shot Roger as he was fleeing from the wreckage. The good thing was that it was pitch dark and nobody recognized his blackened face."

"I would like to thank Marceau and Bridget for their contribution and help," said the surgeon. Then he added, "I wrote in his chart that the operation was a tumor removal in the left lower lung which required immediate surgery. This should satisfy the Gestapo."

"Thank you doctor, we really appreciate it," said Marceau.

"We must go now, Fleur, and I hope you'll inform us about his progress," said Marceau.

Marceau drove home and they talked about everything to stay awake. When they arrived home, Marceau went to his secret room and listened to his coded messages which usually were repeated every half hour until it was received. There was again one waiting for him that he acknowledged. The detailed message will be delivered by an MI6 agent who will introduce himself as Shaw's friend from MI6 school and will identify himself by Marceau's and Bridget's birthdays.

Shaw and Parker were informed by Bridget about the MI6 message and a tentative meeting was scheduled pending the arrival of the British agent. Bridget was given telephone numbers where she could contact them. Marceau requested that the meeting should be held in Shaw's car somewhere out in the countryside.

Two days later, they met. Shaw recognized him immediately. He identified their birthdays and introduced himself as Robert.

"AI needs to know what the German High Command knows and what counterattack plans they have. It is an urgent request," said Robert.

Then he added, "MI6 has been experimenting with a small radio transmitter and variable frequencies that is classified as top secret. It is the size of a boot's heel and consists of tiny transistors. It is neither patented nor available on the commercial market. We would like to insert it into one of the boots that Marceau is preparing or repairing for one of the German generals."

"How about the power and antenna?" asked Parker.

"Good questions. We thought about them. If we could have the antenna embedded in the sole, or better than that in the upper parts of the boot, the reception could extend for a mile or even several miles depending on the location of the building. The power supply would last about two weeks and is voice activated. The microphone is a super tiny hole in the back of the boot by leaving out one stitch in the sewing process."

"Is there any fail-safe protection for Marceau?" asked Shaw.

"I am sorry but the answer is no," said Robert.

"Your turn, Marceau," said Parker.

"The question is time. When would I have the opportunity to repair or prepare a boot? It could be a day, or a month. Who knows?"

"Well, there is no way to tell. But we know that Bridget's

boyfriend is a German officer and he could help us in the event we don't have a boot to insert the device in," said Robert.

"How did you obtain this information?" asked Parker.

"Well, it is common knowledge. Our agents have seen Bridget with Michael in Caen and Paris. There is nothing unusual that a German officer dates a French girl," said Robert.

"I don't believe that Michael regularly attends Generals' staff meetings or has the privilege to obtain minutes of those meetings. He could, however, inquire unofficially about plans and counterattack troop movements," said Bridget.

"What happens if the transmitter fails?" asked Marceau.

"We only have two prototypes and one we must keep at home," replied Robert.

"Who will be on the receiving end?" Marceau asked.

"I believe the assigned janitor for that day," said Robert.

"How soon do you want an answer?" asked Marceau.

"In a couple of hours," replied Robert.

"You have the transmitter with you so I can see if it will be possible to place it in the heel of the boot?" asked Marceau.

"Yes sir. Now, you'll be careful Marceau, these are expensive instruments," said Robert as he handed over the little transmitter with a listening device that fits the ear and a special copper coiled antenna.

"I'll be careful, but accidents can happen with this kind of insertion," said Marceau.

"We trust your workmanship. Your craft is par excellence," said Robert.

"Well, thank you for your confidence and compliment."

Shaw started the car and they drove back in the direction of Port-En-Bessin.

Two hours later, Robert entered the shop and Marceau told

him that it will fit into the heel of a boot and that he is accepting the assignment. Bridget, however, had some reservations and concerns but was proud that Marceau accepted the assignment. The only thing left was waiting for the occasion.

Marceau had reached the zenith of his potentials not only as the finest craftsman of his trade but as a compatriot, an ingenious and courageous courier of the Resistance, a humanitarian, and most of all as a dedicated stepfather. His philosophical orientation about life came from his father, who was a lay minister in a small village of France. He taught Marceau about the sense of freedom, values, justice, and about the importance of taking care of his fellow man.

The Gestapo did not know what to do with him because there was nothing on him that warranted his arrest. His supporters, the German generals, officers, and the public at large, offset the few accusations against him by his enemies. But most importantly, he survived because of his faith and luck. He was a God loving, religious Catholic who prayed every night before he went to sleep and observed the great holidays within the means of his circumstances.

His personal life was private. Since his wife passed away he spent most of his personal time between his girlfriend, Colleen, and stepdaughter, Bridget. The rest of his life was devoted to his craft and the liberation of France. Crab fishing was an avocation but it was mostly a means to connect with the Allies.

It was Marceau's greatest wish to make a substantial contribution to the Resistance and save France from the brutal German dictatorship. Robert, from MI6, was a Godsend to Marceau. He really felt that his cooperation with AI could be an important input in the Allied planning of the invasion.

Marceau resigned that his work as a stepfather, cobbler,

a Resistance courier and recruiter were the three most important aspects of his life and anything else was enjoyment and sideshow. Marceau, however, offered much more than he realized. He was a Resistance operator, a procurer of resistance manpower, an advisor in underground activities, and a good friend to many who needed his help, companionship, and solace for their souls.

It started out as an unusual morning. The store was jammed with customers and everybody needed repairs. It was if there was a premonition of the masses that something was in the air, that something was going to happen, and it was better to get prepared for the unknown events.

General Furstenbrenner came along with the throng and greeted Marceau with a big smile on his face, like someone who had not seen his best friend for years.

"Marceau, Marceau, bonjour mon ami! Comment allez-vous? Good morning my friend. How are you?"

"Bien merci,-Good thanks," said Marceau. "Please come in to my salon, make yourself comfortable. I will be with you in a few minutes, let me take care of these people because Bridget is not available."

"Don't worry, do what you have to do. I can wait. No problem."

Within minutes Bridget reappeared, and the traffic of customers started to slow down. Bridget took over some of his customers, including the General.

"General Furstenbrenner, we did not have the pleasure to see you for sometime. So nice to see you."

"Oh I am so glad I found you working today. You are my favorite shopkeeper, besides the cobbler!"

"That is very nice of you to say. How can I help you?"

"Maybe this is a premonition, but I don't think I'll be able to order a pair of boots from you for a long, long time."

"Why are you saying this?"

"Well, the war is coming closer to the Western Front."

"What do you mean, Herr General?"

"I hope you'll keep this between us, but the invasion is around the corner."

"May Marceau retake your measurements while you explain?"

"Just go ahead, my foot may have changed a little since you took the last measurements."

"We have information from the Abwehr, our intelligence agency, that the Allies are ready to launch an attack, but we are uncertain of the location and time. Normandy would be ideal for the Allies because we lack the necessary strength."

"I don't know who will win, but we are not prepared the way we should be."

"But you are a strong army."

"Not so strong. Our fighters are a mixed bunch of people, and so is the equipment.

Hitler is holding back the panzers, because his logic, despite his instinct that the major invasion will be in Normandy, is that the invasion will be north from here, Pas de Calais or farther up, and anything that happens in this region will be diversionary. He runs the show, we are not in command. I think we'll be badly beaten and the Allies will be in Berlin next year."

"I am not a military woman and I cannot assess the situation. I would like to know, however, how soon will we have to move from this location if the invasion is imminent?"

"Oh, I cannot tell you that. Nobody knows except for a

few people in the Allies High Command. We Generals have no idea. We are guessing. But as a friend I will tell you when to move. Our intelligence is mixed as far as the location and time is concerned. Some say the invasion is going to be next month, others say two months. Others are equally confused about the locations. Some officers are concerned about the moon and the weather. There is not one cohesive plan that we can base our defense posture on. To top off all this guesswork, Rommel is planning to go home and celebrate his wedding anniversary. Now, you can understand why we are going to lose this war."

"How soon do you need these boots?"

"Well, it would be nice if you could have them in two weeks."

"I will have to ask Marceau about that."

Bridget asked Marceau to give a timetable for the completion of the boots. He came over and told the General that he'll do his best to deliver them in two weeks.

"That is fine. If I were you, I'd start packing all the fragile things. Things can happen rather fast and your place can be shelled before you know it. You also want to have your papers and documents in a safe place. Try to find out who has an air raid and shell proof bunker. Let me know when the boots are ready, and please keep our discussion confidential. Thank you, and adieu."

"Bridget, I am speechless. I can't believe what I heard from this General. He actually told me that the High Command has no idea where the invasion is coming from and that Hitler has the panzers in the Pas de Calais area. That is where the military expects the Allies will land and everywhere else is just subterfuge. So why bother to insert the transmitter when he already spilled the beans?"

"Well, what the General has said is one opinion. Allied

Intelligence would like to have a more comprehensive view, and for all practical purposes, you have already promised to insert the transmitter. This is an excellent opportunity."

"Good thinking, but he sounded so convincing to me. It was like the consensus of many military men. Maybe or maybe not, I will try to put in the transmitter. By the way, I am going to visit Colleen tonight."

"That is a good idea, Marceau; you have not seen her for a couple of weeks. You need company, a little diversion, not to mention time cuddling with her."

"I better get going and prepare the base of this boot; it is a different construction. I must strengthen the heels on both so they would feel the same."

Colleen prepared his favorite marinated chicken for dinner and crepes for dessert. He was absolutely elated with the flavors that were created in the marinade.

"Colleen, my sweetheart, you have a penchant to titillate my sensory organs. You not only made a delicious dinner tonight, but excited every nerve fiber in my body."

"Well, that was the whole idea. I want you to be excited."

"But, my love, I am. You create a flame just by looking and touching you."

Marceau embraced Colleen and kissed her passionately. They left the dining area and they slowly undressed each other. He looked at her while his fingers wandered slowly up her left thigh, and her hand caressed his body. They loved their very gentle touch, their tender care. It was exhilarating excitement of pleasuring. Both of them were great friends and lovers.

Marceau usually left in the early hours, long before sun-up to prepare for the next day's work and contact his Resistance colleagues for their assignments. Colleen was always up when Marceau was ready to leave and she made sure that he ate a sumptuous breakfast. Usually he had juice or fruit, eggs, bacon, sausage, bread, coffee, and some sweets.

"Darling, did you sleep well?" asked Colleen.

"I slept wonderfully in your arms."

"You were just wonderful last night. You made a great dinner and gave me a lot of pleasure. I will terribly miss you until next week."

"So will I."

"Please let me know when you are coming so I can shop and purchase the best food for you."

"Bridget will call you. This was a wonderful breakfast. Love you, darling. Au revoir."

"Adieu, my sweetheart. Drive carefully."

Marceau continued his daily chores without any problems, but it was the calm before the storm. He received a threatening letter. It was a typed letter, mailed from Caen, and was rather empty except for a telephone number. He was told to call the number at ten in the morning.

He went next door and called the number. A young sounding male voice picked up the phone and asked with a Parisian dialect, "Who is this?"

"I am Marceau Badeau and who are you?"

"You are not permitted to ask questions. Colleen was detained by us. If you want to see her alive, do what we are asking."

"What do you want?"

"I want you to write down all your illegal activities, Resistance connections, and all your intelligence functions. We will give you twenty-four hours to complete your task. After that you call again at 10 am and we'll tell you where to drop off the package."

He hung up the phone. Marceau calmly assessed the

situation. After a couple of minutes he returned to the shop and told Bridget that Colleen was abducted and she should connect with the Resistance Emergency Team and inform Shaw and Parker.

While all these contacts were assembling, Marceau made another call from his other friend's house to find out the location of the telephone number that was given to him on the paper. The telephone centers office manager, who happened to be another Resistance operator, looked up the number that turned out to be a public phone in Caen.

"We got the street and number of the phone. It is near the Gestapo headquarters."

The team members arrived to Marceau's one by one, five males and one female. By noon Shaw and Parker showed up and the discussion started by Shaw saying, "There is nothing we can do until tomorrow. We have to wait until ten in the morning."

"What if the call is short and we can't determine the location of the call?" asked Marceau.

"We stall and stall until we can find those creeps," responded Parker.

"What are we going to do after we find out their location? Can we develop a tentative plan?" asked Renoir.

"Yes, we can, providing everything happens according to our scenario," said Shaw.

"Let me illustrate," continued Shaw, "Marceau calls and he'll be told to call another number. So, he calls another number. Then he'll be warned that if his partner is apprehended Colleen will be killed. Which I don't believe, it's a bluff. Then he'll be told where to drop his confession letter. Marceau will stall by asking to talk to Colleen. There may be some delay. She could tell where she is by saying yes or no. We could develop the dialog which can determine the location. Also, Marceau's friend must stand by in the telephone office. But the important thing is to gain time, so we can locate the bastard."

"What are we going to do with the captors?" questioned Yvonne.

"We'll fry them, like before," answered Parker.

"Do you have any other questions before we hunt down those bastards?" asked Shaw.

There was an eerie silence for a minute, then, Marceau excused himself to call his friend in the telephone office. Parker asked the group to assemble the next morning at 0830. The group broke up, but Bridget, Shaw, and Parker stayed for a little chat.

"We should inform Philip to prepare the fire," said Parker.

"How about the guys in the Emergency Team?" asked Marceau.

"The Emergency Team will apprehend the culprits and hand them over to Philip," suggested Parker.

"What is wrong with the Emergency Team carrying out the execution?" questioned Marceau.

"Philip is a specialist. He has the experience, and he has never failed to carry out his assignment," replied Parker.

The next morning the group assembled and some additional details were on the table.

"What if the pick-up guy is just delivering the package and has nothing to do with Colleen?" asked Marceau.

"It is a good point. We follow the pick-up guy to the point of delivery. Then we jump. All communications' will be by signaling. Four people will split up into two groups and drive separate cars. The rest will observe. Oh, yes, and everybody must carry a pistol and silencer," said Shaw.

Shaw and Parker accompanied Marceau to his friend's

house and at two minutes after ten Marceau dialed the given number.

"Hello there," said Marceau.

"Please call the following number in twenty minutes," said the voice on the other line.

"I have to get a pencil and paper."

"I give you two minutes."

"Okay."

Marceau jotted down the new number, turned around, and said, "This was definitely a female voice."

"I believe we'll be dealing with couriers, but let's wait and see," said Parker.

"The cars should spread out and each group should use binoculars to observe from the car. One finger means jump, and two fingers mean to follow," said Shaw.

Marceau made the second call, but this time he talked to a male voice. He was instructed to leave the document in a car's trunk. Before he received the location, Marceau was trying to stall the call by complaining that the connection was poor and the abductor has to repeat every word three times. At the same time, the female Resistance operator called the friend in the telephone office and told him to intercept the call while Marceau was stalling. It was a partial success. His friend found the location, but unfortunately the call was made from a public phone.

The drop was scheduled exactly one hour later in a busy section of Caen. They all whisked to Caen at 130 km per hour. Halfway there, Shaw stopped the car and they had a five minute conference in a hay field. Shaw asked Marceau to check the bag which was stuffed with white empty sheets of paper. Then, he faced the group.

"There is a possibility that they will use an old trick and

give the bag to a second car, or pretend to give it away. This way, they think, we will be confused. But they will not be able to shake the tail. They don't know what kind of bag we are submitting. They cannot buy it in a store. It is large and painted with blue and red reflective paint that is easily visible for two kilometers. In addition, it is sealed with red wax and stamped with a round old brass plate that has two swords crossing each other. We'll be watching with binoculars from different angles. These people are amateurs, hired by Kohler, and he himself is limited in intelligence matters. Just follow my body language and we'll catch them."

The group parked the cars in strategic locations. It was virtually impossible to tell that the delivery person was being watched. As they took up their respective positions, and looked into their binoculars, an old Renault was spotted parked about 300 meters from the group at about the designated place.

Marceau slowly approached the car, exchanged a few words, nodded his head while facing the driver and gave him the bag. The group was watching the driver. He did not attempt to open the bag. He looked around and carefully left the location.

The group followed the delivery person, who did not suspect that anyone was following him.

The Renault stopped in front of a small café and Shaw pulled up next to him. He walked into the café with the bag in his hand and Shaw and Parker sat down to a nearby table. There were a few tense moments of waiting until the real culprit arrived and took the bag. He looked at the package with a curious smile, gave the delivery man some money, and left the café.

Shaw and Parker were right behind him and Shaw signaled

with his finger to jump at him. It was a very brief scuffle. The group dragged him into one of the cars and drove to a vacant area on the road.

"Well, well, so you are the brave abductor," said Parker.

The guy kept quiet and just looked at Parker. Parker slammed his fist into his stomach so hard that he could not breathe for a minute because of the pain.

"Talk you bastard or I swear I will smash your masculinity," yelled Parker.

"If anything happens to me, my partner will kill Colleen."

"I hope it will not happen, because we are very skilled in torturing you to death," said Shaw.

Parker gave him another knock-out. When he managed to get up, Parker kicked his testicles so hard that he cried with pain.

"Enough. I'll talk."

He gave the address where Colleen was being held.

"What was the agreement between you and your colleague when you received the package?" asked Shaw.

"I was told to look around and drive back to the apartment."

Parker hit his testicles again with a stick that he picked up from the field.

"You are lying. We warned you to tell the truth otherwise you will never use your penis again," said Parker.

This time Parker really hurt him and he begged him not to hit him anymore. His testicles were causing him unbearable pain. He agonized over not wanting to reveal the agreement with his partner, but he knew that he could not tolerate anymore pain.

"I was told to call him as soon as I received the package."

Parker put him in his car hand cuffed and tied him to the

front seat. He was accompanied by the group and they drove to the nearest public telephone.

"What's your name?" asked Shaw.

"Gerard."

"And your partner's name?"

"Robinau."

"Who hired you at the Gestapo?"

"Kohler."

The group arrived at the public phone that was in a small village. He made his call in front of Shaw and Parker. He was told not to answer in yes or no and to tell him that he was late because he had the runs. Apparently Robinau bought the story and they drove to the apartment where Colleen was being kept.

When they arrived no one got out of the cars. It was a tense situation. Shaw visualized several possible outcomes and like a chess play, which he was very good at, Shaw carefully calculated his moves to win the game. He was extremely careful and drove into a side street so that Robinau would not be able to detect them with his binoculars.

There was one more step to watch out for. Robinau was at the window and he had to be sure that Gerard came alone and was not followed. Being hand cuffed, it was going to be tricky. Shaw and Parker were dressed in Todt uniforms. Walking behind Gerard would not mean danger to Robinau. Gerard was told that if he makes a wrong move he'll be killed but if he follows the orders by Shaw and Parker he has a chance to be spared.

Robinau became suspicious when he saw Gerard walking in front of Shaw and Parker. He left the apartment with Colleen tied in a chair in the small living room. The first three men entered the apartment house and the rest of the group followed them in from various directions. Shaw and Parker drew their Lugers and had them ready under their coat. They knocked on the door and when no one answered Parker kicked the door down. Much to their surprise Robinau was nowhere to be seen.

Colleen gave a description of what Robinau looked like and what he was wearing to the group. Shaw stayed with Colleen to free her from the ropes while Parker started to look. The group would not let anybody leave the building until Parker had searched the entire building. Parker began by searching the apartment but Robinau was not found. Parker continued to search every apartment and found him in the adjacent flat masquerading as a tenant. He was hand cuffed and both men were driven in different cars to a countryside location.

Colleen was accompanied by a young Resistance lady along with a few members of the group to one of Marceau's friend's barn in the countryside, 30 kilometers from Port-En-Bessin to wait until Marceau and everyone arrived.

The three members of the Emergency Team and the two culprits ended their journey in a country house which belonged to a Resistance operative. Philip was informed of the location of the resistance operative house. He and the crew took the garbage truck and drove to meet the culprits.

They were all seated in a circle and Shaw began the interrogation.

"Who hired you and what reward was offered?"

"We do not have to answer any questions, because if anything happens to us the Gestapo will kill everybody who is connected with Marceau," said Robinau."

"Who told you that?" asked Shaw.

"I am not going to answer," said Robinau.

At that point Parker stomped Robinau's foot so hard that he fell out of the chair, then he kicked him in his chest with enough force to break a couple of his ribs, and finally kicked him in his testicles. Robinau was in agony and promised to talk and to tell the truth.

"We were hired by agent Kohler from the Gestapo. We were told that if we do not cooperate he will arrest our girlfriends who worked as cashiers in a food store and allegedly overcharged two Gestapo agents and pocketed the money. If we cooperate, each of us would receive hundred thousand francs," said Robinau.

Shaw, Parker, and Marceau accepted the explanation, but the culprits had to sign a confession for the future trial of Kohler. Some additional questions were raised and Shaw wrote their answers in a makeshift document. They both signed the papers.

Gerard and Robinau were given to Philip who led them outside the house into an open field. First they were both given cyanide pills and then shot in the head. Their bodies were dumped in the truck and were taken to a dump where they were burned beyond recognition and buried six feet deep. Parker covered the spot with grass that he cut from the field and poured some water over it.

Marceau was terribly upset by the abduction and hoped nothing serious had happened to Colleen. As it turned out, Colleen was only slapped in the face to be kept quiet but was spared from any sexual assault. The group, Marceau, Colleen, Bridget, Shaw, Parker and the Emergency Resistance Team celebrated the happy ending and saving the life of Colleen.

A sign in Marceau's shop window read, "Closed for the holiday."

Colleen stayed a couple of days with Marceau. She felt terribly insecure and told him that she would leave to be with her sister until liberation. She did not trust the Gestapo, especially under the circumstances when two of their collaborators were killed in the most brutal fashion. She was afraid that the person who was behind her abduction would try again. Her sister lived in Paris. She is married to a wealthy businessman with a lot of political clout and invited Colleen to stay with her until the liberation of Paris. She accepted the offer and suggested to Marceau that from time to time they could meet in a secret location. Marceau was delighted for the arrangement but it was heart wrenching to be physically apart from each other.

The Gestapo Headquarters experienced an unusually large number of arrests, mostly connected with the Resistance. Kohler, however, felt paralyzed in the Marceau affair since he had been recognized by the German Generals during the testimonial dinner. He had two major failures which ended with the death of the participants. His clandestine operations were out of bounds and subject to major complaints by the powerful Generals who were involved in the Normandy military operations. Kohler was driven by hatred, envy, jealousy, and pride to justify his suspicion without any regard of the possible consequence.

Kohler was terribly power hungry. Being a desk agent deprived him of the ability to arrest people and persecute them. He was like a wounded animal. He could not complain to other agents about his problems and failures. He secretly hoped that his provocations would yield some retaliatory actions against him by the Resistance and so then he could justify the arrest of Marceau, but it never happened. He was outsmarted and he knew it. He also knew that if the German Army were to be defeated in France he'd be held accountable for his actions.

Shaw, Parker, and Marceau recognized early on that they are dealing with a power-seeking pathological sadist, but unfortunately they could not eliminate him. He was not worth the sacrifice to have a hundred French men massacred in the middle of the park in Caen. Michael whose hatred toward Kohler became even stronger after Colleen's abduction was waiting for the opportunity to finish him off. One day in the company of Bridget, as he was driving to Bayeux for dinner, he said, "The termination of Kohler would be the rebirth of Germany."

Kohler was absolutely furious that he had not heard from the abductors in two weeks. There were no signs of their whereabouts and he could not start an investigation. He sensed something went wrong but there was nothing he was able to do. He was between a rock and a hard place. The overall military situation became tense as the days became closer to the invasion. Allied bombings and sabotage became more frequent. German soldiers talked about the invasion as the coming apocalypse. Kohler made some inquiries at the police stations, hospitals, and funeral homes and the answers were all negative. He finally and reluctantly wrote them off as losses, hoping that some day he would have the opportunity to have a face to face confrontation.

To make Kohler's wish even more difficult to fulfill, a decree from the Gestapo Paris Headquarters ordered all non-essential documents to be burned or relocated. Kohler could not believe that his clandestine operation must come to a halt. He had so much to do and prepare that there was hardly any time left for private affairs. Michael had an opportunity to talk to Kohler about his soldiers protecting secret files and Kohler was more concerned about Marceau than protecting German documents. Michael always believed that Kohler was sick, but the magnitude of his paranoia was new to him. He knew that the man was capable of killing Marceau and it was just a matter of time before he'd be transferred.

The heavy pounding of the Normandy beaches and vicinity by the RAF and USAF signaled the preparations for the landing. Saturation bombing exploded the mines around the bunkers and twisted the rail and wood obstructions that were supposed to protect the shores from boats, tanks and amphibious vehicles. Michael was reasonably sure that if Kohler remained during the invasion until he received the order to withdraw, he would kill Marceau.

To protect him from Kohler Michael decided to personally intervene. However, the German Military cannot cross the Gestapo. Michael, however, must protect the secret Gestapo papers and could keep an eye on Kohler.

Should Kohler behave irrationally, and threaten Michael with his paranoid personality, Michael can defend himself as well as his soldiers by shooting him. It was an extreme precaution, but Michael wanted to prepare for a possible show down.

As a precaution, Marceau received a disturbing caveat from Allied Intelligence that the German Military High Command was aware of the compromises in the Wall and ordered the Gestapo to sanitize the shore population and people working in construction of the Wall.

Everyone in Normandy was being watched day and night. Organization Todt foremen, engineers, supervisors, and officers were checked and some of their papers were reexamined by the construction company personnel files.

According to Abwehr, Allied Intelligence knew what to expect when the first wave of infantry and motorized units were to come to shore. The heavy bombing of the camouflaged bunkers, casemates, beach obstacles, and mines gave a preliminary inkling that the Allies were up to something. That is why some German generals suggested that the mobilized infantry units along with panzers be moved to complement the Atlantic Wall, but Hitler stuck to his guns and kept the panzers at the Pas de Calais area.

Both sides put pressures on intelligence. The Allies wanted all the details about the Atlantic Wall and the Germans needed all the information about what the Allies knew and where and when they would strike. It was a brutal war game. It was the survival of both armies.

The heat was on Shaw and Parker. They needed just a little bit of time to collect all the necessary details, but to conduct inspections in the non-construction areas had became increasingly difficult not to evoke the suspicion of the Germans. Michael was preparing his unit for the big assault by the Allies and had little time left to look into top secret files, memorize the contents, and pass them on to Bridget.

Bridget's role suddenly became magnified as she assumed the lifeline between Shaw, Parker, Michael, and Marceau. Her contribution as a courier, shopkeeper, homemaker, and Marceau's caretaker became invaluable as conditions changed for the worse.

Suddenly Bridget felt the enormity of expectations by all the players who surrounded her life, with very little time left for personal joy and happiness. Michael was on duty most of the time because of the Army's alert status. Shaw and Parker reserved their presence only to those areas that required additional information. Marceau's general health began to deteriorate. He felt sullen and weak most of the time.

What kept Bridget functioning was her spirit and devotion to the cause, her love for Marceau and Michael, and her strong belief in a better tomorrow.

"I feel the tension that surrounds our shop and home," said Marceau.

"I feel it too, but the notion of being liberated gives me courage and vitality," responded Bridget.

"I wish to be healthier and more energetic, but my illness makes me so weak and depressed."

"Did you check for messages from Allied Intelligence?"

"Not yet. Thank you for reminding me."

"Because of the extra German security, are our operations now paralyzed?"

"Yes, to a certain extent. We just have to be very careful sending messages and recruiting new operatives."

"I am worried about Michael. He has not come to visit me in over a week."

"That does not mean that he is in trouble."

"I know that, but I can't help to be concerned."

"I understand."

The lady from across the street called for Bridget. "You have a telephone call my dear."

"Thank you. I'll be there in a minute."

"Hello, this is Bridget. Hello, hello. I am having a bad connection."

"This is Michael. Can you hear me?"

"I can barely hear you. Please call again."

"Hello, hello. I can hear you now. Where are you calling from?"

"I am in Paris for a military conference. I'll be home tomorrow. Can we have dinner together?"

"Of course, we can. What time can I expect you?"

"Around six o'clock."

"Thank you, Michael."

"You are very welcome, my love. See you tomorrow."

"That was Michael. You were right, Marceau. I was just having a free floating anxiety attack."

"This is what happens when you're in love."

"Yes, I am in love. He means a lot to me."

"I need to send some messages. I am afraid my signal will be traced. Would you be kind enough and get in touch with Shaw and Parker? They are using a portable transceiver from various locations."

"I will make a call to them."

"Good girl. Thank you."

"Marceau, for you, it is my pleasure. You're welcome!"

"Hello, this is Bridget."

"Hello, this is Shaw. What can I do for you?"

"Marceau would like to talk to you. We'll meet you at noon at the same place."

"We'll be there waiting. Bye."

"I talked to Shaw, Marceau. We'll be meeting tomorrow."

"I think our lives will be very boring for awhile. I am trying to be frugal with messages. Partly, because of personal fear, and partly, there is too much at stake. We have accomplished quite a bit and why jeopardize our future operations. In addition, I will not give Kohler the opportunity to make a charge."

"Marceau, you are right and I admire and respect you for it!"

The moment Bridget responded to Marceau, Allied aircrafts dropped bombs all over the beaches and hit a number of homes. The explosions were so devastating that Marceau's place suffered moderate damage. Fortunately, nothing serious happened, but it took several hours to put things back to their respective places.

The anticipation of meeting Michael caused elation for Bridget. The daily chores went quickly and before she knew it, Michael arrived with a dozen roses.

"Where did you get those beautiful roses?"

"I bought them in Paris."

"How did you keep them so fresh looking?"

"I asked the flower girl to wrap them for a long trip, and she did it. It is so simple. Tender loving care can preserve the flowers for a long trip."

"How are you my love? It is so wonderful to see you. I was really concerned about you. You did not mention that you were going to Paris."

"It happened too fast. I had nothing to do with it. I was told to go. So I went, I listened, and heard what I did not want to hear. They are convinced that our superior forces and war experiences will totally obliterate the Allied beachheads and drive most of the Allied forces into the sea. Hitler told them how to win this war. What a joke!"

"I made a reservation for half an hour from now. Is it too early for you?"

"I am ready my dear, but before we leave, I want to be sure that Marceau is taking his medication."

"May I say hello to him?"

"Please do say hello to him. He'll be delighted to see you again!"

"Bon soir, Marceau. How are you doing these days?"

"I am fine, and how are you Michael?"

"I couldn't be better. I have the pleasure of taking your beautiful daughter out for dinner. I am in seventh heaven!"

"What is happening in your neck of the woods?"

"Not much, Marceau. The top brass still thinks that beating the Allies will be a piece of cake. I think they are nuts."

"Why do you say that?"

"Because it seems that they are living in a fantasy world. We have no air force to counter attack the Allied aircrafts. We have very immature soldiers and second rate armaments. Those 88s are the exceptions. The morale is low. The spirit is fading, especially, among the generals. The panzer divisions are under Hitler's orders. No general has the courage to tell Hitler how to defend our army. He says we must fight. We must sacrifice for the good of Germany and the Nazi Party. He has no military background or strategy. He is all rhetoric. I have a map about the defense of Pointe du Hoc. I hope you have a chance to send it to the Allies."

"That is fantastic; we have conflicting findings concerning the cliff."

"I know why. They keep changing the defense strategies to confuse the Allied reconnaissance planes. This map is the latest, but who knows, they may change the locations of the small arms fire."

"Thank you, Michael. I don't know how I am going to transmit this map now because of the increased security. But may be I'll be lucky and be able to send it."

"I am sorry to leave you, but we have to go now. Have a pleasant evening, Marceau."

"Thank you and have a good time. Bye."

Bridget and Michael went to a nice place close to his residence near Caen. The meal was simple but tasty. Michael ordered fish and Bridget steak with roasted onions and potatoes. They had wine and salad with the meal. For dessert, they had crepes with apples slices.

"So, tell me how is everything with you?" asked Michael.

"We have had a very stressful period since Kohler decided to nail down Marceau."

"I am sorry, but I have no reason to kill him right now. He is well protected by the Gestapo. Should he step out from his cubicle and engage in a personal vendetta, I might be able to get him for good. But he is too cunning and thinks twice before he ventures out in person. That's the reason why he uses lackeys."

"I hope the Allies will be landing pretty soon."

"Let's hope your wish comes true."

"Do you want to visit my place?"

"I don't think Marceau would mind if we went to his place. I think we could be quite comfortable in my bed."

"I am so happy to see you again. I have had a hard time waiting until I could hug and kiss you again."

Michael drove to Marceau's place with his left hand while his right hand embraced Bridget and she put her head on his shoulder. They were quiet most of the time but their body language spoke their deep love for each other.

They were very quiet entering the shop. Both took off their shoes and tiptoed into her bedroom. It did not take more than five minutes to undress and hop into bed. They kissed and kissed with a ferocious hunger for love and affection. Michael began to kiss her nipples while Bridget petted his head and encouraged him to keep going. Michael then French kissed her until she was terribly excited and asked him to make love to her. They were together without any movement. Just being united with each other was an immensely enjoyable sensation.

"I love you Bridget. You are my whole life."

"And you are mine."

"I love to feel you. It is indescribable how the various parts of your body affect my senses."

"I have the same feeling Michael."

"You have a totaling mesmerizing affect even when you touch me."

"Michael, I can say the same thing. Just one finger of yours can turn me on. Darling, my love, try to pleasure each other without really moving," asked Bridget.

"I am with you, sweetheart."

It was a glorious completion of their love making. Bridget put her head on Michael's chest and they both fell asleep.

Bridget was up early in the morning. The clock registered six o'clock. She made breakfast for everybody. By six-thirty both, Michael and Marceau joined the breakfast table.

"Well, how did you sleep?" asked Marceau.

"We slept just great," answered Bridget.

"How about you, Marceau?" asked Michael.

"I don't sleep through the night. I was up several times. I had some stupid dreams.

I also had to visit the bathroom, but I like to make up for my loss of sleep by napping after lunch."

"Marceau, what chores do we have for today?"

"I hope we can complete our repairs and perhaps finish the boot for the General."

"When do we see you again, Michael?"

"I hope this weekend. I would like to invite Marceau for dinner also."

"It would be our pleasure, but I would prefer to dine here. After the break-in, I am hesitant to leave the premises."

"I perfectly understand your concern. So why don't I contribute my share for the dinner?"

"That is a good idea," said Bridget.

"See you soon. Bye."

Michael kissed Bridget and gave a warm handshake with both hands to Marceau and left with a happy face.

Life in Port-En Bessin became extremely difficult. The German security forces made every effort to discourage any information about the German defenses, the Atlantic Wall, to pass to the enemy.

Surveillance of the port and beach, wireless radio, pigeons, French skilled workers and forced laborers increased significantly. There was an alert status for possible small scale, diversionary invasion. The local residents were watched like hawks and everybody became a suspect as a spy whose behavior was questionable to the military intelligence. Under these circumstances Marceau had a very difficult time communicating with Allied Intelligence.

One of his customers, an officer of the Kriegsmarine, invited him for a fishing trip. He could not believe his ears that this invitation was possible. He did not accept the invite at the time of offering and asked for a few days to give his reply.

"How on earth are you able to take me as a partner for a fishing trip when no boats can leave the port?" asked Marceau of the officer.

"Good question, Marceau. We are allowed to leave port for Channel surveillance."

"But I am not in the Kriegsmarine."

"You don't have to be. I am taking you as a tour guide of the Normandy shores."

"It is a very ingenious idea."

"But why did you think of me when there are so many professional fishermen?"

"Because you are the best cobbler I ever had in my life. You built a fantastic pair of boots for me and I would like to reciprocate by giving you some fun time."

"Let me talk it over with my daughter."

"Please do that. We have time as long as the weather cooperates."

"Come back in a couple of days and I will give you the answer. I must, however, be sure that I am not in violation of your military policy. I prefer a boarding permit from your commandant."

"Don't worry. I have the authority to request such a permit. Bye, Marceau. I'll see you later."

Marceau was absolutely surprised to have such a rare opportunity to send messages to MI6. He asked Bridget to summon Shaw and Parker for an urgent conference. They met at the same location and Shaw and Parker picked them up.

"The story is that I am invited by a customer of mine who is a Kriegsmarine officer on a fishing trip. He claims that I can get a written permit from the Commandant as a tour guide of the Normandy shores to develop a new defensive perimeter."

"I am concerned. This could be an entrapment," said Bridget.

"This officer is just offering. It is a soft invite. Take it or leave it. He wants to thank me for the boots that I made for him. He wants me to have a good time because he knows I love fishing."

"Go for it, but we have to ask MI6 to devise a new plan to meet you at sea," said Shaw.

"We will make contact tonight and let you know as soon we get an answer," said Parker.

"Thank you for your cooperation and now we must go back to the shop to work on the specially designed boot for the general."

Marceau and Bridget walked back to the shop and found a note under the door. It was from a customer who urgently needed her shoes. Bridget's heart was racing just looking at the note without reading the content. Ever since Kohler's threats, posting messages became nerve wrecking for Bridget.

"I don't understand what happened to your nerves of steel?" posed Marceau.

"I don't know. I just worry about you every time I experience something unusual. We don't have messages posted in the door slit."

"Relax my dear, you'll live longer."

Marceau began to work on the shoes and the boot while Bridget waited on customers. The day went by uneventfully. Around ten in the evening Bridget received a call from Shaw to meet the next day.

They met at ten o'clock in the morning two streets over from where they usually met. They had a long talk in the country about the complications of sending the messages.

"The fishing is not the problem. The pick-up is. Since you don't know where he is going to drop the anchor the mini sub will have a difficult time to follow. We must also have some form of vessel identification and we need a departure time. He must tell you what kind of fishing he is interested in.

"Where would you hide the messages? It would be a little strange for him to answer these questions."

"Your safety is more important to us than the messages. I would have two Resistance operators accompany you on this trip. I don't know how we can solve these issues without creating some type of suspicion. I would be more inclined to meet a commando at 0300 and hand him the messages in codes. It is much simpler," said Shaw.

"How do the rest of you feel about the offer of the officer and the response by Allied Intelligence?" asked Marceau.

"I am with Shaw," replied Parker.

"I am also with Shaw," said Bridget.

"Well, accordingly, we'll follow plan B. Thank you for your cooperation. The conference is over and we must get back to our work. You can let us out here. We need a good walk. Bye."

CHAPTER NINE

Bridget felt that time had come for Marceau to have a checkup to monitor his blood and called the doctor for an appointment. She took Marceau to the hospital and he had a thorough examination. He stayed in the hospital for three days, totally bored, and disgusted with life. Colleen went to her sister's in Paris. His work at the shop was at a standstill, Allied Intelligence messages had to wait to be delivered, and his friends in the Resistance were picked up one by one by the Gestapo

The laboratory reports confirmed that Marceau was in the advanced stage of leukemia. It was bad news to everyone, but Marceau had plenty of time to take care of his business affairs and receive treatments. After leaving the hospital, he went home for a couple of days and told Bridget to limit the shop hours for the next ten days.

"I believe I'm entitled to have a well deserved vacation," Marceau told Bridget.

"Are you planning to go somewhere?"

"Yes, I'm going to visit Colleen and have fun."

"That's very smart of you. Finally you are realizing that you need a break."

"Should any emergency arise, I think Shaw and Parker can handle it."

"I agree with you. The most important thing right now is you. When are you supposed to see the doctor?"

"I was told that the doctor will see me in a couple of weeks. I'll call him when I return from Paris. In the meantime, I'll take the medications and follow his orders."

"I am glad that finally you're having a vacation. Although it'll be short, but knowing you, you'll be restless after a week."

Marceau sent a message to Allied Intelligence and told them about his medical condition, the decision to take a vacation, and requested that all communications should be addressed to Bridget until his return. He was given an affirmative and AI wished him well. Marceau left with certain amount of trepidation, realizing that the invasion was imminent and his help would be absolutely vital. But from the radio messages he deducted that more information must be sent before the D-Day was announced.

Bridget kept the store open but only in the morning. She had to make a lot of phone calls, went on errands and intercepted and translated cryptic radio messages that were directed to Shaw and Parker. During the weekend, however, her time was spent with Michael, but much closer to home than in the past. They still went out to have fun, but upon their return, she always checked for messages.

There were tense moments for both of them in terms of providing critical information to Allied Intelligence. Michael supplied valuable documents concerning the German defenses as well as offenses. His information included not only details of Batteries, but V1 and V2 sites.

They were launching sites for the German rocket planes. V1 and V2 stands for Vergeltung-Retribution for Allied bombing of German cities. These were pilotless planes directed toward British cities. Bridget sent coded messages to Allied Intelligence from various locations via a borrowed portable radio. They risked their lives together by procuring and sending messages, but both were determined and dedicated to the cause to defeat Hitler. Bridget managed to borrow the latest mobile radio transceiver through MI6 that Shaw and Parker provided. To use Marceau's equipment was too dangerous due to the volume of information, the time it would take to send the messages, and of course, the fact that his radio was stationary and would be easy to locate. In addition, Michael had to return the original documents within a half a day. Copying was an option, but there was no room for mistakes. The originals had to be returned without the slightest suspicion.

Bridget wanted to spend time with Michael and both agreed to meet for the weekend before Marceau came back. They did not make plans and decided to play it by ear.

It was an unusually busy morning for Bridget in the shop. Most customers accepted the fact that Marceau was not around and that he finally took a much needed vacation. But a very few people expressed resentment in more than one way. Bridget, being a natural diplomat, eased the lament by offering shoe laces in appreciation for their patience. She did this for every customer who brought in shoes for repair.

One morning, however, Michael showed up for an urgent talk with Bridget, who was terribly busy with customers, especially with the General who needed undivided attention about his foot problem. Michael had little time and promised to return, but Bridget sensed the nature of urgency, something had to be more important than just a visit to say hello.

"General, would you be kind enough to excuse me for a minute?

Without waiting for the answer, she rushed after Michael and asked how she could help.

"I can't talk now. I will come back later. It is top secret."

"I am sorry, general, but I was afraid to displease the officer who seemed to be in a hurry."

"You are a kind girl I understand. Now let's get back to my problem."

"General, I feel a nail inside the boot is causing your problem. I will remove it, but I need a little time."

"How much time do you need? I have a very important conference in a couple of hours in Caen."

"I need ten minutes, but I have so many people waiting, I must take care of the customers who have been waiting for an hour."

"They can wait ten more minutes."

Bridget at this point loudly said, "Ladies and Gentlemen, I have an emergency repair. Please wait a few minutes. Thank you for your patience."

She went to Marceau's repair shop, took a curved pair of pliers and tried to pull out the nail. It did not come out. She then took a hammer and hit the nail as hard as she could, but it did not budge. She was determined either to remove or insert the nail. She looked around and found a machine that taps the leather together. Bridget carefully inserted the boot and engaged the machine. It worked this time, but the heel loosened. There was enough space between the heel and sole to saw off the nail. Finally, she succeeded by hammering the heel back and removing the nail from the inside. She rushed back and looked for the General, but he had walked out. Bridget ran after the General and yelled, "I got it, I got it!" The General took the boot, opened his car door, sat inside, and said, "Thank you, but why did it take so long to pull a nail out?"

"Sorry, but I'm not as crafty as Marceau."

"But you did it at the end. Adieu."

Finally, Bridget got back to the crowd and took care of the customers one by one as quickly as she could. A few minutes before twelve o'clock, Michael showed up, and asked Bridget to be available tomorrow afternoon.

"What's happening?" Bridget pried.

"I have a lot of documents of the defenses and V1 rocket sites for Allied Intelligence. You must put the transceiver in a double bottom luggage to hide it. I'll meet you here at one o'clock."

"I shall be ready, my darling."

Bridget went to Marceau's radio room to check for messages. There was a strong warning about a German agent in Normandy who acts as a MI6 agent and sounds like a British born native who is investigating the leaks about German defenses. Find and terminate him. He has authentic British papers but his MI6 code numbers are false. His nickname is 'Poobe,' with the last name, Bernhardt. He is dangerous, psychopathic, devious, and a bisexual sex freak. Because of his good looks, suave character, and highly seductive behavior he can easily charm people. He is eloquent and sophisticated. He is 37 years old, 6 feet 2 inches, and weighs 160 lbs.

Bridget drove to Shaw and Parker's place at 2030. She was careful and watched for anyone tailing her. She noticed one car following her, but she easily got rid of it with her expert maneuvers.

Shaw was a little surprised by her visit, but Parker sensed something was wrong.

"Did you receive news from Allied Intelligence?" asked Parker.

"Yes, I did. It is bad news."

Bridget recited the content of the message. Then took a deep breath and talked about hiding the transceiver.

"You must be careful how you are storing and using the transceiver. The Germans will trace your signals. You must transmit in thirty second bursts and each burst must have a different locale. Do you want us to help you to send the messages?" offered Shaw.

"It is not a bad idea, but I must check with Michael. He feels funny about witnesses.

"Check it out," said Parker.

"About the make believe agent, just be careful of yourself. We'll find him before long, but he might cause some damage. You can call this number and we'll be in contact with you in 30 minutes, if you let us know where to call you."

"Where did you get this number? I would like to have one too."

"I cannot tell you details of this number, it is a MI6 secret," said Shaw.

"There are no secrets between us are there?"

"There is a secret between you and MI6," said Shaw with a serious voice.

"This number was given to us by MI6 for emergencies and we were told that nobody can use it but us," said Shaw.

"Maybe I should call Michael now and ask about your presence."

"Good idea," said Parker.

Bridget called Michael and there was no problem with them being present. As a matter of fact Michael felt safer having them there. Shaw and Parker promised to meet at 1300 hours tomorrow at Marceau's.

"By the way, how is Marceau doing? We haven't seen him for some time," asked Shaw.

"The good news is he's on vacation with Colleen in Paris. The bad news is that it was determined that Marceau is in an advanced stage of leukemia. We can use all the help we can get."

"We'll try to find out what new medications are available in the UK and US," said Shaw.

"While he is there, he should visit the Pasteur Institute," added Parker.

"I'll call him and let him know. It is getting late, I'd better go home. See you guys tomorrow."

Michael, Shaw, and Parker arrived about the same time, dressed immaculately in their German officer uniforms. They were exceptionally clean and crisply pressed, looking like young cadets attending graduation. They all got into the car and drove toward the countryside, making sure they were not followed and had no radio detector mobile units around. But no matter how careful they were, German patrol cars stopped them and ask for identification papers. As they drove farther away from the beaches and villages, Shaw was looking for a desolate area, where a short talk could take place before they sent the messages.

"I am going to stop here examine what we are going to send. It makes no sense to duplicate information that is already in the hands of Allied Intelligence," said Shaw.

"That makes sense, but what I am giving to you is more than just maps and armaments," said Michael.

"Good, let's look at them," said Shaw.

Michael carefully opened the secret papers and gave them to Shaw and Parker. Having read the introductory paragraphs, Shaw put his hand to his forehead, and loudly yelled, "My God, this is good, very good."

"What is good?" Bridget inquired.

"What we have here is a blow by blow plan of military action in the Pas de Calais area, and the stand by forces in the

Normandy area. The Germans have the 352nd Division in the Omaha Beach area waiting for the invading forces. In the Caen region, the 21st Panzer divisions have a dual role: concentrate around the Orne to support the 716th Infantry Division against Allied invasion in that area of Normandy and keep them to the rear as a tactical reserve force. I think this information will strengthen the deciphered Ultra codes at Bletchley Park Code Center."

"According to this information," Shaw continued, "the Allies must be prepared for about 540 German tanks waiting for them in the Normandy area. In addition, we have maps of the port bunkers and casemates with quite a variety of ordnances and mines.

"I suggest that Bridget and Michael have their own transportation. It is not a good idea that we shall be together in one car. Michael can have a romantic affair with a lady. The German patrol could wonder about the secret exploration and measurements in the presence of Bridget. We can function together for the duration of transmission, but must leave in two separate cars. Should Michael be implicated, he can act as an advisor." "I think we can shorten all these into telegraphic sentences and send them by paragraphs from various locations. Each message should last no more than thirty seconds," said Shaw.

"I will prepare the telegraphic messages. Shaw will send them, and the two of you will assume the sentry roles. You scream when you see a German patrol, or radio detector car," advised Parker.

Each time they completed the transmission, Shaw put the transmitter into a special compartment of the car which required special knowledge to open. But every time the German patrol searched the car; there was anxiety that they might be caught. Most of the patrols were polite, respectful, and understood their excuses when asked what they were doing in the country. It was after the seventh transmission when one of the patrols extensively drilled the officers. The interrogation got to the point that Shaw had to turn the tables around and started to drill the patrol.

"Please explain why our presence in the country is so very suspicious," said Shaw.

"You said that you are doing a survey for the Organization Todt to build more casemates, but you don't have any instruments with you to survey the land," said one of patrol members.

"Because you are inspecting us after our original study was completed we found it unnecessary to have instruments with us again. We had already packed the transit for another day. This time we were just confirming our findings," Parker barked.

"We received reports from the mobile radio patrol that signals were being sent from this region," said the other patrol.

"When we are measuring, it is not uncommon for us to use a military radio because we are some distance from each other," said Shaw.

"I want look at your vehicle."

"You may certainly inspect the vehicle," said Parker.

The patrol looked inside the vehicle and started to knock with his fingers all over the seats, the sides, the floor, and the roof. He found an old beat up hand held military transceiver that cannot transmit over a mile in the left corner of the trunk wrapped in a dirty cloth. He saluted and said, "Thank you," then went back to his patrol car.

Bridget and Michael met with Shaw and Parker at the prearranged time and place. They agreed to wait for each other if one of them would be late. Shaw and Parker were a little late for the meeting because of the patrols' questioning and inspection.

"We are only about halfway through. Would you like to have dinner, and we can continue later?" asked Shaw.

Everyone seemed to be ready to take a break and agreed to have something to eat. It was late afternoon, but still daylight. The weather was nice, bright and sunny, low humidity, and excellent for radio transmissions. Michael suggested a quaint restaurant nearby and they all headed toward the Port-En-Bessin direction.

It was the first time that Shaw and Parker sat down with Michael in a restaurant and talked about everything while they were waiting for the dinner to be served. Bridget really enjoyed the company of good friends and working together on a worthwhile project.

During dinner they were quiet, however. Everybody seemed to enjoy the food which was prepared by an experienced chef who learned how to make the best of the least expensive dishes. All the sauces had an exquisite aroma and delectable taste. The desserts were phenomenal, not too sweet, and were pleasing to the eye. Coffee and tea were part of their meal. They spent an hour dining and just before sunset they left the place in a northeast direction.

They found a few sites where they felt relatively safe to continue sending messages. Shaw managed to send all the information that Michael presented and completed the transmission at 2230 hour. Everybody clapped their hands and all thanked Michael for his cooperation and help.

Bridget and Michael drove to Marceau's place. Shaw and Parker headed for home. Another segment in their lives was about to begin the next day, finding the impostor British agent.

It was the greatest manhunt since Shaw and Parker set foot in Normandy. Bridget was instructed to keep her eyes open and watch every word and move he made. This chap does not work alone, but with a lady friend who is pretty and fleshy. He'll seduce women with romantic verbiage and sensual and sexual skills that most women have hardly experienced. Once she becomes captivated by his spell, he uses her to find the squealer. He will do the same with a man, providing he is a bona fide homosexual and desperately needs sex. In addition, he provides orgies with drugs and alcohol. Money is his other incentive and he rewards good information.

The stakes are high because he is after Marceau, Bridget, Shaw, Parker, Michael, and other primary suspects, every resistance operator and Maquis.

Shaw and Parker have a formidable task of tracking him down because he is like a chameleon, changing his color to blend into a particular environment. He can dress like a French civilian, Maquis, fisherman, German officer, Gestapo man, and British agent. He speaks fluent French and English with the perfect accent. He can alter his facial features with special rubberized skin to look young, middle aged, old and with or without a beard. He was one of the better trained counterintelligence agents, perhaps, a professional rival to Shaw and Parker. There was, however, one big personality difference; he was a clever but dangerous psychopath.

What was constant was his insatiable appetite to track down leaks and destroy the enemy of the Reich. Poobe was trained for years by the Sicherheitsdienst, or SD, the SS

Security Service, a spy system which had activities outside of Germany. He was selected to protect the Atlantic Wall from being destroyed by foreign agents, commandoes, and members of the Resistance, including the Maquis.

Bridget volunteered to help Shaw and Parker in the hunt and termination of the agent. They met daily in various places to share information and develop strategies. Michael also helped to collect information about Poobe's inquiries.

By sheer coincidence one day his cover was blown. He was in a French pub drinking his heart out when a young lady invited him to a party next door. He hardly knew the lady, "But what the heck," he said to himself. "The more people I meet, the closer I get to my goal of finding those damn leaks."

At the party he slept a little bit. When he woke up he found a lady in her thirties petting his hair. He felt good about it and kissed the lady's hand. This led to more petting, but he stopped this flirtatious indiscretion to meet a gentleman who talked British English.

"I believe we met awhile ago," said Poobe.

"I don't seem to recall the pleasure of your acquaintance," said the Briton.

"I'll will not retract my impression, but let me introduce myself. If you can keep a secret, I am on a mission to help the British," said Poobe.

"Aren't you afraid of being caught by the Gestapo?"

"Frankly, I don't think so, because I am smarter than they are."

"What makes you think so?"

"I was trained by the MI6. Here is my identification card with my picture on it."

"You have a very impressive background. I must excuse myself. I must visit the bathroom, I have an upset stomach," said the Briton.

He went to the bathroom and jotted down the last four numbers of his ID card. Poobe did not suspect that he was talking to a real MI6 agent who was working in Paris as a nurse anesthesiologist.

"I feel much better," he said to Poobe. "It was nice meeting you, but I must go now."

The Briton rushed home, took the transceiver from his hidden floor space and sent a message to MI6 with the last four digits. Within ten minutes, he got the answer: fake document.

MI6 informed the agents in France about the impersonator and requested more information about him. Within one month MI6 received a detailed profile about Poobe activities. For the past three months, he went underground as a British agent and then resurfaced, with considerable facial alterations and beard, as a French medical doctor. His fake office and German nurse took patients by appointment only. He did not see the patients, but a German associate did.

The warning of his dangerous character was transmitted to every agent and courier.

Bridget personally informed every cell member from Cherbourg to Caen to be on the lookout and not get into his trap. Poobe has been known to blackmail people and torture subjects.

This went on for weeks, but he did not come. He did surface in Port-En-Bessin as a fisherman and made several connections. Then, he left again, and became a cook in Cherbourg. Poobe was a restless man and did not stay too long in a job. He tried to stay close to Normandy and the next places he picked were Bayeux, Carentan, Quistreham, and Caen. The reports of his impersonations came from various sources. On one occasion, he was almost apprehended by an OSS agent but he slipped out the back door of a restaurant.

Shaw and Parker were one step behind him, but he was too clever to be caught. He had succeeded in sending some Maquis and Resistance operators to the gallows and came close to finding the cell members who reported to Shaw and Parker Poobe decided to take a little vacation in Paris and met Susan, a member of the Resistance affiliated with the OSS in a bar. She was one of the most astute characters he had ever met. She saw through him in no time. She played with him like cat would a mouse and devised a plan to trap him. Since Poobe was always bragging about his sexual prowess, Susan contacted another friend, Martha, who was an OSS agent working for the Vichy government.

Susan and Martha were born and raised in France. Martha was recruited by the OSS. Both were trained by the OSS and sent to Paris to collect information. They were vivacious, young, thirty, blonde, blue eyed women with oval faces, moist protruding lips, petite noses and figures with medium sized bosoms. They were 5 feet 7 inches tall with shapely buttocks.

Both had college educations, OSS intelligence and physical defense training. Their parents lived in Paris; both of their mothers were Native Americans married to French citizens. Both girls were bilingual with slight traces of a French accent.

Susan and Martha were told about Parker at the time Poobe was discovered. Parker was to be introduced as a possible back-up and emergency help.

Susan was educated in sexuality in terms of sensuality, physical attractiveness, and emotional involvements. She used sex to gain information and she did it very well. She was versed in the various techniques to stimulate male desires to achieve orgasm. She was patient with men and took her time as it was needed. The age of a man did not matter to her. Sexual dysfunction was her specialty. She could play with a guy for two or three hours before allowing him to be pleasured. She also received training in therapeutic massage. Martha became her student and she learned many techniques from Susan. They were not embarrassed to pleasure a man together or perform some sex play to amuse their victim. It was all part of their show.

According to the plan, they would invite Poobe to a special sexual experience where they were going to play strip black jack with marked cards. For drinks, Susan would serve the finest cognac. Martha and Susan would drink wine that was diluted with colored water.

Martha would prepare the cognac with anesthetic that was supplied by an anesthesiologist friend. The bottle was sealed. The anesthetic was a very potent and special chemical that had no taste. Martha had an extra bottle in her purse camouflaged as a perfume, just in case he insisted on drinking his own cognac. Two drops of the anesthetic would render anyone unconscious.

Poobe found both girls to be intellectually and sexually stimulating for him. He was eager to play the game because it was new to him. The date was set for the weekend in a country home that Susan rented for the occasion. Shaw and Parker were waiting in a nearby house along with a couple of other MI6 friends.

He came alone and looked around twice to make sure there were no other cars following him. He was slightly drunk, but careful. He entered the house, looked around inside, and allowed the girls to search him. He did the same to the girls. They all made themselves comfortable by taking off their shoes, shirt, and blouses and began with kisses, hugs, and embraces.

Martha served sandwiches, drinks and both girls snuggled with him for a few minutes, when the stimulation began. It was very erotic. When all had considerable excitement, Susan called for the cards. Two brand new decks were presented. Martha showed him the sealed old cognac and Poobe was just delighted for thoughtfulness and courtesy.

Before the play began, Susan poured a little cognac into a medium sized glass and presented it to Poobe. Then they poured their own wine.

"To your health," said both women.

"To our health," said Poobe.

The girls watched as he gulped down the cognac and Susan declared, "Let the play begin."

As Martha was dealing the cards and looked at Poobe, he noticed that the women were looking at him.

"What's the matter?" he asked smilingly.

The first sign of trouble became noticeable as he was spreading the cards. He was sluggish and Susan asked him if he wanted another drink.

"Yes, pour me another drink, I lost my pep."

He drank the second drink and was looking at the cards, but said nothing. Then slowly leaned sideways and turned on his back. Martha, who studied nursing before joining the OSS, looked at his eyes and touched his neck for a pulse.

"He is unconscious," Martha said.

Susan ran out and rushed to Parker to come over and help. They lifted and carried him to his car and placed him to the driver's seat. Parker tied the accelerator in the full throttle position and started the engine. He turned the steering wheel toward the nearest tree and put the gearshift into the forward motion. He crashed with enough force to smash his head into the windshield. Then Parker poured gasoline over him and tossed a lit match that instantly ignited his body and the car.

As the car burned, the gasoline tank exploded and the car was totally engulfed by the fire.

At that point everybody was ready to leave. Susan grabbed the cognac, food, and anything that did not belong in the house. They straightened the chairs and removed the slightest clue of a drinking party. Then Susan poured the cognac and wine down the toilet. She tossed the bottles and food into the fire.

"I hope to see you soon, Parker," said Susan.

Susan and Martha returned to their home in Paris.

Parker, Shaw and Bridget returned to Port-En-Bessin. They all had a lot of errands to take care of. For Parker and Shaw it was meeting with the cell members, collecting additional information and listening to Allied Intelligence messages; Bridget needed to take care of the shop, home, various Resistance errands and meeting with Michael.

The Gestapo and German Military were surprised by the death of their agent, but they knew that he was a heavy drinker. The Gestapo did some investigation by questioning the people he had associated with up to the time of his death. They did not know what happened after he had left the bar. The description of Susan, however, caused some concern. She changed her hair color and wore tinted glasses. She left Paris and settled in Cherbourg as a hairdresser. Parker and Bridget watched over her welfare and she was in good hands. She lived with another French girl who later became her friend. She needed a new birth certificate and identification papers to reflect her new name, birth place and current residence. It was Parker who really cared for her. They became serious friends and he was in contact with her every day.

Marceau came back, still tired and weak. He decided to work three days a week. Only his very inner circle knew about his illness and he wanted it to stay that way. Bridget did not allow him to exhaust himself and helped him with the stitching and buffing the boots and shoes. She also handled customer sales and repairs. She took care of the billing and paperwork. At the end of the day, she went shopping for food or other items.

She made dinner, washed the dishes, and made the calls that were necessary to keep the Resistance functioning. Before they retired, she made sure that he took his medication, gave him a backrub and chatted and laughed together for few minutes.

Friday afternoon they closed the shop and they either visited the doctor or went to the hospital for a laboratory checkup. Saturday was reserved for Michael and Sunday for Susan.

Marceau was still handling the transceiver operation with Allied Intelligence, but sending messages became mobile with the help of Shaw and Parker.

Allied Intelligence had a fairly comprehensive picture of what was going on with the Atlantic Wall, but still needed details of the casemates and bunkers which were painted and decorated to resemble beach houses or resort cottages. Michael volunteered to assist Parker and Shaw to gather as much information about the German construction sites as he could. Bridget accompanied Michael while he inspected some of the sites. Upon returning to the car, Michael would give a detailed picture of those camouflaged places to Bridget. Those houses were noted and later reported to Allied Intelligence.

When Michael and Bridget were visiting the bunkers, walking the streets of Port-En-Bessin, Bayeux, or any of the coastal villager and inner cities like Cherbourg or Caen, the tension and anxiety of the possible invasion permeated everywhere. The increased intensity of the aerial bombing made everybody concerned about the imminence of coastal warfare, which was envisioned as bloody, brutal and savage. The majority of the French people were ready to make the sacrifice for the liberation, but the Germans were not ready to give up the holds of power.

Marceau was asked to pay attention to the radio messages from the BBC World Service and translate the codes for those who did not have access to radios. The Resistance and Maquis had to know what to prepare for before the forces got to shore. It was Bridget who contacted the Resistance members and spirited their souls. She was very good to call or travel in the middle of the bombing and tell them what they were to do.

It was one of those calm evenings when there was no bombing, Marceau felt reasonably good and they were listening to Debussy. At 2200 hours, BBC World Service sent several messages which Bridget had to deliver to a few Resistance operators who had no radio. She walked to the nearest restaurant to make her calls when two Gestapo agents entered the place. She was in the middle of the call when she was interrupted and asked for her papers. She presented her papers but she was questioned about her calls. She explained that she has no phone at home and she just wanted to talk to her friends. At that point she was asked to take a seat for further questioning. Fortunately, Michael visited her at home and Marceau told him where she was and he drove there at found her being detained by the Gestapo.

"What is happening to my friend?" asked Michael.

"We would just like to question her," said one of the Gestapo agents.

"I have to worry about the invading forces and you guys are questioning my friend about why she is calling her friends?

Honestly, do you believe that we will win the battle with this kind of stupidity?" asked Michael.

"How dare you put your nose into our business!" spat the other agent.

"Do you realize that in the middle of the battle I could ask you to fight and defend our position!" said Michael.

"We don't have to take orders from you," said the first agent.

"That is precisely what I am saying. We can't depend on you when it comes to fighting with us and for us because the only thing that you can do is investigate. Well, in the middle of the battle there is nothing to investigate. You need to fight and this war is going to be sudden because we do not know where the Allies will land. You may not have enough time to remove yourself, because the enemy can parachute behind your headquarters. I will be your officer because you know nothing about warfare. So remember this because I will remind you when the time comes, which could be tomorrow morning," said Michael angrily.

"You don't seem to understand that we are under orders to find out who supplies the Allies with Atlantic Wall defenses. Our defenses are compromised unless we find the perpetrators," said the same Gestapo agent.

"You have been harassing my girlfriend, who is trying to talk to her friends because her father does not have a telephone. She is the daughter of the cobbler and she takes care of your boots to repair them, helps her father to make new boots for the Generals, sews, polishes, cooks, and tries her best to survive. She did not do anything illegal for you to accuse her. You can check her friends, names, addresses. They are French nationals from this area," said Michael.

"I will let her go if you vouch for her," said the first Gestapo agent.

"Yes, I do," said Michael.

The Gestapo let her go, saluted Michael and left the restaurant.

"Now what?" asked Bridget.

"We'll find another place where you can complete your calls. The hell with the Gestapo and the Nazis. They make me sick," said Michael.

Bridget and Michael found another restaurant, both had some dessert, and she made her calls. They chatted a while then he drove back to her home and stayed with her until she calmed down from the anxiety she experienced from her ordeal. She was worried sick that she might have revealed the names and conversations with the Resistances operatives. She knew the Gestapo method of torture and everybody would have been compromised, including herself.

Michael petted her hair and kissed her forehead and lips. He was compassionate and loving. Slowly Bridget got back her feeling of security and wanted nothing more than a snuggle with Michael.

"Darling, my love, I just want to be close to you, touch you, feel you, and love you with all my heart," said Bridget.

While snuggling, Michael fell asleep and woke up in the early morning hours. He apologized for having to rush back to his place for early morning inspections.

Bridget gave him a warm embrace and saw him out of the house. She tried to go back to sleep, but the aerial bombardment had a terrific raid on the bunkers and beaches. The planes hit first and hardest on the Pas de Calais region, but the second wave concentrated on the Normandy coastline. Some protective fighters who flew alongside the bombers spotted a German rail transport and strafed them as hard as they could. The German anti-aircraft gunners were shooting at them mercilessly, but the fighters managed to escape.

Suddenly there was a huge explosion, fire, and smoke was coming from the railroad direction. Ambulances, military medics, and military police vehicles were rushing to the scene. Bridget couldn't sleep any longer and went to see Marceau.

Marceau did not sleep either. He was in pain. Bridget gave him pain medicine and then made breakfast for him. He ate in bed, had a short chat with Bridget and began closing his eye lids. He slowly dozed off, and Bridget stayed with him for awhile.

Michael knocked on the door and with an excited voice asked Bridget to come and help the injured. Scores of German soldiers, forced laborers, and civilians were wounded and dead. The scene was an indescribable carnage, with dead bodies all around, blood on the rails and ground, and body parts strewn in every direction in the yard. It was difficult to treat without bandages and first aid supplies, and everybody grabbed whatever was available. To Bridget's surprise the two Gestapo agents who gave her a hard time the night before were there removing obstacles to free soldiers from the debris.

"I did not expect you to be here helping," said one of the Gestapo agents.

"What a surprise," said Bridget in a cynical voice, "We French civilians are helping German soldiers to survive."

"I'm sorry, if I was mistaken, but I had a job to do last night. But I must commend you for what you're doing. You are a kind person."

"Thank you."

"Please help me to free this soldier who is buried under the shells," asked Michael.

Bridget pulled the guys legs out of the unexploded shells while Michael picked the shells off one by one. The soldier was almost crushed and was bleeding from pieces of shell casings. Bridget made a tourniquet from Michael's shirt and bandaged some of his bleeding body. This first aid help continued till midday. Additional help came from Bayeux, Cherbourg, and Caen. She worked feverishly for several hours before she returned home to take care of Marceau.

"My God, you look horrible. There is blood all over your body, torn clothing, dirt on your face and head. It's a miracle you're in one piece," said Marceau.

"I know that. The explosion killed dozens and wounded hundreds of people. We are at war, Marceau, and war is merciless. I better take a bath, because I must go and take care of another situation."

"And what is that, my dear?"

"I must take some food to Susan. She is a darling, and I promised to see her."

"How far do you have to travel?"

"Only to Cherbourg. I'll be back before dark to cook dinner."

"You'll be careful, you promise?

"Marceau, don't worry. I'm a grown up girl!"

"I'm worried. The German patrols and Gestapo are a pain in the butt these days."

"I am aware of that. But I am your daughter and that means something. Plus I was a good girl today and helped a lot of people to survive, not to mention, God is on our side!"

After Bridget cleaned up and dressed, she drove to a market first and bought a number of goodies plus a gift for Susan. She arrived just in time to her place, because Susan was ready to go shopping after a day's work.

"Well, hello there. What are you up to?"

"Just came to visit you as promised. I also brought you some food and a surprise gift."

"You did not have to. You're nice. My God, this is my favorite wine. How did you know that? You saved me a grocery shopping trip. You're a real sweetheart."

"How are you managing?"

"I'll get by. I earn some money and the OSS sends me money through other agents."

"How about Parker?"

"He comes around from time to time. We are very happy together. He is a nice guy. I am very fond of him.

He is like me in many ways. We have similar philosophies, thoughts, desires, and cravings for each other. Parker is considerate of my feelings, moods, and idiosyncrasies. We enjoy snuggling and being passionate. I hope we stay together, but one must be realistic, we are at war, and times are turbulent. We live for the moments."

There was a pause. Then Susan asked, "How about you and Michael?"

"We are also very content with each other. Michael has grown tremendously in every respect since we met. He changed his views on Nazism and has become one of us. We gradually fell in love with each other and developed deep feelings for each other. He's a very honest and sincere person. Our relationship is based on many commonalities that we slowly discovered as time passed by. There is a strong psychological and physical bond between us. I only hope that God will have mercy and we'll survive the invasion, because I think it'll be brutal and savage."

"And how is Marceau?"

"He is a very sick man. His case is terminal. Some days are

better while others are worse. I have a difficult time to bear the burden of not showing my terrible sorrow for him. He means a lot to me. I simply adore this man. I love everything about him. He is the epitome of goodness. Marceau is in many ways close to perfection of mankind. He is a rational thinker, has a superb control of emotions, and a special sense on how to make you feel good. Marceau taught me how to be a real human being, apply my education, and develop a life philosophy that can serve as a beacon for the future."

"You're a lucky girl. What you have is hard to come by."

"I know, and I'm thankful to God for that."

There were two short rings of the doorbell signaling Parker's arrival. Susan opened the door, gave him a big hug as he came inside the apartment.

"Hello, Bridget, how are you? I am pleased to see you."

"Hello, Brian. It's good to see you again. You're looking good."

"So do you. How is Marceau?"

"He is having a hard time coping with his illness."

"He is in my thoughts."

"I have to go now, see you guys soon. Bye!"

Susan saw her to the door. She gave her a warm embrace and thanked her for everything.

Brian and Susan looked at each other for a few seconds, and then she slowly approached him and gave him a light kiss on his mouth.

"Care for Scotch?"

"Yes, please. Give it on the rocks."

She poured his Scotch and handed it over all the while looking at him.

"Is there anything new about the MI6 masquerade's death?"

"The Gestapo is still investigating his contacts, but they are running out of time to do any detective work because there are more important matters for them. It is too late to be concerned about the leaks. They must pack, burn documents, and destroy any evidence of their torturing the citizens, the Resistance operators, forced laborers, and saboteurs and the many deaths that resulted. The invasion is around the corner and they can't waste manpower to find the people who had any contact with their agent prior to his death. The safeties of the Gestapo agents are more important right now. You still have to be cautious and stay put after work, except for grocery and pharmacy shopping. What I'm concerned with are the damn French traitors who would sell their mothers for a dime."

"Don't trust anybody! You can be polite and friendly, but say nothing about yourself. Use the background that we already agreed upon. Don't invite anybody over. I don't have to tell you this, because you're a damn good agent, but we can all make mistakes."

"Thank you for reminding me again of my course work. I did not forget, but it is a good idea to refresh your memory."

"You look tired, my dear. Do you want to rest?" asked Susan.

"Yes, but I would prefer in your arms, sweetheart."

He removed his pants and she took off her dress and both were lying side by side on her large bed. He touched her fingers and she turned toward him as if to say something. Both were in synch and there was no need to say anything, at least for a while. They felt each other's desire to commence their sexual overtures, but they also enjoyed the prolongation of their temporary celibacy.

"I am so glad that I met you, Susan."

"I feel the same my darling; you light up my life, which was so routine and empty."

"But your job has certainly been adventurous, creative, exciting, and meaningful."

"Not as far as my private life. Yes, I met some handsome characters. I had various sexual experiences, but when we parted, it had little meaning. They were just moments, the satisfaction of bodily hunger, but the soul, the deep feelings were missing."

"You, on the other hand, are fulfilling my insatiable appetite for love, sex, intellect, and belonging, not necessarily in that order. I feel complete with you. You gave me meaning to life. You know, I can talk to you without uttering a single word."

"I don't know how to respond to your eloquent and sensitive expressions, but all I can say is touché, I feel the same."

Brian kissed her on the lips. They aroused themselves to the point that their hands touched each other all over, and she asked to become one with him, which he gladly responded to by uniting with her in ecstasy and pleasure.

They were really in synch with each other. Having had a great time together, both fell asleep in each other's arms, which lasted for a couple of hours. Then, both looked at each other, and almost said in unison, "I'm hungry."

Susan had all kinds of food that Bridget provided. But both wanted something light and nourishing. She made a large omelet with mushrooms, green peppers, and some sausage. Fresh French bread, butter, and jam were served along with the main dish. Brian made some fresh coffee. They were ready to sit down and eat when her roommate, a vivacious, blonde, blue eyed twenty-something, entered the kitchen declared her hunger and asked for permission to join the company.

She extended her hand and said to Brian, "I'm Collette. I am hungry for food and a nice guy like you."

Susan smiled and said, "You can have eggs, but not him. He is mine—body and soul."

Brian felt flattered and laughed at the young girl, whose breast were almost showing in her low cut dress. Her shapely breasts did not need a bra and she was enjoying her opportunity to coquette with him.

"What do you do, Collette?"

"I work in the x-ray room as a radiologist assistant."

"It must be quite interesting."

"I like it. I meet all kinds of people. It is quite rewarding to find out what is wrong with someone."

"How did you get into your business?" asked Brian.

"I am a problem solver. I wanted to do something in engineering."

"You must love creative work."

"Yes, I do."

"How was your work today?" asked Susan.

"Full of excitement. We had a number of cases with brain tumors."

"Can these people be helped?" questioned Parker.

"It always depends on the location and severity of the tumor."

"Let's change the topic. After a hard day's work you must have been quite hungry?" asked Susan.

"Yes, I had no time to eat. We were terribly busy. I really enjoy your cooking, Susan."

"Brian helped also. He is a great cook."

"What are your plans after dinner?" asked Collette.

"We don't have any plans, but if you have a good suggestion, we may consider it," said Susan.

"Why don't we just chat about anything that comes to mind?"

"What comes to mind right now is adventure and excitement," said Collette.

"You want to talk about some of your adventures?" asked Susan.

"I recently dated a man who was married but had an irresistible desire for me. I felt the same for him. We had some tentative plans for our future, but unfortunately he was one of our patients today with an advanced brain tumor."

"This must have been terrible for you to learn," said Susan.

"Yes, it affected me the whole day."

Parker and Susan looked at each other and felt sorrow for Collette.

"We are very sorry," said Parker.

"I will survive. It is just sad to find somebody who means so much to you and all of a sudden you lose that person."

"I understand you need for company tonight," said Susan.

"Thank you for keeping me company."

The three of them chatted and drank wine until midnight. Susan politely excused herself and retired to her bedroom. Parker did the same, but before he left for the bedroom he embraced Collette and wished her the very best.

When Bridget returned home, she found Marceau in pain. Instead of resting, he tried to allay his terrible discomfort by listening to Allied Intelligence messages in his secret room.

"Let me ask your doctor about the dosage of your pain medicine. May be he'll double it," said Bridget.

"I hope it will not incapacitate me. I must work. The invasion is around the corner and I must know what is going on. I am responsible informing the Resistance when and where the invasion will take place."

She called his doctor, and he suggested one and a half pills for the time being. She must call him back in three days and give an honest report of his condition.

"I think the doctor is being considerate. He knows I have commitments."

"I am getting tired Marceau, there is a long day ahead of me tomorrow, and I must have a good night sleep. I think you should do the same."

"Have pleasant dreams my dear Bridget, I shall follow you soon."

Marceau was reading to put himself to sleep, but he just couldn't fall asleep. His sixth sense was working overtime and he decided to listen to the messages coming in from Allied Intelligence. He walked into his secret compartment, turned on his receiver, and there it was, an urgent call. It was requesting to find the German fuel depots in and around Normandy. The depots can be on the surface, underground, in bunkers, or camouflaged. The find should cover a two-hundred kilometer radius from the Atlantic Wall. He thought it was a tall order, but the job had to be done.

He went to wake up Bridget and asked her to summon Shaw, Parker, and Michael.

Bridget called Michael but Shaw and Parker were unavailable. Michael said he would be in sometime tomorrow. She trotted back, half asleep, from the bar where she made the phone calls and headed straight to bed.

"Please, Marceau, don't wake me up. Call me only if it cannot wait. I am really exhausted and I have to be ready to function tomorrow." With these words she gave a kiss to Marceau and went to sleep.

The next morning there was an extraordinary rush of

orders by the Generals who openly expressed their doubts for a future stay. Marceau was delighted to hear their pessimism and the probability of losing the war. He kept quiet and non-opinionated which aroused some curiosity among the generals.

"I can understand that you are getting fed up with the occupation forces, but we Germans like to keep what we fought for. It will be a bloody battle, but I don't know if we can throw them back to sea. It all depends where the Allies will land," said one of the Generals.

"I think they will land at the Pas de Calais region," said Marceau.

"Is this affirmative?"

"I cannot promise. It is a hunch, just like finishing these boots."

"Do you foresee any difficulties for these boots?"

"I don't know about the supplies from Paris, the schedule and location of the invasion, and the damage of the aerial bombardments. It is getting to be very rough."

"Your assessment may be correct, but we must be optimistic. I'll see you in two to three weeks. If your supplies cannot be delivered during that time, let me know."

Marceau reluctantly called for the supplies, but he sensed that the delivery would be interrupted by the invasion. Later in the day, Michael came and they had a serious talk about finding the various fuel depots for the Allies. The exact landing sites were still a closely guarded secret, but Marceau did not say more than he had to. Michael, however, began to suspect that the invasion would be somewhere in Normandy. He promised to be careful in his inquiries and report back to him as soon as possible.

Michael asked Bridget to go out to have dinner together,

but she invited him to stay and eat with them instead. During dinner, the conversation returned to the fuel depots.

"I must have documents and maps to find the locations for you. Fuel depots are not under my supervision. The question is how to get this information without arousing suspicion," said Michael.

"Would you rather see Shaw and Parker getting involved, since they are traveling all over to inspect existing structures," asked Marceau.

"It would certainly be more appropriate," replied Michael.

"Are there any maps around that you could look at without being questioned," asked Bridget.

"Yes, there are, but you know human nature, somebody is always nosy and might ask, 'What are you looking at'?"

"So, you can make up a story," responded Bridget.

"I guess I could come up with a logistical story about the safety of the depots in case of a bombing."

"I shall call Shaw and Parker again."

The moment she said that, both entered the store and there was a warm welcome.

"We were just talking about you guys," said Bridget.

Marceau took over the conversation and explained the urgency of finding the fuel depots.

"You have two days to do the job," said Marceau.

"Within about two-hundred kilometer radius, I don't think so. But we'll supply as much as we can in two days," said Shaw.

"Michael, what are your invasion plans?" asked Shaw.

"Hold the line with limited tanks, infantry, and supplies. Some areas have more manpower than others. There is a division among the Generals about the main invasion site. Pas de Calais region is where most tanks and infantry are concentrated and Normandy is viewed as diversionary. Some Generals, however, think that Normandy will be the main theatre."

"I hope the Allies have enough information about the landing sites. Between the aerial surveillance, commando reconnaissance, Resistance operatives, and our input they should have a map of expectations, but there is always the unknown," said Marceau.

"You said it well. I would like to resurvey the Pointe du Hoc area. I believe we must warn the incoming forces to be prepared for the worst unless they could decimate the top layer of the cliff and leave nothing but ashes there. I would love to get permission to learn about the dug in places, pillboxes, 88mm gun position, heavy artillery sections, and bunker penetrations. I am sure that there have been major reinforcements of gun and artillery positions since my last visit of the battery inspection," said Parker.

"I am certain that there will be a bloodbath in the air and naval bombardment cannot destroy the German defenses. The 716th and the 352nd Infantry Divisions are an absolutely formidable force to defeat by the incoming invasion forces. They will need heavy reinforcements to save their souls," said Michael.

"I am not sure that Allied Intelligence is completely aware of what you just said," said Parker.

"I agree and we must do something about it," said Shaw.

"All you can do, at this point, is to warn the Allies. But their weapons are limited when it comes to German Batteries. They do not have any concrete penetrating super bombs or any naval super shells. What they have, however, is courage, bravery, and excellent marksmanship to overcome the technical limitations," said Marceau.

The discussion was adjourned for another day and Shaw, Parker, and Marceau bid good night to each other. Michael stayed until the early morning hours with Bridget. Every minute they spent together was precious for them. The feeling of uncertainty about their survival was a constant in their lives. As Michael once said, "Our lives consist of moments, and the ones we have are gifts from God."

The next morning Marceau and Bridget were heading to the hospital for lab work and a medical checkup. Lately Marceau was feeling more weak and tired than before and Bridget was worried that his condition had worsened since the last checkup. They spent several hours at the hospital and the traveling back and forth took a toll on Marceau. She, being his lifeline, however, pumped some vitality into him, and both had an amicable chat about love, life, and friendship.

When they returned home, Marceau felt totally exhausted and after grabbing a bite to eat took a nap. Bridget, on the other hand, took care of some household chores, washing clothes, cleaning dishes, sewing, paying bills, and cleaning some of the rooms. The windows had to be washed and the floors had to be cleaned. Bridget was efficient at keeping the home in order. It was not only because of aesthetics, but health reasons also. She was terribly concerned that Marceau would develop some kind of infection, pneumonia, or some other disease that could further debilitate him.

She spent some time in the radio room receiving messages. Shaw and Parker received further orders to report locations of ammo storages within the battery compounds. Bridget decided to make dinner and personally deliver the messages later.

Having found Marceau awake, a little chitchat, and playing of cards was in order.

"Playing cards is good for you. A little entertainment and winning is good for your spirit," said Bridget.

"It all depends on what kind of game you want to play. In some I'm good, but I'm bad in baccarat."

"How about playing black-jack?"

"That is fine with me."

"If you wish we can change after twenty minutes to something else."

They played black-jack for a while then changed to poker. They had a lot of fun and many laughs. Bridget had to run down for medicine to the local apothecary before he closed his place, and apologized for interrupting the game.

"I know you have to go and I forgive you, we must continue when you return because you're winning heavily my dear, and I'm losing my shirt. Go, my love, before it's too late."

At the pharmacy she met two German military officers who recognized her as a first aid assistant for the wounded at the railroad cars explosion.

"Bon jour mademoiselle Bridget, we recognized you as a tireless first aid worker, saving the lives of many of our soldiers. We never really had a chance to officially thank you for your heroic gesture. May we take this opportunity to invite you to our battery for a celebration? We'll take you on a tour and show you our Atlantic Wall defense structures," said one of the German officers.

"I don't know about that. We have a lot of work ahead of us, but thank you anyway."

"May I write down my name and place where you could reach us? Just in case you'll find some time?"

"That would be very nice and I will keep you in mind. Thank you again."

When she returned home Marceau was feeling a little

more tired than when she left and excused himself to go lie down. She told him about the invitation, but he just closed his eyes and did not respond.

"Marceau dear, I know you are tired but we have to eat dinner. Please come to the table and have some of the goodies I made for us."

Marceau opened his eyes and in a tired voice he replied, "I will have a little. For some reason I am not very hungry."

"You eat as much as you like. Sometimes while you eat your appetite comes back."

"This is a good enticement. You remember my words from the past."

Bridget put the food on the table and just the smell whetted his appetite.

Marceau helped himself and began to eat and drink his red wine. Bridget did the same. Marceau had a second helping of the roasted potatoes and expressed his feelings by kissing Bridget's hand and saying,

"Darling, this meal was one of the better ones. This is Hotel Ritz quality."

"Marceau, thank you, but this was a very plain dinner."

"But, you put in all your love and affection."

"Thank you. I must go now. Help yourself to the sweets."

"I know, you have to see Shaw and Parker."

"Yes, I have one more errand to make."

Bridget gave them all the information from Allied Intelligence and briefly mentioned the invitation from the two German officers to view the Battery.

"I wouldn't go if I were you," said Parker.

"What is your objection?"

"You cannot trust those guys. They need women desperately. If you want to go, go with Michael. I'll bet they will show you very little."

"I just wanted to help you guys, but you're right. It is not worth it to expose myself to unpleasant situations."

"Besides, we have already covered almost all the batteries in Normandy, and AI should have a good idea what the boys will encounter when they come to shore," said Parker.

"However, we are still in the process of mopping up all the details, but there will still be surprises. The bombers will miss some well buried places, the fighter planes will strafe but with limitations, and the hidden mines will decimate quite a few in the first wave. But, we all try our very best to minimize the casualties. The reality is that there will be losses before there will be winners. But I'm sure as I'm speaking to you, that we'll have a beachhead in the first 24 hours," said Shaw.

"I certainly hope so!" said Bridget. "I must go; Marceau will be worried if I'm late."

When Bridget arrived, to her surprise, she found Michael taking care of Marceau. He was making tea for him and served cookies that he purchased in a local bakery in Bayeux. Also, Michael was taking his temperature, fixed his pillow, and played chess with him that Marceau found it quite refreshing and thought provoking from his present dull life.

"This is very kind of you. I'm impressed," said Bridget.

"Just trying to be humane, Marceau is a great man," said Michael.

"Well, thank you, it's very nice of you to say that."

She gave a kiss on Michael's cheek and a loving smile.

"I'll be with you shortly but I must check the mail," said Bridget.

She left for the radio room and attentively noted the

various messages that were sent by the British Broadcasting Corporation and Allied Intelligence. Marceau received a few messages and the Resistance was informed to stand by daily for various messages of great importance. Some of the messages for Marceau were not urgent so she decided to wait until tomorrow to tell Marceau since it was his bedtime and he was tired and sleepy. The BBC messages were general and had no major importance for the day. Michael and Bridget stayed together until one o'clock in the morning. They were eating cookies, drinking fresh milk, making love, and holding onto each other in bed. They were at peace and relaxed, at least for the moment. Michael had to leave to supervise some early morning defensive training exercises.

Very early in the morning, before the church bell tolled six o'clock, one cell member from the Ste Mere Eglise area woke Bridget up to inform her that Therese was in trouble with the officers of St. Marcouf. She apparently did something to be arrested.

"How did you learn about it?" asked Bridget.

"Therese and two other girls were picked up by the officers to offer a birthday party for Therese. They did not suspect foul play. She did go however, not to celebrate, but to find out the defensive locations and calibers of guns. She was concerned about the cache of pillboxes that could annihilate the invading forces."

"So what happened? How did she get herself into trouble?"

"The officers wanted to have an orgy and Therese refused. One of the officers tried to rape her and she bit him. He kicked her out and sent her home. She was walking out but in the wrong direction. Another officer warned her that she was in great danger by walking in the forbidden zone. That area was reserved for sentries only. Plus, many sections of the ground were mined. Another officer spotted her and offered to show her the area but she had to be nice and cooperative."

"She promised that she would be a nice girl and they hit it off pretty well. He showed her every little detail, from guns to cannons, and they ended their sightseeing journey in his private office. There she allowed him to fondle her and there was a reciprocal loving gesture. They both ended up making passionate love with each other, but he had so much to drink and was so excited that he passed out. She called the medic and she was charged on various grounds of assault and espionage."

"The arresting officer who made the charges was the same officer she bit earlier. He threatened her with all kinds of charges and she was absolutely petrified. In the meantime, the officer she made love to began to feel better and started looking for her. He was told that she must have some identification before she can be released."

"Who are you and how did I get into this picture?" asked Bridget.

"One of the girls, who went home, told me to contact you. I am an old friend. You can find out about me from the Maquis. I am a saboteur and work together with the Resistance. My friend is an old friend of Marceau's. You can check me out before you want to help her."

"Thank you. We'll check you out and see what we can do."

Bridget called Michael and asked him to come to the store. He came down as fast as he could. Marceau checked out her background and indeed she was a saboteur working for the Maquis and her story was believable.

"We cannot compromise Shaw, Parker, Marceau, and

Michael to help the girl. That leaves me to step into the picture with a strong possibility of being raped," said Bridget.

"Not necessarily," said Michael.

"You can arrive with a couple of German military police officers and they will not touch you," said Michael.

"How do I convince the military police about the innocence of this girl over the officer's statements?"

"I will take care of that," said Michael.

"No, you will get into trouble."

"I don't think so, not when you have friends in the military police. I saved the career of a military officer who did something very wrong and was almost court-martialed. I helped him by talking to his commanding officer. He owes me one."

Michael called his friend in the military police and he was happy to help him out.

Later in the day Bridget was accompanied by two military officers and drove to the St. Marcouf battery.

"What a big surprise to see this charming lady. May I offer you a drink? You really made my day by coming here, but you do not need an escort," said the 'bitten' officer.

"Yes I do. I am here to vouch for the identity of Therese who you are holding here in custody."

"What is your name? I must have seen you somewhere in a shop."

"I'm Bridget. My father is Marceau, the cobbler."

"Oh yes, now I remember. Your father makes those fabulous boots that the Military Brass is raving about."

"My dear Bridget, this is none of your business. This is a military matter and I shall take care of this."

"No, not anymore. We are under orders to take the girl into our custody. You can make the charges if you wish in military court and present all the details of your escapade along with it," said one of the military police officers in charge.

"How about you, Bridget, would you stay? I'll exchange you for her."

"You know I could arrest you for that offer," said the military police officer.

"No, I don't think so. This battery is under my command and you guys have no jurisdiction over me."

"Yes I do have jurisdiction over every German soldier. I can arrest officers and Generals. It would not take me long to marshal a truck load of military police and take you into custody in one of our jails," said one of the military police officers.

"I don't think we have to have a power play. It is not worth it. You are an officer of the German Army and your reputation is important. We don't need a stand off. You'll never know what tomorrow brings and how this war will conclude. It is always a good idea to have a French citizen on your side," said Bridget.

The officer looked at Bridget, kept silent for a second, than ordered a soldier to release Therese.

"I'm letting her go because you vouched for her. From now on she is your responsibility."

The two military officers accompanied her outside the battery. Therese thanked every one for their help. Therese sat next to Bridget and both hugged each other and drove to Marceau's place. The military police officers went back to their station.

When they arrived Marceau greeted them, hugged them, and offered a half a dozen accolades for her endurance and Bridget's help.

"I could not have accomplished this feat without Michael's help," said Bridget.

"Thank you Michael and Bridget," said Therese.

Marceau opened a bottle of wine and they had a little celebration. Bridget prepared some cheese, smoked fish, and French bread.

"Therese, you must have some important observations to share with us?" said Marceau.

"Can I do it later in the day?"

"Of course you can. I just don't want you to forget anything," said Marceau.

Therese was a Parisian girl in her mid twenties. She had long brown hair combed to cover half her face. Her figure was rather slim relative to her height, which was 5 feet 7 inches. Her breasts, however, were disproportionately larger to her body. Michael couldn't help notice her coquetting posture. She sat on the top of the couch like a model posing for an artist—legs crossed, skirt up halfway, leaning back and supporting her body with both hands.

Therese was hungry and she appreciated the food that Bridget prepared.

"This fish tastes really good. I was really hungry when we arrived, but now I feel satiated," said Therese.

"I am glad. You can have seconds later," said Bridget.

"How long do you expect me to stay?" asked Therese.

"You may stay over if you wish. I'll take you wherever you wish tomorrow," said Bridget.

"Thank you. I am a little scared right now. I really appreciate your support."

"Don't thank me, you went through an ordeal, and you need a restful sleep. You can sleep in the guest bed," said Bridget.

"We can talk tomorrow morning my darling. I don't want to deprive you from resting your mind and body," added Marceau. "Besides, I was planning to write my memoirs."

"Well, that is just wonderful," said Bridget.

"I must go now. I have a lot of work tomorrow. Good luck writing your memoirs Marceau. Adieu everybody," bid Michael.

Both ladies kissed Marceau on the cheek, wished him happy writing, pleasant dreams and left the room. Marceau took a pad, a number of sheets of white paper and a pencil and began to collect his thoughts. His first two words he put down was "My Memoir."

When I was sixteen, I had a very good year. I did well in school, romancing my girlfriend of seventeen and making money on the side as a delivery boy for a grocer. I lived according to my circumstances. My parents were conservative and frugal. They did not tolerate my lack of orderliness. My room was a disaster for my mother and she did not allow any friend, especially a girl friend, to come to visit until the room looked clean and uncluttered. My father hated loud music and talk. The door of my room had to be open when a girl visited the apartment. Sex was in the mind but not in practice.

Despite for all these restrictions we lived a happy life. My parents were supportive of my decisions for the future. They did not get involved in my vocational choice and the girls I dated. Fortunately some teachers became my mentors and helped me to find my goal in life.

The life I dreamed about was unrealistic. I read too much about political ideology. It took me sometime to shed some thoughts which were anchored in a dream world. I voraciously read from Darwin, Kierkegaard, Freud, novels by Roger Martin du Gard and Chekov's Short Stories. Reading books became my past time between work, dates and family.

I loved to walk the streets of Paris. I adored window shopping, looking at people as they were watching the passers-by on Avenue des Champ-Elysees. I walked until I dropped. When my legs gave out on me, I would frantically look for a seat on a bench which was at a premium at certain times of the day. Young lovers and the elderly were taking most of the seats and I often offered my seat to an elderly or pregnant lady.

Hours of walking made me conscious of the importance of good foot wear. I began to read about the role of shoes in walking. A friend of mine referred me to an orthopedic doctor who was a widower and close to retirement. He spent some time explaining to me the mechanics and pathologies of walking. In return, I was asked to take care of his cats in his absence.

I became fascinated with the craft of shoe making and signed up as an apprentice with a first rate store in Paris. They paid me very little and I had to work on weekends in various jobs to supplement my income. Of course, after graduation, I wanted to live independently and had a small room in a rooming house. There were six rooms on the second floor and only one bathroom. It was awful when you had the runs and the facility was occupied. The key to the bathroom was only good for the floor on which you had rented the room.

My high school romance did not last long because I was a year younger and she wanted men who were over twenty-one. I was heartbroken for a while, but I got over it. I found other girls but they did not mean too much for me. One day I was helping out the salesman in the front and met a lady in her late thirties. She appreciated my effort to try to fit the best shoes for her feet and invited me to her apartment for tea.

I was absolutely stunned to have the privilege to visit her place which was located in one of the most expensive locations of Paris. I had to be announced by the concierge and accompanied to the elevator. She was waiting for me in unexpected luxury. The apartment consisted of seven rooms, including two bathrooms, a waiting room, guest room, living room, large bedroom with a king size bed, and a kitchen with all the modern amenities.

She asked me to share with her my past and told me how much she was impressed with me by pointing out her well formed feet and legs. She was titillated by my observation.

She was dressed seductively .We sat down to have tea and cookies and she began to talk about her unhappy life and recent divorce. She was very blunt and without being skittish she revealed moments of her private life with her husband. She talked about her bedroom problems. She told me that she was a virgin when she got married and her parents never instructed her about intimacy. She stated that she had no pleasure to be with her husband and he could not care about her feelings. She had to learn how to pleasure herself with the help of a therapist who became her friend.

This relationship had to end because he had many ladies with similar problems and she did not want to share him with other women. She learned to trust her instincts and invited me to begin a new relationship. She did not want any compensation other than my faithfulness to her. She came from a rich home and her divorce settlement afforded her a comfortable living.

I was absolutely flabbergasted what she told me and did not know what to say. I was attracted to her and she did not come to me, touch me, or have any physical contacts until I expressed my feelings for her. Needless to say that as a young man looking at a seductive lady, my blood pressure rose. I had to tell her in every detail my excitement about her and describe what fantasies I had with her for the future. She looked into my eyes and expected me to do the same. I was in such ecstasy that I had a difficult time holding it back. I told her about my pain after two hours of revelations about my feelings.

She told me that she was totally overwhelmed by my narratives and she also had a difficult time restraining herself. But, she promised *that wewould have a wonderful time together and that all my fantasies would come true.*

By the time we kissed each other, I had to pleasure myself. She told me that this was a natural consequence of our verbal stimulation and French kissing. We rested for thirty minutes and continued to enjoy each other until the morning hours.

I never dreamed in my life to have a lady who would teach me the most intimate desires of a woman. I had my second apprenticeship with her. This lasted for two years and I was totally under her spell. But one day she told me that our relationship must come to an end because she found a man who wanted to marry her. I was crushed and asked her to be intimate the last time. She refuse;, it was over.

I was disheartened and wanted to travel. I enlisted in the Army but to my greatest disappointment I was disqualified on the basis that there was something wrong with my blood. I asked the Army physician what was wrong and he told me that I had too many white cells and I must first take care of my problem before I tried to reenlist. Honestly, I felt fine and decided to open a shoe shop on my own. I had saved some money and started to look around.

From my first apprenticeship I learned the trade of shoe repair, how to make custom made shoes and boots. Later, the experience gained in a shoe store was very different. I learned how to treat customers and run a shoe business including shoe repair. But, I wanted to leave the big city and settle in a small town. My first preference was Normandy. I found a tour guide who took me everywhere. We traveled every day for eight hours and covered most places from Cherbourg to Caen. I fell in love with a fishing village. It was Port-En-Bessin.

My second apprenticeship taught me about a relationship with a woman, what love means, and how to make love to a woman. She made me aware of the differences between physical pleasure and interpersonal love and the combination of both. She spent considerable time explaining and showing how to sexually satisfy a woman and vice versa. She told me that marriage means different things to people and sometimes we are completely unaware why we get married.

Three years later I was very fortunate to find a wonderful lady to share a happy life with. We were honest and sincere with each other. We talked about how we felt about each other physically and personally. I dated her for over two years before we got married. There was a deep respect for our individual needs and deeds. Her unexpected departure from my life was a terrible loss and I will long for her for the rest of my life.

My children grew up in a happy home but both of them wanted to live in a big city where they could acquire culture, music, education, and varied personal experiences. We did not protest their wishes and allowed them to pursue their lives according to their choices.

When the war broke out and life became uncertain and difficult for many families, I volunteered to help people in need through various organizations. I offered free shoe repair, hospital work, social work, teacher aide, and various charitable chores.

The fall of France had a devastating effect on my psyche. I felt as a wounded patriot. I had to do something. It was my great pleasure to enlist to the Resistance and offer all my skills to help the cause, which meant to win back France. About that time, I was asked to help a young lady, Bridget, another Resistance operative, to accept her as my 'daughter'. Her parents, devoted Resistance operatives, were found guilty by the Gestapo for their activities and were sent to a German concentration camp. The Gestapo was looking for Bridget to find out more about her parent's operations. Of course, I accepted her without hesitation. Thank the Lord, we saved her life!

My contribution to the Resistance, Allied Intelligence and liberation of France has been demonstrated in my tireless devotion as a courier and recruiter. I would have to cite each of the hundreds of cases where my work played a major role.

My present outlook on life, which is not too different from others, was shaped by experience. The quotation by Herbert Spencer, 'Survival of the Fittest' would apply more to the concept of Freedom and Democracy than National Socialism. I cannot envision a nation that is founded on exclusion, hatred, confiscation of wealth and material, absolute totalitarianism, concentration camps, and no freedom of speech! To love only the blue eyed, blond hair Nazis cannot and will not survive. There are others who have been contributing to mankind in many ways and forms. Should we abstain our love from others whose skin is brown, black, yellow, or red, with black, brown, or green eyes? Absolutely not! No nation can survive without respect of individual differences. As Comte De Bussy-Rabutin said, "L'absence est a l'amour ce qu'est au feu le vent; Il eteint le petit, il allume le grand.- Absence is to love what wind is to fire; it extinguishes the small, it enkindles the great."

I don't know if the good Lord will allow me to witness the glory of victory of human freedom and democracy, but it is my humble prediction that love and respect for each other will prevail and good will win over evil.

It was past midnight when Bridget got out of bed and went to see Marceau. His head was down facing his knees and snoring lightly. She removed the pad and pencil and put it on the nearby lamp table. She had to wake him up to get him to go to bed.

"What, what is going on?" asked Marceau half sleep.

"You fell asleep my dear Marceau. It is time to go to bed."

"Yes, I fell asleep."

Bridget helped Marceau to put on his night gown and waited until he was under the blanket and gave him another kiss on his cheek.

"Have a very good night, Marceau."

"Thank you, my dear. Good night."

They met at the breakfast table at seven-thirty. Therese

looked more relaxed and composed. Bridget and Marceau looked at each other with smiles on their faces.

"So how did it go?" asked Bridget.

"I think, not bad for an amateur writer."

"I am very proud of you, Marceau. May I read your manuscript?"

"By all means read it."

"What are your plans, Therese?" asked Marceau.

"I have no plans. I don't know where to go and what to do. I am still afraid. These are turbulent times for me."

"I want you to relax. We will help you to find a place where you can work and stay, Therese. In the meantime you can stay with us," said Marceau.

"This is very kind of you. I don't know how much to thank you for all your help."

"You can thank us by describing what you saw in the battery," replied Marceau.

"Do you want me to tell you or write it down?"

"We would prefer it in writing."

Marceau handed her a pencil and some paper. Therese began to cite from memory what she remembered. It took her three hours to describe in detail where and what she saw. Meanwhile Bridget made several phone calls to various Resistance locations to find a place where Therese could live and work.

The revelation of Therese was indeed useful. She described the battery in good detail. Therese remembered the various gun emplacements, caliber of guns and mine fields.

"Well, this is important information but, of course, we must verify everything before we can process it," said Marceau.

"Well, this is the best I can provide you with. If my

perception and memory are inaccurate, I would like to apologize beforehand."

Bridget came back with good news. One of the Resistance operatives offered her a place to stay and work. It was a bakery in Bayeux. Therese had to share a room with another girl, however. Her job would be preparing the dough for baking.

"I think I would like to work there and be out of sight, at least until the invasion is over."

"I will take you there this morning and you can discuss the details with Mr. Sartre, the owner of the bakery," said Bridget.

"Thank you."

Bridget and Therese gave a hug to Marceau and drove off toward Bayeux.

CHAPTER TEN

L iving for Marceau and Bridget became more difficult as his health worsened. Demands for shoe repair and handmade boots increased, messages of Allied Intelligence doubled if not tripled, and Resistance operators, Maquis, and foreign agents became daily targets for the Gestapo.

Marceau's appetite diminished, his strength deteriorated, and he felt tired more than usual. His condition required him to cut back his working days, but people kept coming to have their shoes fixed. Some people anticipated an extended battle, others wanted an extra pair of boots from Marceau, and still others believed that a pair of shoes made by Marceau was like owning a picture from a famous painter.

Success for 'Overlord' required more intelligence. The time table of invasion was about a month away, which depended on logistics, weather conditions, combat readiness of the troops, the bait and effectiveness of Fortitude, the German military strategy, and last, but not the least the intelligence. Thousands of the Resistance and the Maquis were waiting for the code verses to dismantle telegraph and telephone lines, to change the direction of railroad tracks, to explode the railroad ties and tracks and to help planes locate towns, in order to drop bombs, commandos, and parachuting infantry to the designated areas. Every evening they stood by their hidden radios and listened to the messages from the BBC News Service. They were ready to fight like they never had before. Although there were twenty—

one cell members of the resistance, only a few were combat ready. Shaw and Parker were ready to serve strategic assistance to the invading forces but needed last minute information from the Allied Intelligence.

The most disturbing and frightening information came from the Resistance and Allied Intelligence. For the German Military and Gestapo leadership the leaks of the Atlantic Wall defenses became intolerable. They blamed the Resistance forces for the frequency of aerial attacks, commando operations, sabotage activities, and assassinations of German officers. They had sufficient reasons to hit back and hard on the enemy, before the Allies sent their troops ashore.

Marceau received several calls for help because members of the Resistance were being rounded up, arrested, interrogated, and executed. Shaw and Parker suspended all cell operations and asked all members to stay far away from information gathering. Although they still needed to inspect the structural components of batteries, bunkers, and casemates, as Todt officers, they were careful of every move they made and every question they asked. This time the Military Police and Gestapo watched every person who entered the batteries and at the slightest suspicion arrests were made. Over a hundred forced laborers were arrested and tortured beyond recognition. Retributions were rampant.

Shaw was particularly interested in the St. Marcouf and Azeville fortifications where the guns were facing the invading soldiers. They went there to inspect the cracks in one of the concrete walls which had been leaking each time it rained. The officers had been complaining about the sloppy workmanship, but actually it was the wrong mixture of concrete that caused the problem.

Parker was studying the problem intensely trying to determine the necessary repair when he noticed that somebody from an enclosed yard was hanging upside down naked. "What's going on," he asked one of the soldiers.

"He's a forced laborer who walked away to urinate in a forbidden area. The military police grabbed him and charged him with espionage. He was interrogated, but nothing came out of his mouth that would have indicated his guilt. He is undergoing torture by hanging upside down, without water, and has been receiving continuous beating," said the soldier.

"What's next?" Parker inquired.

"He'll receive more beatings on his feet and shin bones until the skin breaks and bleeds."

"What if he's telling the truth?"

"They will not believe him and he'll die of pain and dehydration. The officers are trying to set an example for the others."

"And what is happening at the other wall?"

"They are raping women who are being punished for entering the battery without permission. They wanted to sell cigarettes and wine to the soldiers," answered the other soldier.

Parker summoned the attending construction officer and told him about the repair.

"Well, do it as soon as you can," said the officer.

"It is not that simple," said Shaw.

"Whatever you'll need, we'll provide you with. Forget about bureaucracy, requisitions, paperwork, permissions, et cetera, et cetera, et cetera. This place will be in Allied hands by the time the cement arrives, not to mention the steel rods," said the officer.

"I'm glad that you have a good understanding of construction operations. Please procure the necessary materials. Here is the list. Be sure you have ten good workers for the project. We'll be back tomorrow to start the preliminaries," said Shaw.

Shaw and Parker left the place with some satisfaction. At least they can observe what the infantry is about to face and suggest how to approach and neutralize the guns.

It pained Marceau that with all his friends and contacts he was unable to help his fellow members of the Resistance. The Gestapo was merciless at the slightest suspicion of espionage. Security precautions had reached the highest level. When information had to be passed from one member to another, it was done in the open at public places and without noticeable human contact. It got to the level of magic. As a matter of fact, some of the more sophisticated members were magicians. They worked as cooks, barmaids, mechanics, plumbers, and in other various roles. They hid the messages in cigarettes, toilet paper, wine glasses, copper pipes and destroyed them as soon as they read them. But sometimes mistakes happened and they paid a terrible price.

One incident occurred in a hotel bar in Caen. Julie was a friend to Marceau, and quite often she helped to forward messages to the Resistance. She worked at the bar as a part-time barmaid. There were seven people sitting close to each other at the bar drinking all kinds of liqueur. There was a highly classified message written on cigarette paper about commandos landing and signal lights were needed for direction and clearance. This unassuming gentleman was smoking and drinking wine totally wrapped up in reading a local paper and never looked at anybody. Another young gentleman, sitting with an attractive lady ran out of cigarettes and asked Julie if she had a pack to sell. She politely refused, but offered two cigarettes. Before he had a chance to take the cigarettes, the man with the paper grabbed it, and opened both cigarettes on the top of the counter.

It all happened in seconds. By receiving a signal, another man at the bar approached the young man and showed him the Gestapo badge. He was arrested with Julie and taken to the Gestapo Headquarters in Caen.

Both were separated, put into a solitary cell and were asked to shed their clothes. They were left naked for hours before the interrogations began. The man, who conducted the interrogation with Julie, was a frequent visitor at the bar and had wanted to make love to her for a long time.

"This is a chance Julie to make up for the lost time."

"You can do anything you want with me. I am in your custody. I'm your prisoner."

"Did you know anything about the message written on the cigarette paper before you gave the cigarettes?"

"No, I did not hand him the two cigarettes, he picked the two, and the Gestapo officer grabbed them."

"How did you obtain the package?"

"The hotel manager gave me several packs that I was to use for special customers."

"Please, put your dress on. I will escort you outside. You can go home. If you want to see me, give me your address and phone before you leave."

Julie was lying, of course. She was a good actress and a believable witness. She thanked the Gestapo man and asked him to call her. She went home, packed her suitcase, traveled to Paris the same night. Julie had all kinds of identity papers, wigs, facial makeup and friends to hide her all over in France.

The young man, by the name of Paul was not that lucky. He suffered unbearably torture and implicated Julie and others.

"What was your role in the Resistance?"

"I was a messenger and provided save havens for the fugitives."

"I don't believe you! I think you are a saboteur and spy for the enemy."

"I am not and you can ask Julie."

"I will read her report later, but I am going to find out your role first."

He was taken to the next room which was the so called "operating room" where all tortures took place.

"Before I begin to find out your role in the Resistance, you have a chance to write down what you did, who were your contacts, and what your next assignments were supposed to be. I will give you thirty minutes. If you fail to confess and not give me all the necessary information, I will see to it that you do."

His confessions were unsatisfactory and first he was given the water immersion and then the electrical shock treatments. This was followed by the surgical removal of his finger nails and toe nails. He was sprinkled with salt and acid over the raw skin. He screamed his lungs out. After that he was hung upside down and his shin bones were broken and his ribs were cracked with hard rubber sticks. He was in such agonizing pain that he told things about himself that he never did. He gave all names that he was in contact with. When all the information was jotted down he was pulled by his hair to the courtyard and hung by a thin wire until he bled and suffocated to death.

An order was given to arrest Julie in the morning, but she was nowhere to be found. The Paris Gestapo was informed about her possible stay, but Julie left Paris and headed for

Spain. She had different passports, money, and connections. A week later the Gestapo gave up on her and concentrated on the other individuals.

Members of the Maquis were preparing to destroy German supply routes by derailing the major tracks leading to Normandy and setting bombs with high grade explosives in railroad tunnels. The German Army officers were furious about the Maquis and when a saboteur was caught, the whole village paid for it.

A seventeen-year-old, by the name of Louis, was milking his cows and working diligently on his farm. He was just a kid with a well built body and a kind smile. He was transporting hay to another village, sitting on his carriage and holding on the reins with his innocent look. He was whistling a tune that he had made up and was looking ahead at the road for German patrols. He was instructed to hide dynamite and other explosives in his cart and deliver it to another farmhouse where the Maquis was preparing for a big explosion of a German munitions supply train.

The German military police stopped the cart and asked Louis to get off and show his identity card. Louis was expecting this to happen and he was cool and composed. The military police started to look for explosives and systematically dismantled the cart. They found the explosives and arrested Louis.

He was taken to the military headquarters and interrogated for two days going without sleep and water. They made him confess all his connections with the Maquis and were able to arrest five men and two women. With the help of the Gestapo, they found out that the same outfit bombed two supply trains and caused the death of three soldiers and wounded twenty.

The military summoned every man in the village to line up in front of the church while all women and children were put inside the church. Every Maquis in the other farmhouse were also lined up. They were ordered to dig a twenty-five by twenty-five foot hole that was four feet deep. It was a long process to dig all the soil out of the ground, but they did it. At night fall every man and woman of the Maquis along with every man from the village was shot. Those women who were spared were told to bury the dead.

The fear and anxiety spread like wildfire and most people stayed in their homes for many days. But the spirit to be free again did not die and Marceau sent various messages to the Resistance members to watch their intelligence activities. The big difference between the Resistance and Maquis was function. By and large, the Resistance, or the Century as it was called in Normandy, was involved with intelligence, while the Maquis, was identified with sabotage and assassinations. However, agents of the Century did engage in sabotage, retributions, and assassinations at times, especially close to the invasion. Marceau desperately needed intelligence shortly before the invasion forces rushed the shore in Normandy.

"I am lost without contacts," said Marceau in a desperate voice.

"I know, but you'll be totally lost in jail when your contacts are rounded up, interrogated, tortured, and confess that all information is directed to you," said Bridget.

"You're right, my dear, but my work is at a standstill now...now when the Allies need me the most."

"The Allies are getting information from Shaw and Parker. You cannot risk your life. You have done more than enough. The Gestapo is just waiting for the chance to arrest you and charge you with espionage. Kohler, your arch enemy, will be jubilant to prove that all the leaks were caused by you and your friends."

"I am sorry my darling, I am losing my patience and logic at times. My emotions and intelligence are out of synch. Inside in me I'm crying, vive la France, liberte!"

"Marceau, you must get a hold of yourself and wait for the opportunity. Your day is coming sooner than you think. Your hard work will present itself and you'll be proud of your accomplishments!"

"Merci, merci, you are just wonderful. You are giving me so much encouragement!

God bless you!"

"You must get in touch, my darling Bridget, with Dr. Louis Charot."

"What's the matter? Aren't you feeling well?"

"It is not about my condition. He is one of my conduits with the agents."

"What is so important that Shaw and Parker cannot deliver it?"

"There is no time. They are too busy. I received coded information of French, British, and American landings tonight. Special Forces are landing in strategic areas. They will carry out the necessary demolitions prior to invasion."

"I will personally see the doctor. I don't trust the phone. It is possible that the Gestapo is tapping the neighbor's line and the conversation will be heard."

Bridget drove to the doctor's office to talk to him. He promised to come after office hours, which he did.

"What is the matter, Marceau? I understand you went to the clinic."

"I went to the clinic to see a specialist because my condition was serious and I wanted to combine the lab work, x-rays, and a medical consultation."

"I understand. You did the right thing to save time. How can I help you now?"

"You must contact the best people to help a special team that will land tonight to direct other jumpers later to find the strategic locations."

"I'll do my best, but you realize the Gestapo and Military Police are making life very difficult for our agents."

"What time frame are we talking about and what are the coordinates?"

"The jump is between 0100 and 0200. Weather is a factor. The agents will be informed about the coordinates by the usual transmission frequencies at midnight."

"I hope you'll feel better. If you need my help, please call and I'll come over. We have some new experimental medications for leukemia of your type, but you must be monitored daily. I am confident that your specialist will do the best for you. Au revoir, Marceau."

"I am glad, Marceau, the doctor seemed to be a very nice person," said Bridget.

"Bridget, my dear, he will contact some agents, but, security is very tight. I can only hope that the mission will succeed."

There was a small commotion in front of Marceau's place. The military escorted five people from the neighborhood restaurant to their truck and two Gestapo agents followed them in the car. Later, witnesses stated that they were just drunk and cursed the occupation forces.

"These are the last days of intimidation. They must show who is in charge," said Marceau.

The next business morning Marceau was asked to repair three pairs of shoes for one of his old pals. Marceau had not seen him in the shop for the past six months, but met him from time to time at the bar in their favorite restaurant, Chez Jolie. He was always there when Marceau needed him and they kept in touch through messages sent back and forth by Bridget.

"My friend, Comment allez-vous, ca va- How are you, how is life?" asked Marceau.

"I am perturbed about all the terrible events. Accusations, arrests, executions, it is getting worse every day. Take the latest story, for example. The Gestapo tapped the Central Telephone Exchange and heard a conversation that was considered relevant to the disappearance of the latest British airman. So they accused our friend Dumas the housepainter that he was hiding the airman. Dumas had been painting for the past three months in Paris. His wife Jeanette is seldom home as she is aiding her ailing mother. It took Dumas three days to convince the Gestapo that he was away and only through his boss, the German General, was he able to be freed. He went home for a few days to see his wife and have a happy reunion and he ends up in jail. I am telling you it is terrible."

Bridget had just returned from her friend's house, excited, and upset, and had to tell Marceau and his friend what she heard on the phone from another friend.

"The Gestapo arrested five Belgians in Paris and charged them with sabotage. They found explosives, grenades, and rifles in their car. The other news was that in Lyon the Gestapo executed eleven Maquis for derailing three ammunition trains and exploding two of them. The third news was devastating. In Rennes, the Gestapo hung three women naked upside down for two days because they stole maps from German officers. They survived, but suffered terribly from exposure."

"I get sick to my stomach hearing this, but hopefully it will not last too much longer. These sacrifices will bear fruit. Liberty, however, is worth all the suffering," said Marceau.

It was noted by the Allied Intelligence that the German

Military, Gestapo, French Milice -militia that sided with the Germans- and the Abwehr were working overtime to stop the leaks concerning the German defenses and sabotage activities. Severe punishments served as deterrents, but the German efforts did not impede the peoples will to liberate France from the Germans.

All over France the purges and tortures continued. Resistance leaders and well-known associates suffered terribly. Pierre Brossolette, and Jean Moulin were among them. Some committed suicide, others died in prison or on the way to concentration camps and in the infamous "no return" concentration camps. But Marceau's spirit was undefeated. He was still ebullient and enthusiastic. He found new recruits who found other agents and the information to Allied Intelligence continued despite the arrests and restrictions imposed on the intelligence gathering population.

Shaw and Parker had an extraordinary opportunity to inspect the batteries as the various construction engineering problems required immediate solutions.

As they were directing a particular cement patching operation, Shaw noticed somebody in wet overalls pretending to fix a tank barricade. Shaw whispered to the man a Scottish code word that he recognized immediately. The code word was a Scottish beer product. The agent looked around, and asked in perfect Scottish, "Can you help me?"

"Yes, I can help you, but you must wait there until my partner comes."

Shaw left to get Parker and they managed to grab some garments from the bunker that were found in one of the rooms and placed them in a small paper package which they smuggled out to the agent. Shaw and Parker surrounded the guy and he hurriedly changed his clothes. They left the area and Parker helped him to get in their car while Shaw went back to continue a repair in progress.

"What a heck are you doing here?" asked Parker.

"I was detached from my unit. We came ashore last night to check the ground for the invasion forces."

"I need your identification numbers to inform your commando unit," said Parker.

"Who the hell are you masquerading in this Todt uniform?"

"OSS. We are inspecting the units also, but in greater depth."

"Well, lucky you. How long have you been doing this?"

"Two years and plus, give or take a few days."

He gave his name as Oliver Browman, along with his code unit number and group number.

Parker drove to an isolated area, opened his trunk and using the transceiver made the call for proper identification. Everything checked out and Parker was delighted to have rescued a comrade.

"I cannot shelter you, but we'll find people who will until you get back to your unit."

"Thanks pal. We will need space, food, and good beer because more of us are coming tonight. and every day until the invasion forces come ashore. We have a lot of work ahead of us. We must destroy a list of tank barricades, mine fields, radar, radio towers, lines of telephone communication, and prepare for the real battle."

"How do you expect to accomplish this?"

"We'll do the same as you. In German uniforms, we'll disconnect their precious phone lines, short circuit the radar, direct the planes to dismantle the barricades and explode the mine fields. We are very good at these things. We have been well trained."

"I hope your German is as good as theirs."

"Don't worry. We have a team of German speaking comrades who will know how to talk."

"You'll need identification papers and security codes for each battery."

"We'll have papers. The codes will be difficult to obtain, but we plan to grab a few guys who will talk as we squeeze their balls and give us the daily codes."

"Good luck. I will hand you over to my partner, Brian Parker, and he'll help you to safety."

"Thanks, pal!"

The nights were no longer the same in Normandy. The relatively quiet evenings turned into tremors and rumblings of the earth from Pas de Calais to Cherbourg. Bombings were more frequent at the Pa de Calais area and more people parachuted into the Caen and St. Mere Eglise region.

The anti-aircraft and machine gunners were busy every night and the explosions of bombs and mines along the shores kept the people aware of the imminence of invasion and the awesome battles ahead.

The commandos were dropping from the sky and surfacing from the water by the dozens every night. Marceau, Shaw, and Parker were busy savings some lives, but most of them were on their own. They hid wherever they found shelter and French hospitality.

The infiltration, at some points, became critical and many of the commandos were killed on the spot.

There was no rescue in place and these soldiers were the forerunners of the invasion forces. Shaw and Parker were still supplying information to Marceau. Instead of sending data via transmitter to England, he was giving direct information to the soldier-commandos dressed in German uniforms posing as shoppers in the store. Bridget however had to check everyone's identification so that it could authenticated by Shaw and Parker. It was a new twist in the courier operation, but it worked. At times, however, it was hairy.

It was 0830 when four guys came in the store dressed in German infantry uniforms and asked Bridget to see Marceau. At the same time the German Military Police was on patrol and asked the guys for their ID's which they claimed they left in the battery.

"I think, I can solve their problem," said Marceau.

"You have some identification for these soldiers?"

"Yes. They were here last week and asked me to fix their shoes. They had no money to pay for the repair and I asked for their identification papers. Today they are here to pay me."

"I will let them go this time, but only because of you, Marceau. We trust your word," said the officer in charge as he was leaving.

"Thank you," said one of the infantry soldiers.

"Well, there will be no next time. You must have your papers with you at all times."

"Yesterday, I received information from two of our agents that you need to direct the planes this morning to bomb certain areas," said Marceau.

"Thank you. We shall do that," said one of the commandos.

"We are also going to cut all the wires and destroy the radar tower in addition to the night's bombing. The invasion forces might be coming through this area," said the foreman of the unit.

"You guys must be exhausted. Do you want to eat and rest somewhere?"

"That would be nice," responded one of the guys.

"Bridget will help you to get accommodations with one of our Resistance friends who runs a hotel," said Marceau.

"Very much obliged. We haven't had a decent meal in days," said the other soldier.

Bridget made a few calls and the commandos were picked up by a group of Maquis who worked on the fishing docks. They were squeezed in between the fishing nets and scallop boxes in a semi-open truck. All landed in a country home under the care of five Resistance women who made them undress and take baths. They all smelled from the fish truck and were dirty from being at sea for days. The women were sympathetic to their female desires, but destroying the German radar was more important than momentary sexual satisfaction. As soon as the men were ready to leave, two women took them to their explosive arsenal and equipped them with the explosives that they were using to blow up two radar installations. After that they waited as wounded bodies as the German military police threw a net around the area. It was a sheer miracle and the gauntlet of three Resistance women that they made it to freedom.

The three women dressed in German military nurse uniforms drove right into the middle of the twisted metal and bleeding bodies and picked up the guys one by one, throwing them in the ambulance, and sped away without a trace. Mission was accomplished.

The German Military, Gestapo and Milice were on the case within hours after the destruction of the radar. The investigation covered every aspect of the explosion. The Gestapo was furious. They searched every house within a fifty kilometer radius from apartments to farmhouses. The soldiers looked in every nook and cranny to find any clue that would lead them to find the perpetrators. All the agents were merciless and arrested hundreds of people. One school of thought, mostly Military and Gestapo, was that the guilty parties were commandos, the other focused on an internal, Maquis operation.

The commandos crossed into Switzerland and the nurses went to Spain. They traveled with lightning speed and with the help of the OSS, MI6, and native sympathizers they were all in safe houses by the second day.

The German roundup produced all kinds of information, but the truth was hammered out by betrayal and Gestapo methods of torture. Some women who housed the commandos remained in the farmhouse while others left for Paris. A neighbor reported to the Milice that several guys were in the house and the Gestapo began to investigate it. Two women were arrested and subjected to various forms of questioning.

"Did you know the background of the men you housed,?" asked Mr. Hauptman, a Gestapo officer, in a calm voice.

"I was told that these people were German soldiers and wanted to have companions."

"Did you have sex with any of the men?"

"I certainly had sex with two of them."

"Did they pay you money?"

"Yes, they were very generous."

"I have different information from your friend. According to her, they were smelly and dirty and they were told to take a bath and get going."

"She was fussy about smell, but I did not care."

"I want you to tell me the truth about it; I want to know every detail."

"I cannot tell you what I don't know."

"Yes, you can."

The officer knocked her down with the chair. Her two legs were resting on the chair and spread apart. Her hands and legs were tied by a rope. She was hardly able to move.

The officer pulled her panties down and told her to think about the truth while he was preparing to get some instruments to make her talk. When he returned he asked again.

"Now, who were those people?"

"I don't know. The only thing I remember is the name of the guy I had sex with."

"Well, I have a way to help you to remember."

"Please don't hurt me. I cannot take pain."

He put a small tube in her vagina which had an acidic-irritant itching solution that was partly derived from bugs and other chemicals to cause excruciating pain and unbearable itching. After the insertion, he left her there to suffer and scream for mercy.

After twenty minutes, she screamed so hard that the officer decided to let her talk.

"Well, do you have something to tell me?"

"Yes, please stop the pain."

"You tell me first. I will then stop the pain."

"They were commandos from England, Scotland, and America in German infantry uniforms. They did all the damage to the radar. Please, help me. I cannot bear the pain and itching. It is killing me."

The officer took his pistol and shot her in the head. Then shot her again and again.

The Gestapo began to look everywhere for the commandos, but it was too late. They ordered the execution of twenty-five men in the vicinity of the destroyed radar as a lesson for anybody who harbors commandos or destroys German defenses.

In the middle of this madness one of the German Generals, Rudolf von Rechtenwald, entered Marceau's place to order a pair of boots. He came in with a big hello and greeted Marceau with respect.

"Marceau, Marceau. It is so nice to meet you again! The last time I had the opportunity to talk to you was at your testimonial dinner in Caen. I came to order a pair of boots from you before this whole region goes up in flames."

"Well, it is nice to see you too. But what makes you think that we are going up in flames?"

"Well, well, come on, Marceau. We built this monstrosity defense structure for some reason. This was not built for kids to play with. We are fighting for something. I don't know exactly for what, but the world went mad and we'll be finding ourselves in the middle of total destruction. I think we wasted a lot of lives for stupid ideas. But being a German, and a high ranking officer, I should acknowledge what we are fighting for, but I do not, I am a rebel! I want to enjoy life in peace and harmony. I want to walk in good boots and enjoy nature around me! Please accommodate my wish."

"I would be more than happy to do it, but I hope you realize, that we are in the middle of a big war that is destroying my supply and I don't know how soon I will be able to get you all the necessary material."

"That is nonsense, my friend! I will get you what you need by a special courier."

"In that case, I would be more than happy to craft a pair of custom made boots for you."

"I will see to it that you'll be rewarded. What do you do for relaxation?"

"I love to fish."

"Anything special you like to fish for?"

"Mostly scallops."

"I realize you have had zero opportunity to leave the harbor, but I will give you a one time authorization to leave the port. You will, of course, be accompanied by our patrol for your safety and security."

"I am grateful for your offer and I hope to deliver your boots shortly after I receive the materials."

"Just one more thing: I also like scallops, and you must save some for a couple of dinners."

"I shall do that. I promise."

"Here is a list of materials that I must have."

"You will have these materials in a few days, even if I must procure them personally."

"Thank you General."

"You're welcome and have a nice day!"

Marceau was suspicious of the offer and wondered about the fishing trip. But, on second thought, he figured there had been no problems in the past with the artificial lure. He further pondered, that even a thorough search would not find the messages because the German patrol doesn't know the sorcery of the trade. The messages in the artificial lure are handled like a shell game. One drops the lure into the trap with lightning speed which is hard to follow for an untrained eye. So, Marceau decided to ask Shaw and Parker to provide all the necessary information possible for the last fishing trip before the invasion.

All leather goods and sewing materials were hand delivered two days after his requisition. Marceau asked the General to come in to make the impressions and take measurements. Marceau felt a sense of completion with his hard work in collecting and transferring information.

"You called us to meet with you. What's happening?" asked Shaw.

"I have an opportunity to make one more fishing trip, probably, the very last one before the invasion."

"How safe is your trip?" asked Parker.

"I have a special permit from an unknown General to make the trip and I anticipate one guard, as customary, to accompany me."

"I am suspicious, but that is my job," said Shaw.

"It crossed my mind, but I figured the odds are in my favor."

"Don't be so sure. A Gestapo agent, dressed as a guard, could ask you to return the basket as you dropped it into the sea, and reexamine the trap and lure, or better, impound the whole thing. They are as shrewd as they come. It would be a gold mine to find that you are one of the major suppliers of information about the Atlantic Wall," said Parker.

"It is a probability. I could always kill him and throw him overboard."

"I believe the guard will search you and the boat for hidden weapons this time," said Shaw.

"I take it that you recommend aborting the mission."

"The risk is too high. I think you are better off to cease operations at sea," said Shaw.

"I understand your concern. Times have changed. The Germans are desperate. We could also compromise the Fortitude strategy by giving information about the Atlantic Wall. Thank you. It is a no go on our part!"

"We will transmit the final findings by radio from various locations. We acquired a new cryptic language that is transmitted by super speed that requires no more than ten second transmissions at a time. By the time they fix the location of the signal, we are gone," said Shaw.

"What else is happening?" asked Shaw.

"The Gestapo continues to do terrible things. I was told that one of the women who helped the commandos to hide was tortured by placing chemicals into her genitals and then shot after she confessed to hiding the commandos."

"I will personally take care of him," said Parker. "I will teach the Gestapo what happens when somebody commits this kind of heinous crime. I will track him down wherever he goes as soon as the invasion begins," said Parker.

"I was informed this morning that the General who ordered the boots and sent for the materials left for Paris in an ambulance. It is my understanding that he required emergency surgery to stop the bleeding from a tumor. Now I have all the materials but I cannot make the impressions."

"I wouldn't worry about it. By the time he is ready to come back, Normandy will be liberated," said Parker.

"I certainly hope so."

Michael entered the store with a big smile on his face.

"What are you so happy about?" asked Parker.

"Everybody is packing. The word is the Allies are coming, get ready to run," said Michael.

"You know more than we do. Share it with us," said Shaw.

"Pas de Calais is still a high priority, but the intensity of the bombings, the commandos, and parachute landings suggest something else. The High Command is divided between diversion and major invasion. Of course, Hitler has the final word of releasing the elite panzers. But, I think, we have a mixture of fighters when it comes to background, age, strength, experience, and patriotism. At this point, I believe, the Allies know more about the Atlantic Wall and strength of the defenders than we do. Normandy will lose and the Allies will win."

"Interesting assessment and prediction, Michael," said Shaw.

"Well, hello Michael," greeted Bridget. "I haven't seen you lately."

"Darling, we are busy losing the war."

"I sincerely hope so," said Bridget.

"Are you here for business or pleasure?"

"Both. I can stay with you for awhile."

"Good. I missed being with you. We could grab a bite together."

"That is a splendid idea. Thank you for the invite."

"I hope you have something good to tell us Michael?" said Marceau.

"It is getting very close to confrontation," said Michael.

"It looks like it, at least from the intelligence point of view," said Marceau. "Gentlemen, you are free to comment," he added.

"Let the Germans ponder. Hitler will have a big surprise party!" said Parker.

As he said that, thunderous anti-aircraft fire opened up in all directions, which was followed by explosions and fire all over around the town. The planes came in waves of one hundred and dropped their bombs along the coast and beyond to the east.

Shaw yelled for everybody to lay low and cover their heads with their hands.

"We better protect our heads from flying debris. It is getting quite rough around us," said Shaw.

"I told you guys, we are getting a little taste of it," commented Michael.

"You are not kidding. It is getting serious," said Bridget.

The bombs were falling closer and closer and the explosions were close to rupturing their eardrums. There were some encounters when it was impossible to hear anything for a few minutes because the blast was so strong. Things were dropping off the shelves to the floor and table. The counter top was full of everything that could conceivably fly. The whole place was in chaos. But it was a welcomed mess.

After the bombing, which lasted forty-five minutes, everybody helped to clean up and put the pieces back where they belonged.

"Is everybody all right?" asked Michael.

Since nobody complained, there were no casualties. Marceau grabbed a bottle of fine wine from the cellar and poured a bit for everyone. With glass in hand, Marceau made a toast and thanked God for everybody's survival.

After the brief celebration, Marceau called a meeting. It was an impromptu get together and Marceau felt that now was the time for closure of their activities.

"Bridget, please put the closed sign in the window," said Marceau.

"We have almost completed our work as far as intelligence gathering and courier service are concerned. You did an outstanding job and a 'thank you' is hardly a grateful expression of gratitude. You not only risked your lives but saved other lives which were above and beyond your duty. I don't know how long I'll be around. My cancer is quite pervasive. I hope you'll keep in touch with each other and carry the torch well beyond the liberation of France," said Marceau.

"Your contribution to OSS, MI6, and the Resistance has been invaluable. There are not enough words to adequately express our deep appreciation. You have also been a savior of thousands of lives of residents, of soldiers, commandos, members of the Resistance, Maquis and all those who fought the battle inside France. You have been a humanitarian, a coach of the mind and soul, and the backbone of human spirit. We'll be with you, support you, and look after you in the days ahead and you'll always be with us as a member of our family," said Shaw.

"I don't know how to begin, because that speech is hard to follow. I am at a loss for words because my feelings are choking my thoughts. I don't believe that we can adequately thank you for the sacrifices you made in behalf of our mission, OSS, MI6 and the French Resistance."

"I cannot imagine under what circumstances we could have amassed and transmitted all the invaluable data without your contribution. The breaking of the German code was a milestone, but our intelligence work within the Atlantic Wall came close to a benchmark. Marceau, you were the foundation of our success because without your recruits and courier service we would not have been able to penetrate the Wall. You risked your life along with Bridget's all the time. Therefore there are no words to describe your contribution to the cause."

"Our hearts ache because of your illness. It is another burden that you will have to bear. We pray for your strength and determination. God Bless," said Parker.

Parker, Michael, and Bridget held each other's hands and expressed the same in their silence standing motionless. Shaw joined them with Marceau who then said a short prayer.

They sat in a circle for a few seconds and Marceau broke the silence by asking Bridget to bring up from the cellar a bottle of champagne and open the box of caviar from Russia. Bridget having complied with Marceau's request also served cheese, salami, and canned goose liver, bread and butter.

They were hungry and thirsty. The mood became sanguine and Shaw began to sing an old Scottish song about a happy family reunion. This was followed by another song which was sang by Parker, then another by Bridget, and Michael and Marceau sang a French song together.

There was a soft knock on the entrance door. Bridget opened the door and saw a good looking young lady with a smile.

"I'm Susan. I am looking for Mr. Parker."

Parker seeing Susan, rushed to her, embraced her, and asked her to join the party.

"What's going on?" asked Susan.

"We're celebrating our accomplishment and toasting Marceau for his guidance and tireless effort to help liberate France," said Shaw.

"Where have you been?" asked Parker.

"Did you miss me?"

"I missed you, darling."

"I was, believe it or not, on a mission."

"How did you make it?" asked Michael.

"I have a Swiss passport. It was a piece of cake."

"What's new?" asked Parker.

"We are very close to the invasion."

"How close?" asked Shaw.

"It is a military secret. I cannot give you the exact date and hour because it is up to the meteorological forecast, and the decision of Eisenhower's and his men. But we are days away."

"Go on," said Shaw.

"The OSS and MI6 are no longer sleeper cells, but the moment we are given the cryptic signals via the BBC, we are to become a part of the US and British Army."

"In what way?" asked Shaw.

"We are helping the soldiers with the invasion, like tour guides."

"How do we coordinate this?" asked Shaw.

"They will ask for our identification and after authentication we'll be assigned."

"Do we become part of the military intelligence unit?" asked Parker.

"Yes, but in a leadership role."

"Tough assignment," said Parker.

"You bet. We'll be dancing to a different tune."

"I'm so happy to see you, sweetheart!" said Parker as he put his arm around her.

"You made me come back. I could have been reassigned but my heart belongs to you Brian. You are consuming my soul and my body. I need you."

"You have to wait until the party is over. We have to talk and make plans. This group is like a family," said Parker.

"At least you can kiss me, hold me, and caress me as a down payment," enticed Susan.

Parker kissed her soft hair strand by strand then both lips met and they started to passionately kiss each other in front of the others.

"I love to see you guys loving each other. That's the only way to live," said Marceau.

"I wish I could join you," said Shaw.

"So what's the problem?" asked Parker.

"I think I can reveal it now. My wife and kids are in England."

"I hope you get liberty," said Parker.

"Just give me a three day pass," added Shaw.

"You'll get it. I'll ask for it in your behalf."

"Nice try, but you're US we are UK," said Shaw.

"I'll do my best to charm them," said Susan.

Michael embraced Bridget, hugged and kissed her, and then he said, "These are precious moments in our lives."

Marceau took over and asked for another toast.

"This time the toast is for the safe return of Susan," said Marceau.

They all lifted their glasses. Parker was looking for an extra glass for Susan. After finding one and filling it with champagne, he said, "Cheers to everyone, but especially to my only love and our lives together in the US."

"Hurrah! Congratulations!" enthused Marceau.

Susan turned to Parker. "Are you serious?"

"We'll make it official later. This announcement was just for our family here. I don't know anything about fraternizing laws, but we are going to serve under Army regulations for awhile."

"What are you talking about? I am an affiliate."

"I have completely forgotten your background. You are so much a part of us, but until the war is over you are one of us and we cannot fraternize. We have to be careful until we are noncommissioned by the army," said Parker.

"May I interrupt?" said Marceau.

"By all means," invited Shaw.

"Bridget, please take notes. We need some articulation of our accomplishments for the Allied Intelligence and Resistance."

"You need them now? Can each of us send in a report?" asked Parker.

"You certainly can, but how about sharing the views. Since time is growing short before the invasion and this may be our last opportunity to be together. Why not now?" said Marceau.

"You want this to be informal?" asked Shaw.

"Yes, very informal. I am tired of long tedious reports," replied Marceau.

"I think we did a damn good job given the resources, manpower, and the strength of the enemy," said Parker.

"We accomplished more with human intelligence than with technology. Of course, we had the advantage of language skills, cultural backgrounds, an excellent education and training, and some natural givens, such as problem solving," said Shaw.

"How about saving thousands of lives by preparing the various branches of armed forces for the battle," said Marceau.

"You guys risked your lives many times by helping reconnaissance operatives, commandos, and allied agents," said Bridget.

"You were successful in penetrating the German defenses, totally exposing the Atlantic

Wall, sites of the V1 and V2, and amplifying the deception of 'Overlord' with 'Fortitude,' and helping many of the forced labor camps to survive the German atrocities," said Michael.

"You have saved the souls of our Resistance by exposing the enemy, those who betrayed us, and tried to destroy our operation," said Susan.

"May I interrupt the flow of assessment because I just have received a coded message through my transceiver? From now on, you must tune in to the BBC night service and listen to the messages. Some of them will be in verses. Some messages are for us and others for the Resistance including the Maquis. For meanings, please consult your code book," said Susan.

"We are really at the threshold of invasion. Good. We have prepared the Armed Forces and I am terribly proud of the intelligence community. Bletchley Park code breakers have been doing a splendid job with the aid of the Enigma Machine. This has been the cipher backbone of the German Army planning, but there is another one. 'Fortitude', is a brilliant deception to divert the German forces, by holding the fifteenth Army in place at Pas-des Calais. I am proud that our intelligence community played an important role in the process of disseminating this deception," said Shaw.

Susan got closer to Parker and embraced him from behind. Michael held Bridget's hand and she put her head on his shoulder. Marceau poured some wine for himself and Shaw looked out the distant window while holding his half empty glass of wine.

"May I refill your glass?" asked Marceau.

"Thank you. I am just fine. I drink slowly while my thoughts wonder away. Right now I'm with my family in England. I am getting homesick," said Shaw.

"I can understand that. It has been a long time since you saw your family," remarked Marceau.

The shouting of the German soldiers and gun fire interrupted the conversation. A bunch of soldiers commandeered people from their homes into the street. They were lined up in the middle of the street and were questioned one by one.

When everything quieted down there were no arrests but the people were petrified by the roughness of the soldiers. The Gestapo was looking for commandos and spies. Evidently they were out of luck.

Marceau commented, "I think for the next few days these kinds of round-ups will be a daily phenomenon. Living in a port city that is strategically located, while having a four-gun battery, big fortifications, and a number of ammunition depots, we are excellent targets to blow up before the invasion."

"I hope this miserable waiting is going to be over soon

so Brian and I can go back to the States and resume normal living," said Susan.

"You'll be needed here until the European theatre is closing the curtain," said Shaw.

"Well, maybe we'll get a few days of liberty. I really need a rest," replied Susan.

"I'll buy a hammock for you," offered Parker.

"You're so funny! You're really generous! But, you know what, buy me a hammock with a two weeks vacation in Nassau and serve me rum and coke. Plus hold my hand and give me a thousand kisses every day and I'm game. So, what do you say?" asked Susan.

"Terrific idea, but first we have to survive the invasion, then we must submit our liberty requests, then wait patiently until somebody in the military will read them," said Parker.

"You're such a pessimist," said Susan.

"No, sweetheart, I'm a realist. We'll be needed right here after the invasion," said Parker.

"I'm sure you will get some days off and you'll be having fun on the French Riviera," said Marceau.

"Good Man! We are going to Cannes, the French Riviera," said Susan.

"I'm happy that you found your niche. I am with you. We are going to the Riviera," said Parker.

"My friends, may I have your attention for some thoughts I want to share with you? History writers may minimize our contributions to the liberation of Europe and the vital importance of the functions of intelligence. But don't let this influence and affect us. Only time will tell what intelligence contributed to the total success of the military strategy, how many lives we saved, and in the end what role intelligence played in the total victory. Everybody likes to promote his or her own turf, but the theory and practicum of intelligence transcends all military science, logistics, and strategies. Intelligence is the nerve center of all military operations and our work by its very nature is rather invisible. So, recognition often comes last and indirectly. The reward is insidious but climactic," said Marceau.

"Well spoken, Marceau. We love you for your wisdom and foresight. God Bless," said Shaw.

"It's getting late. How about we adjourn our meeting?" said Susan.

"I second it," added Michael.

When Shaw, Parker, and Susan left to go to their vehicles two officers approached them and in perfect German asked them for a little discussion inside one of their apartments.

"What's it all about?" asked Shaw.

"May we talk about it in your place?" said one of the officers.

They all entered Shaw's place and without sitting down, one of the officers introduced his partner as Mr. John Riley from OSS and himself as Walter O'Keefe from MI6.

"Do you have identifications?" asked Shaw.

"Well, of course," said Walter. He presented his identification numbers and opened up his small briefcase that contained an MI6 transceiver.

"You're welcome to place a call," said Walter.

"I certainly will," said Shaw.

Shaw called England from the car and at different locations. Everything checked out.

"I received some numbers from AI and I need to translate them into mathematical formulas. Please give answers to the two separate numbers," requested Shaw. Walter and John responded well to all mathematically coded identifications.

"Well, you seem to be all right. What is this all about?" asked Shaw.

"I have to say it, I gave my word. It's really top secret if we can pull it off," said Walter.

"We are all ears," said Parker.

"We are expecting the invasion within days and must protect the Allied forces before they are decimated in the water, on the shore, or on the cliffs. It would be unrealistic to assume that we can pull it off without casualties, but we can minimize it and this is why we are here."

"We plan to relieve the two commandants of St. Marcout and Azeville Batteries for a week. We'll tell them that they must have some rest before the big battle. If they take the bait we'll have a dozen paratroopers in German uniforms take the key gun posts and turn them against the German infantry," said John.

"Where do we come in?" asked Parker.

"You know the layout for St. Marcout and Azeville," replied Walter.

"It is a brilliant idea…if it works. You need great logistics. Radio support, preferably Klaxton, or J/E type for planes. You should have plane to ground radios and vice versa. You must be prepared to have German High Command stationery papers, exact copies of signatures, and authentications. The Germans are not stupid. They are fanatical about details, and compulsively check everything. The parachute drops may be a suicide mission. The guys may not touch the ground alive. If they catch one alive, the Gestapo or military police will torture him until he confesses the mission, which could jeopardize the invasion," said Shaw.

"We calculated the potential risks. The mission was favored and accepted," said John.

"How did you manage to come here and where did you get the car?" asked Parker.

"We have Swiss passports and we came from Spain and Switzerland. In Paris I stole the vehicle and that's all," said Walter.

"How about the documents?" asked Susan.

"We have them and they are perfect," said John.

"How are your German and French?" asked Parker.

"We speak fluent German and French," said John.

"When do you want to start?" asked Parker.

"Tomorrow at 0700," said Walter.

"Do you have all the necessary equipment and is it functional?" asked Shaw.

"We are ready and all devices are functional," replied Walter.

"What is your fail-safe plan?" asked Susan.

"Good question. Should anything go wrong during the execution of our plan, we're doomed in the batteries without support. That is the chance we must take," said John. "But, we are so close to the invasion that there is always a chance to escape to the Allies," added John.

"By the way, where are you staying?" asked Parker.

"In a safe house on a farm," replied Walter.

"Just be careful and polite when you get to a check point," said Shaw.

"Very well. We'll see you tomorrow," said John.

During the morning meeting, Riley and O'Keefe listened carefully to Shaw and Parker about the layouts of the bunkers, casemates, pillboxes, and mines. They reviewed some of the details of the takeover and possible escape routes in case the subterfuge failed.

Riley and O'Keefe met the Commandants, presented their credentials, and convinced them that they were selected by the German High Command to relieve them for one week. The agreement was that they will return on the third of June at 0600 for a six hour introduction. At noon, the Commandants will be relieved and then go on vacation.

Riley and O'Keefe left with the firm belief that the bait had been taken and they would have to wait forty-eight hours to execute their plans, which involved the parachute drop and strategic takeover.

They met with Shaw and Parker in the afternoon and told them about the successful meeting with the Commandants. There was a feeling of satisfaction but some valid concerns.

"Did the Commandants take notes of the papers?" asked Shaw.

"Yes. They wrote down all relevant information and the name and rank of the person who authorized the documents," said Riley.

"Do you think that they will authenticate the documents by a phone call?" asked O'Keefe.

"It would be risky to find out," said Shaw.

"What is your fail-safe recommendation?" asked Riley.

"Watch for surprises. Look for suspicious vehicles. Call the Commandants twenty-four hours in advance and ask if they have any changes in the agreed timetable and if they are ready to go on vacation. Listen to their tone of voice. Should you suspect any problem, please share it with us. But be careful, very careful returning to an unsafe battery under enemy control!" said Shaw.

"Thank you for your suggestions. We'll be extremely careful. This is a very complex operation and if we fail there can be multiple consequences," said Riley.

"What you just said is very true. The Gestapo will be merciless. They would torture you until your last breath, before they kill you. This happened to one of the Resistance operators and she suffered horribly. Once the Gestapo agent found out what he wanted to know she was killed by two bullets in her head. I'm waiting to take care of him during the invasion," said Parker.

"I trust you guys; you'll be smart enough to make a wise decision. Bye," said Shaw.

As the two men were driving off, Susan arrived.

"I need you, darling. I want you. I crave you," said Susan.

"I feel the same for you, but we had some distractions and it just happens that we are facing the biggest battle in history," replied Parker.

"I know my dear. I just wanted to steal some time for us."

"How about we stay home tonight and enjoy each other?"

"We'll buy food and make dinner for the three of us."

"Brian, you're saying what I'm thinking. Give me your lips."

"Let's go. Matthew, are you coming with us to shop for food?" asked Susan.

"Now how can I refuse your company?"

They went shopping for all kinds of food and came back home with two bags. They bought a few canned delicacies, French bread, sardines, snails, mussels, veal, beans, potatoes, and lots of fruit. Susan cooked the veal in her own special gravy. She made pommes frittes and fried the potatoes twice to make it crunchy the way Brian liked it. She then made creamed spinach. Mussels were for appetizers and crepe suzette in brandy topped with apple slices for dessert. The taste of every item was out of this world.

"If and when I marry you, this dinner will never be forgotten and I will insist on having it for our honeymoon dinner. Who needs sex after this meal? You have satisfied all the pleasure centers in the brain. You're awesome, Susan!" said Parker.

"I must admit this dinner was more than delicious, you must have put your heart into it," said Shaw.

Susan embraced Shaw and kissed him on his face. "You are very nice and kind," said Susan.

After dinner everybody hit the sack. She sat at the edge of the bed and had a good look at Parker.

"What's the matter?" asked Parker.

"I can't think of anything really special. I just love to look at you. You're the love of my life."

"Why don't you get undressed?" suggested Parker.

"I'm waiting for you to do it."

"Where do you want me to start?"

"You may begin by slowly removing my shoes and stockings. Then, you may caress my toes with one finger. Gently unbutton my blouse and kiss my breasts and mouth. Then proceed very slowly, by removing the rest of my garments, but leave my panties. I'll do the same for you and we'll meet in bed. We may gently touch each other. Whatever happens later depends on our creativity and staying power. Agreed?"

"Agreed, my love"

Bridget and Michael have been terribly busy with their lives. She has been helping Marceau with the shop and home chores while Michael was told to take care of part of the military preparedness of the Atlantic Wall. This was an awesome order but Michael's qualifications earned him this responsibility.

Specifically, he was responsible for all ordnances requested by the battery commandants.

They wanted to spend an evening together before the big battle to talk about the inevitable separation from each other and then their reunion. This was a requisite topic. They decided to meet the next evening, have dinner, and spend the night together.

The evening dinner was in Quistreham. They dined in a small restaurant.

Bridget and Michael selected fish cooked in butter with boiled potatoes and baked tomatoes. They had a bottle of aged French wine and mixed fruits on biscuits for dessert.

"I am worried, terribly worried about your safety, darling," said Bridget.

"I am not fighting on the front line, nor sitting in a plushy office or bunker. But I will try to survive and become a British or American prisoner."

"But you could be ordered to fight if it is necessary."

"Anything can happen, but there is no safe haven for anybody. A bomb or a shell could destroy your house and both of you could perish."

"I know that hard times are ahead of us and the invasion is going to be brutal, but I am just petrified at the thought of losing you. You are in a German uniform and the Allies will aim their guns at you."

"Darling, I can't predict the circumstances, but I hope I'll be captured and not shot."

"But some are merciless killers, vicious German haters who will not take prisoners but collect dead bodies."

"Then I will be out of luck."

"I will search for you and ask the military about your whereabouts."

"Good luck. You have no idea what the first forty-eight hours of beachhead will be if there will be a beachhead. The

German Army is going to put up a horrendous fight and defend the Atlantic Wall till the last man," said Michael.

"And so will the Allied forces. The psychological edge is on the Allied side. They want to throw out the occupiers and liberate France and Europe. They will be just if not more brutal, and that is why I am so concerned."

"I have a proposition. Whoever has the chance to look for the other one will take the initiative. It may take a few days or weeks to get some information. You may inquire at the hospital or with the military police. I'll do the same if your house is destroyed and I can not find you."

"I think this is a good idea."

"Are you ready to go?"

"Where are we going?"

"What's your preference?"

"You can stay in my house. I don't want to leave Marceau in his condition."

"I am completely with you. I just didn't want to intrude."

"You're silly. He knows we are lovers."

Michael drove to her home. Marceau had fallen asleep while reading. Bridget helped him to his bed, served him a glass of warm milk and gave him his medication.

Bridget offered some wine but Michael felt they better stay sober and make love. Bridget used the bathroom while Michael made tea for both of them.

"I should turn on the radio for BBC messages," said Bridget.

"It is getting late darling."

"We may be having the invasion by morning."

"You're an optimist. Our strategist does not think that the weather is on the Allies' side. It's pretty stormy over the Channel and I was not ordered on stand by."

"Thank God, you are with me tonight and in my heart always."

She gave him a warm kiss, took his hand, and led him to her bed. They snuggled passionately and continued just kissing and hugging each other. Bridget felt his burning body and heightened eroticism would not last for long, so she asked him, "Do you wish to rest a little bit, hold a little bit and then slowly begin to pleasure?"

"You want to lead?"

"I can try. Come into me but don't move. I want to feel you. I want to sense your rhythmic pulsation. I'll touch you tenderly into ecstasy, creating a never experienced sensation. I want to pleasure you."

"Darling, my love, you are so exceptional tonight. You are unforgettable."

Having rested for a few minutes both united their bodies and had an unbelievable sensual experience. Totally exhausted, both fell asleep in each other's arms.

Riley, as agreed, called the Commandant of the St. Marcout battery and after the exchange of pleasantries, he felt an electrifying shock throughout his body. John told that the General who signed the liberty document would be visiting the battery in the afternoon. Therefore he was unable to be relieved until the evening. Riley sensed trouble ahead and politely withdrew his offering with an unforeseen death in the family which required him to go home to Germany.

Riley immediately called Shaw and told him what happened. The plan had to be changed rapidly because a lot of soldiers were readied for the expedition. The four of them decided to meet at Marceau's place in two hours.

Marceau was waiting for them because Parker had contacted Bridget by phone. He was briefly informed of what was happening. Marceau was quite concerned about the outcome of this military adventure and suggested immediate damage control.

Riley summarized what happened and Marceau responded fast and vigorously.

"You must leave on the double for Switzerland. You have less than twenty-four hours before the Gestapo is going to seal every border and look for you in every city. You must shed your German uniform and leave your car anywhere. Just go. Of course, I'm taking the most pessimistic view. It's possible that the General does not remember what documents he signed, but you cannot take the chance."

"I'm sorry about what happened, but I'm glad I listened to your advice. I think by calling ahead we saved our hides. We must call off the parachute mission and another suicide mission must proceed before the invasion begins. We'll make the call first before we leave. Thank you for all your help," said Riley.

It was early June. The morning air at Post-En-Bessin was warm and humid. There was a feeling of apprehension among the early shoppers. The coming invasion was in the air. The frequency of air bombing and the intensity of explosions suggested softening of the German ground defenses. There was every indication that the battle for the shore would come very soon and the liberation of Europe was on the way.

Susan came to see Marceau in the early afternoon with a bag of shoes to be repaired. It was a reasonable subterfuge to deliver a message.

"Well, hello Susan. Comment ca va- How is life?"

"My dear Marceau, ca va bien- life is fine."

"I came to see you about an important message."

"Go on my dear."

"I talked with someone from MI6 and he said that your construction of the boot for the general turned out well. Whatever that means?"

"Well, thank you. It certainly makes me feel good. It was a special custom made boot. I worked on it some time ago, but honestly, I had so many things going on, including my health, that I totally forgot the completion date and did not make any inquiries about it.

"Have you seen Parker?"

"Not lately."

"Well, well, how are you, Susan?" asked Bridget.

"I am fine, as a matter of fact, couldn't be better."

"Are you busy, Bridget?"

"What do you have in mind?"

"Just a little chat. I must leave in thirty minutes."

"You girls go and have a talk. I'll get busy with the shoes," said Marceau.

Susan and Bridget entered the living room. Bridget made some coffee and served some cookies with it. Marceau took out the old shoes that Susan brought in for repair and started to work on them. Out of nowhere Michael came in and wanted to talk with Marceau.

"Forgive me, my love. Bridget, I have a little time between two inspections and thought to have a visit with Marceau."

"That is awful nice of you. I'm having a little chat with Susan."

"So what is happening?" asked Marceau.

"I am trying to find out what the German pharmaceuticals have, even if it is experimental. I really want to help you and get you the medication."

"This is very nice of you, Michael."

"Marceau, I am petrified of the Allied invasion. They really hate us."

"Michael, I am sorry but you really don't know what kind of pathological animals are running your government. They asked innocent children, women, and men, of all ages to remove all their belongings, undress, and go to the so called shower to inhale Cyclone B gas."

"I know about the horrible things that have been taking place, but not every German is a pathological animal."

"Michael, we are talking about the government officials who are deciding what to do with the undesirable people. Besides, the German people voted for Hitler and enjoyed the confiscated wealth."

"I agree. The German government and people must pay for all the atrocities and stolen goods. The problem is that those individuals who did not side with Hitler or denounce his policies must also bear the consequences."

"Whenever a dictator sets unethical and inhuman policies on behalf of his or her nation there is little that the people can legally do. But in democracy the people can legally impeach the chief executive."

"We were brainwashed by advocates of National Socialism. We were presented a different picture than what has transpired since Hitler came to power. Evil took over. I am thankful that Bridget helped me to see the light at the end of the tunnel."

"Michael, you are a good person. You are a victim of the brainwashing and false promises. But, thank God you came to your senses. You understand the value of freedom and democracy. There is much to be desired to have a perfect democracy. People must learn to be tolerant and respectful of others."

"Do you have any hope for the human race? Do you think we'll survive or become extinct like the dinosaurs?"

"We are developing the most devastating explosives and bombs to annihilate a large number of people in a long term. Future explosives may contain radioactive materials that will disfigure and eventually kill you. We are talking about an atomic bomb. The extremists including the dictators may have only one thing in mind and that is destroying everybody who does not agree with their philosophies. If sanity prevails humanity will survive, if not we are doomed."

"So how could we protect the sane from the insane?"

"You must acquire a special communication technique, which is an art, science and profession. It is used by politicians, psychotherapists, counselors, policemen, and detectives. When you deal with fanatics and suicidal maniacs you opt for self-defense first and foremost before you start a dialogue. Of course, in the worst scenario, you eliminate your opponent. This applies for individuals, groups, and nations."

"Do you think Hitler would have listened to anybody?" asked Michael.

"The answer is probably not. But he looked around and found that France, Russia, UK and the USA were militarily complacent and could easily be defeated with the help of Italy and Japan."

"Should the Allies win how would transition come about into democracy?"

"It would take a number of years to change from Nazism to Democracy, but education and experience will help to improve the political attitudes of the people. If you were born into Nazism and Fascism, you don't know any better. Time will prove, however, that it is much better to live in freedom and democracy than in a dictatorship."

"The future looks very bleak to me. Do you think we are ever going to have peace among nations?"

"That is a very good question. I think the nature of homo sapiens does not seem to have changed since the dawn of civilization. There is something restless in us as humans that make us want to engulf other people and then impose our beliefs on them. It is unfortunate that nations believe that they are better than other nations and the less powerful must conform."

"Marceau, thanks for your wisdom and time. A Chinese philosopher, Lin Yutang, quoted in one of his books a comment from an old Chinese scholar, 'Talking with you for one night is better than studying books for ten years.' "

"This is very nice of you to say. I am really impressed by you applying this quote in reference to my comments. May I continue our conversation by asking some questions?"

"Marceau, please ask me, by all means."

"What are your long term plans with Bridget after France is liberated?"

"Providing I become a POW and regain my freedom, I would like to marry Bridget."

"Did you talk about this with her?"

"Yes, we did talk about our future. Bridget accepted my offer to be my future wife."

"It would be nice if we could have a private engagement party before I pass away."

"Because of the uncertainties, I was cautious to have a celebration."

"I think we could risk this event. Of course, we must do it in utmost secrecy. I suggest we should only invite Shaw and Parker."

"I hope she forgives me if I postpone buying the engagement ring. It would jeopardize our secrecy."

"Naturallment-naturally, we understand."

"What are your vocational plans?"

"I would like to continue in my field as a civil engineer. I want to build big office buildings and apartment houses."

"Where would you like to reside?"

"I will not return to work or live in Germany and Bridget would never settle there. We talked about it. We would like to stay in France."

"I believe the next step would be to invite Shaw and Parker for the celebration."

"I can ask Bridget to make the call."

"Thank you, Michael."

"You're welcome and thank you also, Marceau."

Susan and Bridget joined Marceau and Michael. They exchanged a few pleasantries, but Susan had to leave for an assignment. Michael's time was up also and after Susan parted, Michael asked Bridget to call Shaw and Parker to celebrate their engagement.

"I am speechless, Michael. What prompted you to celebrate so soon?"

Michael whispered in to Bridget's ear, "Marceau."

"I am with you and absolutely delighted."

Michael had to leave and Bridget saw him to the door. They hugged and kissed each other. Bridget ran across to her friend's to make the call. The engagement party was set for the next day. Bridget spent her next morning shopping for food and drinks. She was happy and took great effort to hide the news in front of others. She tried to have a normal everyday face that the customers and friends knew. But her glittering eyes revealed something that seemed to be unusual for Bridget.

She was mum and didn't answer questions and played the role of a patient with imaginary eye problems.

In the meantime, Marceau was cleaning his gold plated, distinctive china plates and silverware. He was singing like a young kid who was about to celebrate his birthday party.

The mood was very jovial in Marceau's place. The customers were totally perplexed about the way he behaved. Marceau's answer was simply, "I feel good. God is good to me."

The table was set with a maroon table cloth with white lace and two candelabras in the middle. On the plates he put upward curved maroon linen napkins. He prepared two sets of crystal glasses, one for wine and the other for water. The candles were long and white. Everything looked very festive.

When Bridget returned from shopping, she was totally surprised of all the preparations for the evening.

"My dear, when did you have the time to do all this?"

"I did it between customers and repairs. When you are happy, nothing is difficult. God gave me extra energy for this special occasion."

"This is awfully nice. You must have stored everything very carefully from your marriage."

"Yes I did, my darling. And I am so glad that I preserved them for you!"

"Marceau, you are awesome! My parents would cry to see what's happening!"

"I better start cooking for the evening, so if you excuse me I'll stay in the kitchen."

"And I will put out the sign, 'Closed.' "

The hours passed and the clock chimed seven-thirty. Michael, Shaw, and Parker arrived.

After a few minutes of pleasantries, they all sat at the table. There was no special seating arrangement, but everybody respectfully offered Marceau to sit at the head of the table. Vintage wine was poured into every glass. Absolute silence followed the small chatting. All faces turned toward Marceau, waiting for an announcement to begin.

"I am not a preacher, an orator, or a public speaker, just an ordinary cobbler and a family man. I am going to be brief and to the point. I called you together to celebrate Bridget and Michael's engagement. It is a small party because we didn't want any publicity. I do not need to explain the secrecy. I offer a toast for the future health, happiness and togetherness to Bridget and Michael. Congratulations and God Bless!"

They all lifted their glasses and chanted, " 'Long live the pair,' Congratulations!"

It was an emotionally moving moment in their lives. Marceau, Shaw and Parker got up, embraced and kissed the pair on their cheeks.

Bridget began to serve dinner. It was a simple menu. On a big plate she brought in stuffed champignon for a starter. This was followed by boiled soft shell crabs, gravy, boiled potatoes, and mixed salad. For dessert she made apple cobbler with cognac poured over it.

"Michael, your fiancé is not only a great friend, Resistance operator and business lady, but a terrific cook," said Shaw.

"I second that, plus she is one of the most devoted daughters I have ever met!"

"I agree wholeheartedly," said Marceau.

Marceau excused himself for a minute and went to his cellar to pick a hundred year old champagne. Parker opened up the bottle and let the cork fly to the other end of the room. There was another toast by Shaw and Parker.

Marceau turned on the record player and played some music from his old collection of records. The first dance belonged to Bridget and Michael. After that everybody danced with Bridget. The celebration lasted until midnight.

Michael stayed overnight. Marceau spent a few minutes with Bridget and Michael. To their surprise he presented in Michael's name a diamond ring which used to belong to his late wife.

"Under the circumstances, Michael cannot buy you a ring. It is my honor to give you this ring and wear it in health and happiness," said Marceau.

Bridget, in tears, hugged Marceau and said, "There is no other man except Michael who means so much to me, and I love so much. Thank you, thank you, my dear. With your permission, I will wear this ring on my necklace until the liberation of France."

"Thank you from the bottom of my heart. You could not have given a better gift, especially in my behalf! God Bless you, Marceau!"

Then Michael embraced Marceau with tears in his eyes and said, "Marceau you are a great man!"

It was well past midnight when all three retired to their bedrooms.

CHAPTER ELEVEN

Although the subterfuge to take the batteries prior to the invasion had to be abandoned to save the lives of the agents, the Allied paratroopers successfully penetrated German defenses and carried out the most heroic suicide missions prior to the invading forces.

Marceau was glued to the radio in his home's hidden room and noted every message that was meant for Shaw, Parker, Susan and the Resistance. It was the fourth of June. The BBC World News gave the usual news broadcasts but after the news and commentaries the messages were longer and more compelling.

Bridget left Marceau only twice to receive two short phone calls and Shaw, Parker and Susan stayed an hour after the midnight news and messages. They were practically glued to the Allied radio broadcast.

"I seriously believe that we'll be told to prepare for the onslaught tomorrow morning," said Marceau.

"I really wonder about that because of the impending storm and heavy seas," replied Shaw.

"However there is the factor of low tides and a full moon," commented Parker.

"Things can change. The weather can be on our side by tomorrow," said Bridget.

"I think Bridget is right. I'll bet by tomorrow we'll have the messages," said Susan.

"We better get a good night's sleep then," said Parker.

"Bye. Have a good night's sleep. See you tomorrow," said Shaw.

Shaw was at the wheel. Parker and Susan sat in the back of their car. The mood was quite somber, not knowing what tomorrow would bring. Susan put her head on Brian's shoulder and he looked out the window pensively as the car jerked up and down on the bombed out road.

"Do you hear prop noises in the distance?" asked Shaw.

"Loud and clear," answered Parker.

"I hope we'll survive the next raid," said Susan.

The car was stopped by military police and everybody had to exit from the car. The German military searched through the car and asked everybody for identity papers. The examination of the papers took longer than in the past but the whole process had to stop because the bombs were falling all around them and the explosions were unbearable. The Germans ordered them to return to the car and drive away as fast as they could.

"Sometimes these police guys do the right thing," said Parker.

"I think they were worried about being shot by low level fighter planes," commented Shaw.

"Who cares? The important thing is we are on the way home," added Susan.

She put her hand on Brian's lap and stroked it gently and he in turn with a warm embrace kissed her on the lips while he put his hand under her skirt on the thigh.

"Can't you wait until we get home?" chided Shaw.

"No," said Susan and continued, "We may not make it. Our guys in the sky may bomb the hell out of us."

As she said it, a low level fighter plane was just above them circling. Shaw stopped the car and turned off the partial headlights. The plane suddenly swooped down, flew up again, and disappeared into the clouds. They turned on the ignition and continued their drive home.

"You see, one can never tell. We could have been sitting ducks by our own guys," said Susan.

"You're right, my dear, continue your snuggle," Shaw said facetiously.

Another wave of night bombing made Shaw park the car and turn off the headlights. One bomb fell pretty close to the car and the explosion deafened them for a few minutes.

"I think we are experiencing the prelude of the invasion. By tomorrow there will be hundreds of paratroopers all over. When we get home, I'll bet we'll hear the code message to get ready," said Parker.

They waited for thirty minutes until the raid came to halt and then Shaw stepped on the gas and drove home in a jiffy. Susan and Parker entered Shaw's apartment and Shaw, without saying a word, opened a bottle champagne and poured a glass for everyone, lifted his glass for a toast and said, "Cheers, good luck, and long life to everybody."

He opened the transceiver and listened to the cryptic messages: Stand by...Stay alert...Be ready. He repeated the messages to everyone.

"I believe we have twenty-four hours for the assault," said Shaw.

"Very probable. I'm almost certain," said Parker.

"I have a proposition. Why don't we have a good night's rest, rise late in the morning, and save our energy for tomorrow night and the days after," said Susan.

"Well, that is a splendid idea, my dear. Let's do it," replied Shaw.

Susan and Parker spent half the night making love, like there will be no tomorrow. They fell asleep around four o'clock in the morning, but slept until eleven, ready for a hearty brunch. Shaw listened to the radio, a mixture of music and news, had a little cognac and fell asleep around midnight.

It was June 5, 1944. Shaw, Parker, and Susan had an elaborate brunch. They cut out the small talk and were ready for action. Around 1400 Shaw opened the transceiver and listened to the cryptic messages. All forms of liberties were revoked for OSS and MI6 agents until further notice. Mandatory wireless silence was enforced. They were told to secure safe houses for themselves and others.

Nothing specific happened or came through the pipeline until the later hours. The weather was bad in the morning. The howling winds whipped up the sea with white caps and frightened even the most seasoned sailor. It was a touch and go situation. The Royal Air Force meteorologist, J. N. Stagg, predicted clearing skies for the sixth. This optimism changed the mood and allowed Eisenhower to decide the course of action and gave the "let's go" order.

Shaw turned on his transceiver every two hours but no definite orders came from Allied Intelligence. At 2200, however, the cryptic messages were loud and clear: the word was "go." Further instructions were to follow.

After the news, the announcer of the British Broadcasting Corporation (BBC) in French began reciting a number of personal messages directed to the Resistance: "The dice are on the table," "It is hot in Suez," "John remembers Rita...the compass points north," "The children get bored on Sunday." From Verlain's, "The long sobs of the violins of autumn." However, it was, the second line of the same verse, "Wound my heart with a monotonous languor" that the Resistance was long waiting for.

"I need some interpretation. I'm not familiar with these Resistance codes," said Susan.

"To my knowledge, these messages are relating to groups who will carryout various sabotage acts, from exploding railroad tracks to cutting telephone lines, creating chaos around the northern sector to confuse the enemy about the invasion site, and distributing arms. The last one had to do with the imminence of the invasion and to unleash the wave of violence," said Shaw.

"Well, what's next?" asked Susan.

"I know what's next. We have to get rid of our German uniforms and put on our civilian clothes to assist the paratroopers," said Parker.

"Are we ready yet to shed our cover now?" asked Shaw.

"It all depends on the landing. If they miss their mark and disperse all over, it'll be a mess," replied Parker.

"We must get the drop coordinates. But if the pilots encounter problems, the coordinates become meaningless," said Shaw.

"Well, we just have to play it by ear and see what happens," said Parker.

"I can always be a nurse, dress in white, and have a red cross armband," said Susan.

"Not bad, not bad at all. We just may enlist Nurse Susan," said Parker.

The planes were overhead and the drops were executed. Shaw and Parker only wore shirts and pants under the Organization Todt uniform. They carried two sets of identification papers along with pistols.

It was shortly after midnight when the first pathfinders dropped from the sky and hit the ground. It was a miracle how some paratroopers managed to survive between the intense German anti-aircraft and ground fire. Parker spotted a paratrooper five feet from the ground and about ten yards away from him. He quickly took off his German uniform and ran toward the guy as he tried to untangle his parachute.

"Don't shoot," he yelled, "I'm from OSS helping you guys."

"Well, hurry up, help me to get out of this contraption and show me your ID."

Parker helped him to remove the parachute, showed his ID and quickly described the map coordinates.

"I have only twenty-five minutes left to set up the light and radio beacon to aid the incoming planes and guys dropping from the sky."

"We have been waiting for these drops for the last two years, finally its reality. We want to help the other members of the advanced team."

"I don't think you have the time to scout around, but you can help to set up this homing equipment."

"No problem. Just tell us what to do."

Having helped with the device, Parker and Shaw began scouting the area and assisted three other paratroopers to evade the German infantry and with their homing devices.

The C47's came about thirty minutes after the pathfinders set up their beacons. Parker, Shaw, and Susan were ready to help the hundreds of paratroopers who inundated the sky and descended amid the German anti-aircraft and ground fire. Some soldiers were hit while coming down while others were shot on the ground. Parker and Shaw ran toward the wounded and brought them under the cover of heavy brush, while Susan prepared makeshift bandages using the uniforms of the soldiers.

Marceau and Bridget hunkered down in their hidden shelter and Michael had to take an active role in the 716th Infantry division. Some time ago, Michael provided defense papers to be passed on to Allied Intelligence in reference to the defense exercises by the 352nd Infantry Division. They had moved into the Omaha sector three months earlier. Accordingly, there were two divisions defending the Omaha beaches. He also mentioned that the division had experienced fighters, warriors from the Eastern front and that the Allies had better prepare for the assault against an overwhelming force.

Marceau talked about this information with Shaw and Parker, but they considered this information redundant and did not send it to Allied Intelligence. It was assumed that other agents assigned to this task, agents of the Resistance, and the continuous air reconnaissance already had informed Allied Intelligence of all the necessary German troop movements prior to invasion. Shaw and Parker found this information outside their mission. This obvious assumption turned out to be a colossal blunder and unlike the Utah beaches which were sand dunes, it cost the invading forces heavily in the number of casualties.

For some reason the 352nd Infantry Division was not calculated by the military planners into the Omaha equation. Omaha terrain was about four miles with steep bluffs, in some places two hundred feet, it was an awesome challenge. By the time intelligence came in the Military HQ about the 352nd Division, it was too late.

Shaw, Parker and Susan were all over helping the descending paratroopers while the German infantry were searching and shooting at will. At the areas of St. Mere-Eglise and St. Marie-Du-Mont thousands of young Americans found themselves struggling in the wilderness, swamps, and hedges to find a path to their assigned rendezvous. They were dropped many miles away from the designated mark.

Parker and Shaw assembled small groups, and hunkered down on the ground. With flashlights in their mouths they pointed to their existing positions on military maps and how to get to their points of engagement. It was confusing and hapless being miles away from your company, finding the route that leads to the assembly point, and fighting the Germans that were all around you.

Susan was helping the wounded, bandaging and making tourniquets. There were so many hurt and fallen, it was impossible to provide all the help that was needed. For those who suffered unbearable pain she used the one-shot disposable morphine syrette which she found in each paratroopers medical kit along with other first aid supplies. Susan also had several boxes of first aid supplies from those who didn't make it. She was very good with all the soldiers she cared for. Her gun was always next to her and there were moments when she had to use it.

Shaw, Parker, and Susan kept about thirty yards from each other so when one needed help they could yell to the others for the provided support. One of the paratroopers landed in a seventy-five-foot treetop. The Germans were shooting all around him while he was trying to cut his parachute cord. When he finally succeeded his body dropped 35 feet straight down, but his foot got caught in one of the branches. Shaw tried to extricate him while Susan gave cover and Parker responded to Shaw's yelling. Between the three of them he survived with only a broken ankle.

In another near fatal accident, Parker was cornered with three other paratroopers and he was yelling for help.

"Come on, Matt and Susan, it is hell in here, an inferno all around!"

"We're coming!" replied Shaw.

"Well hurry up! Guys are falling left and right."

Shaw, Susan and a dozen guys started to shoot from behind the advancing Germans and it was all over in twenty minutes. Twenty-five Germans were shot and laid in agony on the grass and hedges yelling for help and a medic.

They joined Parker who was exhausted protecting the descending paratroopers from the Germans.

"Thanks. I didn't think we were going to make it. Those krauts know how to shoot."

"Help, medic, help," yelled one of the paratroopers.

Parker ran toward the guy who just descended and got stuck upside down ten feet from the ground on a tree.

"Hold your horses! I'll come and get you," Parker shouted back.

He helped him to get down but the paratrooper strained his ankle in his twisting and turning in the parachute ropes which tangled his foot and hurt him immensely.

"What's your name, corporal?" asked Parker.

"I'm Joe Stangel. Thanks for helping me down."

"You have a swollen ankle, but you'll live!" said Parker.

"Swollen or not, I must find my unit. Thanks pal." Stangel took out his compass and started walking toward the Northeast.

Another group of six paratroopers landed and the German were closing in on them. It was hell all over. The paratroopers formed a circle and hit back with devastating fire power. One of the guys threw the grenades while the others were shooting the approaching German soldiers.

Parker, Shaw and Susan were shooting at the backs of the German soldiers and suddenly the Germans found themselves in a crossfire. The paratroopers finally managed to break through the German defenses and were heading toward their assembly point.

The leader of the small unit thanked for all the help and remarked, "You guys are great Resistance fighters. Those krauts know how to shoot. But with your cooperation, we made it."

"We are OSS and MI6. We were glad to help you. Good luck!" responded Shaw.

As Shaw spoke the Germans started to machinegun the area and mortar shells exploded nearby.

"Take cover now," yelled Parker.

The bullets whizzed and ricocheted near Shaw and Susan. They were protected by a crater made by Allied bombing. As the Germans were heading toward the crater, another group of descending paratroopers strafed the ground and killed the running German soldiers.

"I see a terrible carnage," said Susan

"It was them or us. Thank God, we made it!" said Shaw.

"Until the next round," replied Susan.

The killing fields in the forests, hedgerows, and villages created a powerful stench which was a combination of mortar, grenade, gun powder, and dead bodies of humans and animals. The paratroopers gained small pockets of land and occupied some of the places that were assigned to them.

Parker called Shaw and Susan to check on their status and decided to meet in a nearby barn of a farm house. It was getting close to dawn, but the sky was still dark. To walk any short distance was dangerous as German patrol cars still crossed the area. The shoreline of the invasion coast was lit by flashes of exploding shells that came from naval bombardment of the German defenses.

Parker was looking for Shaw and Susan in the early fog. As he was walking toward the crater, he spotted both of them.

"How are you all?" asked Parker.

"Couldn't feel any better," said Shaw.

"It's hard to believe, but we're still alive," said Susan.

"We'd better go to sleep for an hour before the major invasion starts. One of us will be a sentry while the others sleep," suggested Shaw.

"It's a great idea! The two of you sleep while I'm guarding your souls," replied Susan.

"Splendid, my darling, you're the savior of all mankind," said Parker.

He was the first to shut his eyes. Shaw followed him a second later. They were so tired that it did not take them even a minute to fall asleep. Susan held on to her semi-automatic rifle and looked out the window into a wide open field. There was some sporadic gun fire but the paratroopers held their positions.

Parker woke up an hour later and asked Susan to change places.

"We have another important assignment when you guys wake up. I am very concerned about Marceau and Bridget," said Parker.

"I agree," said Susan.

In less than five minutes, she was sound asleep. Shaw was completely out, deep in his sleep, and snoring heavily. Suddenly, he jerked and hit the ground with his fist. Then he screamed, "Kill him, kill the bastard." Parker woke him up before he really hurt himself.

"What happened?"

"You had a bad dream."

"I must get up and keep the watch," said Shaw.

"I am doing the watch. You just rest."

"I slept long enough, it's your turn."

"We must get up in a half an hour and see how Marceau is doing."

"OK Go to sleep."

Nothing irritated the Gestapo officers more than the enemy making a fool of them. They were convinced that their knowledge about the enemy's plan was superior. The torturous interrogations of Allied soldiers in captivity and Resistance fighters lead them to believe that they were well prepared for any assault. The surprise of "Gummenpuppen," rubberized paratrooper puppet drops to the north of Normandy, sighting of live British paratroopers by the hundreds on French soil, gliders coming down with ramming force, experiencing the breakdown in telephone service, increased sabotage activities, and the reported landings of British infantry by the thousands on Normandy coastlines made the Caen Gestapo absolutely furious. They could not bear the insult. They had to retaliate.

On the day of the Allied invasion, the Gestapo killed one hundred Resistance prisoners who were held in the town jail. They were hauled down into the courtyard by groups of six and eight and mercilessly shot.

The Gestapo agents were mad as hell. French Resistance operators were priority targets. They wanted to choke the insurgency before the Allies formed a beachhead. It became obvious that the Gestapo would arrest anyone who they deemed to be a part of the Resistance.

Words of caution reached Marceau early in the morning of the invasion. Bridget received a telephone call that a Gestapo officer, Mr. Hauptman, was on a rampage arresting people by the dozens. Bridget asked Marceau to take refuge in his hide away place which was well hidden, but he refused because he wanted to protect Bridget.

Unexpectedly, Michael came from out of the blue. He had a contact inside the Gestapo and was told that Hauptman was after Marceau. He also asked Marceau to keep out of sight but to no avail. Michael promised to protect Bridget, but he still refused.

Shaw, Parker, and Susan arrived shortly after Michael. Shaw and Parker were wearing civilian clothes. All three had automatic rifles in their hands and were prepared to meet any hostilities from the Germans. They rushed to embrace Marceau and hugged and kissed Bridget.

"Thank God," said Shaw. "We were worried about you."

"Michael told me that Hauptman is after Marceau," said Bridget.

"That son-of-a-bitch who tortured and later killed the female resistance agent who saved the lives of many commandos, I swore to kill the basted if I ever saw him," said Parker.

"It is not that simple. He is well protected by his Gestapo entourage," said Michael.

"I have enough bullets to kill them all," said Parker.

Shaw, Parker, and Susan sat down on the sofa and excused themselves for a short nap. They were exhausted from the night before.

About an hour passed by when a black sedan arrived in front of Marceau's place with two Gestapo agents in the front and three in the back. Two agents, including Hauptman, knocked strongly on the door and demanded the door to be opened.

"Auf machen, snell auf machen.—open up, quickly open up," yelled Hauptman.

Bridget was pleading with Marceau to go hide in his secret place and tried to convince him that she had enough protection. Finally Marceau yielded to Bridget's plea.

Parker got up and went to the door and in perfect German asked him to calm down.

"What is it that you want?" asked Parker.

"I am Gestapo officer Hauptman and I demand entrance to the premises."

"Ah so! I expected a more polite tone from a Gestapo officer."

"Who the hell are you?" asked Hauptman.

"I was with the Organization Todt as an engineer."

"So what are you doing here?"

"I am waiting for you," said Parker.

He opened the door and allowed the agent and Hauptman to enter. He escorted them to the waiting area and asked them to sit down and be polite. Parker summoned Shaw and Susan and told them how to support him silently while he was finishing off Hauptman.

"Herr Hauptman. I understand you were involved in the interrogation and killing of a Resistance worker who hid commandos," asked Parker.

Hauptman and the other Gestapo agent stood up straight and looked into Parker's eyes.

"What right do you have to question my duties and involvements with the Resistance?" challenged Hauptman.

"I asked you one simple question and I want one simple answer," asked Parker.

"Who are these other people with you?"

"He was my colleague, an engineer with the Organization Todt and she was a secretary."

"Why are you talking in the past tense about your occupations?"

"I will answer your question when you answer my question about the interrogation and execution."

"You mean the vaginal chemical interrogation. This must turn you on. You must be a sexual pervert. Yes. I induced slow pain and slowly increased the dosage until she screamed. Then I relieved her of her miseries by shooting her in the head. Are you happy now?"

Parker held back his anger, stayed silent for ten seconds, then turned toward Shaw, and looked again at Hauptman for another five seconds. Shaw positioned himself behind the other agent. Parker unexpectedly grabbed Hauptman's throat and Shaw hit the other agent on the head with a rubber stick. As Parker was choking him, he ordered Hauptman to kneel down, while the other agent lost complete consciousness.

"I have no way to arrest you for murder. But in the name of humanity, I'll carry out your sentence in behalf of the Resistance. I shall quote from the King James Bible. Galatians 6:7

'Be not deceived; God is not mocked: for whatsoever a man soweth, that shall he also reap.'"

As Parker continued to squeeze his throat he asked him how it felt when he increases the pain.

Hauptman wanted to scream for help but he could not. Parker choked him to death. He then turned to the other agent and choked him until his last breath.

Susan then opened the door and asked the three other agents to assist in the arrest of the belligerent Bridget. All three agents walked into the house, Parker finished them off with his submachine gun.

"We have five corpses and the Gestapo will be suspicious by tonight," said Parker.

"No problem. We'll have a bona fide explosion of the vehicle by incoming enemy fire," said Shaw.

At nightfall, all the corpses were put into the black sedan. Shaw drove the car far from Marceau's place to a desolate area opposite the coastline. Parker and Susan followed in their own car. The Gestapo men and the car were soaked with gasoline. Parker had two grenades in his car that he had taken from the German soldiers the night before and placed them in the front and back seats. Shaw lit a gasoline soaked rag and tossed it to the car. The flames expanded rapidly and a huge explosion followed.

Shaw, Parker, and Susan returned to Marceau's place in the middle of exploding shells. On the streets German soldiers were running back and forth, shouting for medics and ammunitions. The Allied attacks were massive and destructive.

Michael reluctantly had to return to his post but it was clear to him that the Allies had superior forces and materials to crush the German defenders. He promised Bridget to contact her as soon as he could.

Shaw, Parker, and Susan hardly talked in the presence of Marceau about their ordeal with the Gestapo men. They asked Marceau to allow them to stay and provide them with the minimum accommodation. There was no problem with their requests. Shaw and Parker slept in the guest room and Susan with Bridget.

"Marceau, please forgive our manners for not being sociable, but we were helping guides last night and fought with the German Infantry while protecting the paratroopers. Our bodies are about to collapse if we don't rest a few hours," said Parker.

"You don't have to excuse yourself. We are in the middle of the greatest warfare mankind has ever experienced. You need all the energy you can muster up. Shaw, Parker, and Susan you can stay here as long as you want. My home is your home," answered Marceau.

"I will prepare some nourishing food for you," added Bridget.

"Thank you all. We'll talk later," said Shaw.

"And I'll help you in the kitchen and with washing the dishes," added Susan.

Shaw, Parker, and Susan had a very short sleep. It was more of a catnap. The Allied Naval vessels bombarded the Atlantic Wall and surrounding German defenses between six and seven o'clock in the morning. In addition, the 50th division was firing artillery pieces. The Bunker on the Hill was responding with an all mighty force. The sounds of big explosions were augmented by the 88mm and rapid machinegun fires. Hell was breaking loose. They used their pillows over their heads to muffle the sounds, but it did not work.

It was around 0700 when three commandos of the 47th Royal Marine Commando banged on the door and sought Marceau's help.

"Damn it. I can't get a few minutes rest," said Parker.

"In the hospitals the interns are on a thirty-six hour duty. They are also engaged in a fight between life and death. Don't complain," replied Shaw.

He got up and opened the door. Shaw immediately recognized the very British chaps.

"Hello, good morning. What can we do for you?"

"We survived the onslaught on the beach and we would appreciate the help of Marceau," said one of the commandos by the name of Roger.

"How did you get his name?"

"We got it from Allied Intelligence. We were told to look him up for help."

"Come in fellows. We'll make you coffee."

"We can't stay long. We are in the middle of the battle. We already lost twenty-eight of our buddies and twenty-seven are missing. It is hell out there."

"I'm Marceau. How can I help you?"

"We're planning to attack Port-En-Bessin from behind. This includes the fortifications and bunkers. We need an updated map and knowledge of how to attack the bunker at its weakest point," said Roger.

"By the way, this is Paul and this tall man is Howard."

"I'm Captain Parker, OSS, he is Captain Shaw, MI6, and she is Susan McCoy,OSS affiliate. Shaw and I have impersonated Todt Organization officers for the past two years so we are quite familiar with the construction of the bunker in question," said Parker.

"Well, that's splendid. We can learn from you guys and kick the 'Krauts' in the rear," said Roger. He took out a military map from his shirt's waterproof inner lining, put it on the table, and started asking questions.

"We must take Port-En-Bessin as soon as we can to supply petrol. We intend to have a pipeline under the ocean and our mission is to capture this port," said Paul.

"We'll help you as much as we can, but you still need men to take the bunker," said Shaw.

"We have 340 men to take into action," advised Howard.

Shaw and Parker explained the soft spots of the bunker and the surrounding defenses.

They also talked about the various approaches to take the port. Shaw was excellent in mapping details, describing the various routes, hills, and shortcuts.

The commandos left Marceau's place under fire and tried to reunite with their group. They made several attempts but under heavy fire they were forced to return to Marceau's abode.

Finally, under the protective armed cover of the Maquis, they fought their way through dead bodies, houses, partly demolished buildings, burned trucks, and hedgerows but made it back to their units.

Port-En-Bessin became the frontline and the Germans did their best to protect the place but the 47th Royal Marine Commandos also did their best to take it. Shaw, Parker, and Susan felt trapped in Marceau's place, but there was no way out until the British secured the beachhead.

"I'm a little concerned about this place because Marceau has been well-known in military circles. Some enterprising soldiers might enter our premises for money, food, and sex, but I'm ready for them with my automatic," said Parker.

"Anything can happen in war. Some bastards can easily turn into savage beasts and as a last hurray indulge themselves in any uncivilized act that under normal circumstances they would not do," said Marceau.

"Rape and mayhem occurred quite frequently on the eastern front. A lot of stories were told by various people coming from Eastern and Central Europe," said Shaw.

"I'm ready to emasculate any deranged blokes. They better stay away or my training will be put into practice," added Susan.

The machineguns and mortars were all over the streets. German soldiers were shouting as the killing field got closer. A big explosion collapsed a nearby building. Cries for help were heard all over in French and German. But the intensity of the fire kept civilians in their homes. It was a full scale war of attack and defense.

As the sun went down and darkness approached the horizon, the commandos decided to stop the fight for the night. The guns became silent on a hill at Escures, a mile distance from Port-en-Bessin. The following day, however, the attack continued with vengeance.

The German defenses suffered heavy casualties on the Bayeaux Road and the commandos advanced their positions. They were ready to commence a major charge toward the harbor half way up the slope with everything that they had, when they discovered that they had the wrong intelligence.

According to the commando's information, the ships in the harbor had no guns to be afraid of. However, just before D-Day, a couple of flaks were installed without the knowledge of Allied Intelligence.

This was a real catastrophe. On the Omaha and Utah beaches, the US Army had to face two divisions instead of one, because of faulty intelligence. It was well understood that the purview of Shaw and Parker was the development and maintenance of the Atlantic Wall. Susan had general collection of information as she was provided by the German officers and generals. Military intelligence including Army, Air Force, and Navy logistics, ordnance, weapons, and weapons of mass destruction fell on specialized OSS, MI6, and Resistance agents. Marceau was the center of information collection and transport. His courier service was limited to the input that various agents provided.

One must, however, never to underestimate the German secrecy, subterfuge, and shrewd military planning. Why Michael's reports failed to acknowledge the changes of the German Military Planning will remain a subject of inquiry. Human nature and other factors, however, always must be taken into consideration. Was it possible that his findings and caveats arrived too late—after the initiation of military encounter? Timing was always the essence of military winning. It could have been that Michael had no privilege to top secret logistics, or problems collecting information on time,—meaning well before the D-Day started.

While Michael was inspecting several units, he came to visit Bridget at the night. There was some sporadic fire but by and large it became reasonably quiet.

"Hello my love, I missed you terribly," said Michael.

"I can't believe it! I'm so happy you came."

They embraced each other, and passionately kissed their lips, face and neck.

"This is beautiful and memorable, a true love," said Susan.

"We are truly happy that you made it," said Marceau.

"I wish I could stay and become a prisoner, but if the SS should catch me here, I'll be shot as a deserter and would also risk your welfare. The SS is merciless and mad because we are losing."

"How much time do you have?" asked Bridget.

"One hour."

"Can I fix you something to eat?"

"A couple of slices of homemade bread, butter, and coffee."

"I'll fix them with great pleasure, my sweet heart."

"Did any of my soldiers bother you?"

"We've had no problems so far."

"I had some report of rapes and robbery."

"Here my darling, eat well, bon appetite. We could go and lie down for a while before you leave."

"I can't wait to have you in my arms, my darling Bridget."

Michael who likes homemade bread more than any other bread or croissant enjoyed every morsel with butter and fresh brewed coffee. Soon after his meal, they retired in the bedroom.

They shed their clothes with lightning speed and just snuggled for awhile. Then Bridget began caressing his entire body, then climbed over him and slowly allowed Michael to unite with her. Both remained motionless and silent. Only their lips communicated their love for each other. Michael and Bridget continued their kissing until both opened their mouths and in reciprocal motion touched each other's tongue. Both became extremely aroused and Bridget began wavy motions of her lower body. This evoked ultimate pleasure in both of them.

"Can you hold it a few more minutes?" asked Bridget.

"I'll try, but it's very difficult."

"I need a couple of seconds to come together with you."

Michael then began caressing her buttocks and that put her into absolute ecstasy. They convulsively came together with an enormous sigh. They were still together kissing each other, when somebody with a rifle butt banged on the window and shouted: "Auf machen, Auf machen," meaning open-up, open-up.

Michael grabbed his pans and shouted back in German.

"Was wollen sie?" "What do you want? You are talking to a German Military Officer."

"I have orders to evacuate this building," said the German soldier.

"You show me the papers when I come out."

Michael dressed fast and was ready to open the door when Parker grabbed his hand and told him not to believe these guys and along with Shaw he'll be protected with their submachine guns.

"I sincerely hoped we would not have to resort to this."

Michael opened the door and found five soldiers facing him. He was surprised that out of the five, two were from the SS. They saluted each other. Michael asked for the papers.

"We don't have papers. The orders were all verbal," explained one of the SS soldiers.

"Sorry, this place is under my jurisdiction and there will be no evacuation. If you want to clarify this matter, you could talk to General Hochendorfer. I must also have your names and the unit you belong to."

One of the SS soldier pointed his submachine gun at Michael and in total disgust replied, "I don't feel like discussing this topic any further. You will have to face the consequences if there will be any harm occurring to the occupants of this premise. We are at war. Street by street war. We are leaving but this location will be yours and only your responsibility."

"I can deal with that. Now get lost!"

Michael returned to Bridget and apologized for the rude interruption.

"You did what you had to do. Thank you," said Bridget.

"Honey, I must return to the base. I hope this battle will not last long and we'll be reunited again."

"I wish you could stay. Port-En-Bessin will fall shortly."

"I can't. They will look for me. And I could create problems for everyone here."

"I'll miss you."

"I'll miss you too."

"Please be careful."

Michael gave her a big hug and a kiss and left in a hurry toward his car.

"I will. Bye, my darling."

"Bye."

Small groups of the commandos continued their brave fight against enemy positions. They attacked a major bunker, and suffering limited casualties managed to capture it. The commandos were reduced to 280 minus the wounded. They fought against the superior, top class German division, but their determination to win over the enemy was stronger than the morale of the Germans. The enemy positions were captured one after another.

They accomplished what they set forth to do, to take the Port from the rear. By the night of the 8th of June, Port-En-Bessin fell and the US 1st Infantry Division joined with elements of the British 50th Division. It was a celebrated event and Marceau, Bridget, Shaw, Parker and Susan rushed into the street to join the others. Marceau had a small American and British flag in each hand and was singing and dancing in circles with a Commando captain and an American black beret lieutenant.

The streets were full of people singing, dancing, hugging, and drinking champagne that they had stored in hidden places to celebrate freedom. The church bells were tolling with rhythmic allegro and the music of French ballads and American jazz were blasting from windows all over. It was like a carnival of freedom.

The Allied forces were swarming in by truckloads and the people in the streets and leaning out of the house windows were throwing all kinds of flowers and confetti at the soldiers. It was the most gratifying feeling of liberation after years of occupation, dictatorship, intimidation, deportation, incarceration, and torture. People were shouting, "Vive la France," and Liberte!

It was hard to believe what the people saw; it was a long awaited dream of hope. People were crying from joy and happiness, but also for the lost ones. Those who were sent to the concentration camps, tortured and killed by the Gestapo.

This was an all night celebration. Marceau and Bridget, however, had to excuse themselves. His illness made him very tired and Bridget had to help him with the routine bed time preparations. Shaw, Parker, and Susan were engaged in socializing, sharing stories, and just enjoying the company of others. It had been a long time since they were free to talk and meet some nice people who shared the same or similar values.

It was dawn when they returned to Marceau's place to sleep. They did not have any problems falling asleep despite the exploding shells and machine gun fires in the far distance. The war was expanding toward Caen and Cherbourg and many battles had to be won to liberate France.

It was eleven o'clock when all five were joined at the breakfast table. Bridget made a super meal of sausage and eggs with home fried potatoes, home made bread, butter, orange jam, coffee, and English tea.

"So what's next?"

With the invasion in progress, Shaw and Parker's mission had ended.

"Why don't we share some of their and our past experiences?" asked Susan.

"Splendid idea," said Bridget.

"I nominate Marceau to be our master of ceremonies" said Parker.

All hands went up.

"It is unanimous, Marceau," said Shaw.

"Thank you for your confidence. I shall try my best."

"Captain Shaw, would you be kind enough and begin?" said Marceau.

"I would like to go back to Shrewsbury, UK, in September of 1942. The meeting with Parker was an unforgettable episode. It was scheduled for the latter part of September when the leaves were still basking in the autumn sun of Shrewsbury. We met at 0900 in Coleham Primary School's Teacher's Conference

Room. The school had the traditional brick siding and gable roof. It was located at Greyfriars Road.

"As I was walking toward the school a middle aged good looking man asked me if I was lost. He offered his help by accompanying me to the school entrance and gave me his business card and told me he was a theatre agent and he was looking for pretty showgirls like me.

"I was cross-dressed and had heavy makeup on. Of course, I gave him a sensual smile and thanked him for the compliment and invite. One never knows who is a German agent.

"By the time I arrived, the classes had already begun and there was hardly any traffic in the corridors. Both of us arrived a few minutes earlier and entered the secretary's office to get directions. There were a couple of teachers, a head teacher and the secretary present. They were looking at us as two call girls who were about to change their professions.

"Major Rugby, MI6, and Teller, OSS, laughed their hearts out. Teller commented that if we were going to be as good of an agent as we were camouflage experts we'd win the war."

"Mr. Parker, you're next," said Marceau. "Any questions?" asked Marceau.

"How effective was the German espionage that you had to cross-dress?" asked Bridget.

"The Abwehr, the German espionage organization tried to identify every agent who entered the Axis states. They tried to photograph every MI6 agent. They were particularly concerned about agents entering France, especially the Normandy region."

"What was your background? asked Susan.

I received my PhD from Oxford in material science. I was employed by a large chemical company in Bristol. I had extensive training by the MI6. I am married to a lovely lady and we have two children."

"Now we can understand why you were so skittish with women," said Susan.

"I was like that even before I was married."

"You had missed a terrific opportunity to be on the stage, "said Susan.

"Maybe, but I was in a different theatre. Something that I am very proud of," replied Shaw.

"Thank you for your presentation. Mr. Parker, your next," said Marceau.

"Thank you. I only have one episode to report and that was my night flight from England to France. It was a LysanderIII modified aircraft and we bounced back and forth in terrible turbulence. Before we reached the coastline, we encountered anti-aircraft flaks of the worst kind. I was ready to pee and puke.

But the girl who was sitting next to me offered her help and I threw up in her lap. It took several minutes to wipe the smile off her face. I was so embarrassed that I wanted to jump out of the plane. I was sure that she never wanted to see me again. It turned out that the girl I soiled was Susan, the love of my life."

"Any questions?" asked Marceau.

"What was your education and training?" asked Bridget.

"My undergraduate degree was in Civil engineering, my Master's and Doctorate degrees were in Mechanical engineering from New York University. I designed bridges and tunnels for a large firm in Manhattan, New York. I received an excellent training from the OSS."

"Thank you, Mr. Parker."

"I believe Susan would like to share some of her experiences. Susan."

"I am French born but of a mixed parentage. My father is

French, but lived in the US. My mother is German and lived in Paris. I graduated from Wellesley College and Columbia University and attended Sorbonne. My majors were chemistry, mathematics and philosophy. When France was occupied I joined the Resistance. Somebody from the higher ups asked me to meet a gentleman who was an OSS recruiter. Within a couple of weeks he made an offer in behalf of OSS to become an affiliate. I was asked to fly to the US and go through a second check of security and training. I was assigned to learn about German generals in every possible way I could.

"My most intriguing experience was a middle aged general who was impotent because of psychophysical complications. I was his therapist but without sex. As a matter of fact sex was seldom the issue. The emphasis was companionship. Yes, I was naked and the generals climaxed without coitus. This middle age general, however, fell in love with me, and wanted to divorce his wife and marry me. He was extremely thankful that he regained his manhood and was able to climax. But I was trapped in the worst way you can imagine. He shared with me many secrets that I was able to forward through Marceau to OSS. I was supposed to travel to Berlin to stay with him during the divorce procedures.

"What saved my life was that his wife shot him. I immediately returned to France and had a month vacation in Spain. The OSS suggested staying away from public functions until the storm over the homicide was over. They were afraid that I'd be implicated in court. I flew back to the US and had a splendid vacation in the Caribbean for several months. Then I was called back to France. The case with the deceased general was over. The rest of my stay was dangerous but rewarding. Of course, my greatest gift was meeting Brian."

"Thank you, Susan," said Marceau.

"I will spare you talking about myself and Bridget. Most of you know about us in terms of our lives and operations. We could spend a couple of days just citing all the excitement with all the ups and downs," said Marceau.

Bridget served refreshments and the mood was exuberant. Still there was concerned about Michael's safety. Suddenly there was a loud knock on the door. Parker opened the door and a man in civilian clothes with a French flag armband introduced himself as a lost Resistance agent and wanted to know how he is going to get back to his unit. Marceau looked at him with piercing eyes and did not like his voice.

"Are you French?" asked Parker.

"I am as French as you are."

"You have an accent," said Shaw.

"I was born at the border town between Germany and France."

"What is your name?" asked Parker.

"Louis Savogne."

"I think I saw you somewhere," said Parker.

"I don't think so."

"Your face and eyes have the shape of the man I heard about," said Parker.

"You are confusing me with someone else. May I speak with Marceau in private for a few minutes?"

Parker put his hand in his back pocket and lifted his pistol. He pointed it at him.

"I should not be surprised that you would masquerade as a Resistance agent. Your hair and mustache are false. You are wearing a wig Mr. Kohler. How dare you come to visit this house?! You are under arrest," said Parker.

Shaw approached him and wanted to tie his hands with an

electric cord. He tried to pull his Luger pistol out but Parker hit him and knocked him to the floor. Shaw took his pistol and there was a short brawl. Kohler started to call Marceau dirty names and kicked and hit Parker. Parker had enough and shot him in his head. He stumbled to the floor and his eyes became transfixed.

There was an eerie silence in the room. They just looked at the dead corpse.

"He will not hurt anybody anymore," assured Marceau.

"Thank God," said Bridget.

Again, there were two knocks on the door. Four Allied soldiers, two American and two British made inquiries about Marceau, Shaw, Parker, and Susan. Two of them were from military intelligence. They properly introduced themselves with military papers and were asked to be seated.

"I am Captain Mulberry, US and my partner is Captain Lehigh, UK military intelligence."

"Please excuse us for the dead body on the floor, but he was a Gestapo agent, Kohler by name, and tried to assassinate Marceau. In self defense he was shot."

"You may remove the body and we'll ask a couple of soldiers to bury him," said Captain Mulberry.

"You can write a report later about the incident," said Captain Lehigh.

"We are here to request your presence on our command ship to meet with your supervisors," said Captain Mulberry.

"When do you want us to go?" asked Captain Parker.

"We were told to accompany you to the return vessel as soon as you can accommodate us," said Captain Lehigh.

"Would you mind if Miss Bridget, Marceau's daughter and aide would come along? Marceau has leukemia and she may be needed on the trip," said Shaw.

"By all means, please let her come with Monsieur Marceau.

Thank you for telling us about his condition," said Captain Lehigh.

They gathered some important documents. Bridget packed a few medications for Marceau. Within fifteen minutes, they all headed for the transport vessel that was moored at the harbor.

The sky was reasonably clear but the wind made the trip uncomfortable for Marceau. There was a three foot swells with ominous looking white caps. Marceau threw up several times, but fortunately the trip lasted only twenty minutes.

Upon their arrival, there was a stupendous reception for the whole party. The medic brought some medication for Marceau which made him feel immediately better.

"This medication must be magic," said Marceau. "I feel so much better."

They entered the situation room with all the comforts surrounding them. The buffet table had the most exquisite assortments of food and drink delicacies. It was saying, "Welcome home and thank you for your services."

They were all overwhelmed by the reception, attention, and gratitude. They all had a glorious feeling of homecoming with some tears in their eyes.

The door swung open, and the top brass came in accompanied by the music of the navy band. It was an unforgettable moment. The dignitaries of OSS, MI6, and the military shook hands with everybody. One of the Generals suggested having the goodies served at the table.

After brief introductory, remarks the chaplain offered a grace. A toast was offered by an OSS representative. The total feast lasted an hour, including appetizers, entrée, dessert, and beverages. Immediately after the meal, there were two speeches.

One had to do with the unqualified success of intelligence, the other of the success of the military forces.

This was followed by individual consultations. The OSS representative had debriefings with Parker and Susan. In the same order, MI6 debriefed Shaw and Marceau. There was a French Resistance representative and he talked separately with Marceau and Bridget.

Parker, Shaw, and Susan were offered a two week furlough to the US and UK respectively. After that they must report back to OSS and MI6 for further duty. There was a sense of disappointment in everyone's eyes. But as it was explained, the brief vacation time was due to the present war situation.

It was unclear what kind and where the reassignment would be, but guessing by their backgrounds, it looked like France again. Judging from the conversations, there was a hint by the Allied Intelligence representatives that it would be necessary to identify pockets of French and German insurgents.

The debriefing lasted two and a half hours for the US, and UK and France. The whole hearing ended before dusk, so they were able to return to their apartments to listen to the soccer game in England.

Susan was holding onto Parker's arm and in a bittersweet voice inquired about their departure and travel plans.

"Darling, we have to decide when, where, and what," said Parker, as the boat was bobbing toward the port.

"Besides, we have several obligations to our families. Your parents, my mother, sisters, brothers, are all expecting us to be there. I would love to have our engagement in my mother's house. Yet, we need some personal time," said Parker.

"So why don't we spend one week with our families and the second week together?" said Susan.

"This is a splendid idea my sweet heart. Let's go for it!"

The boat started to dock but the current of high tide was quite strong. Parker jumped over the gate to the dock and pulled the docking rope with all his energy. He managed to fasten the rope of the bow to one of the cleats and did the same for the stern.

When the boat was steadied with several ropes, all passengers were allowed to walk ashore through a narrow ramp.

"Our trips are not so simple. We must first go to England and then take the train to London's airport," said Parker.

"I'll take care of the details," replied Susan.

"Good. Let's start packing. Knowing her, we'll be sailing tomorrow morning," said Shaw.

"Yes, but we don't have a timetable for departure," replied Susan.

"I'm heading to the port. There must be some kind of military transportation," said Parker.

"Good thinking. May I go with you?" asked Shaw.

"OK, let's go," said Parker.

At the port there was some reluctance to give any information until they were supported by navy officers. They were told to arrive early and wait at the port until a vessel was ready to sail. There were no timetables or promises, just spur of the moment departures.

Parker and Shaw went back to pack and told Susan that they were not sure when there would be a vessel to take them to England.

"One thing is for sure, and that is, we must be at the port by 0700 hour every morning, until we can catch a ride," said Parker.

"OK, I'll be ready," promised Susan.

They spent the night listening to soccer on the radio, ate delicious food catered by the local people, cracked funny jokes, and just enjoyed each other's company.

The next morning, Shaw, Parker, and Susan waited at the port to be called. Nothing happened for two hours and their patience started to wear thin. Shaw approached one of the fishing vessel captains and asked him what he knew about military vessels departing to England. There was little response. So they kept waiting. Around 1000 hours a military captain was inquiring about Allied Intelligence agents.

"Are you the guys interested in crossing the Channel to UK?"

"Yes sir," was Parker's response.

"May I see your Agency identity? It will take a few minutes until I check with the Military Intelligence HQ to get you aboard."

"I think we are going to London's airport," said Shaw.

The Captain came back with a smile on his face and invited them to come aboard.

"We'll be leaving as soon as some of the American and British soldiers show up and we check their identities. We must do that because some Germans are trying to escape in British or American uniforms."

The time was ten minutes to noon when the ropes were untied and picked up by the sailors on the boat. It was an American military cargo ship. The sea was calm and the sky was blue with few clouds. Shaw, Parker, and Susan leaned on the camouflaged colored railings looking at the parting panorama of the semi-circular entrance of Port-En-Bessin.

The vessel slowly sailed to England.

Marceau and Bridget were happy and sad. The departure

was overwhelmingly sentimental. Although they will come back, life for everybody will be different.

"I will always miss the inner circle," lamented Marceau.

"The feelings are mutual. I hope Michael will return unscathed."

"If God's willing, I hope he will, but it will not be easy," replied Marceau.

"I wish to find him as a prisoner of war; at least he survived the onslaught."

"You'll find him, but it will take some time and effort. You must make contacts and ask many people. The POWs will be scattered all over. We'll have to contact the Military Headquarters."

"I suggest having our telephone connected again," said Bridget.

"I wholeheartedly agree. We must have contact with the world. But Port-En-Bessin is not ready yet to install telephones in private homes. Give them a little time."

"Forgive me, Marceau, I am very impatient. I have Michael and you on my mind all the time. I am concerned about your welfare. I am worried about Michael. Maybe we could have the privilege and perhaps the priority to have a telephone."

"I'll see what I can do. I have to contact the person who is in charge of the residential telephone service. I don't want you to walk on the streets until the beachhead is secure enough. They are still fighting in the distance and a stray shell can explode and kill you. It is still dangerous, my darling. Please trust me; I know what I am talking about."

"Marceau, I know you make sense but my emotions are overriding my intellect."

"My dear Bridget, you are a strong person and you must get a hold of your impulses.

Michael is thinking of you just the same as you are. He will need Bridget as a whole person in mind and body, not a crippled heroine."

"Thank you, Marceau. You are a wonderful father!"

Bridget brought out the radio from the hiding place and placed it in the living room. They were listening to the BBC broadcasts. The war produced a lot of pain and suffering on both sides.

She tried to get in touch with her neighbors but because their homes were badly damaged, she was unable to see them. The doors were locked and knocking did not help. She assumed that they sought refuge in their basements. Every time she ventured out for a few minutes, Bridget was glad to return. The streets were desolate. Mostly military personnel were walking with their fingers on the trigger of their rifles and trucks were zooming by in all directions. The war in Port-En-Bessin was not completely over yet.

A military jeep arrived at Marceau's place. Two officers entered the premises.

"We brought you some food, drinks, and medicine. There is concern about your welfare, Marceau and Bridget. Would you care to relocate to England for a while?" asked one of the officers.

"Thank you. It is very kind of you to think of us, not to mention all the goodies you have brought. But we are managing here the best way we can. Besides, Bridget has been waiting to hear about her fiancé."

"Please let us know if we can help you in any way," said the second officer.

"We certainly will, and thank you again for all your concern and food packages."

"Before you leave can you tell me please how I must go about finding my fiancé's whereabouts?"

"Do you know his division?" asked the first officer.

"He is with the German military. Michael is an officer in the Army but he was helping the Allied Intelligence. I am terribly concerned about his welfare."

"It is too early to find out what happened to him. We do not have the German list of casualties completed yet. It is in the process. If he is being held as a prisoner of war, he must go through debriefing and paper processing. It all takes time and we must ask for your patience. As soon as we find out something, we will let you know immediately.

Please give us his full name and rank," asked the first officer.

"Thank you ever so much. His name is Michael Woerner; his rank is Hauptleute- Captain."

"Well, well, maybe this is the contact. Who knows, we may find out about him sooner than you expected," said Marceau.

"I wouldn't hold my breath. It is too soon."

"Don't be discouraged. You must be positive! We have at least a glimmer of hope."

"Thank you, Marceau. You must take your medicine now and take a nap."

"Thank you, my dear. I'll see you later."

CHAPTER TWELVE

Bridget woke up rather early, walked to the window and had a hard, long look at the sky. It was liquid sunshine. The raindrops made their presence by the rhythmic sounds as they were hitting the pavement. She always liked to hear the falling raindrops, something that fascinated her since childhood.

She was far away in her thoughts, wondering about what was happening to Michael.

Did he withdraw with other officers; was he captured by Allied forces, injured, or killed?

She learned a long time ago that guessing leads to nowhere, but she couldn't stop her wandering thoughts.

Marceau stayed unusually longer in bed than in the past. When he finally came to the breakfast table it was past ten o'clock. He hardly ate anything Bridget prepared and the only acceptable excuse was his lack of appetite.

"I don't like your tiredness and not eating breakfast."

"I can be tired and have a stuffed stomach, couldn't I?"

"Marceau, I don't disagree on that, but this has been progressing for some time. The past two weeks you are sleeping longer and eating less. You know it."

"So what do you want me to do?"

"I want to take you to the doctor."

"We can't travel to Caen now, the battle is brewing."

"I know, but we can find another doctor."

"I need a specialist who knows how to treat leukemia."

"I am aware of that. Therefore, I must take you to Cherbourg."

"Cherbourg was liberated only two days ago. Wait a few more days and we may be able to connect with the specialist by phone."

"In the meantime, we should consult with the local practitioner."

"If it makes you feel better, do it. But I don't think he knows too much."

"He knows more than what we know."

"Very well, get in touch with him, my dear."

Bridget called the local doctor who came to see Marceau. He was not surprised how badly Marceau deteriorated and offered temporary panacea until he had a chance to see a specialist. He recommended, however, blood transfusion which must be taken place in a hospital under stringent supervision. He was somehow skeptical about the availability of matching blood because of the war conditions and injury priorities.

Bridget did not waste time and got on the transceiver and asked for help. Allied Intelligence urgently ordered blood and a military ambulance to take Marceau to the Cherbourg Naval Hospital.

The situation however became complicated because of the large number of casualties and priorities. His type of blood was not immediately available and the ambulances were also tied down at various fronts. It took three weeks to get his blood and he was in bad shape by the time the ambulance arrived. He was very weak and dizzy. Marceau lost ten pounds in three weeks. His face was pale and he had difficulties breathing.

Bridget drove behind the ambulance and stayed with an old friend of the Resistance until he was allowed to come home.

Her friend, Jill, a kind and charming lady of twenty-seven, went out of her way to accommodate Bridget. She not only provided lodging but fed her breakfast and dinner. Bridget hardly knew about her intimate life and was surprised by her gracious generosity.

Marceau's health improved considerably and he was released on the third day. But he still felt weak, and there was a slight concern of relapse. Jill offered Marceau to stay in her home for a few more days. Reluctantly, Marceau agreed, only because he felt more secure being close to the specialist and the hospital.

Jill was a gracious host and Bridget was grateful under the circumstances in a war torn city. Marceau slept in the living room and Bridget and Jill in the bedroom. Although Bridget was comfortable and had a good night's sleep, she preferred to go home next day. There was a major conflict between staying and going home. Bridget was desperate to hear about Michael because all information went to Marceau's place.

Marceau was sensitive to her conflict and without talking about it, suggested to leave for home. Bridget, however, needed some time in the morning to revisit the hospital, talk to his specialist and get his recommendation about returning to Port-En-Bessin. It was there she found out that Michael was admitted there sometime ago. He was badly injured and the doctors removed a piece of shrapnel from his abdomen. He was then transferred to a POW camp, but nobody knew where.

"So what did you find out?" asked Marceau.

"First, you can go home, but if your condition changes, even if it is a slight change, we must immediately inform the doctor and return to the hospital. Second, Michael is alive! He is alive Marceau! Oh, thank you God! He was seriously injured, but by miracle, taken to this hospital. He underwent surgery and the doctors saved his life. After his recuperation, Michael was transferred to a POW camp, but they don't know where."

As they were driving home, Bridget said again, "At least he is alive."

"Thank God," replied Marceau.

"You should contact military intelligence to find him," said Marceau.

"I will definitely contact the US Military Intelligence tomorrow."

"How do you feel Marceau?"

"I'm getting stronger. But, as I was told, I must return for more blood transfusions."

"We must be hearing from Parker, Shaw, and Susan," said Marceau.

"Perhaps we will soon."

Marceau closed his eyes and fell asleep. Bridget was told that he will be more tired as his cancer progresses and it will not be unusual to see him sleeping more and more. She looked at him for a second and his pale face and lost weight made him look older and seriously ill. Bridget had tears in her eyes and tried to wipe them off to see the road, but more and more were shedding and she had to stop the car.

"What's the matter? Why did you stop the car?"

"I was reminiscing and tears blocked my vision."

"We all have some soft moments sometimes. I had it in the hospital. I know that I'm dying and it is very hard to leave you and my friends."

"I wish you would not talk about it. My heart goes out for you and Michael."

Bridget started the ignition and proceeded toward home. They arrived within a half an hour. She helped Marceau to exit from the car and enter the shop. There was a note on the floor from Shaw, Parker and Susan.

Bridget read the note out loud standing in the shop and Marceau listened sitting on a chair.

"Dear Marceau and Bridget: Having enjoyed a little vacation abroad, we are back in France but reassigned to different places. Hope to see you next week. Love from Susan, Shaw and Parker."

Bridget was a little disappointed by not hearing from Michael. But she understood the complications that Michael was facing to get in touch with her.

The first thing she did was to help Marceau take his medication. Then she helped him lie down on the couch. The third thing was to make dinner. The food was sparse, so she prepared a simple but nutritious meal. She was always a skillful cook and managed to make delicious meals out of few ingredients. For Bridget, nutrition and taste came first over aesthetics.

Marceau felt strong enough to repair a few shoes that were left there to be mended. He had to do something to keep his mind off from his condition. Marceau asked Bridget to take care of her business and leave him alone for a while. She needed a couple of hours to talk with the officials at the US Military HQ in Port-En-Bessin. Bridget, however, was terribly concerned leaving Marceau without supervision. She called her neighbor to stay with Marceau but she was nursing her husband who was injured by a stray bullet. By sheer luck, one of his customers, a nurse, came to pick up her shoes and asked Bridget about Marceau. Having learned about his condition, she was more than happy to stay with him until her return. Bridget accepted the offer and in no time rushed to the US Military HQ.

There she waited impatiently for the officer in charge. Civilians had a difficult time making inquiries about a missing POW soldier of German origin. Bridget was quite determined, however, to talk with someone of the higher ups. She felt that Michael deserved special consideration for his cooperation with Allied Intelligence. Finally, having waited for forty-five minutes, the sergeant asked to state her business.

"May I talk to someone of Military Intelligence?"

"What is it about?"

"It is about a German Officer who is now a POW and he worked for Allied Intelligence."

"What do you want to know about him?"

"I would like to reunite with him. He was injured and after his release from the hospital he was taken as an American prisoner of war."

"Do you have papers, to prove your claim?"

"I don't have to say too much to the Intelligence Officer. He will know who I am after he checks out my story."

"What is your name?"

"Just say Bridget Badeau, the daughter of Marceau."

"You have to wait a few minutes until my relief comes."

The soldier was relieved. After ten minutes of waiting, entered the Military Intelligence room and talk briefly with one of the officers. The officer left the room and went to see Bridget at the entrance of the building.

" Mademoiselle Bridget, I am captain Howard from MI, please come in to my office."

"You are the daughter of Marceau who worked for AI, trained by MI6, and was a courier of the Resistance?"

"That is correct."

"What can I do for you?"

"I would like to find out what happened to a German Officer Michael, my fiancé, who also worked, although indirectly for Allied Intelligence. I would like to reunite with him. I understand he was injured and hospitalized. After leaving the hospital he was put in a POW camp."

"Your request is not so simple. Madam, you must present documents of his full name, rank, and serial number. Marceau also must be identified by his full name, occupation, MI6 number, and Resistance identification. It would be preferable if he could come to this office for picture taking and other forms of identification checking. He must also sign documents in person before two witnesses."

"I hope you realize that we are in a war situation and there are priorities that come first. We must check all documents and statements. Please allow some time, one or two weeks to collect your documents. I will see you in a couple of weeks with Marceau at the same time. It will take roughly two to three months before we can give you some answers. Please be patient," said Captain Howard.

"But it will take you very little time to verify Marceau's identity. MI6 and OSS will acknowledge his intelligence participation during the development of the Atlantic Wall in a short time."

"I have no doubts that we will verify his identity on a double, but you have to realize that we have thousands of German POWs in various locations. Some still have to be properly processed and it takes time. I do understand your concern and I promise we will do the best we can to find him and check out his contribution to the Allied Intelligence."

"I thank you for your reassurance and hope we'll hear from you soon."

Bridget walked to the car head down, on one hand comported, the other sad and daunting.

"Hello, my dear Bridget," said Marceau.

"Hello, Marceau."

"I hope you have some good news."

"I am afraid not. It will take some time until they will find Michael. We have to go and give them our identities in papers, codes, and whatever documents you find. The verbal identifications are not acceptable. Marceau Badeau, the Cobbler, is not known in the local US Military Intelligence HQ. But word will get around with the help of Shaw, Parker and the Resistance."

"My darling, we are still at a shooting war and France is not liberated yet. As long as we are alive, there is hope! Let's just wait. I know you want to help Michael, but you are thinking with passion instead of logic."

"I can't help that. I love Michael. I miss him terribly."

"I can understand, my dear. Something good will happen, you'll see!"

Ten days went by and a US soldier came to the shop and asked Marceau and his daughter to come tomorrow morning at 0800 to the Military HQ Intelligence Section and meet with Captain Howard.

The next morning Marceau and Bridget left for the meeting. They prepared a sufficient number of documents to verify their identities and affiliations with the Allied Intelligence and the French Resistance. Both of them looked exhausted and disgusted. They had more than enough with the search for documents on the top of Marceau's illness, treatments, and the stresses of the war.

"Good Morning to you both. You are very punctual," greeted Captain Howard.

"Good Morning. We hope it will not take too long this interview. I failed to tell you that Marceau is in the advanced stage of leukemia and I don't know how long can he function in a sitting position," said Bridget.

"We planned for, give and take, three hours for the entire interview and checking the documents," said Captain Howard. "But under these circumstances, we will expedite the hearing and verification of the documents. I have done some preliminary research and MI6 said nothing but the best of Marceau and highly appraised Bridget for her devotion, cooperation, and tireless efforts. But I must present to our Military Intelligence a coherent picture of your involvement of intelligence during the past two years."

"I think the best and fastest way to get Marceau to rest is to start the interview now in the presence of a stenographer," said Captain Howard.

"I'm ready," said Marceau.

"Please tell us when you want to rest. I have some water, coffee, tea, hot chocolate, and cookies for you that will be on the table next to you shortly. Should you feel sick, we will stop and continue later or on another day. Is that o.k. with you Marceau?" asked the Captain.

"It is all right with me. You are very kind and considerate."

"My first question is who trained you to become a courier for the Allied Intelligence?"

"I was trained by the British MI6."

"How did you collect and transmit all the information?"

"I was connected with the French Resistance, British MI6 agents, and OSS agents, and a German Officer who provided all the messages in person, courier service, and my assumed daughter, Bridget. You will hear her story in a separate interview.

"I was allowed by the German Generals to go crab fishing and the artificial bait contained the microfilm that the Allied Intelligence mini-sub picked up."

"What role did the German officer play in your collection of military information?"

"He supplied verbal and written military strategies and documentation of the batteries, guns, camouflage casemates, military plans, and Gestapo raids in the planning stages.

"Did you authenticate his information?"

"Yes, I did authenticate it with the help of OSS, MI6 and the Resistance."

"I assume the various forms of information checked out positive?"

"Yes, indeed. He tried very hard to give us the most authentic and valuable information."

"In your assessment, why did we succeed so well in the Atlantic Wall intelligence?"

"Well, we had two highly intelligent, well-prepared, perfect French and German speaking OSS and MI6 agents, who brilliantly masqueraded as Todt Organization engineers. Our French Resistance organization provided terrific spies who collected detailed information about various batteries, bunkers, casemates, pill boxes, mine fields, and underground interconnecting tunnels. OSS and MI6 field agents independently searched for information by making friends with German generals and officers. These well prepared agents were also protectors of the operatives of the Resistance. We had the best trained commandos and reconnaissance pilots. We were able to decipher the German codes because we had the Enigma machine. But our human intelligence and cooperation with each other played the most important roles in succeeding to beat the Atlantic Wall."

"Your identity documents are being processed right now. Your secret number of your MI6 affiliation will be my confidential inquiry and I shall contact them at the end of our discussion."

"I would like you to have a few minutes respite and enjoy our refreshments."

Marceau and Bridget started to snack a little bit when Captain Howard informed Marceau that his identity papers and affiliation with Allied Intelligence checked out.

After a half hour respite, Captain Howard continued the interview.

"Monsieur Marceau, do you have any additional comments?"

"Yes. We had a very fortunate turn of events. I very strongly believe that Michael, the German officer, should not only be pardoned from POW status but decorated with an award for his heroic deeds."

"I will need all the information and documentation about him. I will personally act on behalf of your request. This is the best I can offer about Michael."

"I trust you, Captain Howard, that you will do your best. Thank you very much for your cooperation."

"Thank you, Monsieur Marceau, for coming here in your condition and participating in this interview. We wish you the best, good health, and recovery from your illness. Our meeting is over. Would you like to lie down on a cot or return home with our medic?"

"I'm fine. With all the refreshments, I think I can wait for Bridget until she completes her interview with you. This chair is good enough. Thank you. You are very considerate."

It was Bridget's turn. She was ready to answer all the questions when a soldier handed an envelope to Captain Howard. The envelope was a message sent from MI6.

"Marceau as well as Bridget, Marceau's 'assumed daughter,' are under our protection.

Some of their answers to your questions may be sensitive. Please extend utmost courtesy since their contributions to Allied Intelligence, especially to MI6 have been invaluable. Captain Howard called back the soldier and asked to authenticate the message. It was approved within five minutes.

"Mademoiselle Bridget, we have verified most of the information about you and your honorable activities for Allied Intelligence. We have only a couple of questions to ask. One has to do with your friend Michael. Have you considered petitioning the US Army for his release?" asked Captain Howard.

"I did not have the knowledge on how to go about it. But if you would be kind enough and inform me on how to proceed, I would be very thankful to you."

"My other question is about the news organizations. Did you tell anyone about Michael's conversion and collaboration with the Allies? We are concerned about his welfare. Some of the German POW's may hurt him if they find out about his activities. The safest thing is to have all yours and his intelligence activities on hold until Michael is freed and France liberated from the Germans and insurgents."

"Thank you for this suggestion. We shall hold our tongues until it is safe. I would appreciate it if you would be kind enough to supply me with the official POW petition documents. We would also like to get in touch with you for future reference. Is there a quick way to contact you wherever you are going to be stationed?"

"Just contact the Military Intelligence Services. They know where to find me. Do you have any other questions?"

"I don't believe so."

"Thank you for our conference. Our meeting is over."

Bridget drove home with Marceau in relatively good spirits but physically fatigued. They were happy that the interviews were cut short and less stressful than they had anticipated.

Their stay was cut short because Marceau badly needed a blood transfusion. She told Marceau that they would to the hospital in Cherbourg. Bridget suggested that he should lie down in the back seat of the car and go to sleep until they got there. As she opened the door, there was a note on the shop's floor. It was from Shaw, "He, Parker, and Susan were planning to visit them tomorrow afternoon. In case you are busy, phone us in this number."

Bridget drove to Cherbourg quite fast because Marceau's condition worsened. In the hospital, he received emergency treatment and the doctors insisted that he should stay overnight. She stayed with Marceau and slept on a gurney because there was no other accommodation. She did not want to go back to her friend's place, and there was no empty bed in the hospital.

By the morning, Marceau felt a little better. The doctors were quite concerned with his deteriorating illness. Unfortunately, there were no miracle drugs to cure his leukemia.

He was sent home, but she was told to bring him back early next week. Bridget was very upset and had a hard time to hide it. She wanted to cry but not in front of Marceau. It was a blessing to have their friends coming that day.

Shaw and Parker came early that afternoon, but Susan couldn't make it till early evening. The reunion was very emotional. They all hugged each other. For minutes they just looked at each other but their silence bespoke their concern about Marceau who looked yellowish, pale, thin, and breathing slowly.

"Oh, cut it out. I know, I have a sickly look, but my mind is still functional. You guys, however, look fabulously good and rested," said Marceau.

"You are still sharp and kind. We know you are fighting the disease and we understand your circumstances. Bridget, however, looks good and keeps your spirit up!" said Shaw.

"Well, sit down, and tell us what's happening in your lives," asked Marceau.

"Where is Susan?" asked Bridget.

"She'll be here in a few hours. Her boss asked her to take care of an errand," said Parker.

"I went home and had a wonderful time with my family. My God, it was almost two years ago that I had hugged my wife and kissed my children. Returning home was an awesome feeling. The kids have grown, my wife looked more beautiful than ever, and the food tasted delicious. Apparently, as the saying goes, absence makes the heart grow fonder," said Shaw.

"I flew home on a military plane to see my family. We had a great time together. We talked about Susan and our forthcoming engagement. But the time was extremely short. Traveling took half the vacation time, but I had a chance to be with my sister and brothers," said Parker.

"So what are you doing now?" asked Bridget.

"We have been temporarily reassigned to watch the insurgents by mixing with the people. This job will last until France is totally liberated. After that who knows."

"Susan has a similar position but she is a collector of information. I am right now in various places and Susan is more centralized, and in one place," said Parker.

"How about you, Shaw?" asked Bridget.

"I was also reassigned into France. I am working on secret German nuclear projects that were well hidden," said Shaw.

"Well, let's wait for Susan, we'll celebrate our reunion together," suggested Marceau.

"How about all of us going out somewhere for dinner?" asked Parker.

"I honestly don't know if any restaurant is open. The gunpowder still smells in the air," said Bridget. "Well, we can try calling a few places," said Parker.

"The lines are still broken," replied Bridget.

"I can drive to the nearest places," suggested Parker.

"But if you don't succeed, we can eat here," said Bridget.

"That is a good idea," added Shaw.

Parker went for a ride to find out about the availabilities of restaurant dining, Marceau excused himself and laid down for a nap, and Shaw turned on the radio and listened to the BBC world service for the news.

Parker came back and happily announced that he found a small mom and pop place which offered limited dining. This meant mostly fish. He tentatively made reservations for seven o'clock.

Susan happened to come earlier than expected and there were lots of hugs and joy. She was happy to see Marceau in any shape or form as long as he was alive. She was fond of Marceau as a human being and loved to hear him talk about his philosophies.

"Come and give me a hug and kiss, Susan. You are my favorite listener, like a little child in kindergarten," said Marceau.

"Yes, I'm your student and you are my favorite teacher. Marceau, you are the most aspiring person I've ever met. I hear your voice wherever I go. You really light my fire! I am so happy to see you again. I was afraid that I would be reassigned to another country and we would occasionally see each other. I am sorry that you're not feeling well but hope that some new drugs will be released soon and I'll be the first one to get it for you," said Susan.

"This would be just wonderful. I hope your wish will come true. In the meantime, however, I must have transfusions to keep me alive."

Susan sat closer to Marceau and took his left hand with a passionate touch. She began gently to pat his hand and sang a song about hope. It was a very moving scene and Shaw and Parker joined Susan to sing along. Bridget was standing in the corner and watching how the three of them made his pain more bearable. Marceau's eyes filled with tears, he opened his arms and tried to give a hug to everybody around him.

"I love you Marceau," said Susan.

"I love you too."

It was time to leave, and Bridget helped Marceau to put on a jacket. Marceau always liked to dress up for dining in a restaurant. He was formal and respectful for his company. Bridget has always been cognizant of Marceau's wardrobe needs. She has never selected a jacket without his approval.

Parker was driving the car and Marceau was flanked by Susan and Bridget in the back seat. It only took ten minutes to get to the restaurant. They arrived a little bit earlier, but the owner had a table for them.

"Bon Soiree Madame et Messieurs," said the owner. The table was decorated with candles and some artificial greens. He provided a simple menu and suggested a vintage wine from the cellar which happened to be his only bottle because the German soldiers practically emptied his inventory.

The choice of food was simple. Everybody comported to have onion soup, flounder, potatoes, veggies, and crepe suzette. They also had homemade French bread with butter.

"I am just delighted that we have such a good common taste. The food indeed was prepared and cooked superbly," said Marceau.

"I couldn't agree with you more," commented Susan.

"Who are the insurgent?" asked Bridget.

"Insurgents are German officers who speak fluent French, shed their uniforms, and mix with the citizens, or French citizens who supported the Vichy government and are pro Nazi," explained Shaw.

"So how do they make trouble?" was her other question.

"They can incite the population against the Allies, engage in sabotage and killing, spy on military matters, and in general, impede the liberation of France," replied Shaw.

"What do you do with them?" asked Marceau.

"We have to assess the situation. Not all liberated towns are normalized in terms of law enforcement, others are fine but lack jurisprudence. We have a tough situation. So in the interim, Allied military police must do the arrests and holding of the prisoners. As soon as the French court is established in a particular town, the prisoner is transferred and prosecuted," said Shaw.

"Our job is to catch them, sometimes to hold them until police or military police takes over. During the hold, we are identifying and interrogating the prisoners. It is surprising how many Nazi sympathizers we find," said Parker.

"We are also discovering a lot of atrocities committed by the French under the Vichy regime. People were brutal. Some Resistance operatives, French Jews, and Allied Commandos were hidden in private homes, apartments, farms and hospitals. Some French Nazi collaborators took all kinds of valuables from the keepers to not reveal to the Gestapo their hiding places. Others demanded sex and beat them with sticks. There were some random killings by some hate monger psychopaths," said Susan.

"What happens to these perpetrators?" asked Bridget.

"We'll transfer them to the liberated French civil court at the appropriate time," said Susan.

"Why are they terrorizing? It's a lost cause," said Bridget.

"These people don't want to think that it's a lost cause. They call it a temporary setback. They believe in ultimate victory. Hitler told them never to give up; hope for a better tomorrow. The Allies will have a devastating defeat and they will be driven back to the sea," said Parker.

"Fool, fools, what fools. The Axis already lost the war. Between the Russians and the Allies, they don't stand a chance," said Marceau.

"The Nazis believe that a super weapon will prevail and wipe out the enemy," said Shaw.

Two guys entered the restaurant and without asking the owner to be seated, demanded to have dinner. The owner explained to the guys that he is technically closed and this was a private party and he has no more food to serve. They did not accept the decline of service and began to curse the owner and the Allied landings.

"Do you have any problems with the Allied forces?" asked Parker.

"You bet we do," sneered one of the guys. He continued "We had no problems under the Vichy regime. We like National Socialism, and will do anything to chase out the Allies."

Parker asked them for their identifications while Susan called the military police. The guys refused and became belligerent. One of the guys tried to knock out Parker but Shaw stepped in and pushed the man away while Parker reached for his gun and made both guys put their hands on their heads.

Shaw handcuffed both guys and told them that they were under arrest.

"Who the hell are you?" asked one of the guys.

"We are agents of Allied Intelligence and you'll be transferred to the military police," said Shaw.

"You have no jurisdiction over us," said one of the guys.

"That is why we will transfer you," said Parker.

"What is the charge of my arrest?"

"You wanted to strike, meaning attempted battery and disorderly conduct. Plus we have to check your insurgency background. Right now you are under military rule," said Shaw.

The two guys were taken away by the MPs and their reunion continued without any trouble. The owner turned on a radio that was tuned in to a British station, playing jazz. The radio played 'Serenade in Blue.' Parker asked Susan to dance and Shaw did the same with Bridget. Marceau was delighted to see how these young folks were enjoying themselves. After the dance they all chatted and drank wine.

Marceau began to feel more tired than usual and asked Bridget to accompany him home. Bridget recognized the signs of his fatigue and asked Parker if he would be kind enough and drive them to the hospital for an immediate blood transfusion. They all joined in to go to the hospital.

Marceau received an emergency treatment in the hospital. The attending doctor called Bridget into his office where he expressed concern about his deteriorating health. Not much was offered, however, in terms of treatment other than what he had been receiving. He suggested finding Marceau his specialist in Caen.

Parker offered to drive to Caen but in the war torn city there was little hope finding the doctor. Telephone connections were still out of service in many places. The hospital in Caen could not locate the doctor. Marceau and Bridget, upon the suggestion of the attending physician, decided to stay in the hospital overnight and Parker offered his help to pick them up the next day. Shaw and Susan could not return because special assignments were waiting for them.

Parker was accommodated by military intelligence overnight on an undisclosed military base. He was able to get in touch with some officers in Caen and they made some inquiry on behalf of Marceau. It was found that his specialist returned to the city but had no office to practice. His place was bombed out. Parker was told that the doctor would see Marceau in the hospital. They set the time for 1100 the next day.

Parker arrived to the Caen hospital at 0800. Marceau had a brief exit exam before his release. Before departure they all had breakfast in the hospital's cafeteria. Parker was concerned with the hospital facilities, availabilities of medication, and treatment opportunities in Caen. The city was pretty much destroyed by all the shelling from both sides.

"I wonder if we could send Marceau to London?" said Parker.

"Waste of time and money," said Marceau.

"Why do you say that?" asked Parker.

"Because my condition is fairly advanced and there is no medication that could reverse the process," replied Marceau.

"There are always some experimental drugs. You don't have the access here to find anything at the present time. You have to be in a British or American hospital to receive the support of pharmacological specialists. You need the consultation of a cancer specialist, hematologists, and internists. You don't have these opportunities here," said Parker.

"So how do we go about it?" was Bridget's question.

"Shaw and I will take care of his admission. Shaw knows his way around in medical circles. His brother-in-law is a medical scientist in London. Let's get through this visit in Caen and I will contact Shaw to get the ball rolling."

Marceau kept quiet. Bridget saw a glimmer of hope.

"God bless you, Parker! I think you should go for it," said Bridget.

Marceau had a one hour examination by his old physician and he very much concurred with the idea to transfer Marceau to a London specialist.

Parker contacted Shaw and OSS for help. Shaw called London MI6, and requested urgent medical assistance for Marceau. The replies came astonishingly fast within three hours. The OSS offered fifty percent of transportation, hospital, and medical expenses, while MI6 picked up the other fifty percent plus arranged the recruitment of a specialist, hospital admission, and military medical air travel transportation which included a nurse, two aids, and two pilots. For the return flight, however, Bridget may accompany Marceau. She can travel by military plane to London, stay in a designated hotel, consult with the medical doctors and nurses, receive adequate supply of medication, and fly back with Marceau a few days later.

This sounded like a dream. Without any hesitancy, Marceau and Bridget agreed to the offer and began to prepare for the departure. Thanks to both agencies, they were absolutely superb in expediting Marceau's treatment. Shaw and Parker also deserve commendation for their prompt intervention and action.

A military messenger delivered the departure schedule, the name of the hospital and the content of the luggage as a carry on. For Marceau's return, Bridget has to call the hospital from a British Military HQ.

Marceau's departure was scheduled for the next day at 0500 from his home. He'll be driven by military ambulance to the Cherbourg US military airport. From there, he'll fly to London. There he will be accompanied by a military nurse and taken by ambulance to The Institute of Cancer Research of The College of the University of London.

Upon his arrival, he was well received by the physicians and nurses. He was told the first day that his condition had reached a terminal phase and they would do their best to prolong his life.

Being a patient in a research hospital, however, suggested a glimmer of hope. The second day, he was subjected to a powerful experimental drug. This made him very sick. But he was told in advance, that most experimental drugs will induce some side effects and he will not die from them. The test continued for three days and the results were promising. A week went by without any serious side effects. Bridget was informed of Marceau's progress and was told to prepare for his homecoming. She was asked to take Marceau home. She was ready to fly the next day, but because of a storm, they postponed her departure until the weather cleared up and a seat would be available on the military transport plane.

Marceau, however, again became sick, but his leukemia started to improve. His white cell counts went down considerably. For the medical community, this was a scientific breakthrough.

But, the doctors were puzzled by the nature of the drug that made him so ill. He lost most of his appetite and hardly ate. There was a fear indeed that he'll emaciate to a critical point where the drug and not the leukemia would kill him.

Unfortunately reduced dosage of the drug will allow the cancer to advance. Bridget was notified to hold off her departure for a few more days because Marceau was not in any condition to return home.

Marceau had to gain some weight before another experimental drug was applied.

By the end of the week he was given another try, but the preliminary results were negative and the doctors discontinued with the second experimental drug until Marceau's condition improved.

There was a suggestion by some doctors that the first experimental drug should be given periodically to prolong his life. But the toxicity of the drug was so overwhelming that the doctors were afraid of the consequences. The dilemma on how to help Marceau became an academic and political issue.

The consensus of the doctors was to find some means to reduce the drug's toxicity and to let Marceau go home. Since the drug was working well, there was a chance that reduced toxicity could prolong Marceau's life. Marceau will be immediately notified when the research pharmacologists solve the toxicity problem and he'll be brought back to the Institute.

Bridget was optimistic but Marceau doubted that he would survive long enough to benefit from the modified drug treatment.

"I'll never make it. I am too sick to wait for the result."

"You never know. We'll take care of you in the meantime. You'll receive some more transfusions."

They both thanked the doctors for the try and superb care. The plane was waiting for them and both were taken by ambulance to the airport.

At the last minute, one of the doctors offered a small bottle of research pills with instructions and asked Marceau to take it twice a day. He must report back by phone in two weeks about the result.

"I promise to call you in two weeks. You are very kind and really are trying to save my life."

The doors of the ambulance were shut and the soldier drove quickly to the airport. The plane ride home was bouncy and uncomfortable. The turbulence over the Channel was quite bad and Marceau threw up a couple of times.

Bridget kept busy with the household and nursing Marceau. Her thoughts, however never left Michael. She made several inquiries about his capture and whereabouts from US Military HQ but she failed to get any promising information.

She was getting depressed when news came from Susan about her search for Michael.

She came to visit Marceau and Bridget for a couple of hours.

"We know that Michael is a POW in France. We found some documentation that indicated that a number of German officers are in POW camps scattered in coastal towns. At this point, in time it is a secret to release names of officers because some of these officers were engaged in V1 and V2 bombings, or in other military technology that is valuable information for the Allies. The German military tries to kidnap these guys under the guise of Allied uniforms so their technological know how can be utilized again," said Susan.

"Well, I wouldn't know where to begin with searching for Michael. Besides, I will not leave Marceau. Definitely not in the condition he is in."

"So take him with you."

"He cannot travel now. He is too weak."

"Well, maybe he will regain some of his strength."

"Susan, you are very kind. But, I am not optimistic. He has been taking experimental drugs and so far there is little improvement. The side effects are killing him. What's new with you?" asked Bridget.

"I am going to be decorated for saving the lives of the commandos and risking my life."

"Congratulations. When is the ceremony?"

"No ceremony, just a medal. I will be a notch from Captain."

"I am proud of you. You and Parker will make a nice couple. Any future plans?"

"We are in the planning stages now. Sometime in early fall we'll fly home and have an engagement party in my parent's place."

"I wish Michael and I could be there."

"You will. You are my closest friend."

Marceau woke up from his sleep and excused himself from being asocial. Susan pulled up a chair and set next to him, holding his hand and looking at him with a smile.

"I hope you had pleasant dreams."

"Oh, yes my dear. I dreamed about angels, like you."

"Aren't you sweet, Marceau. I love you so much that I had to see you, even for a short time. You are our sunshine. You have always something positive to say. You break through the darkest clouds."

Susan hardly finished the sentence when she heard a strange rough hoarse noise. He fell back on the couch. Susan tried to prop him up by holding his back and making it easier for him to breath.

"Marceau, what's the matter?" asked Susan with a frightened voice.

Marceau did not give an answer. Bridget came over looked at his eyes, palpated his neck artery and said, "He fainted. It is quite common with him in the past three months."

"Is there anything we can do?" asked Susan.

"Yes, we can pray. His brain is getting less and less oxygen. I am afraid Marceau will not last long."

"I am calling Shaw and Parker to have another union before he passes," said Susan.

"Thank you."

"When will your telephone be installed?" asked Susan.

"The telephone company promised to come tomorrow."

"Where is the nearest phone?"

"Next door. My neighbor would not mind if you use her phone."

"It is long distance, but I am under military compensation. The operator will connect me."

Susan gave a kiss to Marceau's forehead and said bye to Bridget. She walked over to the neighbor, made the call to Shaw and left for home.

Shaw, Parker, and Susan agreed to see Marceau the next evening. She drove to Marceau's the next morning and told Bridget that they will be visiting in the evening and will provide for dinner. Marceau, surprisingly, was cheerful but only for minutes, because he collapsed again on the couch. Bridget gave him his medication but he was still gasping for air. It was a pathetic moment of roller-coaster emotions for all of them.

Susan left the place hurriedly because she had a meeting to attend. In the late afternoon she went to see her hairdresser, and then went shopping for dinner. She did not forget Marceau's favorite French wine, mussels, and whipped cream pastry.

It was seven-thirty when everybody sat down to the dinner table. Mussels with butter were the appetizer. Bridget made an excellent French onion soup with cheese. She served it in a special soup bowl that she seldom used in the past. While she poured the soup, Shaw lit the candles. The table, decorated with a white tablecloth and flowers, looked extremely festive.

While the filet mignon was broiled outside on an open fire, Marceau became overwhelmed by the gourmet dinner and fancy serving. He could not help but to remark,

"My friends, I feel that tonight is our last supper together."

"Come on Marceau, you should not say that," said Shaw.

"I want to make a toast," offered Marceau.

"Let's hear it," said Susan.

"I want to make this toast to everybody's health and happiness. Many thanks for your tireless sacrifice you exhibited for the liberation of France and Europe. May God bless you all," said Marceau.

There was a loud applause by everyone. Susan went to Marceau and gave him a kiss on his cheek.

Parker brought in the filet mignon from the fire which looked absolutely divine.

They were glazed with butter and served with pommes frites and asperge with crème sauce.

"The wine tastes superb. I just love it. It is my medicine," remarked Marceau.

"Good, we are so happy to please you," said Susan.

"May I have your attention, before you serve the dessert," said Marceau.

"By all means," answered Parker.

"I really appreciate this elaborate and delicious dinner, but in my condition, I have a difficult time finishing what was served. For this I apologize. But I want to talk about something else. I know you can observe that my illness is about to end my life. It was a long and painful struggle. Maybe some day doctors will be able to cure bone marrow leukemia. But for now, they don't have the means to tackle the problem."

"I want to thank you from the bottom of my heart for what you have done for my country and the rest of the world to overcome tyranny. I am terribly grateful to Bridget, who was my closest support at work, home, and the Resistance. She was more than my daughter, she was my confidante. I wish her a healthy long life and happiness. I hope she finds Michael and will reinstate him before the Allied Command so he can be recognized as one of the fighters for the Allied cause."

"I want each of you to carry the torch of freedom, because we are heading toward a very difficult time. Although science is trying to replace human intelligence by electronic means, you must never sacrifice electronics for human one-to-one intelligence.

"Please fight for freedom, democracy, and human dignity. I know you will do it!

May God bless you all!" said Marceau.

"We'll promise to keep your words in our mind and heart. We shall carry out your wish to our best abilities. We'll never let you down! God be with you!" said Shaw.

Bridget and Susan went over to Marceau, embraced him and they all cried together.

There was a ten minute silence and Parker proposed to serve the whipped crème dessert that Marceau liked so much, Crème plaisir. It was a square piece of thin, fluffy top and bottom pastries, sandwiched in between an inch layer of custard and the same layer of whipped cream.

Marceau looked at it, and stared at it for a while. He took the dessert fork and had only two small bites.

"What a shame, what a pity, but I cannot enjoy the rest. Thank you," said Marceau. "By the way, where did you get this filet mignon?"

"It's a military secret," replied Shaw.

"We have no military secrets among each other. You should know better," said Marceau.

"We found a farmer who was butchering his cow," said Parker.

"Was she blonde or brunette?" asked Marceau.

"We love your humor. Yes, she was a blonde. A delightful daughter of a farmer who offered the meat as a token of appreciation for the liberation of France," said Parker.

"I knew it, I knew it. With Parker it had to be a woman. He knows how to charm. And Susan will vouch for it," said Marceau.

"You are something else," said Susan.

Marceau waited for ten minutes then asked Bridget to help him to lie down on the couch. He became quiet. Susan took her chair and sat beside him. She held his hand when Marceau began to gasp for air. He became silent. His fingers slowly turned white and his hand felt cold. His face gradually changed from white to ash white and he stopped breathing. Susan tried to sit him up and yelled his name twice. Bridget joined her to help him breathe but to no avail. At that point, Bridget bent down and gave Marceau mouth to mouth resuscitation, but nothing helped. He had expired.

Parker touched his neck artery and declared him dead. Bridget and Susan were sobbing and Shaw and Parker had tears in their eyes. Everybody remained silent. After twenty minutes, Bridget declared that they had to make plans for his funeral.

"I will inform MI6 about Marceau's death," said Shaw.

"I will do the same for OSS tomorrow," said Parker.

"I am also going to call the head of Resistance," said Bridget.

"The best plan is to wait until we hear from the Resistance and Allied Intelligence in terms of their contributions to the funeral," said Shaw.

Everybody seemed to agree with Shaw's suggestion. Bridget called the funeral home and Marceau's body was removed within one hour and stored for the preparations the next day.

There was a feeling of tremendous loss in everybody's heart. Shaw and Parker stayed for a while, but Susan remained with Bridget overnight.

Bridget put a sign in the shop window about closing the store because of a death in the family.

It was a restless night for Bridget and she awoke several times during the night. The feeling was unbearable to lose Marceau, the uncertainty of Michael's whereabouts, and to live alone. She asked Susan to stay, but she had to go back to her post.

The next morning at ten o'clock, Shaw and Parker informed Bridget that all funeral arrangements will be underwritten by Allied Intelligence. At the same time, a special delegation from the Resistance offered a plot and flower arrangements.

Bridget went to Marceau's attorney for her eleven o'clock appointment and asked him to open his will. There were a few surprises that Marceau never talked about. One of them was his burial site. Marceau requested to be buried at sea within French territorial waters. Most of his assets went to Bridget and the rest was divided between his children, past girlfriend and charities. He left a fairly detailed description that his lawyer had to work with. Marceau even included the attorney's fee in the will.

She did not spend any more time at the lawyer's than she had to. Bridget rushed back home to meet the telephone service men to reconnect the phone. With the new phone she called Shaw and Parker and told them about Marceau's burial request.

Shaw and Parker came down in the afternoon to discuss the funeral arrangements. Shaw suggested having him buried from a fishing vessel by three British sailors, three American commandos, and three Resistance agents. This idea was unanimously accepted. Shaw got on the phone and started to make the preparations. Parker embraced Bridget who broke down in tears and became despondent. Susan came to help Bridget and take over some of the chores that Bridget set forth for the afternoon. Bridget had to make several calls to inform the Resistance about the funeral arrangements, representations of Resistance dignitaries, Marceau's friends, and relatives. Because of several technical difficulties it was complicated to get in touch with people in a short time. Transportation was another problem because of war conditions.

The funeral arrangements, however, progressed smoothly and the plans called for a burial at sea in forty-eight hours. The time was set at 10 o'clock in the morning.

One of the largest fishing vessels was offered by a fisherman. At the pier, the crowd began to assemble around 0915 hour but only the members of the family, best friends, delegates and dignitaries were allowed on the ship.

When the hearse delivered the body, it was put on six scallop traps and covered by a long French flag. The MI6, OSS, and Resistance delegation made a five minute speech.

It was followed by Shaw, Parker, and Bridget, whose heart wrenching words made everybody cry. The service ended by a prayer and eulogy of the local priest.

The body was flanked and lifted by three British navy seamen, three American commandos, and facing the front, three Resistance operatives. They slowly moved up on the gangplank, followed by Bridget, Shaw, Parker, and dignitaries from Allied Intelligence, Resistance, and the priest. There were British, American, and French soldiers with rifles behind the body bearers.

The ship's whistle sounded off three times and the vessel slowly began to move out of the harbor. An accordion player accompanied the departure by playing the French National Anthem.

The ship sailed a few miles from the harbor and stopped. The body was lifted, slanted and held toward the sea. The priest made a short prayer and it was followed by a three gun salute. The body bag held by the Resistance operators was lowered and splashed into the sea. First Bridget, then Shaw, and Parker threw a summer bouquet into the sea. There was a moment of silence. The ship's whistle sounded off three times again and the vessel returned to the harbor.

The people began to disassemble, but Bridget stayed and sat down in her black dress on one of the harbor benches. Susan, Shaw, and Parker accompanied her. They were all silent, and the feeling of permanent loss began to sink in. Bridget stared at the sea with a very sad and longing heart. She began to sob louder and louder. Then, she called his name "Marceau, Marceau, my dear Marceau."

Parker embraced Bridget. She began to calm down and allowed him to take her to his car. They all left the harbor for Marceau's house. There were three food baskets sent by OSS, MI6, and the Resistance waiting for Bridget in front of the store. They were delivered by the US and British Military HQ. Neighbors and friends of Marceau and Bridget came with food and flowers to express their condolences.

The visitation lasted well into the evening, but Bridget had to excuse herself. She began to feel emotionally exhausted and went to the other room to lie down. The friends slowly began to depart and the house became quiet. Shaw and Parker kissed her good night and left. Susan stayed overnight with her.

Bridget had a restless night and Susan helped her to bear the loss. In the morning both had breakfast and went for a short walk. Susan was allowed to stay for three days, but she was allowed to stay longer if Bridget needed assistance. It was part of the Office of Strategic Services contribution.

By the third day, Bridget composed herself well enough to stay by herself. Susan promised to return the next weekend and stay with her for a couple of days. A phone call from Vivian, her close friend from Port-En-Bessin cheered her up and they spent the evening together at another friend's house for dinner. Eve was a fellow Resistance operative who often helped Bridget with difficult tasks.

"It would be a good idea just to go sightseeing in another part of the liberated France," said Vivian.

"I agree wholeheartedly, it will do Bridget a lot of good," added Eve.

They decided to pack up that weekend and head for Ste. Mere-Eglise. Bridget was quite excited about the trip. She could not remember the last time she had been on an excursion. She also had an enigmatic superstition about the trip. Bridget spent most of her days on paying old bills, executing parts of his will, and finding a shoemaker to finish the jobs Marceau accepted and started before the invasion.

As the weekend approached she became preoccupied with memories of Michael and Marceau. She knew Michael was alive, but since she had not heard about him as promised, she became less emboldened and more anxious. She was, however, holding on, like someone holding onto a twig in a fast current. A new place to visit meant a faint of hope.

It was a few minutes after nine on Saturday morning. Vivian and Eve were already waiting outside when Bridget, with a small luggage, left the house.

"Come on, Bridget, we are waiting for you," yelled Vivian. Vivian put her luggage in the trunk and asked her to sit next to her. All three girls looked fresh and charming, ready to take on a little adventure.

"Are you hungry, because I had no breakfast," asked Eve.

"Not really. I didn't have too much for breakfast, but I will gladly join you," said Bridget.

"I am not familiar with this area, so I'll stop at the next coffeehouse," said Vivian.

She drove about ten miles when she saw a sign 'Chez Charles Coffee' but as she approached the diner there was a 'closed' sign in the window. Vivian stepped on the gas and drove a few more miles when she saw a bunch of cars, trucks, and US military vehicles parked in front of a diner.

"How does this place strike you?" asked Vivian.

"I hope we can get fast service! I am starving," replied Eve.

They left the vehicle and entered the diner. Some guys whistled, turned their faces, and one jumped out of his seat, put his napkin on his elbow, and politely asked, "Can I help you?"

"We need a table for three," said Vivian.

"This is no problem," said the make believe waiter and directed them toward his table with two more guys already sitting.

"We need a private table," said Eve.

He withdrew and left the girls to hunt for a table. The owner of the place helped them by bringing a table from the storage and removing three empty chairs from other tables.

"Anything for pretty ladies," said the owner smilingly.

The waitress, however, was exceedingly slow setting the table and taking orders. After fifteen minutes of waiting, she brought three glasses of fresh water, coffee, and croissants.

Eve ordered eggs, Vivian crepes, and Bridget muffins. The food was excellent and each of them savored every bite.

The owner of the diner approached them again and asked them about his food. Of course, the answer was positive. From his look, he was attracted to Eve, and asked them to consider returning for dinner, but on the house. Vivian answered, "Maybe," to which the owner kissed her hand and handed to each a little pastry package for the road.

"Come again, you charming ladies. We are waiting to serve you!" said the owner.

"What a charmer," said Bridget.

"You have a chance, Eve. He could not take his eyes off you. I think he was very, very attracted to you," said Vivian.

"Did you see the ring on his finger?" asked Eve.

"That does not mean a thing until you know why he is wearing it. Perhaps he wears it because it belonged to his mother, he is a widower, separated, divorced, or who knows," replied Vivian.

"Do you want to come back to find out?" asked Eve.

"It all depends, what route we'll take to come back, or where we'll dine tomorrow. Besides, you already have a guy who knows how to please you," said Vivian.

"There is always somebody better. He is just for pleasure. I don't know if I love him because he is not a devoted guy. I think he likes variety in women. I cannot trust him. He is good for a couple of hours," said Eve.

"I think, sex without love is never lasting," commented Bridget.

"Unless you are addicted to the guy," replied Eve.

"There is no perfect situation," added Vivian.

"Sex addiction is like craving for the smell, taste, touch, sound, and sight. All the basic sensations and perceptions are involved. It can be totally satisfying and pleasuring," said Eve. Then she added, "I have this guy right now, but I feel empty in my heart when he leaves. He only lasts for a short time after pleasuring. But a couple of days later, I began to imagine, and develop the desire to see him. He comes and drives me nuts with his touch."

"I did not know that you are so much into sex," said Bridget.

"Not less than you are with Michael," said Eve.

"There is a difference. I love Michael," said Bridget.

"But you also love his body, don't you?" asked Eve.

"You can bet I do very much. But love fused with sex is a different experience. You are longing for the body and soul simultaneously," said Bridget.

"We are at the outskirts of Ste. Mere-Eglise," said Vivian.

"This place is historic in terms of US parachute drops. Many guys were killed on the way of descent and when they landed. One soldier's parachute caught on the steeple of the church, another landed in a burning house and exploded, still others were shot while they were hanging on tree branches," said Bridget.

"What happened to the guy whose parachute was caught on the steeple of the church?" asked Vivian.

"Private John Steele played dead, but the Germans saw him moving and removed him. A stray bullet hit his foot and he was in agonizing pain. He became a German POW. Later on he was rescued by US forces," said Bridget.

"Poor guy, but at least he made it," said Eve.

"Anybody want to have another coffee before I park the car?" asked Vivian.

"I don't mind having another coffee and maybe something else," said Bridget.

"Very well, I will drive into town and find a coffeehouse," said Vivian.

She found a little unobtrusive roadside café, stopped the car, and all got out.

Bridget was the first to enter the café and she headed toward the powder room. Upon her return she stopped at the display window and was completely taken by the delicious looking pastries. She ordered a whipped crème chocolate torte and coffee. The rest had some coffee with coffee cake. They spent about a half hour in the café and Vivian drove into the middle of town, parked the car, and started walking.

It was a cloudy late summer day and still warm to have a long exhausting walk. Each girl stopped at the store windows, looked at the buildings, the bullet holes, the stripping paints, and some dilapidated places that were eyesores. The half-ruined buildings and stores were still left untouched. Some houses, however, were under construction. The invasion and the German forces fought a devastating battle and the war damaged businesses which had to be rebuilt before commerce could continue.

As they approached the site of the church where the massacre took place, everyone's heart began to throb faster and faster. They looked at the steeple and the front of the church and their minds replayed the scene of what happened. This was first hand knowledge and their imagination lit the way to reconstruct what happened.

As they looked up and around, a storekeeper approached them and told them that it was the most devastating fight of the invasion. He was witnessing what happened from his window that was overlooking the church.

"These boys did not have a chance. Some were shot in the air, and others as soon as they hit the ground," said the shopkeeper. "The Germans were mad and brutal, they did not want prisoners. It was their last hurrah," he added.

Vivian, Eve, and Bridget walked away from the church in a direction where they saw a large number of German POWs clearing the debris of several buildings and stores. It was a mixed feeling for them to see the enemy after experiencing the devastation. On one hand, they had to endure the harshness of prisoner status, but on the other hand, some were merciless and unfair fighters.

As the girls approached the sweaty, torn uniformed German POWs guarded by US soldiers, Bridget recognized the silhouette of Michael in the distance. He was picking up pieces of bricks. Her pace got faster and faster. She had her heart throbbing in her throat and the silhouette appeared into a form of Michael's face and body.

She began to yell his name, "Michael, Michael, it is me Bridget." He looked at her from the distance, stopped picking up the bricks, and could not believe what he saw. She was five feet from him and both just stood and looked at each other. Then she ran into his arms and they embraced each other.

At that point, the US guard stepped in and warned both of them to separate. She didn't listen and the guard touched her to split it up. At that point, she became absolutely furious and unmanageable.

"Do you know whom you are talking to? Do you know what this POW did for our country? I want to see your commanding officer right now, on the double. You understand?"

The guard took his whistle and blew it three times. Two guards came rushing in from the distance. They took Bridget by her arms and walked her to the lieutenant's office.

"I am sorry, Madam, but we are under regulations and I cannot permit you to have contact with our prisoners without permission," said the officer in charge.

"I am Bridget Badeau, the daughter of the late Marceau Badeau. I am a member of the French Resistance. Michael had been a very important contributor of Allied Intelligence. The Office of Strategic Services has been on the lookout finding him. Please get in touch with your Superior Officer to release him immediately into my custody."

"It will not be that simple Madam. We have to have verification. I can start the process but it will take some time before we can release him."

"May I use the telephone and contact the OSS right now?"

"You may use the phone, but we do not take orders from OSS."

"I know that. But you will be contacted faster by your military officer."

Bridget called the OSS officer who attended the funeral and told him that she found Michael and would appreciate it very much if he could intervene in his immediate release. The OSS representative assured her that in a few hours he will be released. He suggested talking with the officer to allow her to wait in his office for him.

The OSS representative talked for a few minutes with the POW officer and she was permitted to wait in his office for his release.

Eve was already engaged in talking with an officer and Vivian had a good time talking and laughing with several soldiers. When Bridget came out of the office to inform the girls about her waiting for Michael's release they were very cooperative and supportive.

The officer in charge informed Bridget that American Military Intelligence is about to arrive in an hour or so to clarify matters but it will take some time before the commandant of POW will agree to his release.

Bridget also asked the officer to allow her to call Shaw and Parker which was granted without any problem. She needed all the help for verification as was necessary.

As a matter of courtesy, Michael was allowed to leave his post and join Bridget in a separate room. He went first to the facilities to wash his face and hands then gave a very warm embrace and kiss to Bridget.

"I missed you so much, darling, it pained me," said Michael.

"You were always on my mind. I missed you terribly."

"I love you forever," said Michael.

"The feeling is mutual. I also love you very much."

They were in each other's arms, he had tears in his eyes, and she wept of happiness.

The door of the commanding officer opened and he informed Bridget that the representatives of the American Military Intelligence arrived and would have a consultation pretty soon. It was also added that representatives of British Military Intelligence will also join, but it will take some additional time.

"We have all the time in the world. We waited for the invasion much longer and suffered during that period, enough to bear this inconvenience," said Bridget.

The US Military Intelligence representatives shook hands with Bridget and Michael.

"This is Captain Tim O'Brian and I am Captain Steven McGregor."

"We must apologize for all your waiting and problems Madam Bridget but we have to go by the regulations and orders. I understand you are the daughter of the deceased Marceau, whom we respected and honored for all the help he provided for Allied Intelligence. May we express our heartfelt condolences on behalf of our Military Intelligence," said McGregor.

"We must go through some preliminaries, which means some paperwork if you don't mind," said Tim O'Brian.

"That is understandable. I don't mind at all."

"May we see your driver's license and any additional identification?" said McGregor.

Bridget presented her driver's license, her Resistance identification, and two letters written to her by OSS and MI6.

"I think they are more than enough. Why do you carry these two letters with you, if I may ask?" asked O'Brian.

"I know these are confidential letters, but they give me comfort and security."

While Bridget was questioned, Shaw and Parker arrived on behalf of OSS and MI6. Parker immediately intervened in the process of identification and Shaw followed.

"I put my professional career on the line to vouch not only for Bridget but Michael as well. I am Agent Parker from OSS and I spent over two years in Normandy to make this statement."

"I can say the same and I am certain that these people are who they claim to be. I also spent over two years in Normandy as a partner of Agent Parker. I am Agent Shaw from MI6."

"I want to thank you for your cooperation, but as you know quite well we are under strict regulations just as you are. Your vouchers are appreciated, but we are two separate organizations and I must also ask you for identifications. By the way, this is Captain McGregor and I am Captain O'Brian."

"I hope, sincerely hope, that your inquiry will be fast, because we are tired of this kind of bureaucracy. We put our lives on the line so you guys could come here and conduct this affair," said Parker.

"I am truly sorry if we hurt your feelings, but I must go through the procedures both with Bridget and Michael," said O'Brian.

Shaw and Parker, although agitated by the procedures, tried to compose themselves. They went outside the building and looked around for fifteen minutes then returned to Bridget.

"We will give all the support you guys need. We have been sent by our agencies as representatives," said Parker.

"Very well, please sign the papers here and I'll try to expedite this whole affair," said O'Brian.

"That is nice of you. Thank you," said Shaw.

O'Brian went to the other room and called his superior. He was instructed to conclude the meeting and allow Bridget and Michael to leave. He returned to the room and shook hands with Shaw and Parker. He promised that the whole procedure will end in ten minutes and after that both are allowed to leave.

"I am going to buy a pair of trousers and a shirt for Michael. I want him to throw his German uniform away," said Parker to Bridget.

Both Shaw and Parker began to shop around to find a store for trousers and shirts. A lady in a store overheard Parker's inquiry and offered her late husband's garments. The sizes were just right for Michael and Parker grabbed the offer. Shaw offered some British money but she accepted Parkers couple of dollars. When they returned Bridget and Michael were waiting for them on the street.

"Do you have a ride, or did you drive?" asked Parker of Bridget.

"We have a ride, but my friends are busy with the guys over there and I prefer not to interrupt their fun," said Bridget.

"We'll take you home. You guys deserve to be together and have privacy," said Shaw.

Shaw was driving and Parker sat next to him. Bridget and Michael sat in the back of the car.

"I have these garments for you. Please throw away your German uniform. You can change in the bathroom. I will go with you and ask for permission," said Parker. When they returned, Michael looked more like a tourist civilian, than a POW. They stopped for short a short time in a restaurant and had something to eat.

"I hope they treated you fairly as a POW," asked Parker.

"They did not beat me, but they let me know who I was."

"How about the food and accommodation?" asked Shaw.

"It certainly was not the Ritz-Carlton, but we were not starving. The food was bland. Housing was adequate, some slept on a mattresses, others on cots. They provided us with what was available under the circumstances," said Michael.

"You should have a medical exam and tomorrow I'll take you to Cherbourg to be checked out," said Parker.

"But I have no money or means to pay for it," said Michael.

"Don't worry. Allied Intelligence is paying for you. You will also get some money for your services. This will give you an opportunity to start your civilian life again," said Parker.

"Well, we hope your tummy is full so we can proceed for home. By the way, before I forget, you'll have a visitor in the afternoon," said Parker.

"Who is that?" asked Bridget.

"Susan is coming to town with a large food basket for you starving guys," answered Parker.

"We'll have a party in the evening," said Shaw.

"What kind of party?" asked Bridget.

"Allied Intelligence decided to throw a party for Michael

tomorrow, and honor him for his deeds at seven in the evening in a Bayeux hotel. We'll meet tomorrow around five with the appropriate clothing for Michael," said Shaw.

They left the restaurant and headed for Marceau's place.

"I'm sorry but we had such a hectic day at the Military Intelligence HQ that I forgot to ask you about Marceau," said Michael in the car.

"That is all right. We had other priorities to settle. Marceau passed away recently. He was buried, according to his wish, at sea. OSS, MI6, and the Resistance contributed to the funeral and burial. Before he died, he sent you his best wishes and asked me to take care of you," replied Bridget.

"I hope he did not suffer too long."

"His pain progressed, but the medications, especially morphine, helped him to alleviate much of the discomfort."

"Did he die in the same illness as he was diagnosed for?"

"The cause of his death was acute myelogenous leukemia."

"Please accept my condolences and the very deepest sympathy to you."

"Thank you, Michael. You had enough for one day, and I tried to postpone the news for as long as I could."

They arrived to Bridget's place. Parker promised to call the hospital and schedule the physical exam for tomorrow. He would pick him up at 0700 and possibly return him by noon. Then come back in the afternoon and take them to Bayeux. They wished them happiness and drove to their posts.

"Finally, we are together again, in privacy, after so many months of separation. Those guys are just super. They have been doing so much for you, darling. I truly appreciate that."

Michael took Bridget in his arms and gave her a long kiss

on her mouth. He kept her in his arms, holding her tight, and she said, "I thought of you so much. It was sometimes impossible to bear the pain of worry."

"Darling, I was worried about you and Marceau also. Bombs from the sky, shells from the ground, explosions all over, the invasion kept my imagination working overtime about you. But thank God, we are together again, and right now, this is the most important thing."

"I am going to prepare a good dinner for you, darling."

"No sweetheart, we are going to do it together."

"Are you hungry now?" asked Bridget.

"I'm hungry for you."

"So am I."

Both began to shed each other's garments on the floor and started to kiss each other all over.

"I suggest we are better off on the couch," said Bridget.

Embracing and kissing each other's lips, they slowing moved toward the couch where they made love in total ecstasy.

They stayed together after their climax and they gazed at each other with utmost fascination.

"I can't believe my eyes. I can't believe I'm kissing you, loving you like never before.

It can't be real. It is a dream," said Bridget.

"It is a dream that we are alive and made it to be together."

"I am hungry," said Bridget.

"You had your appetizer."

"So did you, darling."

They both got up, he in his shorts, and she in her negligee, started to peel potatoes and onions. They put some mixed vegetables on the stove with butter and lemon. She opened the refrigerator and took two slices of flounder she purchased a day before and put them into a frying pan. There was some French bread. He opened a new bottle of wine he found in the basement, and they cooked a delicious meal.

Susan arrived with her gift, a large food basket, and embraced both of them.

"I'm so happy for this reunion that I'm quite speechless," said Susan.

"Well, well, you brought so much food; we'll have a feast to finish them up, said Bridget.

"It's our pleasure. Brian and I could not think what to get you. It was my impromptu decision and Brian's blessing."

"Please join us, we would be delighted to share our meal with you," invited Michael.

"Thank you, but I can only stay for a short time."

"Please tell us what's happening in your life?" asked Bridget.

"I am terribly busy with my new assignment. We have little time planning our future with Brian. He would like to spend some time with me, but we are still at war and the OSS cannot spare us at this point in time."

"Is there any time we can be together for an afternoon or evening?" asked Bridget.

"I will talk to Brian about it and get back to you. Now that you have a phone we can communicate easier. I must go now and promise to see you soon. Bye."

"Bye Susan and many thanks for the gift."

Bridget and Michael were quite hungry they began to ravage the food, but as their stomachs began to fill up, they slowed down, drank the wine, and looked at each other as they sat opposite of each other.

"Thank you for your help."

"You're very welcome."

They kissed on their lips again.

"You are a great cook. This was a fabulous meal," said Michael.

"Thank you, but you had something to do with it. You gave love, spirit, inspiration and of course, labor."

"So, tell me, how was it in my absence?" asked Michael.

"It was terrible. I was worried sick. I hadn't the foggiest notion what was happening to you. Were you killed, injured, withdrawn with the other Germans, or had became a POW? I had many sleepless nights, terrible nightmares, and my imagination worked overtime during my waking hours. On the top of it, I had Marceau's illness. We had limited access to medical supervision and medicine. Finally, when the coast cleared and as the American forces liberated Cherbourg, we had a chance to receive blood transfusions for him in the hospital."

"Tell me about yourself, my darling."

"I thought about you and Marceau a lot. You were the focal point of my thoughts. Of course, I was often distracted by the shelling and the invasion forces, but I had no spirit to fight, only to survive. I held your picture to my heart, and each time I was in real danger,

I looked at your picture and that gave me strength and hope. When I was taken POW by the American forces, I thanked God for listening to my prayer."

"I sincerely hope we learned something about ourselves, our love, and our future destiny," said Bridget.

"We certainly did. May our path of life continue together?" asked Michael.

"Forever my darling, you are the love of my life for as long as I'll live."

"I forgot the ring," said Michael.

"My dear, I have one that Marceau us and I have it on my necklace."

"I totally forgot about it."

"Don't worry about jewelry, we are alive and together. Who cares? Your presence is more than a piece of diamond."

To that, they kissed each other again.

They washed the dishes together and Bridget set the alarm clock for six in the morning. After clearing the table, both had a bath and met in bed.

"I forgot to ask you about myself," said Michael.

"What do you want to know?"

"How do I look to you?"

"You lost some weight and hair, but otherwise still handsome. May I pose the same question about myself?"

"You also lost a pound or two. I saw a couple of gray strands in your hair, but it is very becoming hairstyle."

"Thank you, let's go to sleep," she said.

They fell asleep by holding each other's hands.

It was 0700 sharp when Parker knocked on the door. Michael was ready waiting for him. They exchanged a few pleasantries and the two drove away to Cherbourg hospital.

At the hospital the usual wait began, then identification and registration processes started and lasted an hour. Finally, he was cleared and admitted. Since Parker arranged the physical exam in advance, there was little waiting for the doctor. Michael had a thorough exam, including blood chemistry, x-ray, electrocardiogram, a lung test, and the physician's personal exam. After three hours, the doctor gave him a clean bill of health.

They had lunch in the hospital's cafeteria. They chatted about old times and renewed their friendship by naming him and Shaw the best men for their future wedding. Parker was absolutely elated and promised to come to their wedding.

After they returned to Bridget's place, Parker rushed away to pick up everything necessary for the evening ceremonies.

Michael took a nap, being exhausted from all the exams, and Bridget prepared her dress for the occasion. She tried several shoes, but she wanted something more elegant.

Since Vivian had the same size, she called her, and she brought her a pair she liked for keeps.

At twenty after five Parker arrived with a load of garments. A few minutes after Shaw came and they looked over every piece to see how it was fitting to Michael's body. Everything was perfect, even the shoes fit right. It was a single breasted gray suit with a white shirt and maroon tie. He looked absolutely stunning.

Bridget wore a beautiful charcoal gray dress and pearl necklace. She had a pair of dark shoes and white gloves up to her elbow. She was exceedingly beautiful. Parker drove to the hotel and they were greeted by the doorman and the manager of the hotel. In the lobby, some members of the OSS, MI6, French Resistance, and the Military Brass, including General de Gaulle delegation shook hands with Bridget, Michael, Shaw, and Parker.

The musicians began with a waltz from Strauss and slowly the invitees sat down to the table. It was a choreographed affair with all the political trimmings. The food was prepared by one of the best chefs in the area. From wine to champagne, nothing was missing. The delicacies of grandeur served as an appetizer. Some food arrived from abroad by plane.

Between courses there was dance music by a big band. They flew in from England. The guests and their accompaniments had a marvelous time. After the dessert, which was flaming crepes, the speeches began.

Representatives of Allied Intelligence, a Delegate from De Gaulle, and the American and British Military had a short speech. After the recognitions and accolades, a member of Allied Intelligence called Michael to the podium and placed a medal of freedom on his chest and handed over a check for $25,000 US dollars. He was also given the status of a military veteran with hospitalization for life.

Everybody got up from the tables and applauded Michael for ten minutes. He could only choke out, "Thank you."

The ceremony ended, Shaw, Parker and Susan congratulated Michael. Michael and Bridget's eyes filled with tears of happiness. The two embraced each other as they left the hotel for the waiting limousine.

ABOUT THE AUTHOR

A dissident of Stalin's communism and survivor of the German atrocities during WWII, Otto A. Berliner graduated from NYU and later received his graduate degree from the University of Rochester. A psychology professor, he retired after thirty-eight years at Alfred State College. Currently, he is a Professor Emeritus at State University of New York at Alfred.

419707

Made in the USA